THE SKIN THIEF

T. E. MACARTHUR

Indies United Publishing House, LLC

ALSO BY T.E. MACARTHUR

The Volcano Lady Series:
A Fearful Storm Gathering
To the Ending of the World
The Great Earthquake Machine
The Lidenbrock Manifesto
The Doomsday Relic

The Gaslight Adventures of Tom Turner Series:
The Yankee Must Die: *Huaka'I Po*
Death and the Barbary Coast
Terror in a Wild Weird West
The Omnibus Collection of Tom Turner

Anthologies:
Twelve Hours Later: 24 Tales of Myth
& Mystery
Thirty Days Later: Steaming Forward
Some Time Later
Next Stop on the #13

Lou Turner, P.I.:
A Place of Fog and Murder

INDIES UNITED PUBLISHING HOUSE, LLC
P.O. BOX 3071
QUINCY, IL 62305-3071
www.indiesunited.net

Copyright © 2023 by T.E. MacArthur.
Published by Indies United Publishing House, LLC

First Edition
First Printing, 2023
Cover design by T.E. MacArthur

All rights reserved worldwide. No part of this publication may be replicated, redistributed, or given away in any form without the prior written consent of the author/publisher or the terms relayed to you herein. This includes no replication by any electronic or mechanical means including information storage and retrieval systems, without permission in writing from the author / publisher. The only exception is by a reviewer, who may quote short excerpts as part of a review.
All rights reserved.

This book is a work of fiction. Names, characters, places, and incidents are either the product of the author's imagination or are used fictitiously. Any resemblance to actual persons, living or dead, events, or locals is entirely coincidental.

ISBN: 978-1-64456-596-4 [Paperback]
ISBN: 978-1-64456-597-1 [Mobi]
ISBN: 978-1-64456-598-8 [ePub]
Library of Congress Control Number: 2023932002

INDIES UNITED PUBLISHING HOUSE, LLC
P.O. BOX 3071
QUINCY, IL 62305-3071
www.indiesunited.net

ACKNOWLEDGEMENTS

To **AJ (Aaron) Sikes** and **Ana Manwaring**, editors extraordinaire, my heartfelt thanks. To them I owe a big debt of gratitude and a willing friendship.

To **Ethan Hay, Jay Hartlove, M.M. (Michelle) Chouinard, Debbie Young, Chuck Johnson, Pamela Duncan, Shelly Howell, Juliana & Patrick Gaul,** and the ever-splendid **Sharon E. Cathcart,** my collaborative development beta reading team C'est Magnifique!

Many thanks to my Uncle **Bill Christensen** for all the cheerleading and occasional insider information.

To **Linh Tran** proprietress of ***A Cuppa' Tea***, on College Avenue, Berkeley CA, for the hours she allowed me to sit in her shop.

And to **Indies United Publishing House, LLC** for allowing me to join their merry band. What a grand way to start the year 2023.

AUTHOR'S NOTE

I grew up in Colorado, though I was California born and now California living. Places such as Mesa Verde, Canyon de Chelly, and Chaco fascinated me. Like many children, I wanted to know all the exotic supernatural wonders of these magical ancient people. It was never my privilege to visit those sites in my childhood. And perhaps that is just as well – over time we have learned so much more about the actual people who lived in the cliffs and along the mesas, things that are far less exotic and magical, and far more human.

I offer you this story from my inner child to yours, in search of the mysterious and scary, but by no means looking to make any of those real ancient people or people today in the Four Corners region appear to be some sort of "*other*."

The best lesson we can learn is that people are people – they are decent and bad, nice and mean, smart and dumb, and everything in between. Pedestals are for only statues. Human beings were always a mix of good and evil, just as they are now, just as they always will be.

Perhaps that is the scariest lesson of them all.

T.E. MacArthur

DEDICATED TO

My father, **Tay McArthur** * **(1932 – 2022,)** whom I lost last year in April. He was my best beta reader, always being a teacher first, a fan second.
**(yes, missing an "a." It's a long story.)*

My dear friend and almost-husband, **Patrick James Lacy (1950 – 2023,)** a man who never heeded the airline admonition to put on *his* oxygen mask first before helping others. His generosity was infinite. He leaves a big, PJ-sized hole in so many lives.

THE SKIN THIEF

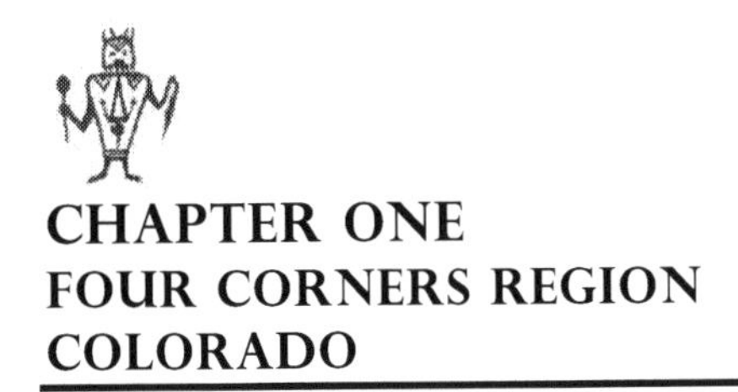

CHAPTER ONE
FOUR CORNERS REGION
COLORADO

AGENT X138 REFUSED TO BELIEVE IN GHOSTS, despite the gnawing premonition he was about to become one of them.

He shook it off, hoping that the tingling in his hands and spine would go away. Imagination was taking over, not facts, and X138 was here for the facts. For the sake of getting his bearings, he stopped, crouched, and dragged his fingers through the coarse gray dirt. Splinters of stone and wood pierced his uncalloused skin.

So much limitless night sky pressing down on him. For a moment, X138 recognized his own insignificance, how tiny he was. Above him were more stars than he'd ever seen in Washington DC or New York. Absolutely nothing competed with the glare of the Milky Way. Desert scrub concealed much of the distant horizon, leaving X138 surrounded by the unknown, bottomless canyons in every direction, an endless sea of looming rock, and vicious creatures with only one purpose — to find something to eat.

Something like him.

Why did his boss send him, a city boy, on a mission to the blistering Southwest desert? At least he'd had the good sense to accept a local kid's offer to guide him in the back way. "I'm going to go catch pot pickers who are selling on the black market," he told the kid. Hey, he read Tony Hillerman's Navajo Police mysteries. It wasn't the truth, but it was a fair lie and got the kid willing enough that it only cost X138 twenty bucks to secure his support. When he told the kid he'd need to go into the ruins after sundown, it cost him another eighty. He'd have to ask for reimbursement when he got back to Seattle.

Going to the site in the daytime like some tourist, had failed for the first agent. Athenaeum Intelligence had sent X456 out here weeks ago and he since dropped completely off the radar.

X138 shifted his footing and moved deeper into the rock formations surrounding the site.

Two loud booms rang out from the canyon near him.

Drums?

No.

Falling rocks?

On the way here, the local kid — who looked like a typical American Indian to him — had warned him to stay off the mesa, especially at night. Keep away from the ancient dwellings. No one liked the place. No one talked about the place.

Who constituted *no one*?

Indian Kid, with his stereotyped long braids, bead necklace, baggy jeans, and frowning face didn't explain further. The kid kept talking about terrible things, sounding just like X138 expected an Indian kid to sound.

God, if someone had ever designed a perfect Indian teenager from his imagination, that kid would have been it. Hollywood movie perfect. Perfect to every detail. Not that he'd ever met a real Indian before.

Native American, he silently apologized.

And man was that kid fixated on *Spirits*. Ravenous, cruel, evil *Ghouls*. *Spirits* of this, spirits of that, spirts of divine retribution, spirits of people so unknown even the local tribes had no name for them. *Ghosts* of those who were betrayed and now wanted to get back at the wicked for everything wrong in the world! They'd have to get in line, X138 muttered to himself. He was an intel operative and knew damn well how many people wanted to punish the world for all the sins they perceived being committed.

Small rock skidded down the path behind him, making X138 spin around.

Nothing. No rocks, no pebbles, no sand.

Must be the ghosts, he thought, laughing inside and seriously reconsidering the wisdom of being out here at night. Alone. Indian Kid had left him at the bottom of the path, refusing to go any further once the sun had passed below the outcroppings around the mesa.

Geez, the kid loved telling him all about those *Spirits* in every gruesome, stomach-turning detail. Wasn't the kid on his side? His nerves were raw by the time they reached the back road into the mesa, where the kid had left him and high-tailed it back to town.

At least X138 was coming out of this assignment better educated in Southwest culture.

Skinwalkers, he had asked the kid, trying to sound smart?

No. These Spirits of the mesa weren't them. Weren't Ute. Weren't Navajo. Not Pueblo or Hopi. None of those people. Nobody knew anything about them.

X138 wasn't sure if he believed any of it, but he was positive the Kid believed. And damn it, the stories unnerved him.

It got to the point where he had to tell the Kid to shut up when they were only halfway to the mesa.

And now, X138 wondered if X456 was a *ghost whatever* now. Would he find the body of the former agent, only to be eaten by his ghoulish spirit? Would another agent be sent out here find *his corpse*?

This was exactly why X138 hated horror movies and scary camp stories. He took comfort knowing that if anything did happen tonight, at least he would be the only casualty. By now, the kid had to be safe and sound back in town.

Enough children were being hurt by the situation here already — hence X138's mission.

He kept thinking of death. Of the sudden, creeping, morgue-like cold overwhelming his hands and joints, making them hurt. Of stillness blanketed in a suffocating layer of beige dust. Of shifting silhouettes seen when the moonlight allowed.

Of being foolish enough to be out here alone, at night. All alone.

Spasms of fear coursed up and down his legs, like icepicks stabbing at them. Goose flesh crawled along his arms.

He was sweating, desperately flapping his coat to cool off. Any field experience he had was useless, wasn't it?

A burst of chilled wind blew dirt and stinging gravel at him, spraying the area with debris and noise. Shit, the landscape didn't want him there anymore than that kid's supposed ghosts. What followed the cacophony was eerie, empty silence.

Agent X138 crept forward, weapon ready. Every breath shallow by half, too quick, and followed by a shake up and down his spine.

The official agency communication he'd received was simple:

> AGENT X138
> INVESTIGATE: TWO AGENTS SENT TO SITE NOW MISSING.
>
> SITUATION UPDATE: TWO CHILDREN KILLED IN WAR FOR CONTROL OF 32ND STREET GANG TERRITORY. GANG LEADER MISSING — REPORTED DEAD — LURED TO REMOTE LOCATION.
>
> STATUS URGENT: DETERMINE DISPOSITION OF MISSING AGENTS — DETERMINE DISPOSITION OF MISSING GANG LEADER — DETERMINE PARTY/PARTIES RESPONSIBLE.
> CODE: YELLOW. LETHAL RESPONSE AUTHORIZED.

Urgent. Dead Children.

In quick strides past sagebrush and rock, his boots sank into the deep sand and dirt.

The entrance to the old cliff ruins was ahead.

A placard, like those at any state park, bore the name of the place in scratched paint on rusted metal. The sign was bent sideways, its pole crimped in the middle by force, and now lying at an ominous angle off the path. Withered, leafless branches stuck out in all directions, and dust drifted into mounds against the boulders. It looked nothing like the fruitful farmland only a couple of miles away.

They had tried to make this a tourist spot?

Tried.

Failed.

No one took care of this place anymore, certainly not since an epic flood had drowned every living bush, tree, and creature, a few years before the drought. Even the land was deceased.

Stop. Wait. Listen. An agent's basic training. The air smelled of rot instead of piñon pine. The kid's warnings iced his nerves. The kid wasn't precisely clear on what could happen to him, only that it was worse than eternity in Hell.

Creeping forward again, one step at a time, barely rising above a crouch, X138's stomach churned. Heavy chains drooped across the path, proving a complete failure in their one purpose. A sign squeaked on its last nail, writhing in the resurging wind. The lettering was gone, scoured away by the elements over time.

The dirt tempest settled for only a moment, giving him enough time to hear the ringing in his ears and the sound of every movement. Mist hung inside the canyon, blotting out its true depth.

Wailing cut through the silence, putting X138's on edge. Was that a human shrieking in pain, or some animal? Or something else entirely? Not a ghost. No such thing.

Pivoting slowly, he concentrated, trying to triangulate where the sound came from. Behind him? No. In front of him? He stilled every muscle, straining to hear the slightest echo. Yes. There it was, the last of the cry. Toward the entrance to the dwellings.

What was that?

Imagination? No. He never imagined that kind of thing before.

A coyote? Sure. That was it. *Just a coyote.*

Overhead, an empty sky, filled with too many stars, blended so completely with the blackened distance that it gave him vertigo. He shifted his foot in the dirt, letting the scuffing and crunch of gravel calm his nerves. Those sounds were real or tangible.

He pushed his hair out of his face and inched his way to the edge of the cliff dwelling's entrance. It was little more than a gaping, black hole on the edge of the ravine, partially blocked by sagebrush.

Sweat formed on his upper lip and at the nape of his neck. *Focus on the mission.* Down the stairs, cautiously, one barely steady step at a time. They'd been hacked out of the rock by someone a long time past and were eroded by blasting sand and, at another time not so long ago, tourist foot traffic. Treacherous and hazardous enough in good light, in the dark they might be deadly. But he didn't dare turn on a flashlight. He'd be spotted by someone nasty. Or something.

Every nerve in his body screamed, *Run back home.*

Those weren't his orders. His orders were crystal clear.

Use extreme prejudice. Code: Yellow. Lethal response authorized.

Agent X138 also knew what his orders didn't address — what other agents were saying back at the Headquarters. *Who cares if gang leaders were dying or missing?* But in the underworld vacuum their absence created the power struggles that emerged and were spilling into the streets. Now, there were mounting civilian casualties.

Two more dead kids.

Two dead innocent kids.

I have kids.

Voices — whispers. Couldn't be. No such thing as ghosts. But no one was here.

More than one? Saying something about him – unworthy – lawless – undeserving.

Muffled laughter? Growling? Hissing. Jesus, what was he hearing?

In front of him. Behind him.

He ran down the last stairs toward the ancient dwellings, weapon poised.

The ancient dwellings were nested in darkness, except for pale moonlight shining in from the vast opening of the cavern. What a place! What a marvel of ancient engineering.

One of the Shadows moved. Human shaped? Imagination? No such thing as ghosts or whatever the hell people called them. They weren't any more real than the Mothman, the Jersey Devil, or …

Quiet. Silence. Emptiness.

The stench. Like garbage. No, more like an open sewer.

Despite it, he gulped in air and took stock of his environment as coolly as possible. The ruins here were a little different from *Mesa Verde* a few miles away. Smaller numbers of round, stone buildings. Smaller footprint. Harder to get to. Lonelier.

Near him on the rock, was something gouged in white …

X138 turned his flashlight on it and jumped back. It had seemed real for only a second. A fraction of a second. Long enough to scare him. A petroglyph in white, maybe hastily scratched into the surface of the stone. A horned, hollow figure, sneering, holding a club and a knife. Inside him appeared a human being, upside down, helpless.

He backed away from the crude petroglyph.

He had to go further inside. He slipped around another old, battered chain and a newer sign that read, *Danger — Keep Out.*

Behind him, a bush rustled. X138 snapped his aim over to the sound.

He could hear his own heartbeat.

A shadow — formed by a bush — changed shape.

Quiet.

Loose gravel fell. Rocks clashed against the floor of the cave dwellings.

X138 gripped his gun with both hands. He was shaking. He couldn't make it stop.

One foot reached out, touched solid ground, and he shifted his weight.

The ancient city was full of holes, both purposeful and accidental. At *Mesa Verde*, they were well lit, confined by chained barriers, and announced by helpful rangers and tour guides. At

Mesa de los Muertos, they were hidden in the shadows. Shadows. Always the shadows.

And more of those angry petroglyphs. Hastily scrawled.

Something laughed. Behind him. It was laughter— or —what makes a sound like that and isn't an animal?

X138 spun around. His eyes had adjusted to the dark. Was it enough?

Movement? He listened until his ears hurt.

Laughter. From behind again. X138 spun back, losing his bearing. Only the open face of the cliff dwelling with its relentless horizon told him he was facing west.

A rock skipped. Jumped. Skidded along the floor.

Thrown!

The laughter came from all around. Many voices. Echoes against the rocks and stones.

Behind. In front.

The shadow swept across him.

He fired two shots. They ricocheted off the walls. The reverberation pounded his chest and head until the echo silenced.

Stillness.

No footsteps. No shuffling. Only his own breathing.

Above, the wind shifted a load of sand over the side of the dwelling roof, sending the grains pouring over the edge like water.

Behind him. A whisper. No one there.

He took three quick steps backward and suddenly found nothing under his footing. Cursing, he dropped down and landed hard.

X138 sat up, stunned. He hurt, but he'd only had the air knocked out of him. Getting to his feet was harder than he'd expected, but then, what did he expect? Groping around, he found he had landed in a round room, with an opening at the far side. He must have fallen into one of the family rooms.

The blow to his head came from behind. His vision blurred. His gun flew from his hand and skittered out of reach.

The grip on his collar was so tight that it choked him.

The edge.

He reached back and should have been able to grab his attacker's hair, or shirt, or …

Nothing was there.

His belt was held and used to move him. Where? Where was he being taken? He waved his arms frantically, striking out at whatever had him.

Agent X138 reached down to his belt and undid the buckle. It slackened and his assailant no longer held him by it.

It didn't save him. He'd been thrown too hard.

Screaming, he dropped down ... and down

... and down ...

... and down ...

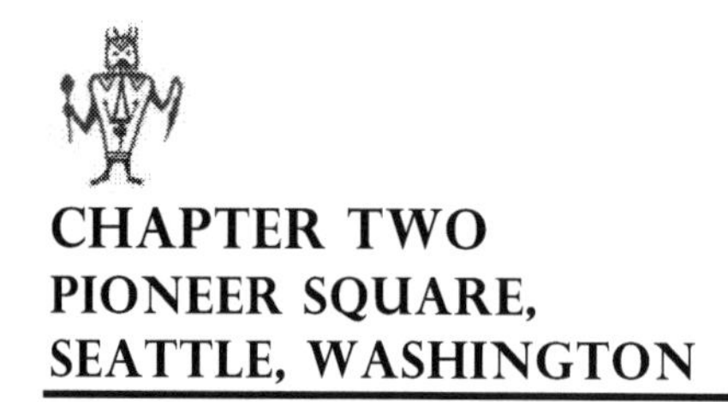

CHAPTER TWO
PIONEER SQUARE, SEATTLE, WASHINGTON

SHE HAD A MISSION AT LAST. Two long years of waiting — working on menial desk projects and praying for a fresh start — she had a mission.

Her sanity depended on it.

Her career depended on it.

Her life depended on it.

Seattle's signature rain had grown from drizzle to steady downpour over the past few hours, chasing most visitors to the Emerald City indoors. A boon for the cafes, a bust for the sidewalk sellers, and a challenge for Athenaeum Agent Tessa Wells-Lancing. With so few people on the streets, she couldn't hide amongst the throngs of tourists. A woman alone, dressed well and carrying a briefcase, on the weekend? Well, if anyone gave her trouble, she could handle them.

Can you?

Tessa's bravado and security vanished, leaving only the sound of someone or something eating.

Not now, she demanded and closed her eyes while tightening her grip on her briefcase handle and reminding herself that the hefty tome, PARAPSYCHOLOGY AND IT'S DEVELOPMENT, waited inside beneath a landslide of documents and papers for her to sign.

After a moment of peaceful city chaos, she opened her eyes again. A deep, humid breath was followed by a soothing list of must-do's. After the meeting, when she *would be given a mission*, she could take lunch near Pike Place. Oh yes, she would definitely be given a mission.

The Agency shrink had cleared her for duty while being amazed at her recovery from the *Unfortunate Incident*, or more specifically, Tessa's chosen methodology for coping. Parapsychology? Why not? If one thinks they encountered something … well, unanswerable by normal science, why not deal with it with un-normal science?

The shrink gave her a few resource recommendations and signed off. Ah well, the Agency shrink wasn't there to make sure Tessa was sane but to make sure the Agency could still make money with her employment.

Work out her first steps for the mission – contacts, equipment – that sort of thing. Perhaps even finish that last chapter. She'd given up hope that the recommended book could answer her … particular … question, but she had another six like it at home. One was bound to have the answer. The flashbacks, though …

The city park décor at Pioneer Square reflected the aesthetic of a *Paris le Metro* subway entrance as opposed to an urban U.S. tourist destination. The Art Nouveau ironwork arbor held dripping vines and flowers over the wet pavement.

Tessa's low-heeled boots tapped lightly against the sidewalk as she darted around puddles. At the corner, she stopped a few paces from a small group of sturdy tourists huddled together under the cheap umbrellas they'd just purchased at a gift shop. Tessa observed the out-of-towners while they all waited for the crossing signal. Traffic sloshed by, kicking up gutter spray. The tourist group stepped back from the curb and into the empty space Tessa had left in front of her.

The day was miserably wet – the sort of wet always shown in movies during funerals..

Sunday. The office building looming ahead was officially closed until Monday. A security guard sat at his station in the lobby, bored, and probably watching the latest sports game. The elevator bank just beyond the security desk only went from the first to the fourth floors. The special elevator went further up, but the guard didn't have an operator's key since clients for the

Agency never visited on weekends. Agents entered from beneath the building with their own keys and elevator.

Looking up, Tessa noticed lights on the seventh floor.

Her Field Controller, code named *Kyriós*, was early — he always was. She was on time — she always was.

Her whole body ached with anxiety, not excitement. Well, either way, she'd finally be out of that limbo an agent finds herself in after two failures in a row. Failures meant loss of revenue for the Agency, and honor didn't retain a high resale value. Still, a field mission rather than excommunication to the Agency's infamous Department 44 was best.

And as usual, the man-with-the-newspaper was sitting in the bus shelter twenty feet to her right, keeping his own clear view of the building. When wasn't he there?

Dizziness, dry mouth, nervous tension. Was Newspaper Man the cause, not the expectation of the new mission? She wasn't sure. Strange, he had no umbrella, only big, dark sunglasses hiding his eyes and a heavy coat. New Italian shoes too. He wasn't trying to be inconspicuous. In fact, he left the impression that he wasn't concerned about being noticed.

Isn't one of ours. Much too respectable to be one of my colleagues. Amongst her associates, it was widely accepted that he posed no immediate threat. He was from some legitimate federal organization or a rival private one. Tessa agreed with that assessment.

From experience, she knew the crossing light was about to cycle through and change. She side-eyed Newspaper Man, the not-so-covert-observer.

She felt him, as if his glare penetrated her skin.

That scent? Sweet, smoky, almost … medicinal. Nothing like the petrichor of the rain or the exhaust of passing cars.

That was when she saw Ben. Laying on the pavement. Blood everywhere. Yes, now she could smell it. Her heart was hammering in her chest. *Christ, not again. Not now!*

Ben's eyes. Glazed over. Clouded. The Figure. Tearing him away. Screaming. Fighting. He didn't want to go. The Figure ripping at Ben – its scent turning from sweet to sour to morgue-like –

Familiar. Frightening. *Danger*, she heard It say.

Tessa looked around wildly before she thought better than to do that.

The street was empty – no Ben – no blood.

Newspaper Man was still watching, but behind him waited the Figure cloaked in black, fading in and out of the reality around It. She'd seen It before with Ben and now, here.

Newspaper Man gave no indication he knew It was there.

It radiated menace, and the sight turned her insides. Moving. Changing. Floating behind Newspaper Man. People walked by the bus stop, oblivious to Its presence.

Danger, girlfriend.

That voice, in her head. She knew It. She knew It.

She gulped in her breath, blinked hard, and looked again.

Newspaper Man sat as usual. Nothing but an ad for a men's cologne behind him.

She'd seen It. She'd heard It. It was playing spectral games with her. Sensation left her arms and her head spun. Her instinct was on alert adding to everything else.

Calm. She would have to stay aware — without panic. Newspaper Man was too obvious to be taken seriously, but smart training told her to keep an eye on him anyway. It was not something she could do anything about. Even the strange scent was gone.

Tessa, jerked back to reality. She sneaked a glance back at Newspaper Man.

Newspaper Man watched her cross the street.

Tessa glared from the far corner..

Newspaper Man glared back at her.

This is ridiculous, her sensibility scolded her.

He's a problem, her gut screamed at her. Wait, was that her gut? Or her anxiety?

The clock tower chimed. She couldn't be late. Her first mission in so long and she couldn't be late. Not for this. The first mission in two years.

He's still over there, and I don't have time to play games with a rival agent, she rebuked the inner voice. Tessa's legs moved on their own, following the known path to the office. Her anxiety multiplied each time she told herself to ignore the hue and cry pounding her psyche.

Crossing the side street, Tessa navigated the downside of the hill that tilted steadily toward the waterfront. She followed the slope as it turned up an alley with a battered door not visible from the street. Her key fit the lock in the side after two fumbling tries.

Steady. Breathe. She slowed her movements with determined force and controlled her hands. *The hands of a professional.*

She wasn't late, not yet. The mission was her only focus. *Professional.* She folded her umbrella, smoothed her hair, and squared her shoulders — comfort gestures.

In the gray light, her rich, auburn hair disrupted the gloom. It was that long, stick straight hair, her heart-shaped face with thick but small lips, and Elizabeth Taylor violet-colored eyes that were her few physical assets. The rest she brought to the party was based on her life as a skilled intelligence officer and an exceedingly well-connected operative, minus the last two years.

Her heart squeezed. At least her father didn't know she'd trapped herself in an unviewable alleyway. Alone. An amateur's mistake. The consummate intelligence veteran that he was, her father would undoubtedly be disappointed in her.

Get a grip, Tess.

Frigid air tickled the back of her neck — spectral fingers alerted her. Decaying alley smells mixed with that familiar sweetness.

Danger!

Her hand dropped to her waistband holster.

CHAPTER THREE

THE UNDENIABLE SENSATION within each cell of her body announced Its arrival.

The Figure as standing right next to her. *Death.*

She and *Death* were too well acquainted now. She knew *Death's* presence. That was the scent that dragged memory back to the present. She knew *Death's* voice, too.

She knew *Death's* sickening laughter, especially when it was directed at her.

Tessa turned to point her 9mm between Newspaper Man's eyes, now threatening less than three feet from the muzzle. "Hands out," she growled, words low and clipped. How could she let this happen? Cornered. Beginner's fatal mistake.

Slowly he moved his hands outward. "Easy, honey."

"Name."

"I'm not—"

"Name!"

"Trono. Phil Trono. Look, I ah ..."

"Who are you with?"

He licked his lips and leaned forward.

"Don't. Even. Blink."

"I think this is a simple mistake. You kept looking at me, so I thought maybe —"

"Who are you with!" She watched his body, especially his fingers, for the slightest tell. *Don't make me kill you*, overwhelmed her thoughts.

The man who called himself Phil pressed moistened his lips again. His breathing was unsteady. Sweat formed above his eyebrows.

Pull the trigger, girlfriend. Death's voice was icy smooth. *Shoot and I'll take him away, too.*

Fire welled up in her chest, carrying into her arms and her hands. This was going to be like Ben – just like Ben. *Don't make me do it! You don't want death. I've seen It – you don't want that.*

She must have spoken her thoughts out loud.

"Shit, lady, it was Jenkins," he spit out. "Jenkins over at the Keepers Group sent me to watch you folks."

Tessa's vision tunneled down to only the man and the tip of the gunsight. "Why are you over here now? In this alley?" She spoke slowly, hiding the tremble of fury, fear, and electricity coursing through her muscles.

"I just told you, honey, so why don't you put that thing down."

His right hand twitched. Left hand swept out to take the weapon from her. He struck the muzzle hard instead, as she pulled it back and held it close to her body.

Shoot, Death insisted.

I can't.

Tessa crouched back as he took another grab for the weapon. It almost slipped from her numb fingers.

His right hand gripped her neck and squeezed.

Girlfriend. Shoot, Death demanded.

No!

Sickening dread flooded her stomach — her chest — her lungs. No room for air. No air!

Shoot!

It wanted *her* to provide *him*. To kill him. To –

Tessa flipped the weapon in her hand and pounded it on top of his arm until he let go. With a backswing, she connected the grip with his face, knocking him backward – stumbling – until he dropped to the ground.

His expression of shock and fear as she threatened to pistol-whip him again was at first a relief, she wouldn't have to kill him, then satisfying.

She heard him try to speak as she searched him for weapons. She watched him struggle with pain and consequence while she called for backup. Moving fast, she made certain he wasn't going to give anyone any trouble. Her gun, she kept low, out of reach and out of sight. The last thing anyone needed was attention drawn to the alley.

She hadn't killed him. Why? She could have. She should have.

"I can't."

But that was the job, wasn't it? Didn't mean she liked to kill, but she'd done it before.

Goddamn it — I hesitated. She'd taken a terrible risk by not dropping him there and then, like any other agent would have.

Again.

And she knew why. That damn Agency shrink knew why too. But Tessa was one of those agents they needed back in the field –

Or permanently out of the way.

In either case, the shrink had cleared her.

And she was sure the shrink had been premature.

Several agents, Agency medical staff, and her Controller's personal assistant responded to her call. With terrifying efficiency, the Keepers Group point man was bundled up and removed to what she assumed was emergency services under heavy security. Statements were given. Judgements quietly passed. Evidence removed. The stink of the alley returned. All routine as though this happened every day. All personnel were ordered back to their own business.

One of Tessa's departing colleagues gave her *that* stare — the one that implied he was amazed her attacker was still breathing. Tessa turned away. She owed no one in that crowd an explanation. No one.

Damn it. Now I'm late.

CHAPTER FOUR

LEAVING THE SITUATION BEHIND HER, she hurried through still, thickened air to the antique world waiting far below the building. To the hidden elevator reserved for Agency staff.

Each footstep sent jarring, metallic clangs up and down the stairwell. A small red scanner light followed her. No one entered the Athenaeum offices unseen.

She was expected an hour ago, and the idea that she'd been picked up by the Athenaeum's security bothered her. Probably because she knew whoever was watching also knew she'd engaged but not taken out an enemy. By now, everyone probably knew. She'd hesitated in the heat of action. In her business, hesitation was a death sentence.

She reached the bottom step and the sound of her presence disappeared into the centuries' old dirt of the infamous Underground City, which served as the entry to the private world of the Athenaeum Agency. Private agents, private funding, private clients with a private entrance from the lobby. Agents entered from the equivalent of the back stairs. Athenaeum was one of a handful of private spy and investigative agencies, employing trained rejects to be fixers, deceivers, and sometimes questionable problem solvers. Tessa knew the other names for her line of work, but she didn't spend time reviewing those.

She followed the familiar wooden sidewalk, between a dirt covered street and shops that had once been Seattle. Above, the modern world rolled on. Here, brick arches, stone walls, old gas features, rubble, and rickety support jacks greeted the senses with handfuls of dust and cobwebs. It was muggy and warm in places. Strings of lights led the way. Passing buses and cars rumbled above, causing a sprinkling of debris to fall from the cracks.

Any other time, the old city would have been charming or intriguing. She preferred the earthiness of the old place. The closeness. The honest pretense and artifice of an earlier era. Brick. Wood. Dirt. Business signs that lied truthfully about what was being sold or hawked. An old city holding up against an onslaught of modern convenience and, in its own way, winning. It was still there. So was she.

There were supposed to be ghosts too. Tessa hadn't seen any … not here at least.

Maybe she would haunt the place, if she didn't leave it today — alive.

As for *Death*? It hadn't come with her. She could sense It and sometimes smell It. Why? There was more to learn, more to read. Just when she'd find the answer to one question – about the Unfortunate Incident – she'd find four more questions revealed to her. And she was no closer to understanding what she saw – what happened that night to Ben.

At the end of the musty walkway awaited an antique elevator, folding gate and all. Dragging the gate into position with a loud clang, she pulled the main door closed behind her. Only one destination button.

Breathe. Calm. She counted from one to ten, knowing the technique worked. No one could know her of her anxiety.

Tessa drew herself up, shoulders back, business mask on. In the Business, everyone covers their weaknesses and fears with a mask of superiority.

No effort was needed to open the elevator when she arrived on the seventh floor. An automated device replaced the old-fashioned mechanism. Brilliant, white light met her and stabbed at her eyes.

Crisp white walls, modern paintings, black furniture, and rows of glass offices. Clean to the point of sterility. The Athenaeum Intelligence Agency, Information and Resolution Specialists, contracting to affluent clients in need of specialist personnel.

The receptionist, dressed to match the décor in a white three-piece man's suit, nodded at her. "Good afternoon, T301. Controller Kýrios is in the Sitting Room. Please join him at once." She flashed Tessa an expertly practiced smile and handed her a sealed courier-box, containing all sorts of goodies needed for the mission.

Tessa flashed back her strategically rehearsed, "Thank you." True names were never spoken. No clever monikers were given to the ground troops — only the directors and above received interesting code names, most in Greek, to match the theme suggested by Athenaeum. Average agents, like Tessa, were numbers — easily redacted statistics. Kýrios, being an upper-level Controller, enjoyed many special perks of his position.

She didn't mind the anonymity. It made pretending much easier.

Ahead, the mythical Kýrios waited, engrossed in a file. He wore a bespoke suit in light gray, suggestive of a country squire.

Behind him sat a young man. Just far enough away to make any conversation with Kýrios seem private, but close enough to inform Tessa that he had already been engaged in whatever she and Kyrios would discuss. He wore an expensive navy suit. His heavily rimmed glasses didn't appear, at distance, to show any change in focus behind them. She smiled professionally while he drew attention to the unnecessary eyewear by constantly shifting them on his nose. *The silly boy must believe that glasses were all Superman needed to fool everyone into thinking he was Clark Kent.*

"Agent T301." Kýrios did not bother to look up. "You're late."

"Good afternoon, sir," her voice was light. "Unexpected traffic delay."

"I suppose." Kýrios had no use for pleasantries. "You certainly know how to make an entrance." Kýrios sat down with a huff. "Why didn't you kill that man?"

Straight to the point – she'd forgotten that he didn't make use of such things as wit or charm. "No need."

"He attacked you."

"And to his surprise, as it is often to my colleagues, physical response is something I was taught to do from an early age. I'm reasonably good at it."

"He attacked you – on *our* doorstep."

"He was sloppy and panicky — and, by his own admission, works for a competitor."

"Hardly worth saving or working up a sweat over."

"But possibly worth questioning. I thought you might like to know what a rival is up to, sir. Or why a rogue element would attempt to put the Keepers Group in our sights."

Tessa believed no such thing. She lied without batting an eyelash. This was the game and had long since learned to ignore the urge to take a shower after these briefings.

Kýrios stared at her for a time. "You've become rather too discerning about how you treat threats. You haven't developed any poor habits due to that Unfortunate Incident with Agent Ben Solomon?" Kýrios pretended to cough. "Excuse me, I don't recall the assigned moniker he was given. You and he were not in my portfolio at the time of his demise."

Ice rushed across her nerves, but she kept her posture and expression neutral. He was trying to unnerve her by using Ben's name rather than his agency designation. This too was part of the game. "B776," she offered, "And, I've always been discerning, sir. I believe in assessing opportunities before squeezing the trigger."

"Hesitation is a weakness."

"Discretion, however, is always advantageous." She drew in a deep breath so slowly it did nothing to keep up with the demand of her pounding heart. Was this why he'd called her in? Was she being reassigned or decommissioned because she was rumored to be a risk? *Control the conversation.* "I understood you have a mission for me, sir."

His eyes only narrowed in response. "Your assignment," he stated bluntly, handing her a tablet.

Tessa took the item but kept her eyes on her Controller. The cold in her fingers burned her nerves. "Which is?"

"Not to Department 44, if that is what you are thinking."

All Tessa gave him was a slight glare through narrow eyes, surrounded by a meticulously curated, neutral expression.

Not Department 44.

Warmth reclaimed portions of her chest. Carefully, she reviewed the information on the tablet. He wasn't lying to her — she had a real mission, not a reassignment to the department from which no operative returned to active status. Her heart climbed down out of her throat.

"Four Corners?" She looked up, still masking any emotion she might or might not feel. "Colorado, Utah, Arizona, New Mexico. That Four Corners?" She set down the tablet. "High altitude desert, exceptional hiking trails. Home to some of the greatest surviving examples of ancient indigenous dwellings as well as some curious new archaeological sites."

"A virtual encyclopedia," Kýrios intoned, annoyed.

"Thank you, sir."

"Hmm." Kýrios leaned back.

"According to the file, this has to do with the drive-by shootings, motivated by turf control wars, culminating in ever-increasing collateral damage. Bit of a stretch, isn't it? Big cities, big syndicates or gangs, and a small, remote, Southwest region most people can't find on a map?"

Kýrios nodded. The young man in the back leaned forward, adjusting his fake glasses.

Tessa folded her hands. *Time to show you never stopped being an agent.* "I'm aware that over the last five months, a handful of major criminal leaders have disappeared, leaving no trace. The vacuum of power gets filled fast, and violently, by rival leadership vying for control of the significant assets."

"Exactly. The whole sordid situation has so-called innocent people caught in the middle. Several civilians were shot in a drive-by last night alone, some have died."

"Including a toddler, sir, asleep in her own bed … stray bullet …" Tessa's voice faded sadly.

"Collateral damage. Our client believes it is getting out of hand and that the damage will ultimately impede his real estate development plans to which he has already committed millions of dollars."

Profit first, of course, Tessa desperately wanted to snarl. *Can't sell executive residences with dead bodies scattered around the parking lots.*

"He's not the only one alarmed by this situation. We're hearing all sorts of odd stories about how and why this is happening. Outrageous stories."

"Information from inside sources?"

"Of course. What intelligence agency is without its well-paid informants?"

"Even inside of gangs. The hypotheses?"

"The criminal leadership is being lured to a place in the remote desert and somehow eliminated. Our better-installed associates have ferreted out unusual, last-minute travel plans and certain unexplainable expenditures by the missing individuals, which have led us to conclude that whatever is happening is indeed occurring in this remote region."

"But why would they go? If after the first two bosses vanished, wouldn't even the least of them know better? Or at least to send in junior captains to clear the place out first? Crime bosses aren't stupid by any means. They must be smart to run the businesses that they do. I'm not sure the hypothesis —"

"Yes, yes, I agree." Kýrios dismissively waved her off. "We need to find out what is truly happening, especially if someone has found a way to 'convince' or 'coerce' these men to ignore self-preservation and travel to a hole in the Southwest to die. Now that's a skill or technology I don't want available to the highest bidder. Other than us, of course."

"That skill or technology being the true end goal of the mission? Are we the only agency connecting all these events to the Four Corners region?"

"For the moment."

"Why? Where is the FBI or Homeland Security?"

Kýrios shrugged allowing his face a smug smile. "We're not precisely sharing everything our operatives have learned. Well placed agents are expensive, and we have every right to expect a return on the investment."

"By obtaining and controlling this so-called mesmerizing device or methodology?"

"Of course. It's not as though they're always sharing vital data with us, so I feel no compunction to be generous whatsoever."

"Of course."

"Oh, don't worry about them. They've found some information about the situation, but … there's an aspect to this case they find … unbelievable. Off-putting." His lips pursed in annoyance. "Something I hear you won't be troubled by these days, at least according to Dr. Phillipa."

Ah, the Agency shrink. "And what is that?"

"For the record, I'd appreciate it if you did not end up dead."

"How kind of you, sir." She batted her eyelashes over her violet eyes.

"Don't be such a wise ass. You know I don't like the paperwork and I don't want to have to explain it to anyone on the Committee. Never ever make me have to explain things. Whatever it is, the less I know, the better."

"I'm glad to hear it. And what is it Dr. Phillipa thinks I am not troubled by?"

"It's time for a USGS survey down in that region. Due to the farming, grazing, etcetera. You can convince them you are a geologist?"

Will you just answer me, she thought. "Of course I can."

"Good. We need you in there sooner rather than later. Play detective — find out what is going on. Make friends and use your connections. You're rather good at making friends as well as beating the snot out of people. Learn the secret behind overriding a crime lord's sense of self-preservation. Skill, machine, or drug — I want it first. And make this whole thing stop."

"Understood."

"Success will go a long way in repairing your reputation. There are those on the Committee who see your reticence and hesitation as a danger. I'd hate to see you reassigned to Department 44."

Ice dripped down her vertebrae. "As would I."

"And T301?"

"Yes, sir?"

"You are taking M021 with you. That is not open for debate." Kýrios indicated the young man at the back of the room, who stood. "He is brilliant with Finance and can find any graft, scam, or skim. He has a remarkable head for numbers and a handful of cleanly closed cases under his belt."

She sat quietly, waiting, counting from one to ten. Kýrios was leaving too much out. Calmly, she asked again, "Sir? Why me?"

Kýrios cleared his throat and lowered his voice. "Before we lost track of the last assigned operative, he reported contacting a local … guide. The area has a long history of … superstitions and folklore … if you take my meaning. Ghosts and ghoulies and such nonsense. Locals say that some sort of ghost murders interlopers rather regularly. Dr. Phillipa you've recently spent a great deal of time learning about such *para-things.* I am hoping it will give you an upper hand."

Ah, there it is. Thanks, Doc.. "You are suggesting that something paranormal may be behind all this?" Her voice was much too innocent.

The deadened pause was long. "Of course not, but … you seem uniquely qualified to dismiss such notions in favor of facts."

Tessa rolled her eyes so hard, she might well have seen a moment from yesterday at the back of her skull. "Sir, I've been curious about the subject, that's all. A brief diversion from the numerous, dry, case files I have been analyzing over the last two years."

"After the Unfortunate Incident with your partner Solomon, you appear to have been very curious."

Don't react. There's no point. Of course they've been watching me – of course Phillipa reported it. "You needn't be concerned. I pride myself on being, as one might say, open minded yet wholly scientific." *I'm so full of shit today.* "Does M021 know about the possible paranormal angle?"

"No." His smile twisted. "M021 is a tight ass who might not be …"

M021 tried cleaning his glasses, only managing to fumble them in the process.

"… Open minded?"

"Indeed. He'll be present because I don't want you going in alone. This mission cannot go … sideways. M021 is chomping at the bit to get out into the field. Don't get him killed, too."

Her nails sank into the palms of her hands.

One, two, three ...

Tessa glanced casually in M021's direction again. "Later on, you'll have to tell me where you got him. None of us are angels here. I'm certainly not. If I were, I wouldn't be here — I'd still be working for the Big Boys."

"Our good fortune," he stated with absolutely no sincerity. "The trouble with angels is that they always want support and acknowledgement. Rogues and loners are much cheaper and ... expendable."

Tessa rose from her chair as Kýrios did. Kýrios nodded curtly to each and left the two agents in the room, alone.

M021 was tall, and on closer inspection, much younger than she had originally guessed. He was around thirty? His hands, as he took the tablet out of hers, were perfect. White. Clean. Manicured.

"T301?" he said very smartly.

"Tessa," she corrected very politely.

He nodded, raised an eyebrow, and announced, "We're inside HQ and I'll call you T301. I'm M021."

Oh great, she thought. By the book and only the book. "Of course. However, outside, when we're in the middle of cowboy country, what should I call you?"

"Manfred." he stated pompously again, acting surprised that she would even dare to ask.

CHAPTER FIVE
BUILDING 5-A, HARBOR PLAZA BLVD
LONG BEACH, CALIFORNIA

CRANES OUTSIDE DROPPED CONTAINERS onto trucks and train cars. The abrupt crash was followed by the roar of a semitruck's engine as it pulled away with a load of imported goods or hazardous materials bound for cheap consumer stores across the state. Inside the building, activities were more important.

Julio nodded with the others while waiting outside the boss man's office. It made little to no sense for their boss to leave town and the safety of their company, especially with all the rumors they'd heard and all the stories about the disappearances. Truth was, Julio felt relief when he heard he wasn't invited on the trip. But if he wasn't going, how would he be able to report back to the Athenaeum? He had a job to do.

Julio, Agent J114, knew why he hadn't been asked to join his boss on some secret meeting. He looked down at his torn jeans, white sleeveless tank top, and overpriced sneakers. He ran a hand through his cropped black hair. His tattoos were especially vivid in order to show on the deep tones of his arms.

Slouching near the boss's door, just claiming to be ready and eager to please, he listened. Everyone thought he had severe hearing issues, and he played that assumption for sympathy and access. Many of his gang brothers found his youthful toughness cute. His command of lip-reading, both English and Spanish, was handy. So what if his ears worked fine and he could turn the faux hearing aid volume up higher than anyone knew?

Thanks to the faux aid, the boss's voice, and some of the caller's, was clear enough, even behind a slightly ajar office door.

"... can wipe out all of them. Like ... of old. A general in the field ... troops ... command. Your deepest dream. Power."

"I like the sound of that," the boss said in a voice tinged with disconnected pride and fantasy.

That wasn't right. Alejandro Suarez was normally harsh, cold, calculating. J114 listened more. It was definitely his boss talking, yet not.

Excitement filled the hallway to his left. The brotherhood that dressed well and looked intimidating, plus those in Suarez's inner circle, were packing to go. They barely knew where. They'd heard some vague rumors of what happened to an associate of Suarez's, and they grumbled that nothing would happen to their man.

Folding his arms and looking untouchable, J114 pushed his back against the wall near the Suarez's door and listened harder.

The voice on the phone was strange, soothing, enveloping. Even without hearing complete sentences, J114 was light-headed yet energized. When Suarez agreed with the caller, J114 violently agreed — to what, he had no idea. He had to agree. He wanted to be there. He craved the journey.

Examining his hands, Julio saw them differently, as though they could shoot lightning bolts at enemies. Or could cut the hearts out of fallen warriors with a knife of gleaming obsidian. Julio could sense the weight of the feathered headdress on his brow and hear the priests chanting their magical spells at the top of the sacred pyramids. His family was old, going back centuries in central Mexico. Their collective memory lit up his nerves.

An ancient call. The hero's sacrifice. A call to follow his god-king into the cenote, into the depths of the underworld, fearless, the warrior in sacred defense of his people. Justice — safety — continuance. It flowed through every cell.

J114 wanted more than anything to go with Suarez. He had to go. The caller, his voice — it begged him to join the holy crusade, to wipe out the unworthy. The words were still scattered but he heard one that sent a shiver of power racing along his spine — *Justice.*

"Hey, little brother! Wake up. Don't let the boss find you napping out here." Tio Montanez teased, slapping J114 on the side of the head as he walked by. "You wanna' be awake if he calls you in … needs you to run an errand."

Wait? What? What the hell had just happened?

The slap had knocked the listening device slightly out of his ear. He couldn't hear the caller's voice anymore.

Tio was going with the boss. Julio knew that was bad.

"Hey man, you shouldn't go," J114 begged and signed.

"I gotta. Don't worry. Boss says we'll be back." Tio signed and replied so that Julio could read his lips. "I'll put in a good word for you with Suarez. I'll take care of you. I said I would." Tio smiled. Tio was a good man.

The door flew open, and Alejandro Suarez strutted forth, looking like a god-king headed into battle. He stopped to grasp Julio by the shoulder. One of Suarez's closer friends handed him a map. New Mexico and Colorado labeled on the top. It was folded to show the most southern and western area of Colorado, with an area circled.

Still shaken, J114 observed but mostly stood with his hands in his pockets, acknowledging comments about his being allowed to go next time with a jerk of his chin. The raging chaos followed Suarez out the door.

In the shocking silence that remained, J114 excused himself to go smoke some weed. Outside he called a contact, who called a relay, who called his controller. The basic report was simple but unbelievable. Destination: Four Corners, Colorado. Why? *Mesmerized* or *hypnotized*? Those weren't strong enough words for what the caller could do to anyone who listened. Goddamn it, he hadn't even heard the voice completely, just a portion, and he was drawn in. J114's hands still shook when he'd finished the report.

He had a bad idea he was about to work with a new boss.

But …

What about Tio?

CHAPTER SIX
ATHENAEUM INTELLIGENCE AGENCY

"*MANFRED*, AGENT M021, we may be going into some very conservative, very folksy American towns. I don't think using your full Christian name is the best plan. A nickname will be better. Something casual. Comfortable. What about *Manny*?"

M021 visibly cringed. "*Manny*? I can't think of anything worse."

"*Fred*?"

He glowered so hard it must have hurt his jaw. Tessa held back her laughter out of something between manners and pity.

"M021, these people are generational farmers and ranchers, who live at a different pace. They are not by any means stupid or uneducated, but they see life through a different lens. A little more laid back."

"And you think these yokels are going to open up to you? You have eccentricities and very ... overtly feminine behaviorisms."

Was that a compliment? "I know how to blend in."

"I doubt you'll fool them."

"I understand a great deal about the area. I know how to go undercover, and you really need to become plain old Manny, or Ted, or Phil. I also know how to talk like a USGS scientist."

"Hold on!" He held up his hands. "I am the USGS scientist. You're just the surveyor. Your job is to distract these red necks who think any woman with all her teeth is a goddess. You keep them busy, and I'll go find the missing agents. And if anyone asks questions, I'll dazzle them with techno-speak they can't understand. I'm far more convincing as a scientist. You just need to ..." He mimicked unbuttoning his shirt a bit.

For a moment, Tessa's mouth went slack. *Focus.* "That's not the plan, Manfred. As the senior agent here I will choose the roles each of us plays. We don't know the conditions and who we're up against yet." She drew up and took even breaths.

Snorting, M021 glared at her

Tessa chose to ignore him. "I can talk soil science. I've done it before. These folks know all about it too — they have to, even if they don't have post graduate degrees in agriculture. Their livelihoods depend on understanding their environment. Assuming your local populace or potential adversaries are idiots or yokels is a recipe for failure."

"No." M021 finally took off his fake glasses and used his height to leer down at her with ice blue eyes. "A recipe for failure is being assigned on a vital mission, for an important client, with someone who fails her assignments because she can't shoot when she has to, and the only reason her last partner didn't fail too is because he's dead."

That stung in ways she forgot she could hurt.

"Well, T301? I hear you have a problem pulling the trigger. That got your partner killed. Or did you develop the problem after? It's any wonder you haven't been reassigned to Department 44."

Tessa was brutally aware of the pressure against her spine, from the gun holstered at her back. In that moment she could easily show him a trigger being pulled without hesitation. *No, no. He's baiting me.*

His face darkened in frustration. "Did you ever find his ghost? Scuttlebutt says you've been looking for it. You've become quite the ghost buster. And you think Kýrios *put* you in charge?"

So much for pretending that client – therapist privilege is a thing at this agency. Her hands balled up, white knuckled, and released reflexively. Her eyes, however, blinked slowly — sleepy with the man's boorish behavior. *We're not going to do this now*, she thought. He was not going to control the moment. *Breathe. Focus. Stick to the Mission. I control the moment.*

"I've been with the Athenaeum for two years now. Spotless record," M021 bragged.

All her fury disappeared in a puff of amused steam. It took all her self-control not to burst out laughing at the accidental relief he'd provided. Should she tell him about her many years of training and experience? But why? She owed him nothing.

Smiling, she held her tablet up to his. "Sorry, mine's bigger than yours." She turned on her heels and headed toward the door. "We're going in *work casual* clothing. Bring jeans, tee shirts, work boots. Nothing new and out of the package. Be ready to get dirty. You might even want to get a cowboy hat. Plain straw is best. Any baseball cap with a truck or machine shop logo will work too."

"Just one moment!" M021 followed her to the elevator and slammed his hand into the gate as it tried to close. "You are not taking this mission away from me like that."

"Get. In," Tessa commanded, in a clipped, low, deceptively quiet tone.

M021 did as he was told.

When the gate shut and the elevator car started down, Tessa hit the big red STOP button. "Manfred let's get this straight. You can have all the credit and glory you want. I don't care. What I do care about are the people who are dying because of what may be going on. I actually also like being alive and want to stay that way. Neither of those should be compromised by any agent's ambition."

"Then, I'm in charge."

"No."

"But —"

"I said no. Now, go home, pack, and I will meet you at the airport. We'll have to fly into Denver or Phoenix, then take a puddle jumper into the local airport. Or maybe Albuquerque or Gallup. I'll find out. I'll also arrange for geo-testing equipment to be waiting for us, along with anything else we'll need for our cover. I know people," she smiled at an old memory, "the right people to call. Do you?"

He opened his mouth but didn't answer.

"Had you thought that far ahead?" She pushed the button again when M021 again didn't answer. The elevator resumed its descent. "You need to develop networks and contacts, Manfred, they are essential. We don't work in a vacuum."

Back in the Underground City, they took a sharp right instead of going down into the walkway and found themselves in a garage. Tessa pulled out a keyring she'd been given with her box and pressed the location button. A car near the building engineer's closet lit up and honked.

M021 located his car the same way but kept walking with her.

What are you up to?

At the car, a lovely two-door, black vehicle, Tessa unlocked the doors, stepped around to the passenger side and put her briefcase and overcoat into the seat. As much as the car was modern and delightful, she knew they couldn't arrive to the mission with such a vehicle. A jeep or an SUV would be more appropriate. Yes, a jeep, with extreme mileage on it, along with some nicks and scratches. Tessa considered, deciding what the next step would be, along with the believable ride.

Her body lit up in energy.

What?

A shadow shifted across her line of sight.

Shit!

M021 moved with alarming speed. He seized her by the waist with his right arm and yanked open the engineer's closet with the left.

She screamed, furious. Pushing, she struggled to get free from his grip. He kept dragging her toward the closet, cursing each time he had to regain the ground he lost when she jerked away.

"Sorry, sweetheart, but this isn't a time for old, effete chicks who can't do their job.' He pushed her into the doorway. "This is a young man's business, and I need this mission more than you."

Tessa reached up and behind her, grasping handfuls of Manfred's hair. With one foot planted on the door frame and the other kicking upward, she forced her body up until her hips were higher than his shoulders. Her skirt stretched to its limit and a seam ripped. Tightening all her muscles, she swung her legs down, hard, and dropped all of her weight into a twisting, kneeling position. M021 folded over and flipped, landing on his back, inside the closet.

A loud huff of air escaped his lungs. While he struggled to breathe, wiggling like an inverted turtle, she slammed the door on him. A short length of plastic twine lying near the trashcan made for an excellent means to keep the door secured.

His banging, cursing, and door rattling would likely get someone's attention. *Eventually.*

That was when she looked down at her skirt, ripped along the seam to her hip. Well, that's what she risked wearing vintage and doing this job. At least it was the seam that gave and not the fabric. Still, it was one more reason of many that M021 wouldn't be added to her Christmas card list anytime soon.

Damn him. This mission had to go right. People's lives depended on it. Children were dying, too, and she could not do this alone. Heading into this situation without backup would be suicide.

The threat of Department 44 was no joke. Agents reassigned to Department 44 were put under outrageous pressures until they resigned or simply vanished.

The mission. It was her last chance to — what? Survive? Succeed? Maintain some sort of honor? Or status quo? Tessa had a laundry list of reasons she needed this mission to go right. Manfred was a guarantee of failure. *Probably why they stuck me with him.*

Who? Who could she take? Who could she trust?

She worked for people who were undesirables. With people who were undesirables. Working for clients with all the wrong money. She had no one but herself to blame for being amongst rogues and villains. These were not the old days. Nothing was like the old days.

She should have started her own agency a long time ago, to become a Fixer and solve people's problems. She was always doing that anyway, so she might as well get paid. And … know that she was living her truth, as they say. The thought weighed on her skull and shoulder bones like the street above.

If she had, she certainly would never have hired any of the agents she worked with now. None of them were like …

Her Cowboy.

M021 was screaming profanities about her now and more than a few threats. That horrible man-boy was not even in the same league with …

Her Cowboy.

Did she dare reach out to him? She'd forced *Her Cowboy* out of her thoughts as though someone might read them and discover that she knew where he was.

Tessa climbed into the car and started the engine, drowning out M021's annoying hollering.

Her Cowboy gone dark.

He was perfect for the job, but would he do it? Would he take the risk of exposure? Would she only lead *Death* to him?

Tessa seized the radio knob and blasted whatever noise was on it. Noise helped her push the images of *Death* out of her mind. She needed to think about Her Cowboy. He was far more important. He was mission critical.

Her employer functioned along the lines of asking for forgiveness, not permission. The Athenaeum Agency and its clients wanted success. How that was achieved was often allowed to vary drastically from protocols. All that mattered was winning. Being first. Beating the other guys. Succeeding. They would look the other way for the sake of success.

Mission success in this case would require skill and experience, not a spreadsheet and an analytical report. The paranormal part would likely turn out to be nothing. And, as long as there was no mention of *aliens*, Her Cowboy would be amenable to the rest of it. Possibly …

She exited the garage, a bit too fast, swerving as she emerged into the rainy weather.

… if he agreed to join her in the first place.

She had only one way to find out.

CHAPTER SEVEN
MONTAGUE VALLEY
MT. SHASTA, CALIFORNIA

TESSA FROZE IN PLACE, her foot held just an inch off the dusty driveway that wound upward from the base of a hill. A slight, blue light winked at her from between mounds of scrub brush. A thin sapphire line ghosted in the dust she'd kicked up. She stepped over the beam. Scanning the slope of the driveway, she noted two, maybe three more lights in her path. *Security, of course.*

Tessa continued her slow meander up the driveway. When the wind blew through juniper and pine needles, it made the pure, haunting, magical sound of rushing water. Near the top of the hill, water lay in shimmering puddles of rain from the morning and afternoon. The air was so fresh, so pure. Natural. Deceptively innocent.

In the creeping twilight, *real* was subjective. Memories had little fact to grip onto. Even a scientific mind could easily wander into the indigo shadows to be drawn back into events that still had no explanation. Out here, sounds were hard for the human ear to pin down and identify. Left with slippery truths, the imagination hastily filled in the answers with childhood fears.

She knew the speaker was there before he spoke a word, and kept her hands held out to her sides.

"He told me lately, he wouldn't mind being found. He isn't one for hiding."

She twisted around to find the man in the shadows. His silhouette was that of an old cowboy — a crippled hat brim from years of being clutched, thick coat to shield his antique bones against the cold, and bowed legs from sitting and watching the life he no longer actively participated in.

The older man walked out to where the last lingering sunset could reveal his features. Early seventies, with dark hooded eyes under brows permanently creased together, and a frown dropped into place by exhausted muscles. "Says he's tired of livin' like a ghost."

"One can only imagine, going from Spook to Ghost. He had quite the career, and reputation. It can't be easy giving that up." Yes, she could feel that extra … someone … out there.

"I took it to mean he's ready to die." The expression that followed asked if she was aware of that or if she was going to be part of it. So much said by a worn face.

"Are you his Uncle Joe?"

He nodded.

"I'm an old friend of his."

"Can't say he'll be glad to see ya'."

"He might," she brightened her tone.

Uncle Joe didn't bite her sweetened bait. "I went to an awful lot of trouble to keep him safe these last couple a' years. I'm not happy to have someone simply walk on in here. Means all that trouble, all those favors, might have been used in vain."

"And yet, you knew I had arrived."

"A safe place is only as good as its security measures. Nothin' happens here if I don't say it does. I don't leave much for him to think about, except the horses. He needs to know he's safe. He needs to know I've done everything humanly possible for him, 'cause he means that much to me. We're all the kin we got left. Just us two."

"That, too, I can only imagine. I have stayed away." The last came out of her mouth a bit more harshly than she'd meant.

Uncle Joe reached up a wrinkled hand, one that still showed some strength, and pressed on something in his ear. "Stand down, boys and girls."

A barely audible voice in his ear responded, "Copy that," followed by a clearly audible rustling of bushes both behind Tessa and beyond Uncle Joe. *Ah, there they are.*

"Do *they* know who he is?"

Uncle Joe frowned heavily. “Nope. They don’t want to know nothin’. Not what they’re here for.”

“The nature of such assignments.”

He cocked his head. “A man who wants to give up and die has either got too much guilt in him or needs something to give him hope.” What might have been a smile on his face came and went. “Welp. You should go talk to him then. I’ve got no idea what’s in his head anymore.”

“He’s probably thinking that he didn’t do anything wrong.”

Uncle Joe didn’t bite again. “Can’t say. I’ve heard a lot. Don’t believe it, but he won’t talk. Not a *yes*. Not a *no*. Not one goddamn word to explain. First time I haven’t been able to get intelligence from someone and it’s my own beloved nephew. Ya’ hear me, Miss? *My beloved nephew*.”

Warning received. “Yes, sir, I heard.”

He raised his chin in salute, touched the brim of his hat as a gentleman should, and pulled his jacket around his throat. Slowly, he slipped into the shadows of the trees.

That went well?

CHAPTER EIGHT

A WASH OF COBALT BLUE painted the hill before her. Night was coming. A ranch house nestled into the gloaming, to the right of the road — light peeking out from behind curtained windows, a rocker and swing on the porch, and a small railing protecting the front. Just beyond the house, trucks, cars, and equipment created silhouettes and shadows in a large, graveled area. To the left, downhill, was a barn, stables, enclosed horse corrals, and a breathtaking view of Mt. Shasta across the Montague Valley. Tessa's steps veered that way, knowing without a doubt that the crumbling barn was her destination.

Inside the barn, the resident ranch hand unloaded bales of hay from a faded-red, 1970s pickup truck. The sound of packed straw thumping against an unyielding surface was one among many common stable noises.

Tessa stood at the rail of the corral to breathe in the sight.

The view was deliciously good.

The ranch hand was a fit man, as she'd expected he would be. As she remembered he had been. His uniform of the day was cowboy simple: well-fit and well-worn jeans, a flannel shirt and thermal Henley that were layered against the cold, and a thick denim jacket. Supple hide gloves protected his hands, and scratched utilitarian boots covered his feet. A scruffy, brown felt cowboy hat was pulled low over his brow. He was unfazed by the ripe scent of livestock, dirt, and decay, blown through the breaks in the barn's wood siding.

His right hand swung down, and the hay-hook latched into an awaiting bale, solidly under a wire. His left hand worked differently. With it, he held the hook oddly and carried the weight of the bale as though he couldn't fully grasp it. Still, he swung the bale up and dropped it into position with the others.

Once behind the truck tailgate again, he stopped, set down his tools and waited, his face directed toward the back of the barn.

Waited.

He knew she was near.

"Hello, Jack."

The wind whistled through the slats of the barn.

He rested his hands on the tailgate, and his head dropped a little. "*Mrs. Peel.*"

He remembered. Oh, how she loved the sound of that: *Mrs. Peel.* "Mind if I join you?"

He said nothing. Instead, his gaze bored straight down into the truck bed. "Do I dare ask why yer here or how y'all found me?" A baritone voice thick with the drawl of the West.

Tessa gingerly stepped through the rails, then down to where Jack, *Her Cowboy*, waited, glad she'd thought to dress warmly in her 1960s, black, one-piece jumper-suit and warm, white cable knit sweater. Her long auburn braid thumped on her back as she made her way to him. Frankly, she could not have appeared more *Mrs. Emma Peel,* from the British TV show, unless she'd worn white go-go boots.

Up near the house, something fell from one of the pine trees with a crash through the branches.

Horses whinnied and spooked.

Jack's spine stiffened. His head twisted and eyes glared toward the sound.

Tessa froze, crouched, hands balling up to fight.

Had someone followed her?

Did anything move? What if it wasn't a person, but a …

The branch finished skidding to the ground. She could see the broken limb and needle-laden twigs as it broke apart in the dirt. The wind must have loosened the already weakened tree branch and sent it crashing down. Nothing more.

Back in the barn, Jack had not moved beyond returning his stare to the truck bed. His shoulders lowered at last with a deep sigh.

Tessa started back toward him, her breath and heartbeat working to escape her chest.

Warily, he nodded but didn't look at her. "I was wondering. Seems about time someone came to get it done."

"I'm not sure why you worried at all. You did a hell-of-a-job of falling off the radar. Everyone thinks you're dead."

"Y'all didn't."

"I know you. If there was half a chance you could survive, you would." She heard the false bravado in her voice. When he remained still and she took his silence as a rebuke for her crappy humor, she added quietly, "For a corpse, you look good, Jack."

He abruptly pulled off his left glove, still keeping his face away from her, and held out his hand to look at instead. "Not quite what one calls *good*."

Jack's hands were strong, with long powerful fingers — digits that did hard work. Browned a bit by the sun, and expected of his mixed, Southwestern heritage.

That left hand of his, however, was pale and incomplete. Healed over scar tissue failed to replace the missing section of his outside palm, absent small finger, and stump of a ring finger. The middle and index fingers, along with his thumb, were damaged but otherwise fine. Usable. Perhaps, even a bit elegant as they always had been. The damage overall was horrible, and it was a miracle he still had his hand considering what rumor indicated happened.

Her hands ached in sympathy.

For a stretch of time, they both listened to the horses prancing in the mud. Occasionally he looked over toward the big mountain.

"Jack?"

"I'm not in the *Intel Business* anymore!" he snapped, letting his arms fall heavily back down to his sides and his shoulders to drop low again. "I'm dead, remember? Formally confessed under torture," he held up his hand, "and executed as a traitor by my own Ops Team, just before they were all taken out. Body dumped in a shallow, unmarked hole. That's what they're sayin', so it must be true."

"No governmental agency does that sort of thing to its own. That's a wild Hollywood trope."

Jack's mouth twitched. "*Darlin'*, we didn't work for a *governmental* agency, not one that's recognized anyhow. Disgraced, despised, and dead." He drank in a deep breath of air that shuddered his whole body, or was it something more emotional he was attempting to keep under control?

"Death is worse. Believe me." She looked around.

"Maybe. I sure don't recommend playing dead. All ya' do is count the seconds before some sniper makes it a reality. Or some old friend shows up unannounced, to take care of things face to face."

She sucked in her breath. "No, no. I came here because I have a mission —"

"Then be careful, Darlin', and come home safe!" A small choke slipped into his voice when he said, 'come home.' He stayed put. "Be the one who comes home, Darlin'." After a moment of desperate hesitation, he whispered, "Don't let 'em throw ya' away because yer inconvenient." A chilled gust cut him off. The horses shied away.

Uncomfortable silences were all that were left.

Tessa walked forward and settled at the far side of the tailgate, staring in the opposite direction.

He put his glove back on.

Tessa muttered a little laugh. "I'm not at the old place anymore. Quit. I am working though at a new agency, with a new moniker: Agent T301." She feigned a salute.

"What? We had more creative names." He settled facing the same direction as she, leaning back on the tailgate. He muttered something about missing the name *Sundance*, and Tessa lightly rubbed her upper lip, hiding her effort to stay steady even as she wanted to giggle. *Sundance Kid.* It had been right for him. He had been such a *bad boy.*

"I need your help."

Jack stared again at the ground, moving broken pieces of hay with his foot.

This isn't his style, she thought. *Demurring, avoiding eye contact?* Sitting up on the tailgate, she leaned toward him. "Come on, let's have a look at you. See if you have aged out of the Business." In his prime, he had been a bit vain and cocky.

The expression on his face told her she'd punched the right button and that he knew it. Jack stood up, stretching his six-foot-two frame to its full height. He wasn't a broad man but built strong all the same. Like many cowboys, he remained lean. Yet he kept a subdued regal air about him — a clue to his mother's ancient Zapotec roots.

Jack still wore the dense, dark moustache he'd always had although the hair on his head was a bit longer and messier than before. Thick threads of grey had sneaked into his sideburns along with a few white streaks at his hairline, just the way an 'aging gentleman' was supposed to get them. He hadn't shaved and the patchy scruff was downright sexy. One side of his mouth turned up in what he'd always passed off as a smile. Other than deeper crow's feet around his gently hooded black eyes, he was the same as ever.

"I need you to come with me."

"Why me," he snarled. "Ya' know damn near everyone on the planet. I swear ya' could be a top-tier *Fixer* if ya' wanted to."

Her eyelashes batted prettily. "And not work with the best *Honey Trap* the Business ever had?"

He moved fast, placing his hands on either side of her, blocking any retreat. He had to know she wasn't helpless, that she could extract herself with little effort, but she knew he wanted her full attention too. He took a deep breath, and in that time, she smelled something earthy about him. "Tessa, ya' can't put your life at risk by dragging me along. I ..." He hesitated.

"Jack?"

"Didn't they tell ya' what I did? About the Ops Teams?" He clearly couldn't finish the sentence. "About Bosnia and —"

"I don't care."

"Ya' should. Being linked with me, even if I'm dead — it could be bad — so yeah, ya' should care."

"I don't."

Could a man's eyes plead on his behalf or beg to tell a story his lips refused to speak?

She couldn't let him give up. "I need you, Jack. *I need you*. In the here and now." That came out more pitiful than she meant, but true or not, she wouldn't take it back if she could.

His head dropped in frustration. He started chewing on his bottom lip, probably holding himself back from swearing like a sailor at her.

He knew some choice words, too.

Why was he trying so hard to convince her of something she clearly refused to accept? "Jack," she whispered so softly he might not have heard her. When their eyes met, she knew he had. "I'm not asking this of you casually. I've heard the rumors, but I know you. And I know this mission could put you at risk of being discovered." She swallowed hard. After a sigh, she grasped his hand. "You should know, I haven't had good luck with missions lately. I feel ..." *Word this carefully.* "Like Death is following me." She let go of his warm fingers. "I'm asking too much."

After a long moment, he asked, "And this mission y'all want me to stick my neck out for? What's behind it? What's pushing you?"

"Innocent people are dying. Street wars are erupting whenever a big-name crime boss disappears, and the casualties are mounting. So far, it's only been a few, but ... But if those eggheads of ours are calculating right, the number is on the verge of growing exponentially fast. We know in general where the bosses fall off the map."

"Somebody is giving a damn about innocents, other than you?"

"No. They want to know how someone is able to trick or coerce crime bosses into acting against their own best interests. They think it's a drug or something. I'm sort of curious too."

Jack smirked. He understood.

"Four Corners. Colorado — New Mexico region. Practically in your old summer stomping grounds. Look, we've sent in two agents and neither have come out. They're likely dead."

His black eyes blazed. "Then why the hell are they sending *you* in? That's red-neck country. Darlin', I don't doubt your brains, but ya' can't pass as a local. Hell, if ya' try to pass as a tourist now, they — whoever *they* are — will see right through yer cover. Do your people want ya' to get killed?"

"That, too, is a possibly," she replied darkly, a little sorry she'd spoken the truth so easily. "See. You and I are thinking alike already, *Steed*."

He gave her *that* look, the one that said he wasn't fooling around. He ran his hand through his hair, messing it up substantially. "Y'all'ave got a real dog in this fight?"

She couldn't stop lightly laying his hair back into place with her fingers.

Jack playfully snarled and messed it up again. "We're like an old married couple, aren't we?"

"How would you know, you've never been married?"

"True. Never met a woman who could compete with the mission," he grumbled, looking away abruptly.

Tessa felt a blush heat her cheeks. "One more thing," she added noting his eyebrow rising, "there are aspects to this mission you won't like. I promise to tell you on the way. Right now I need to know I have someone who will have my back, who can talk-the-talk with the local ranchers and farmers. We're going in as a USGS reps, doing an expected soil testing, so if I come off as a little too urban ..."

Jack smiled and shook his head.

"... I won't set off so many alarms." She could afford to be patient while he rolled everything around in his head. "I'm going with or without you. It's my mission. I have to do this. It's my dog in the fight."

"And y'all need me to make your cover story look and smell more down home and legit?"

"And to help me shoot my way out if necessary." She touched his shoulder after resisting the desire to touch his cheek. "We're going in, incognito. You'll simply stay that way when we're done. As a dead man, you are the ultimate ghost."

He pushed back from the pickup and strolled over to the barn entrance. Tessa watched for any negative body language. Instead, he stood with hands on his hips, feet spread in a confident stance, the last light of the day warming his closed eyelids.

"Darlin', what in God's name are ya' gonna' to tell your employers if they ask who yer with."

"I'll figure that out if and when it happens. They may not want to know as long as I'm getting the job done."

"Y'all're damn right about this being risky. We'll be getting' between rival gangs and messin' with someone's ambitions."

It was her turn to demur. "If this isn't possible, then it isn't." She walked up to him and put her hands on his shoulders. "Truth is, I wish everything was the same as it was before." Taking his arm, she turned and studied the big mountain. The top of the peaks was a shade of orange, reflecting off the yearlong snow, casting everything below it in amber light. "If you don't want to do this, then don't. I'll be satisfied having seen you. And you do look good, Jack."

He took off his hat and held it at his side, so that he could rest his head on hers. "There are days I wish nothing had ever changed. You, me, the others, our missions. It was living — as big as any man could imagine. Today Paris — tomorrow Cairo."

"The good old days."

"Nowadays, I can't tell if I'm dead or just waitin' to be. But this *retired* life isn't for me. Not yet. Hell," he laughed a little, "even Joe can't walk away from the life completely."

"He's not going to be happy if you join me, is he?"

"Ya' kiddin'? I'm sort of surprised he's not down here kicking my butt out to your car, if ya' really must know. I think he's worried I'm going to eat a bullet one of these days."

Tessa pushed back grimacing, her eyes wide.

"Don't worry, Darlin'. That ain't going to happen."

Her heartbeat slowed, ratcheting down to something closer to normal. She hadn't even realized how much it had sped up.

He squared on his hat again as the sun light faded from the big mountain. "One last mission, ya' say? With my *Mrs. Peel*?" He took a long, deep breath, his chest expanding with it. His voice dropped to nearly a whisper. No bravado. "It might not seem reasonable to ya', but, yeah, I'll do it. Let 'em come and get me after this." He tugged his brim. "Innocent lives, ya' say? Maybe our lives too."

She gave him a warm smile.

Regarding her, there was a shameless spark in his eye.

"Can we horse trade? Since ya' seem to think I'm worth keeping alive, I'm going to guess ya' don't know what happened." He stared out at Shasta again. "Don't ask for details and I won't need to decide if I should lie to ya' or not?"

"Gonna' lie to me about anything else?" she asked, mimicking his drawl.

"Nope."

"Then I agree to your terms, *Mr. Steed*."

"I'll get Uncle Joe to take care of things here. And no, he never left the CIA. Retirement isn't an option. Not 'cause the Agency insists, but because some folk just can't leave it all behind.. Joe's permanently *ex officio*. It's called workin' for free." He winked.

"But on paper?"

"He owns a horse ranch in California, if y'all hadn't heard. Retired. Occasionally consulting. Still mourning the death of his nephew."

"His *beloved nephew*," she corrected, and received a raised eyebrow in return.

Jack stopped to take a deep breath of the air.

Please don't let this be a mistake.

"Well," Jack shook his head. "I guess bein' dead isn't enough to get you out of the Business anymore."

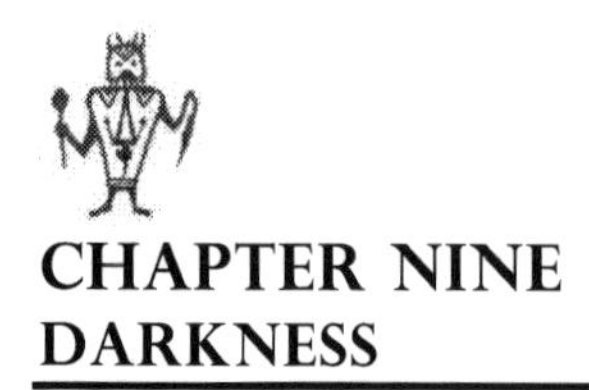

CHAPTER NINE
DARKNESS

ALEJANDRO SUAREZ DIED TOO FAST.

He was lucky.

Tio, paralyzed, stared up at the scorched sandstone rock above him, his backbone crushed. The shadow hovering nearby — its eyes: red beads. There was something else about it. Something hungry, needy, horrible.

They must have been near a sewer – he could smell putrid garbage. Nothing he could do could spare him from the stench.

It stopped hovering for a moment, coming closer to stare deep into Tio. He knew he was dying. They were all dying or already dead.

A human hand reached through the shadow.

Yanking hard, the hand snatched a crucifix off Tio's neck and held up the prize.

Tio watched as other shadows crept towards him.

One shadow stayed back.

The shadows folded, blended, came together creating a solid black void. Tio could do nothing but stare.

For Tio, there was nothing more.

CHAPTER TEN
GALLUP, NEW MEXICO
US HWY 491 BEGINNING AT OLD ROUTE 66, AMERICAN SOUTHWEST

THE TRIP TO THE SOUTHWEST took two puddle-jumpers and one judiciously arranged, private, red-eye flight with the upside being they avoided any intrusive security checks. The downside? By the time Jack and Tessa rolled off a twin-prop plane barely seating six, each hefting their own carry-on, their bones were as rattled as the nickname of the aircraft.

At least their luggage wasn't lost.

Even in the early morning hour, it was hot.

Jack stretched his back and Tessa thought she heard several things crack. Whoever said that the life of an operative was all high-rolling casinos and luxury hotels was either a fiction writer or drunk. Probably both.

The arranged-for jeep wore its age even worse than they were. As the saying went, "What the hell, it runs." Jack noted aloud. He glanced around the vacant parking lot, and the low, flat-roofed building that had been a DIY super store at one time. Unlit lamps stood sentinel, unnecessary for the shuttered business, providing some necessary privacy for their early morning transaction. "Where's our benefactor? I mean, one doesn't just leave a fine automobile like this out for anyone to steal."

Tessa shrugged. "Some contacts prefer anonymity."

The sun crested the distant blue mountains, casting the west side of the region in orange. To the east, rusty red buttes were blanketed in gold or black, refusing to get up. The morning wind was sharp, but Tessa knew from the forecasts such a relief was not going to last. The sooner they left, the quicker they could get through the Navajo Reservation and brutal desert region to their destination. With record breaking drought figures and blistering heatwaves raging across the Colorado Plateau, the only good bit of luck the mission offered was the timing — the disappearances had waited until after the height of summer to happen. *Damn considerate of them.*

Slithering out of the darkness, eyes shining like a snake searching for the first rays of warmth, a west-bound freight train approached alongside the lot. The engines whined steadily as it passed at a moderate speed, dragging empty auto carriers and various shipping containers back toward west coast harbors. It rumbled and clattered away, keeping close to old Route 66.

For a spell, Tessa grasped at a faded memory of two overloaded cars, with an overheated adult, and over-bored kid, making their way along the southern route to avoid driving through the mountains in winter. One of many such trips that she and her father took, racing past areas that promised fun, later on, but never happened. Always another post, another assignment, and off they went to another base and another set of empty promises. It was the life of an Air Force brat. Still, she remembered Gallup. She remembered the tourist junk shops with fake Indian wares, like arrowheads and copper bracelets, the kind of things only nine-year old's want or could afford on allowance money. Hot car rides with the windows down and the dog panting, its muzzle stuck out into the rushing air. Strange days of filling long hours with secret stories she kept in a journal: blood-thirsty pirates, brave Indians, evil princes, lonely cowboys. Yes, cowboys. *Speaking of ...*

Tessa turned to offer Jack their old game of coin-toss-for-first-shift driver. Jack was nowhere to be seen.

Everything had been waiting for them to pick up at Oh-God-Hundred in the morning. She had arranged it. Everything was going perfectly. *Where the hell was Jack?*

Tessa rushed around the jeep, looking frantically in every direction. To the north, where the last of the train slipped past, heading west to Winslow and Flagstaff. East, a blinding sunrise, and empty lot, ending with a battered chain link fence, weed defiled open space, and a highway. South, the closed store, assaulted by free-blowing trash, but with a hopeful sign that a business was coming soon. West, more scrub-strewn open space.

Empty, open space. No Jack.

He couldn't have bailed on her. He gave no sign of doing so. Her training, her experience, and her gut ... If Jack had bailed on her, then every skill and hope had all failed her.

Stop. Breathe. Regroup. Tessa mentally pushed down a sensation of pain and tightness that crawled up her chest from her abdomen. *What if he is in trouble?* That was much more likely. What if a hitman or "cleaner" had finally caught up with him? Or? No. She couldn't think like that. If her finding Jack meant that someone else had also found him, and now that someone else had taken him from her?

Tessa ditched her bag onto the front seat and grabbed the weapon that shook out with all the other significant contents. She kept her aim low and held the gun close to her body. If a cleaner had come for Jack, they would have taken him to the store. More privacy to do the deed. If Jack could have put up a fight, he would have. So that meant he couldn't, and that meant she had to move fast.

But why take Jack at all? Why not pick them both off from a distance? Something didn't make sense.

Death?

It would be there, if only to mock the fear and pain Jack would feel.

She knew *Death*.

Moving quickly, she slid into the shadows nearest the front door. Nothing.

Around the right-hand corner. Listening. Sliding carefully past the trash that piled up. Tessa crept down the west facing, back of the store.

Still nothing. Her heart moved up into her throat.

Waiting and listening for some sort of indication that someone was near, she shoved her back against the cement exterior. Coldness forced a shiver down her back.

Movement. To her right.

Shadow.

Death?

Big enough to be a man?

All she could smell was rancid food rotting where it had fallen out of the industrial bins. Blood? Was she smelling blood? Was the whine from the highway close to the cries she'd heard that night – from Ben? When Ben was ripped away –

No. No. Focus on Jack. Jack needed her,

Her fingers traced along the cold metal of the gun. Yes, it was real. Yes, she was holding it. Here. Now. Go find Jack.

She crept, her back toward the parking lot, holding back a wave of nausea. *Focus on Jack. Where are you?* Around the giant garbage bins. Up to the corner.

Weapon ready, *one, two, three*, she peered out at the lot.

Jack, alone, was leaning over the passenger seat. Something inside the jeep had caught his attention, but all his body language showed was agitation. Whatever he'd picked up from the seat, he tossed back and began his own desperate search.

"Jack," she half called.

He turned, his eyes wide. "What the hell are ya' doing?" He jogged over to where she was calmly stepping out from her hiding place. Clearly, the weapon in her hands did nothing to relax his fears.

"Where were you?" she demanded.

He pointed west.

"I looked."

"Well, I'm glad to see y'all didn't look too hard. There's a ditch and since we're gonna' be on the road for a bit, I thought I'd take care of … business. Not like I can go anywhere else for a couple of hours – once we're on the road."

Tessa snapped on the safety, closed her eyes in exasperation entirely at herself, and shook her head as if trying to bash something around inside. "True. There are some things one shouldn't see their mission partner doing." She walked past him, touching him lightly on the arm as she went by. "Next time, please tell me. I don't want to watch but I do want to know."

"I did. But y'all were off in La-La-Land."

Crap. He was right. "Sorry about that. It's been a long time since I've been here. It's … beautiful."

Jack cozied up to her and watched the continuing sunrise. "No doubt about that."

"I'll be on target, don't worry."

As they parted, she informed him she'd take the first driving shift after she stowed her weapon, and he folded his arms tightly across his chest. "Mind if I ask y'all a question?"

"Go ahead."

He watched her, and for a time, the muscles in his face went through a variety of changes, suggesting he was trying to come up with the wording of that question. At last, he said, "Never mind. I'll remember what it was later."

She shrugged, leaned into the jeep to put everything back into her bag, and noticed all her items on the seat where she'd dumped them. Ah shit. She could see the titles of a couple of the books she'd brought with her. *Advanced Parapsychology*. *Paranormal Investigation*. And if she could see them, then he could.

Those were going to require explanation.

Not now.

Without any further comment, she shoved everything back into the bag, put her weapon away, and climbed into the driver's seat.

Jack made no attempt to argue, and for the first leg of their ride, he continued to play dumb.

CHAPTER ELEVEN
CORTEZ, COLORADO
FOUR CORNERS REGION

JACK KNEW WHEN they had crossed the Colorado state line. The environment changed from rusted, ragged buttes and ancient eroded pinnacles to velveteen ranges of tan and green grasses, shaded by clumps of cottonwood and pinon-juniper trees, yet with the ever-present mesas. Childhood memories which weren't perfectly clear still floated around his brain. Grasping mountains cupped the highway between them, steep and dark against the ever-cloudless sky.

Four hours north on the *Devil's Highway*. And not a ghost or demon in sight.

The only specters to be had were those they tried to one-up each other with from the lore they knew. How Hwy. 491 had briefly been Hwy. 666, hence the name. Jack didn't buy into any of that nonsense, of course, and made that absolutely clear. "Y'all want to believe it was the number alone that did it. I say it's all the accidents. Head-on collisions on a 70-mile stretch of two-lane, stick-straight road where folks'll keep tryin' to break the speed of sound?"

"What about the White Lady?"

She was trying to rib him, wasn't she? The little, coy smile gave her away. "People seeing things they want to see, even if they aren't there. Maybe it's a trick of the sunlight or moonlight reflecting off something. Who knows?"

"Well, what's your favorite, Jack? There has to be at least one ghost story you don't mind telling."

He gave her a sideways look and a lopsided smirk. "Satan's Possessed Cadillac Sedan was and is my personal choice. Can't go wrong with a classic."

The desolate drive was far easier to bear, as Tessa kept needling him, and Jack gave it back as good as he got it. Of course he didn't believe any of the ghost talk, and she knew that. But it wasn't the topic that mattered — it was the conversation, the trust that no insult or harm was meant, the freedom to risk being temporarily fallible.

They were falling back into familiar patterns.

An hour or so past the state line, the vista widened into a broad plane of farmland and grazing. In the distance, indigo mountains and mesas beckoned the traveler not to give up on their journey.

Cortez, Colorado, turned out to be the epitome of *quaint.* Hwy. 491 ran straight through it and served as its main street, too, complete with colorful businesses in Spanish and Southwest style.

At the north end of the city, Tessa pulled into a gas station attached to a mini mall which hadn't had the luck of businesses closer to the town center.

Tessa beckoned Jack into one of the empty store fronts. "Come meet my Maker Extraordinaire," she said with a wink.

He took stock of exposed areas, hiding places, and potential surveillance locations as he slipped through the swinging door. Inside was a wasteland of broken promises — of someone's business that hadn't competed with the sand and snow. Dusty banners, empty drawers, signs of abandonment.

She gestured to a resplendent Black man, wearing dark sunglasses blinking with led lights, something stuck into his ear like a Bluetooth earbud, a pair of ruby studs in each earlobe, and a black t-shirt that was so immaculate it appeared to be pressed. The man didn't seem at all concerned about Jack's presence. Pushing off the counter, he shook hands with Tessa and slipped her a sealed box.

"Thanks, Chey." Tessa beamed as she removed half of the contents and passed along the rest to Jack. "Chey is an old friend with amazing skills."

So, she'd tapped an old friend who knew ... well ... things, such as how to make a set of Synthetic IDs for him, aka *Santiago "Rio" de Sombras*. "De Sombras?"

"Should be easy for you to remember and to respond to without thinking too much," Chey replied in something thick and possibly south or eastern African. "You call me when you need resupply." He nodded appreciatively at a rubber band wrapped envelope Tessa handed him. "Always a pleasure, *Mama Mdogo*."

"Always, *Rafiki*."

Jack offered him a deeply respectful, well-earned nod. The product the man provided was the highest quality he'd seen in some time.

"She knows how to reach me if you run into trouble," Chey added, stuffing the envelope into his satchel, taking up a leather jacket, and pushing his way out the door. "*Baadaye*."

While the door swung back into place, Tessa leaned over Jack's arm, "I thought you'd appreciate the surname."

Why is she still an ordinary operative? He knew she was an outstanding agent, but as a "Fixer." As someone hired to resolve unusual or complicated situations, no one could come close to her magic touch with people, plans, and resolutions.

"I appreciate it being Mom's maiden name," Jack muttered loudly, smiling in his off-center way, shuffling through the credit cards, New Mexico state fishing license, USGS ID, NM state driver's ID, and fake paid bar tabs from months earlier. Everything Joe Average would have in his wallet. "You?"

She held it up for him to see. "Ms. Teresa 'Tess' Wells, PhD. If *you* say 'Wells,' *I know* I'll answer. Most people don't even know me by anything but *Lancing*."

"That'll work."

As they stepped outside, a gust of wind sent dry air and the scent of old desert past them. A childhood memory pricked at him for a second and was gone. A well-used pickup truck pulled into the gas station and up to the pump behind their jeep. An older man, warped and crusted by sun and toil, hopped out. He tugged his hat brim. "Mornin' there." His weathered voice was cheery.

"Mornin'." Jack casually waved at the man, but his attention was on Tessa's *old friend* Chey, who climbed into a decent looking SUV, bearing a thick coating of dust and under-carriage mud.

"Does he live here in town?"

"No." She waved at the departing vehicle. "Came down from Telluride. Loves to ski," she noted nonchalantly, in part to keep impressing him, he was sure, "and decided to settle near the lifts." She leaned against the hood of the jeep and unfolded a map. Strands of her auburn hair escaped the long braid down her back and drifted on the breeze, giving her an ethereal appearance. Perhaps even heavenly or angelic.

"He's quite the pro. What else does he do?" Jack studied the map over her shoulder and caught a brief scent of vanilla.

"If you need it made, Cheyenne Kern can make it. IDs, electronic devices, specialized weaponry ... he's the man." Tessa glanced out at the road. "It's all about who you know."

"And who ya' can afford." Jack stuffed all the new documents into the inside pocket of his suede jacket. He'd prepared the rest of his disguise easily, since it was no real stretch for him. Boots, older brown felt cowboy hat, wide-checked button-down shirt. Meet-the-locals wear. "I don't suppose y'all can expense these off to yer agency?"

"A set of IDs for someone who doesn't exist and isn't on this mission ... hmm ... I think not. Don't worry, *Steed*, he gave me the family discount."

"I'm not gonna' ask." Since it was dusty and dirty, he was glad to be wearing gloves, hiding his disability, though he did occasionally need to shake out his left hand — a matter of poor circulation — preferably when she wasn't looking. He had it under control.

The older man with the pickup truck kept looking up from what he was doing. Most folks try not to get too nosy, Jack remembered. But the map, yeah, that was probably too much of a temptation.

"You folks new around here? Goin' somewhere special?"

"USGS. Just getting' our act together before hittin' the road," Jack replied.

"Know where yer goin'?"

"Pretty much. It's been a little while, but y'all know, not much changes."

The man chuckled. "Change ain't that popular around here, even if you can't avoid it."

His voice was soothing and reminded Jack of his father. "Well, ain't that the truth."

"Need any recommendations?"

"Sure. We got work in Montejo. Where should we eat ..."

The man's face fell into long, sorrowful lines. "Y'all have to go there? I mean, ya' said you were USGS but ... do ya' have to?"

Tessa twisted her body toward him. "Yup. If they tell us to go, we go. You've had a drought going here for a number of years, and we need to know what the impact is. Plus, we're due anyway."

The older man nodded, chewing his bottom lip. "We sure could use all the help and info. People're doing their best not to over tap the aquifer, so I suppose we need all the testin. But ..." He put the gas nozzle back in place and shuffled over. "But I got to tell you. An', I'm not so sure how to put this nice."

"Don't worry about that. What is it?" Tessa was being Tessa, earning the man's trust and likely adding him to her list of contacts and resources. She smiled, gave him her full, sincere attention, and looked him right in the eyes.

"Folks in Montejo, well, they just ain't quite, um — usual. Not for this area."

"How do you mean?"

He shook his head, likely fighting off a memory of his mother telling him if he didn't have anything nice to say, don't say anything at all. His eyes, however, told Jack far more than the words.

"See, that town took a hit a while back. Bad flood. It never recovered. Now? The folks who are there? They aren't like everyone else around here. Nothin' like us. We're good folks up here. I guess, I don't know how to explain it right. I just suggest you stay somewhere up on the highway, like Dove Creek or maybe over in Delores, and only go to do your testing. Stay away as much as you can. It's a depressing place."

"Can't even find the place on GPS. Only on the old map."

The man shook his head. "They're down in a hole, nobody claims. Soil's no good for planting, and its mostly drainage into the canyons so you never know if it's going to flood. Can't for the life of me figure out why anyone put a town there in the first place. Maybe thought they'd make it rich on the dwellings or something." He kept rocking his head back and forth.

Jack exchanged a look with Tessa but couldn't quite read what she was thinking. That was new.

Her delicate hand reached out gently to the older man and shook it kindly. "Thank you. We sometimes get some of the strangest assignments. It helps to know if we should be alert for anything ... out of the ordinary." She clasped his hand in both of hers before letting go. No doubt, she had a convert to her resource club.

Quite gratefully, Jack took his hand and shook it. They didn't say anything — all was implied.

While the older man drove off, Tessa gave Jack her expression of concern and he gave her the Eyebrow of Doom. And a scorching blast of wind, carrying grist and debris, gave them every reason they needed to get moving. The clock was ticking.

Highway signs waited for them on the north edge of Cortez's city limits, coated in pale blond dust, and indicating that, whichever way they decided to go, it was going to be a hot, dry ride.

Jack kept driving into a haze of yellow, beige, and tan natural smog blowing across the roadway. Scrub brush, pinons, rolling yellow grass, and a scattering of telephone poles, all attempted to compete with the high desert's vast, infinite presence — and were left humbled in the dust. Bright green patches of irrigated farmland competed with rusty red or white dirt.

Someone had defiled a reflective highway arrow sign with graffiti, but the wind had already taken bites out of the profane, and it was only a brief matter of time before the desecration would be stripped away. Nothing that the land didn't want, stayed for long.

The sun bore down on all of it, baking truths and lies into the clay with equal permanence.

The region where Montejo salted away its secrets, she explained as they sped up the two-lane highway, was an exciting hub of archaeological activity. "Ruins found of an ancient people that both pre- and post-dated those of Mesa Verde, incorrectly called the *Anasazi* at one time. These were much earlier people, or so carbon dating and pottery patterns suggest." Her voice rose enthusiastically above the road whine. "They don't know who all of these dwellings belonged to. Some are Pre-Puebloan — Basket Weaver people. Some are pre-*no one they know anything about*. But most are those who eventually moved south and became the Puebloan people known today."

For his part, Jack silently nodded in acknowledgment. She knew he shuffled his youth between San Antonio and El Paso. But sometimes his family sent him up to Albuquerque or Santa Fe, even Durango, according to tales he wove for her during their old missions. He already knew what she was telling him about the area, yet he paid her the courtesy of not saying so. No one likes a know-it-all.

She clutched her hat. "From what I've learned, they tried opening some of the sites near Montejo to tourists, like they did with Mesa Verde, but because these are so much older, they didn't pan out to be safe. None are open to the public now. Yet, they hope to learn new things someday."

"Like an answer to the big question — who the hell the unknown earlier folks were?" Jack added.

"Yes … well …" her voice fell below the rush of the road, and she stared off into the distance.

"Well, what?"

The silence was too long for his comfort. "There's some speculation about that, based on recent evidence … and encounters." She refused to look at him. "You remember I said there is an aspect to this mission that is a bit dodgy?"

"Yer not leavin' something out because I might not like it, are ya?" He offered her his big lopsided smile, but when she didn't return it, the smile fell from his face. "Darlin'?"

"You might be uncomfortable with it. Perhaps it could wait until ..."

It struck him hard when he realized what she was going to say. Her books. Her damn books. All *Paranormal* topics. *Paranormal?* He knew what insane notions fell under the heading of *Paranormal.*

No, she wouldn't?

His foot was over the brake pedal before he remembered what a bad idea it was to slam on the brakes at 70 miles per hour. "Oh, hell no!"

CHAPTER TWELVE

THE JEEP SKIDDED TO A STOP on the shoulder of the highway with minimal control and a cloud of dirt spun up into the air.

She wouldn't do that to me?

"This ain't about Roswell because I know that's 500 miles from here in the other direction. But the Southwest has a reputation for ..."

"This has nothing to do with aliens!" Tessa reached out and laid her hand on his. "I would never do that to you. I've asked too much of you already."

"Then what? You briefed me on the way here and mentioned nothin' about the paranormal. Yeah, I saw the books back in Gallup. What they hell are y'all doing with paranormal ..."

"I prefer *parapsychology*. I don't feel so stupid when I say it."

His jaw slackened, followed by his shoulders. "What aren't you telling me? Darlin', we promised not to tell lies. Omission is a lie too." Jack's voice had lost the edge it had before, but he kept swallowing and trying to gulp in as much oxygen as the thin air would allow.

"I can't omit what I don't know enough about yet. And I didn't want to bring it up until I had something concrete to tell you. I know you want facts. And I need to find out if a local belief is involved."

A big rig passed them, roaring as it went by and blasting them with hot air.

"The mission you and I are on is clear enough: stop whoever is killing these crime lords and letting the violence spill out onto civilians. The Athenaeum's mission goal goes further. They want to know by what means is the person or persons manipulating grown men into going against their better judgement and allowing themselves to be killed or at least disappeared?"

He nodded, acknowledging that she had explained all that. But what did paranormal ... parapsychological beliefs have to do with that?

"I don't know yet. Maybe nothing, which I'm hoping for. Hence the books."

"And that's why y'all know too much about this area's ancient history." Jack's head cocked slightly as his thoughts rearranged themselves into something calmer. "Y'all think that some old tradition is part of this?" Frankly, he couldn't manage to say that any other way without sounding stupid to his own ears. *Go ahead, be stupid, better get it over with now*. "Real *old*, as in *ancient*." There, he stated it.

"I believe that the *belief in something old* is part of this and understanding what drives people's ambitions, wants, and motivations, even if it's based on superstition, is too important not to consider. We need to think about everything before eliminating the truly impossible."

"Ghosts? You think ghosts or magic is part of the manipulation?"

"Spirits ... maybe ... yes."

His fingertips were cold. "Yer a rational lady, so why did they assign you?"

"I'm ... I've gained a certain knowledge base to work with." She looked at her fingers.

He asked more tenderly than he expected he would. "Y'all wanna tell me?"

"Right here?"

"Sure."

Tessa stared out at the expanse of challenging land — at mountains that appeared reachable but forever on the horizon. For a moment, she could hear Ben laughing at someone's crappy joke. *Tell Jack — what a relief that would be.* She hadn't told anyone about Ben.

She could also hear Ben gasping from the pain. Dying. Terrified of Death. *Death.*

Death that refused to leave her alone.

"No. Not right now."

The midday air was sheer and strong at 6500 feet above sea level. Even sunglasses hadn't kept him from squinting. His head was starting to hurt and arguing with her had put a knife into the happy familiar moments they had been enjoying. Slowly, he pulled the jeep back out onto the highway.

Tessa gave him as much data as she could over the incessant road whine. For his part, he stayed uncharacteristically stoic and focused. No snarky comments, no wit, no humor. Silence and focus.

She didn't mention the paranormal again.

He didn't ask.

Had this been such a good decision? Or had he been too long out of the field and unused to keeping the little things from throwing him off mission focus?

Had she made a terrible mistake by asking *him*?

It would help knowing what was going on in his own head. But even Uncle Joe said he didn't know.

"There it is. Downtown Metropolitan Montejo," she pointed at the green and white sign whipping by them, declaring MON—JO NEXT —IT.

Important letters were missing. "Montejo, Next Exit," although by *Exit* she was sure it meant, *Make a left turn across the fast-moving highway. Best of luck to you. Don't forget to donate your organs.*

With a little patience and perhaps some quiet cursing, or praying, he cut across the highway and over to a dust thickened road, avoiding an 18-wheeler by seconds. The truck's horn blared at them as it whooshed by and shook the jeep.

Near the top of the incline, to the left, was a dead restaurant, missing its roof, with what were the last vestiges of a couple of gas pumps. The pumps had been removed, though the tanks were probably still in the ground. The windows were broken out or long gone. Paint was either fading or peeling or both. Weeds half as tall as Tessa shot up through the cracks in the cement. The price of gas showed as $0.95 per gallon.

Devil's Highway, eh?

Jack slammed on the breaks — again, forcing Tessa to brace against the dashboard.

The jeep skidded to a stop, again.

Still standing in the spot where he almost got hit, was a young man, perhaps sixteen or seventeen, staring straight at them with semi-stoned eyes. The kicked-up dust swirled around his feet and covered them completely from view. He might as well have been floating.

CHAPTER THIRTEEN
MONTEJO, COLORADO

THE YOUTH REMAINED looking at their jeep, nodding in time to a silent tune, and grinning a little. "You folks lost?"

He looked like a kid Tessa knew.

Fanning the dust tossed aloft from their urgent stop, and mentally talking herself out of a potential heart attack, Tessa gathered her wits. "Heading for Montejo," she called over to him with a false nonchalance.

The young man turned and thumbed down towards the valley. Sticking his hands back into his pockets, he scowled at them. His eyes were black, but his long hair was bleached blond and so were his eyebrows, as one might expect from a surfer on the coast. He wore a bead necklace, probably purchased locally, and like any teenager hanging out, appeared bored.

"Nuthin' down there to see, man," Surfer Teen slurred, with a slight drawl that made Jack's eyebrow lift above the rim of his sunglasses, though his knuckles were still white in their grip on the steering wheel. "Ain't been nothin' down there to see for years. No point in going."

Tessa pushed her hat back an inch or so, to see him better. "Oh, we're not staying long. We aren't even tourists. USGS — soil sample time."

Surfer Teen nodded and twisted his grin into something between a smile and a frown. "Yeah, well, if ya' go down there, they ain't got Wi-Fi. They ain't got nothin', man. Dead zone. Nobody goes there. Nobody wants to go there. Heck, they have their own police down there, with their own laws, so nobody bothers them. They're not like everyone else. Ya' might as well be dealing with zombies and ghosts."

Jack coughed, pulling up the brake but kept the engine going. Turning to the kid, he asked, "So, why are *y'all* here?"

Good question, Tessa thought.

The black eyes and blond eyebrows narrowed. "You not listening, man? Nuthin's down there. Down there ain't good." He pointed. "Up here is okay. Down there just sucks, man. I'd just go home if I were you. Or, you know, like, go somewhere with hotels and restaurants and casinos and stuff. Just not here."

Tessa adjusted her hat again. "I'm afraid we have to- to do our job. But your warning is appreciated all the same. Anything else we should know?"

Jack reached for the ignition, to turn it off, but the jeep stalled on its own, burping and snarling and pinging as if out of gas.

Startled, Tessa turned away from the young man and checked the dashboard dials in front of Jack.

"Well, shit. This is a fine start." He tried the key a couple of times.

"Don't flood the engine," she admonished him.

For that comment, she got the Eyebrow of Doom. Of course he knew better. Then he gave her a look of surprise.

Actually Jack's surprised stare was aimed over her head. Turning in her seat to look too, Tessa knew what Jack was, or wasn't, seeing.

Surfer Teen was gone.

Not simply gone from where he stood. He was nowhere to be seen.

The highway stretched out in two directions unhindered and visually unblocked. With the exception of the steep dirt road down toward Montejo, there were no other exits. Flat farm country stretched out in the distance.

Surfer Teen would have had to cross in front of them and run faster than an Olympian to reach the restaurant ruins in the seconds they weren't looking. So, unless he had jumped down a rabbit hole, he had simply vanished.

The agents stared at one another, Tessa shrugged helplessly, and the jeep started on its own. After a moment of astonishment, she mumbled, "A mystery for another time?"

They sat for another minute, baffled, before Jack gingerly put the Jeep in gear.

Jack nodded, chewing a little on the inside of his mouth. "Yeah. One conundrum at a time please."

The road had a steep grade, one that would prevent trucks of a certain size from coming into town. The next turn was onto a county road that went south again. It began a twist and turn downward, wending its way to the base of the bluff where the township of Montejo rested. The place was off visual range, making the closest miles of the highway invisible from Main Street, which was already hazy with pink and brown dust.

Tessa caught herself mutter-singing, "*Brig-a-doon, Brig-a-doon, blooming under sable skies …*"

"Stop that," he whispered.

Further into town on Main Street, the elements of life and death were better mixed, with a liquor store that was assumed to be open only because there was no front door, two run-down businesses, a diner that looked much less ready to crumble back into the ground than the buildings around it, and what was hopefully a working service station. Had a flock of tumbleweeds rolled past, she wouldn't have been surprised. A man in overalls, spattered with grease, waited half in the shadows, cleaning a tool or something, and watching them as they headed toward the obvious motel.

"That's it." Tessa grinned slyly, pointing at the neon sign. "Ah darn, no pool."

"The 'Seven Little Indians' motel?" Jack shook his head and parked the jeep near the door to the lobby.

The motel's second story sagged worse than a couch-potato's stomach. The blue exterior and white trim failed to hide that it hadn't been painted in years. Flower boxes with plastic, dust covered flowers were a nice attempt, but underneath those, the withered weeds and bits of trash blown against the building spoke more about the owner's expectation of weekly vacancies.

If it wasn't obviously beaten up by wind and sand, it was obviously damaged by water and rot. A dirty high watermark still branded the first-floor exterior.

Despite the motel's condition, it was arguably better than the abandoned hotel down the street, half of which had collapsed from apparent wood rot.

The motel's balcony faced the street but was clearly off limits, with construction tape fluttering in the breeze. The other half of the motel looked to have been a house, converted to commercial use by the same gentle means as a shotgun wedding. The windows facing the diner were at least open, allowing a curtain to tremble in and out. There was hope for semi-fresh air — dusty, but not mechanically recycled.

Jack scratched his head. "Looks like it was built up in the 1960s and hasn't had a maintenance-job since. Nice old motel."

"Ah — correction," she pointed to the printed sign on the door. "*B and B.*"

"Excuse me. We've moved up in the world?"

"One can only hope. It's our home sweet home for a bit."

"Right down to its offensive little name," he grumbled.

She swung her legs out of the jeep. "Aren't you glad I came with you?"

"Did ya' call ahead to reserve our deluxe accommodations?" Jack was completely deadpan, but a quick sly wink anyone else would miss told Tessa he was enjoying the joke. There was the old Jack. "I'd hate to find out that they just can't fit us in at the inn."

Tessa tossed her hat into the front seat of the jeep. "Well, if they don't have any room, we'll just have to rough it out at the work site."

"*Al Fresco*? Boss Lady, that could prove interesting." Jack dropped his voice to a low volume. "We might have to combine our body temperatures to withstand the cold of night."

Flirting? Finally, some normality. Maybe he would get back into the swing of things after all, she hoped. She flicked the brim of his hat as he got too close.

Grabbing the larger pieces of surveying and computer equipment she'd arranged, they trundled up to the front door.

It banged open, allowing three, 20-somethings to spill out. The first was a woman, dressed in a black tee shirt that announced her membership in the *4-Corners Paranormal Research Society* emblazoned in neon green letters that dripped at the edges, as if written in ectoplasm. She scowled and gripped a large black box so hard it turned her knuckles white.

The two men with her sported unkempt beards, Bermuda shorts, socks, and hiking shoes. The equipment boxes they were taking out were as impressive as those Tessa and Jack were taking in. One of the men was white as a proverbial sheet and squeaking a little as he spoke. "I'm just saying, I saw what I saw."

"Did you get any video?" the woman demanded.

"No! I saw it, I turned the camera to it, and it was gone." His face was rapidly shifting from white to green, and he muttered curses as he couldn't get his equipment case to fit into the car. Desperately, he kept trying to force it in place. "Shadow men never stay around for long."

"No video then?" the woman snapped.

"Find anything good?" Tessa asked, her interest piqued.

"Too much," the other fellow replied, sounding a bit shell-shocked, and pushed past them. By his rush, it was clear he couldn't get out of town fast enough.

"Oh," Tessa asked, genuinely. "Like what?"

"Nothing," the woman in the T-shirt responded, defensively.

"Footsteps. Moving objects. Voices. Whispers. Christ, the place didn't shut up." The man must have realized his success in fitting the first case into the car was going to prevent him from fitting the second case in. He cussed and tore things out to repack.

His friend raced back into the lobby as though he was rescuing puppies from a fire. Coming back out, arms laden with cases, he added, "Shadow figures. That's never good."

"Any video," the woman demanded again.

The man didn't reply and ran back to the lobby for a third, overloaded trip.

Jack set down one of his cases and held the door for all the parties. "This isn't a ghost town yet, is it? I think all y'all are a bit too early."

The woman, determined to show her status as leader of the team, ordered the two men to keep putting the equipment into their car, a station wagon of formidable years, and planted her hands on her equally formidable hips. "Oh, this place is just about there. But no, we took our chances with the *Mesa*."

Tessa brightened up a bit. "*Mesa Verde*? We are a bit far from there. Still, I always wanted to see it but never had the time." *Another Daddy-Promise, missed.*

Looking at Tessa with intimated side-glances, the team leader shook her head. "No. That place might be haunted, might not be. Depends on who you ask." She watched her boys like a mothering hawk. "What brings you to this hole in the dirt?"

"The very dirt you mention. USGS. De Sombras," Tessa pointed to Jack, "and Wells."

"Doctor Wells," Jack corrected, watching the team leader. "Geologist — amateur Parapsychologist — something like that," he muttered out loud.

Nice move, Jack.

"Parapsychologist?" Surprised, the woman slowly offered her hand to Tessa. "Bel McGuire, Lead Investigator. The guy cussing at the car is Andy Solomon." Andy waved a hand from his position behind the station wagon. "The guy inside is Sid Franklin, Tech Manager and the guy we can credit with getting us into the Mesa — not Verde."

Sid, on his last trip out of the lobby, thanked Jack for holding the door as he retrieved another of the paranormal group's cases from the lobby. "You can't hunt over at Verde anyway. National Park. They won't let us."

"It's rare to get access out there," Tessa added.

Sid slowed long enough to give Tessa an appreciative nod. "We went out to *Los Muertos*." He added for Jack's benefit, "Not doing that again. Not without a bigger team and a loaded shotgun."

Tessa turned to the leader with wide eyes.

"*Mesa de los Muertos.* Most haunted ancient site in America," Bel exclaimed. "It's so dangerous, the National Park Service gave it up six years ago. And we stayed the night there," she added with a great deal of pride.

"Impressive." Tessa's eyes brightened.

Sid leaned over his leader's shoulder, and added chidingly, "We stayed until just after midnight."

"It was 'A.M.' when we left. That counts as *morning*," his leader corrected him. "We officially stayed *the night*."

Sid rolled his eyes. "We bailed as fast as we could. Especially once that howling started. I'm all for ghost hunting, but shit — there's stuff out there I've never seen or heard of before." He glared at Bel and shouted, "Can we go now?"

"And us with no video!" she shouted back at him. She smiled at Jack; he tipped his hat. "I got EVP recordings though. I'll need to go over those when I get home. Andy's right about one thing: that place doesn't shut up all night. I'm bound to have something on the recorder. We all heard stuff."

"Just no video," Jack added with dramatic sadness. "That's a real shame."

Tessa pulled out one of the cards Chey made for her. "EVP? Listen, if you wouldn't mind, I'd love to hear, literally, what you got. I'm curious if you picked up any music or only voices."

Bel's face perked up. She examined the card for a moment. "Hadn't thought about music, but you're right."

"You aren't using those spirit boxes are you?"

"Ugh!" Bel shook her head. "I don't buy into those and besides, they only work if you speak English. Won't help with someone speaking ancient Puebloan."

"Can we go now?" the men cried almost in unison.

"Hold your horses," Bel shouted.

Tessa coyly looked over at her cowboy colleague. "I wonder if that place is on our map for soil analysis. Now, I'd love to see it. Always had a weakness for things that go bump in the night."

"No, you wouldn't." The gas station attendant walked up, still wiping his tools. A baseball cap covered his forehead and cast a shadow over his face. He stood between the sun and the motel, making everyone squint to see him. "These kids were told not to go out there. I know, I done tell 'em myself."

"We came out here to record video and EVP evidence at Mesa de los Muertos," Bel shot back at him, with plenty of extra venom in her tone. "Not to sit in a diner, stuffing our faces with greasy burgers, and listening to others tell us about it. We're not a bunch of tourists you need to entertain. We're not folklorists, we're ghost hunters. We hunt ghosts." To emphasize her point, and perhaps to suggest the attendant was a bit stupid not to have guessed everything on his own, she waved her hand across her logo t-shirt.

"Yer lucky you all didn' get hurt. People don't go out there and *not* get hurt." He turned to the agents and pointed his tool, possibly a screwdriver, though Tessa couldn't quite tell. "You two stay out. I don't know what yer business is —"

"USGS," Tessa replied flatly.

The Gas Guy stared at her.

"It's been ten years. Soil analysis. Current drought data."

"Uh, sure. Okay."

"And, if it makes you feel better," she cooed, turning on her best charm for the man, "If Mesa de los Muertos isn't on our survey map, we won't be going out there. No time. There's a tight schedule to keep. We're due in Pleasant View, then Dove Creek ... too many sites. Too few of us."

The man nodded, and looked over at Jack, who gave him his best *don't look at me* expression. "Just as well. We had some fool fall there two weeks ago. Sent him off to the hospital. Unlucky, he didn't survive. People gotta' learn when we say it ain't safe, it ain't."

"That's fair enough." Tessa stepped a bit closer to him. "I'm Dr. Wells, USGS. Hello," she offered him her hand. "Thank you for the warning."

He looked at his own filthy hand and stuffed it into the pocket of his baggy, dirty coveralls. "Ma'am."

Undeterred, she smiled at him. "That's Santiago de Sombras. Out of our Albuquerque office," Tessa said, indicated Jack with a tilt of her head. "We call him Rio."

Jack gave that quintessential, man-with-nothing-urgent-to-say nod to Gas Guy. The nod was returned.

"And you're our very first local contact, except for a kid at the top of the hill." She gave him a heart-melting smile. "Your establishment?" She indicated the building behind him and began giving it a pre-approved once-over.

Gas Guy nodded a bit. "Welp, don't forget to fill up on yer way out today. Ain't many stations around an' ya' don't want to run outta' gas anywhere out there."

Interesting, Tessa thought. He assumed they would be leaving — right quick.

She and Gas Guy had to move aside as the paranormal team spun their wheels in the sand and dirt and drove out of town as fast as possible.

Standing close to Gas Guy, Tessa noticed an unpleasant aroma wafting up from his coveralls. Whatever he worked on, it didn't smell like petrol or oil. More like … raw sewage. Still, she needed to ask him questions. "The man who fell? How terrible." Her hand came up under her nose, and she made a point of rubbing to hide that she was blocking the odor. The man who fell, was it one of the other agents? Maybe Gas Guy knew. "Not always fond of heights," she lied. "Who was he?"

Gas Guy shook his head. "Stranger. Strangers shouldn't come here."

"Really?" Her voice had a well-rehearsed tremble in it. "Was he a ghost hunter like those kids who just left?"

The bill of Gas Guy's hat lowered. "He came to find …" He stopped for a long pause. "Maybe he was a pot picker. Don't know, but he found out that you can't mess around out there. The Mesa's cursed as far as I can tell. Won't go there myself. Never mind ghosts, the place ain't stable — it's dangerous. You sure you're not goin' there?"

"If it's not on my map," she lied again without hesitation. "My colleague doesn't believe in … you know … but I do. Thank you for the tip." She gave Gas Guy a confidential, serious nod.

"How's the food?" Jack called over from where he was still acting as the door stop.

"Awful."

CHAPTER FOURTEEN
SEVEN LITTLE INDIANS B & B
MONTEJO, COLORADO

CHECKING IN TOOK LONGER than Jack anticipated, considering the motel had exactly two prepared rooms for exactly two pre-registered guests. Them.

As he pulled his own overnight bag out of the jeep, he mentally saluted the motel manager. The woman had missed her chance to be in the Business. She had asked for every type of ID and tidbit of information. Either she'd been scammed before or was digging for details on who they were.

He assumed the latter.

He leaned on the driver's door, checked the jeep, then surreptitiously glanced into the lobby. Sure enough, the manager was on her computer. By the shapes and colors on the monitor, reflected in the framed photos hung up behind her and on her glasses, he felt comfortable guessing she was on the USGS website checking their stories.

Tessa was too good not to have their covers set up deep.

Stopping for a moment, he closed his eyes. What was he doing? Could he genuinely go through with his plan? Jack leaned back on the jeep's door.

He'd grown accustomed to the green of the northern pine trees and redwoods, the thick forests climbing up Mt. Shasta, and the white snow of the mountain's peak. In the fall, California turned brown and beige, but not like this. This place was different. Montejo was not merely an electronic dead zone, it was lifeless. Cold weather or hot, and it was definitely getting hotter, this place was a desert.

Jack's muscles tightened. Hairs on his neck prickled. His missing fingers ached.

Something was very wrong

The hair on his arms stood up.

The incessant wind had stopped blowing. The air hung heavy, unyielding, thick. And the oxygen was thin. For a moment he also wondered if the motel parking lot was down wind of a garbage dump. The smell of rot was so intense that he coughed. He couldn't hear any noise. No laughing or speaking. No birds. No insects.

Nothing. Dead air.

Wait… He saw it.

In broad daylight, he saw it.

A shadow.

Out of the corner of his eye, he saw it.

A free-standing shadow of a man.

Not cast by a solid thing.

Glaring at him. Red eyes.

Pushing off the jeep's door, Jack took several steps forward.

And it was gone.

Had he blinked and it vanished? Or had it never been there at all?

A woman's voice burst into laughter. Far away, an 18-wheeler began jack-breaking on the incline. The wind whipped up the pale dirt and flung sand at Jack, carrying the smell of garbage with it.

Should he tell Tessa? *No*! She was giving such *unusual* experiences too much credence, and it seemed she already wanted to explore them. No, no distractions. Mission first. This was nothing more than his imagination, spurred on by all the talk about ghosts, local lore, and strange coincidences.

The hair on his arms remained upright.

I don't believe in ghosts, he shouted inside his mind, while getting into the motel as fast as he could.

But she does.

CHAPTER FIFTEEN

TESSA RESTED HER HANDS on the battered sill, where chips of paint splintered away from the wood. She scraped them off, revealing the weathered, sand-pitted surface of the sill boards. The greasy aromas of the old-style diner wafted into her window. Sheer curtains whipped further into the room and tangled with the brass bedstead. The clear, bright sky settled behind Sleeping Ute Mountain to the south, while a piñon juniper tree wavered drunkenly near the corner of the B & B motel.

The door to her room stood open behind her. Jack had insisted on the smaller room, across the hall from hers, with one window facing west-southwest and a full view into her room.

Both rooms, plus the hallway with the broken light, plus the squeaking stairwell, plus the closed off sections of the B & B motel, were all creepy as hell. All this place needed was the pair of twins at one end of the hallway and a man with an ax at the other.

"I hope you're all right with such a tiny room," Tessa said through the open doors, clearly filling the void of silence with chatter, the sort one might expect from working folks just settling in.

Jack looked briefly around his room. "When yer the youngest of seven boys, in one house, a room like this is paradise."

A pair of pines blocked much of his view from that single window, but he seemed quite satisfied. His door faced hers, the foot of his bed pointing to the foot of hers. As he had done many times before, he was setting up as her self-appointed guard dog. He made certain she saw him place the Smith & Wesson 10mm revolver under his pillow. Her knight in tarnished armor was not without sword or lance. A nice weapon, though when and how he'd obtained it in the time between their reunion and departure for Montejo, she left as a question best not asked. She suspected Uncle Joe had something to do with it and, thinking that Tessa guess the 10mm wasn't the only item Jack had brought in the name of protection.

Smiling sweetly to him in response, she waggled a neat little Walther PPQ 9mm M2, then slid it under her own pillowcase. "Seven boys?" she asked, adjusting the pillow. "I had no idea you came from such a big family." She set her one suitcase on the bed, along with what looked like a motorcycle helmet.

"Six uncles too, but no cousins," Jack called from across the hall.

"Seems your father made up for it."

"More than," he chuckled unconvincingly. He was distracted, carefully running his hand under his bed, giving her a thumbs-up signal when he didn't find anything. "These days, it's down to me and one uncle. That's just the way life goes."

"Well, I'm sure glad Albuquerque could spare you, and that you are willing to help with this."

"Yes, ma'am. Glad to get out of the office."

The rest of their audible conversation was professional, simple, and to the point: where to take samples and how to report them. Tessa behaved managerial. Jack behaved blue collar.

All the while, Jack took Tessa's phone and began using an application not found in any app-store. Its signal fanned out checking for familiar electrical impulses or strings of communication.

Bugs.

And not bed bugs.

He complained about the drought and excessive heat while scanning everywhere near the doors, an unused phone line, lamps, and anywhere else the less experienced tended to plant listening devices.

The scanner beeped.

Neither of their rooms had more than two electrical outlets, both were taken up by an alarm clock and lamp. Her room clock wasn't working well.

Watching as Jack checked twice, she unplugged her alarm clock and peeked under the heavy, boxy unit. The alarm clock had something spliced into its power cord. *Bingo.* Surveillance objects need power, at least the older models did. Unplugged, the round object ceased to function, along with the clock. Tessa gestured to him in their spy semaphore, that she intended to leave the clock unplugged. Out loud she added, "My phone has an alarm. I need that plug for my laptop." *In a building this old*, she thought, *we'll be lucky if two laptops don't burn the place down.* "I'm beginning to think someone is suspicious of us," she muttered.

"Probably suspicious of everyone who checks in here." Jack shut the door quietly behind him. "Nothin' more on radar in here," he whispered to her.

Tessa simply nodded.

He smiled. "I suspect the manager is the owner, janitor, maid, and insect expert," he pointed to the bug. "Not a bad arrangement if you need to keep a close watch on visitors."

"All two of us." She held up her phone. "We really *are* in a dead zone."

He gave her his signature, if exaggerated, eyebrow lift. *No shit Darlin'.*

She leaned forward to him but glared at her phone and the words, *No Service.* "Definitely cut off from the real world."

"Funny that," he replied, sitting on the bed near her. "Anything last minute from your home office?"

"Absolute quiet. But I expected that too." Finally sitting, she leaned back in the creaky, old chair. The tied-on cushion provided no comfort at all. "Any communication will either be slow and cumbersome, or we'll have to go back up to the highway to get a clear signal." *Drawing unwanted attention.* "How's your room?"

"Clean enough, and comfortable." He nodded to her, opened both doors, and headed over. "I brought those maps — got them in my bag right here," he announced to everyone listening.

"Hey up there," the manager called to them from downstairs. "Diner's closing between lunch and dinner. If ya' want to eat, go now."

Jack returned post haste, leaned down and whispered in Tessa's ear, the warmth of his breath a bit stirring. "They want a little look-see into our personal belongings. Now that I think about it, I might feel a bit insulted if they didn't."

"Well, nothing says intruder like a refusal to allow someone to grope through your underthings." Tessa brought up a USGS website that Kýrios's team had designed for them to use and closed the computer's lid. If anyone tried to get past that site, the entire Athenaeum would know.

"Are you hungry, Rio?" Tessa asked, loudly, retrieving her 9mm to take with her.

"Yes, ma'am. All that drivin' left me a might peckish." He announced as he slipped his gun into a pocket sewn into the back of his jacket.

Set it up — take it right back down. It was a dance they both knew the steps to.

"Why don't we grab something before they close? We can go over the schedule of the job when we're done."

"Yes, ma'am."

The innkeeper tried not to look interested when they came down the stairs. Tessa said something about seeing Jack at the diner and left him to handle the innkeeper.

At the door, she waited to hear what Jack would say. Not that she was worried, she just liked to watch him work. It was a little bit of a turn-on.

Jack held his hat, now sporting a coat of Montejo dust on it, and smiled a toothy, sexy grin at the woman. She was in her late fifties, a platinum blond, heavily made up, and dressed in outdated clothing. With Tessa still in hearing range, she figured Jack would speak softly to the innkeeper and she might as well go outside. As the lobby door was closing, she could see Jack leaning on his arms, on the front desk, moving loosely and confidently. The innkeeper's cheeks were a bright pink.

That was Jack's true superpower. Never mind fancy clothes or fighting styles, Jack had cool confidence, assurance of victory, and slyness. He was brutally aware that his dark eyes could drag a woman under and drown her in their depths. He knew he was the right height to be impressive without being threatening. The moustache? It gave him that quintessential Western appearance, so nearly impossible to resist.

For a man wanting to be hidden from the world, why did he keep that *soup strainer*? It meant he looked exactly as he did when he was ... uh ... formerly employed. Ego, perhaps? He knew he was even more dishy with it than without, not that there was anything to complain about when he was completely shaven. Frankly, he looked twenty years younger without it and that didn't always work in his favor. Or maybe, just maybe, he kept it as the one thing from before, since all else was lost.

And dear God, he hadn't lost any of his appeal working on the ranch with Uncle Joe. In fact, he'd gained all the more. Tanned. Muscular. Weathered.

Tessa tore herself away and started walking.

In the middle of the road, Jack caught up with her, trying in vain to swat off the dust from his hat before shoving it onto his head in disgust.

"Anything we can use?" Tessa asked.

"Not a damn thing she said is useful right now. But I was amazed she was wearing a Cartier necklace."

"A what?" Tessa took a step or two away, to read his face, to know if he were kidding her or not. His eyes were always a give-away.

"Bought one for a lady, many, many moons ago. I know good quality when I see it. If it isn't Cartier, it's something just as spendy."

"Where the hell does a woman out here in *B.F. Egypt* get anything from Cartier?"

"Now that, Darlin', is a very fine question."

"I suppose it was in the family, or a gift, or she saved up? We can't assume."

"Hold up a minute," Jack darted toward the back parking lot of the diner. Tessa knew not to follow him, but to keep on walking, sauntering even, toward the front of the diner.

Waiting for him to return, she stopped to take in the scenery. Up on the highway, the area could have been mistaken for any farmland in the Great Plains. Down in Montejo, the environment was pure Wild Country Southwest. Colors of grey mixed with purple, rust, and salmon beneath a sweeping, cloudless blue sky. If *Death* wanted to find her here, *It* would have no trouble. If *It* found the place at all. And certainly, she would recognize *Death* coming from any direction.

Shaking off her morbid thoughts, Tessa read the menu posted at the window. It had been updated — that day — as if someone, other than her, was expected to read it.

The diner looked like a set piece from the movies or possibly even a theme park. It was curved at every edge, and neon tubes flowed along in sets of three, across the roof line, door frame, and generally anywhere a 1950s element would be suitable. The place was painted medium blue, like the color of a classic Chevy. It was clean, tidy, and shiny, in the middle of disheveled Montejo?

The newspaper stand in front held a weekly print. The paper was tinted dusty brown, with a headline warning of a major storm coming, a county fair, and some sort of junior rodeo. The incessant wind tossed the dust around. It struck her between her shoulders, as if to push her into the diner, she held back her desire to tell the wind off. She hated bullies. She'd go inside when she was damn good and ready.

The date on the paper's header was from five years earlier. Maybe the publisher went out of business.

Something banged shut in the wind and slammed for a moment. The air was thick, clogging, choaking. The smell of being downwind of a garbage dump permeated everything. All the dryness begged to be relieved with water that hadn't come for a long time. Brown. Tan. Gray. A tinge of artificial color now and then.

Corpse colors.

No one drove through town. No laughter. No gossip. No phones ringing.

The full opposite of the towns up on 491.

Eyes bored into her back.

The fight against panic was real, but she held it together, with tissue paper, sarcasm, and spit it necessary.

Panic was held off – for the moment.

She knew something was watching.

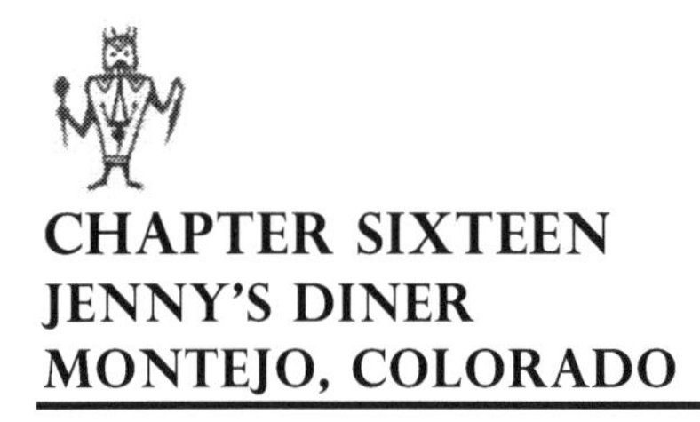

CHAPTER SIXTEEN
JENNY'S DINER
MONTEJO, COLORADO

HER GUT WAS NUDGING HER, urging her to look. Surreptitiously, she put the paper back, allowing her to check.

Over her shoulder, across the street, stood Gas Guy, wiping the same tool, with the same greasy cloth. As he was half hiding behind the door, she decided not to obviously notice him.

Jack returned to open the diner door for her.

"Careful, Jack, we're being watched. Gas station."

"Got him."

She backed up to allow the door to swing open. "Anything interesting back there?"

"Cars," he replied solidly.

"No surprise there, but why do you mention it?"

"Expensive cars. There's a Mercedes, two BMWs, a couple of collector's classics. Several new plates."

"Not to be found in a desert plateau of the Southwest?"

"Could be, as you mentioned, one shouldn't leap to conclusions. There could be a reasonable explanation for them — and the Cartier necklace."

"Of course."

He removed his hat and nodded as the startled waitress noticed them.

"Come on in," she said with a hitch in her voice. The woman kept looking at them, as if she couldn't quite decide who they were. "Pick any place you like. Any. We're just happy to have you." She waved at the seating nervously, turned, and skittered to the back of the bar, looking over her shoulder at them often.

"Do you know her, Jack? I mean, knowing you, it is more than possible."

"Never been here. Don't recall her."

"She keeps staring at us. We are the curiosity *du jour.*"

"I'm thinking she's expectin' someone and is wondering if we're them?"

"Good point."

The smell of fried potatoes and cooked meat filled the place. The cook's pass-through behind the bar gave Tessa a view into the kitchen. The short-order was a younger man, with a shock of reddish-blond hair. He pulled on a hair net, tied his apron, and got to work. Pots and pans were lifted out of the washer and dropped loudly on the stove or prep-counters. Paper bags waited on the pick-up sill, ready to be filled. "I thought they were closing for the midday break," Jack said, sliding into a vinyl booth across from Tessa. "Awfully busy for closing at any moment."

The cook banged through the saloon doors that led to the kitchen, carrying a coffee carafe and two mugs. He set the cups and, hopefully, fresh coffee on their table without so much as a "howdy," and walked back into the kitchen.

The waitress came over and offered menus with the sweetest, forced-on smile. "No more specials until later, which you already know, but if you want more than what was preordered, we can always cook up something special. You bein' *Incomers* an all. We are more than happy to be accommodating. All you need do is ask." She rubbed her hands on her apron, as if trying to get circulation going. "An ... and if you do request something special, me and the kitchen staff would appreciate it if you'd mention the extra service you got from us to the Sheriff." Her gaze went distant, as though remembering. "Quality customer service is vital to the white glove experience. Our clients are of the highest caliber, and we know you have certain expectations." She completed her memorized statement and allowed her lips to settle into a practiced smile.

"Just here to check yer soil, Sweetheart," Jack replied to her. Was his drawl a tad bit thicker, Tessa wondered?

"Come again?" The waitress's face contorted.

Tessa pushed her computer bag over a bit, to make more room. "USGS. We're here to do the ten-year —"

The woman, perhaps in her thirties, with mousey brown hair, scowled, aging herself by a decade. "You're not ..." She began to back away from them.

Jack to the rescue. "USGS. We'll be here for a couple of days and then gone. Say, what do y'all recommend? Especially since we better hurry so y'all can clean up and get ready for the supper crowd."

Her corn-flower eyes, the same color as her shoddy, faded uniform, were wide and unblinking. "Um, maybe ..." She crept back to the agents and started to grab for the menus. "Maybe the kitchen isn't open anymore ... Maybe I should check ..."

The so-called kitchen buzzed with activity. Carry out bags were being filled up along the order counter.

Tessa jumped in abruptly. "My word, that's a gorgeous ring."

Startled, the waitress looked down at her hand. The engagement ring was large, diamond encrusted, and did not go with the coffee-stains.

"Would ya' look at that," Jack replied, taking her hand politely, to look at it closely. Yes, his drawl *was* stronger. "Now, what lucky fella got ya' to put that on? He better be one hell of a guy, to deserve a pretty thing like you."

He was turning it all on. Charm. Off-side smile. Touch of swagger. Good old Jack. The waitress was ready to pull her hand away but chose instead to let him hold it.

"I think I might be jealous," he added. "Bet he's from out of town and just makes every excuse to come visit. I know I would."

The waitress turned beet-red and began to shy back, though not nearly as fast as before. "Ah, no. My Billy is local. He's a good man." She stared at the other woman, Tessa.

Tessa shook her head. "Just a co-worker. Rio here is absolutely shameless when he meets a beautiful woman. But, I promise, I've never seen him hurt a fly," which was true. What he'd done to some people, on the other hand . . .

"Billy's one lucky man," Jack acknowledged, giving the woman a wink. "I don't suppose there'd be any chance for a fella like me? Nah, there isn't, is there? Just my luck."

"Ah, that's sweet." The waitress looked out the window, sighed in relief, then turned to Jack. "You're being kind. But I'd never do anything to upset my Billy."

Jack's hand swept out in a gracious, resigned motion. "I would never think that a nice lady like you would ever do anything terrible to anyone."

Her smile vanished along with any color in her face. "We can make a couple of burgers for you — *to go*." She turned heel and fled the dining room.

"You bad man, I think you frightened her," Tessa said without scolding him at all.

"Guilt. For doin' something terrible? Her hands were freezing. Plus, she keeps lookin' out that window. Whatever it is, she's expecting it to come down the road at any minute."

"It's already here."

A rumble of engines announced new arrivals, and a handful of vehicles swept into view, on a brown cloud.

"My dear, your timing is impeccable as usual."

CHAPTER SEVENTEEN

ON CUE, AN ENORMOUS SUV, with wheel lifts, screamed to a halt, inches shy of the window next to the Agents. A cloud of dust flew up and gravel skittered everywhere.

The waitress, her breath catching in her throat, called over to them. "Don't move. Stay perfectly still. Oh God. Don't say nothing. Don't ... don't, just don't." She clutched her uniform and begged with those cornflower eyes. Tessa felt the need to assure her, if only with a nod of agreement.

Jack and Tessa glanced at each other, then at the diner staff who all magically appeared out of nowhere. Each stood stiffly, lined up behind the bar or the kitchen order window, ready for inspection.

"It appears someone has found our secret honeymoon destination," Tessa whispered.

"Let's hope we're mistaken for locals."

Not a chance in hell.

The diner's door banged open.

Jack casually tucked his hand under his suede jacket. Tessa's calmly pulled her computer bag close so that she felt the bulge of the 9mm in the front pocket.

Hollywood Central Casting couldn't have done better with the fellow barging in the door. The man was shaved from head to presumably foot. His tan was fake. Cold blue eyes scanned the room. The all-black suit, shirt, shoes, and tie were new but old fashioned in cut. A pair of scars cut up along his chin to his bottom lip.

Spotting the waitress, he snapped his fingers. She nodded, fetched up the packages on the order counter and ferried them over to the cash register near the door. Without uttering a single word, she held up the bill. The man in black laughed, if that was a laugh, and pulled out two one-hundred-dollar bills.

"Keep change. For pretty girl," he said in a thick Slavic accent and offered her a leering grin.

"Thank ... thank you."

He picked up all the packages and turned to go. Immediately behind Jack, he stopped.

Tessa kept a menu open in front of her, her attention deliberately showing disinterest in the Russian in black. She made herself think and breathe *small.*

"Two pretty girls today. Maybe I come back some time."

Tessa did not respond, and the Russian laughed, glaring at the cowboy hat on the table.

Jack sat still, drinking guardedly from a cup of coffee. His right hand remained tucked away at the ready.

"*Mestny Svinovod*," the Russian hissed at him.

Jack's lopsided grin showed up, he otherwise didn't move.

Satisfied, the man in black slammed out the door.

"He thinks I'm a pig farmer," Jack added quickly, still calmly drinking his coffee and letting only his eyes move. "Like they have the water around here for that."

Engines and breaks filled the diner with noise and dust. Out the window, Tessa counted cars again. Sure enough, the vehicles had doubled in number. A dozen SUVs split into two groups right outside. Men scrambled out, posturing at one another, fists shaking.

"I think there's going to be an old-fashioned rumble," she whispered to Jack. "Right outside."

"Oh my God," the waitress quaked. "Not again. Not in the middle of town."

Before Jack could turn on his charm for questioning, she fled the main room for the kitchen, pulling out a cell phone. Everyone fled the dining area, leaving the agents alone. Once in the kitchen, the staff all hid behind the kitchen counter, eyes bigger than the plates they served lunch on.

Shouting raged between the two groups outside.

Guns out.

Tessa grasped her 9mm and waited. Jack pulled his gun from the jacket holster yet waited to reveal it completely.

"Do we need to get out of here before Sergio Leone starts directing this picture?" she whispered.

"I think they're mostly just making noise." He slid closer to the window but kept low in the seat. "Recognize anyone?"

Tessa did the same. "The little guy on the left. Anatoli. Replanted Russian Mob. East coast. Jersey mostly. Handles small arms to small tyrants with smaller dicks. No idea who anyone else is."

"There has to be ten, maybe twelve, vehicles out there. Same unimaginative tailor. Think the one with the carrot-top is Anatoli's rival."

The five-foot, five-inch Anatoli stood and casually buttoned his jacket. He showed no sign of concern over the rival gang nor for his own safety. The redhead that faced him and smiled was not worried either. Their gangs lined up behind each man and looked ready to kill if summoned. Hands were positioned under coats and around the back of belts. Knuckles were tested for hardness.

A gun shot exploded in the air.

Both agents and staff all dropped low in the booth.

"Shotgun," Tessa spit out as she landed flat on the vinyl seat.

Jack laid flat on his back, on the booth seat. "Classic 12-guage."

A thundering voice began demanding what was going on here, had they no respect, and someone needed to get going — now!

Daring to peek out, Tessa saw an interesting mountain of a man standing between the two factions, holding the shotgun in question. Even from that distance and position, Tessa knew a cop when she saw one, and this one wore a hat that screamed *policeman*, complete with a shiny star fixed above the bill. The sheriff himself? Behind the sheriff waited three well-armed, uniformed men. Deputies?

"Johnny Law just showed up," she announced under the table.

Jack shimmied over to the window and squinted as he peered into the bright parking lot. "And the Ruskies care?"

"Apparently. Maybe the shotgun has something to do with it."

"Not likely. Any of those boys has something the same size in his pocket. One sheriff, three deputies, and about fifteen Ruskies. He may need *our* help."

"Hold on."

The sheriff stood between the warring factions, but no one moved. They stood there — *mesmerized.* It was the only word she could think of that fit.

Tessa's face twisted in confusion when both gangs quietly went back to their vehicles without another word. She glanced over at Jack, as if he understood any better.

The two mob leaders stood eight feet apart growling at one another, until all their associates were boarded into the SUVs. Neither waited for someone to open their door, choosing to fend for themselves and got into their respective vehicles.

Mesmerized. That was exactly the right word.

Anatoli's gang drove off to the left of the diner. Carrot-top's caravan headed around to the right.

A few moments later, the dust settled.

Only the sheriff and his men were left standing in the road. One leaned close to the sheriff and told him something that did not please him if his expression was to be believed. The deputy pointed with his head to the diner. The sheriff turned to glare in the same direction.

"Surreal?"

"Too real," Jack said, sneaking his gun back into its jacket holster.

"Uh oh." Tessa sat up sharply. "*Prepare to repel boarders.* Here *he* comes."

CHAPTER EIGHTEEN

THE SHERIFF STROLLED INTO THE DINER, shotgun in hand. His quick sweep of the room apparently satisfied him. He nodded and lowered the gun to a less threatening position.

Tessa gave him a quick estimation, keeping her face as if she were at once concerned for her safety and thankful that a man in uniform had shown up to save the day. She put him around six-foot, three inches, and two hundred twenty-five pounds of muscle. If it weren't for the brown shirt, tan work pants, patches and silver badge, she would have guessed him to be a Marine. His mouth supported no significant lips, though they weren't likely to show through the frown anyway. His chin had that punching bag look that probably no one dared to touch. His utility belt hung low, slung well below the natural placement of his waistline.

They locked glances.

Her body froze. No skilled reaction. No danger messaging. In fact, the man had become … intriguing. No. But yes.

Tessa watched the way he moved. He was fascinating in the strangest way. She couldn't quite pin it down. He wasn't her type and yet? She started blinking and finally reached up to rub her eyes.

Jack leaned in. "Dust in your eyes?"

"It's nothing," she waved him off. *Mission. Stay on point.*

Removing his hat and settling the shotgun under his arm, muzzle down, the sheriff arrived at their table. No need to run his hands through his hair, he didn't have enough. The classic crew cut only harshened the angles of his hardened face.

Tessa used a report to fan herself. "Are you and your men alright? That looked intense." She did her best to shiver on cue.

"City folks. Nothing I couldn't handle."

Jack looked up, emoting great relief. "Sure glad that ain't my job." Jack shook his head. "I've been mugged before, but I can't say I ever took on a bunch of folks like that. Maybe I don't know no better, but I'd say you handled that very nicely."

"You're safe. They're long gone and won't be back. Take a deep breath or you'll end up hiding in your room." The last statement was aimed at Jack but put out for her amusement. "Just some fellows getting upset about dust on their fancy cars." His eyes didn't leave Tessa. "Like I said, city folks. No manners. Rich people who never earned a living the hard way. Don't know the desert. Nothing but a bunch of good old boys who got lost." He shifted his weight. "Speaking of lost, who are you two? Tourists?" he asked with more gravel in his throat than the roadbed outside.

"Work." Tessa gave him a soft smile.

For a long moment, the sheriff looked her up and down. "What kinda' work?"

"USGS."

Still ignoring Jack, he leaned against the table, forcing Jack to move over a bit and to slip the coffee pot out of the way before it was knocked over into his lap.

"Where are you from?"

"Reston, Virginia."

"Originally?"

"No." Tessa blotted her lips from drinking coffee and put out her hand. "Doctor Tess Wells, I came out from our HQ back east."

"But you're not from Virginia. No accent."

"Air Force brat. Where daddy went, I lived. And we lived all over the world."

"Yeah, something about you doesn't come off as being a local sort."

"That's pretty good. Most people don't pick up on that from a *hello, how are you.*"

"Don't mistake me for some poor, dumb hick. It's a mistake on both counts. I've seen to that with a lot of hard work. Years of it." His face was growing dark red.

"Clearly, it's paid off." Before the sheriff felt the need to say anything further, she indicated Jack. "May I introduce my associate, Santiago de Sombras." Classic, formal introduction — a recognition, she hoped, of the sheriff's years of hard work to be an educated man.

"Call me Rio," Jack added.

Basic manners demanded that the two men shake hands, but neither appeared to remember it, as though they wanted to stare each other down in the dusty street, one drawing his weapon faster than the other. She'd place her wager on Jack if it came to that.

The taller of the deputies came into the diner, lifted his chin in salute to the sheriff, and headed to the back.

The big man barely acknowledged Jack and returned eagerly to Tessa. "Connor Bergman. Sheriff. People call me *Boss*. Nobody gave me a call about USGS coming into town."

Tessa blinked innocently. "I was not aware such a call was needed to your office. We're only here a brief time. Dirt. Bottles. Labels. Survey. That sort of thing. Then we're off to the next site up the road." She leaned her arms on the table. "I'm sorry if we mismanaged some sort of protocol. We move around so fast sometimes we don't even know where we are, except for numbers on a map."

Bergman twisted until he was completely cutting off Jack. "I don't like not knowing."

Jack leaned over, glancing around the sheriff. She read Jack's expression as either a desire to be useful elsewhere or a need to teach the sheriff manners. He certainly knew better than to create a commotion so early in the mission. Then again, Jack would certainly be in his rights, having been given the *cut direct* by a stranger.

Jack gritted his teeth, set his napkin down, and made a polite gesture for Bergman to move. "Give me a minute, Boss Lady, I'll be right back." While Jack was shorter than the sheriff, he still had enough confidence to look the man straight in the face, smile as though he knew something secret, then headed toward the men's room.

Bergman was quick to lean against the seat back but not to climb into the seat. Too small for him. The whole town was too small for him. "I need to know who and what is going on here."

"Sheriff Bergman, you're positively conspiratorial in your thinking."

"Well, we've been getting unwanted visitors lately. Not only those city boys."

"Like that ghost hunting club we ran into at the B&B? They seemed harmless. Just a bunch of kids."

"Some other folks went over to Mesa de los Muertos and one of them got himself dead. They were told not to go there. I don't expect people to be foolish enough to disobey me. There are consequences."

"I gather you're good at being in charge?" Tessa let her eyes bat once and sat holding her coffee cup expectantly. She hoped her expression read, *your move, Big Boy, brag a little, oh please. Tell me more about you.*

"I take care of things, here and all the way out to the Mesa, and that's why folks here are holding on, where others aren't." Bergman pushed off the booth. "Let's be clear, Doctor Wells, you will not go there. Not now. Not ever. People die there and I don't want you to be one of them." He put his hat back on and held the shotgun with both hands. "If you die over there, I won't get to find out more about you."

"I'm sure you can look me up on the internet. Plenty there to find. Should I look *you* up?"

He stood right next to her and leaned in. "What's the fun in that? I think I'd much rather ... obtain anything I need in more traditional ways."

"Why Sheriff Bergman, are you making a pass at me?"

He smiled at her with a hungry expression. "I'm letting you know that you're going to be telling me a lot more about yourself, and I'm not against an unconventional approach to getting it."

Her nerves tingled, as if all were caressed at the same time. It had been so long since someone had made her feel pursued, even primally desired. "And what will that depend on?"

"How long you resist me."

"That may be longer than you think."

His expression said, *let's find out.*

For a second, it crossed her mind — *yes, let's find out* — until she felt her hand touch the 9mm in her computer bag. Cold. Metal. Real. Tessa smiled and demurred behind her menu, hoping the wave of confusion wasn't changing her expression.

She'd almost given in to him. He was alluring in a way that made no sense to her.

What the hell just happened?

CHAPTER NINETEEN

JACK STEPPED INTO THE DRY AIR. Outside the diner's kitchen, the odor of cooking grease and trash was awful, but expected. The wind blew in the right direction to carry most of the stench away from Main Street. And yet he couldn't help thinking that the county dump was just on the other side of the motel – nothing in town seemed to escape the stink.

Out by the road, a man stood with his back to the diner. A bandana covered his black hair, the strings of an apron were tied messily at his backside, black pants hung loosely around his bent legs, and a white t-shirt sported numerous grease stains. He appeared to be smoking as a billowing cloud of fumes surrounded him, obliterating some parts of him from view.

Jack sized him up: cook, possibly Spanish speaking though one did not assume. Looked precisely like the guy who worked at his father's ranch, back in the day. Damn good cook, he recalled.

How to start a conversation? Bum a cigarette.

"Hey, Buddy. Y'all got an extra?" He held up two fingers near his mouth — smoker's semaphore.

The man turned only enough to see Jack and nodded slowly.

I'm in, he thought. *Let's see what ya' have to say?* He was fully prepared if the conversation moved into Spanish because — *damn* — the guy really did look like the man he'd known so long ago. "Thanks, pal."

The man's ruddy skin was much darker than Jack's, his face heavily wrinkled, and his black eyes were ice picks stabbing outward, viciously, as if to say, "Go away." Yet, he pulled out a pack of Marlboro cigarettes, shook one halfway out of the opening, and stretched out the offering to Jack.

Jack accepted it. "Supposed to quit, but after all that ruckus," he indicated the front of the diner, "I need either this or a drink. Maybe both."

The cook nodded, brought out a worn match book, and let Jack use it to light up.

"That business, with all those cars." He handed the match book back to the cook. "I don't know about y'all, but that scared the hell out of —"

"Water ain't comin'," the cook said, staring again, off into the distance and dragging heavily on his smoke.

"Pardon me?"

"*The water stays away*," he repeated thoroughly in Spanish.

"*Okay.* Gracias. *I'm sorry, but I don't know about that. Does it have anything to do with that fuss a little bit ago?* Amigo, *what were all those cars doin' here?*" Maybe he'd say more if he thought Jack would speak Spanish along with him. It had helped before, in giving someone a reason to relax and speak comfortably, confidentially.

"*Food for Skin Thief, that's all they'll be. Sometimes they're like crows. — They like the shiny things. — Rewards for their deeds. Sometimes, they like to remember how to touch. Mostly, they want revenge for being.*"

"*Being what?*"

"*Stuck, stuck with the Unjust.*" The cook spoke sadly, then perked up. "*Hey, you got Zapotec in you, don't you? Your mother was one of the Be'ena'a, the Cloud People from the mountains of Oaxaca. Yeah, I can tell. Still don't matter. Skin Thief might like you better than the one he's got. You should go home to the clouds before he decides on you.*"

Jack was a little dumbfounded at first. "*I haven't been to Oaxaca yet.*"

The cook slowly took a drag on his cigarette and let the exhaled smoke pour out of his mouth and nose, encircling him like a private fog. "*Or Texas or wherever.*" He was entirely enveloped in the smoke cloud as before. "*It ain't healthy here, ya' know. Go home. Skin Thief will wear you like gloves. Ain't no real people here, all fake.*" He kept nodding, not once turning to look at Jack. "*Shadows who want to be real.*" For a minute he scrounged around in his pocket, near the pack of cigarettes, and produced something.

Jack couldn't see it, but the man inspected it fondly, holding it respectfully.

Holding out his closed hand to Jack, he began nodding again. "*Yeah. This place is bad. Water won't come back 'til it's clean here. You should go home. Take your woman with you too. Don't come back.*" He flung out his hand, forcing Jack to catch whatever it was he'd been holding.

The cook dropped his smoldering Marlboro butt onto the ground, put it out with his foot, and walked away. His cloud went with him.

Jack watched, his debilitated hand clinging to the object he'd caught with barely two fingers and his thumb and wondering what the hell he'd just heard. Had he been warned off? Again? Unquestionably. But why? His cover was intact, so why did the cook say what he did? Why did he give him ...?

Opening his hand suspiciously, he found a long, polished piece of bone — perhaps three inches long, tapering to a sharp point. At the wide end, a hole had been drilled through and a narrow string of something fibrous was threaded through. A needle? It seemed a bit big for one. The bone was aged, turning brown in places.

Alright, he thought, *I've got a bone-thing and a warning.*

Damn. First the man in Cortez, then the kid at the top of the hill, and now this guy, who was more or less a cross between stereotypes of local Native Americans and Latino immigrants he knew.

That's interesting, he realized. *Stereotypes.* Not necessarily real or accurate — *expected.* He hadn't been bothered by the kid's physical appearance up near the highway. A kid like that was average enough for the region, but maybe that kid had been too average.

This could be important later on.

Right now, he wanted to talk to the cook a bit more.

The cook had wandered off toward the back of the motel and out of Jack's sight. He couldn't follow. He needed to stay near Tessa.

Well, shit.

People didn't stay out in the sun here any longer than they had to, which was damn smart. But Jack had work to do out here before he would have to escape back into the air conditioning. He slid the bone object into his pocket and held the cigarette up to his lips.

Gravel crunched under his boots as he found a spot to continue smoking his cigarette. Nothing gave an operative more chances to be nosing around and observing than the ubiquitous cigarette break. He held it and wandered a bit. Smokers move around when snagging their ever-diminishing opportunity to light up.

Tempting as it was to inhale, he blew out any smoke immediately. Time with doctors, recovering from the finger amputations, and then living with his inconveniently allergic Uncle Joe, had rid him of the habit.

Where had the gang cars gone? He changed his wandering path to take him out into the main road. Casually, since only worried people tend to hurry, he wandered along, allowing himself to draw on the cigarette and look about at the same time.

A cloud of dust hovered over the road. Nothing odd about that. But over in the direction of the Mesa there was a significant roiling of dust. Jack looked at his feet, or rather, the deep tire marks in the road. He was certain he was seeing tracks from one of the caravans. What about the other gang? A few yards down, he saw where the second caravan had circled the diner and rejoined the road.

The big dust cloud in the distance had dissipated. Either they'd stopped, or the road dipped down into one of the ravines. Worth looking into.

"Whatcha doin' out here, mister?"

Jack played cool and waved his cigarette over at the deputy at the kitchen door. Again, not rushing. After all, he wasn't doing anything wrong, so why act as if he'd been caught with his hand in the proverbial cookie jar? He let it take him about a minute to meander over toward the deputy. "Bumming a smoke. Figured I'd stay put. Smells better out there on the road," he joked with a grin.

"How can you tell? I light up too and I can't smell a damn thing? Who'd you bum it off of?"

"Guy from the kitchen. Wandered off that way."

"Probably to get shit-faced, if he isn't already. Probably some lazy Mexican." The deputy spit on the dirt.

Jack kept any remarks to himself in the name of protecting his cover. Seemed the deputy didn't think Jack looked Hispanic enough to keep such bigotry quiet.

"If you don't have any smokes, I usually do."

Jack held up his cigarette. "Trying to quit. First rule of quitting is, don't have them too easy to get to."

"Little woman at home demanding it?"

So, the deputy was digging for information too. "No 'little woman' anymore. Divorced, two kids. You?" It was a cover story he'd used many times, certainly often enough for it to sound real.

"Not married but workin' on it." The deputy leaned against the door frame, keeping the door open with his foot. Folding his arms, he gave Jack a look that Jack interpreted as, *get the hell back inside.*

"I don't recommend it."

"Quitting smoking or marriage?"

"Yes," Jack said, dropping his cigarette butt onto the ground and smashing it out with his foot.

"So why quit?" The deputy wasn't exactly warming up. "The smoking. Why quit smoking?"

Good. Keep working him into your circle. Jack stopped at the door and nodded inside the diner. "See the lady I'm here with?"

"You're trying to bang her?"

"No!" He withdrew from the doorway. "She's my boss. She doesn't like smoking and she doesn't like drinking and she doesn't like all these things she doesn't like."

The deputy's shoulder began to relax. "Tough boss?"

Jack gave him a well-you-know expression. "I'm this close to getting a promotion. Then she shows up to manage this trip. I've got a bad feeling about it, so I'm being a real good boy."

Shoulders now relaxed and voice matching, the deputy lowered his voice too. "She's pretty. Might be fun to have her for a couple of nights."

The agent simply shrugged. "After I get a pay raise and move up to Denver. Anyway, I can play by her rules until she gets comfortable. Promotion first, banging second."

The deputy snarled a brief laugh. "Man's got to have his priorities. But I'd hurry up. I think my boss has her on his radar. And Bergman always gets what he wants. And if he doesn't get what he wants, it don't exist, if you know what I mean."

No, I don't know what you mean, Jack thought. *I can guess though.* Keep playing a good ol' boy and a little dumb. He grinned for the deputy. "Hey, what about that mesa all y'all are talking about? What gives?"

The deputy's shoulders tensed up. "Do yourself a favor — stay outta' there. Nobody farms, fishes, grazes, or screws over there. It's falling apart. A guy got hurt when he fell down a hole. The National Parks folks fled the place as fast as a desert rabbit. They don't want the costs to fix it up."

Jack held up his hands. "I hear you, loud and clear. We don't have time anyway. Boss Lady and I have to get soil samples for models on climate effect and overgrazing."

"Exciting."

"Thrilling. But I get to listen to her. Swear she could read a phone book and I'd need a little quiet time — alone."

Looking at Tessa, her red hair dazzling in the light, Jack was sure the deputy was seeing the same thing. She was a lovely woman. The sheriff was leaning next to her and saying something. Maybe she needed a little backup?

"Good luck with that promotion, uh ..."

"De Sombras. Rio de Sombras. Thanks." He offered his hand. A little surprised that the deputy took it, he kept grinning. "Say, what do y'all want? What are yer priorities?"

"Me? I'll tell you what, de Sombras. I want my own town to run. Hell, I'll run this one in good time. Come and see it then. There'll be plenty of changes and we won't be a ghost town in the making. Sheriff's not the only one done being poor."

This time, the deputy put his hand on the door, effectively keeping Jack from going back outside. Jack nodded and sauntered back into the diner. *Town to run?* What the hell did that mean?

CHAPTER TWENTY

SHE SAW JACK WANDER BACK into the diner, do his usual potential adversary count, and saunter over to the cash register to snag a local map in the old wooden rack. Making eye contact with her, waiting for her slight nod, he came back to take his seat again in the booth. The big man — the sheriff — waited at the door, visually inspecting him with frowning distaste and narrowed eyes that read more predatory and competitive than anything expected as legitimate interest from law enforcement.

Bergman shoved the door open and marched out to the parking lot.

As Jack shimmied into the booth, he glanced up, and stated loudly, "I know how much ya' hate it when I smoke."

An odd thing to say, she thought. Tessa then sensed the heavy presence of the someone behind her and felt them thump into the next booth against her back. "I thought you said you were going to quit," she scolded, also loudly. "Rio, you know I despise the smell of those things."

"One stick at a time, Boss Lady. Can't just go cold turkey." He held up his hand, making an oval with it, and placed it on his left chest.

A Deputy. "Alright. But remember, you promised me."

A sharp snicker behind them indicated a minor victory for their cover story. The deputy decided to seat himself at the counter instead and demanded a cup of coffee. Jack tilted his head in that direction when the waitress came flouncing out of the kitchen and began flirting outrageously with the officer.

"I guess we know who got her that ring," Tessa whispered. "That must be *Billy*."

"On his salary? Not likely."

"Interesting, isn't it."

"Ah, young love. What a man won't do for it."

"Did she call him 'Billy-boy?'"

"I do believe she did." Jack tried not grinning. "And they were going to send ya' in here with an Ivy League financier?"

Tessa rolled her eyes while spreading a tourist map flat on the table. "You and Billy-boy best friends yet?"

Jack set up a USGS topographical map to coincide with the tourist version. It would look good if they could point at them while talking. "The ice is thawing but no melt yet. You and the big man?"

She didn't reply at first, but her mouth tightened. With hesitations sneaking into her story, Tessa shared her experience. Jack let his face slide from congenial to quietly fuming. All the while she kept her expression soft, her voice lilting, trying to make it all seem commonplace.

"That wasn't flirting by any measure I know. That was a threat."

"I'm aware of that." She pointed to a spot on the geologic map.

"He's saying he wants to hurt you," his voice dropped to a hiss, and he heatedly pronounced each word. "He's saying he wants to torture you."

"He said several things, none of which are doing more than alert me to potential dangers. For all I know, he likes it a bit rough. He may be more talk than delivery. What is it you boys say, 'more hat than herd?'"

Jack's eyebrow shot up. "And if he isn't?"

"Then, I'll have to deal with that problem."

"*We'll* have to deal with it."

She raised her eyebrow to mimic him and pointed to another random spot on the map. "*We*?"

"If he gets any information out of y'all, our cover is blown. Besides, if he does put ya' on the rack and he does it without style, he'll only make ya' mad." *Poor Jack*, he couldn't stop his lopsided smile showing up, though he didn't keep it for very long. "I'm the one who'll have to calm ya' down. Or bandage you up."

"And you'd enjoy that ..."

They both suddenly sat back and grabbed up their maps as two plates of food descended on the table.

"I thought we had to take this to go," Tessa asked.

"It's okay," the waitress droned. "Just sit tight and enjoy it while it's still hot."

"Really, we don't mind take out if you are ..."

"Just. Sit. Tight." The waitress snapped with a bit 'a sass, smiling at Jack. Deputy Billy-boy looked over at their booth, his face screwed up in confusion. Whatever he was thinking, he let it go.

Sit tight? *Great.* Now they were stuck. The music box was droning out something old and warbling.

Jack shrugged, lifted the bun off his burger, and shook his head. Probably over-cooked,. He preferred his beef on the rare side. So rare that a good vet could bring the cow back to life, he told her once. He looked over the maps noting, she wasn't surprised, the lack of detail on both.

They couldn't stay put; they needed to poke around the buildings in town, then some of the ravines and arroyos. Three days, maximum. That was all they had. Maybe four.

Jack started talking about the differences in the maps, while taking reluctant bites out of his burger. She was ignoring her food.

Tessa had become thoroughly engrossed in a sketch she was making. His voice was comforting and familiar, leaving her free to copy or add to the design.

"Hey, *Dr. Wells*? What did ya' draw there."

Tessa was startled back to the present. "Ah, the cover of the menu. It's unusual and ..." She stopped and stared at the line drawing on the menu cover and now on her napkin. Done in a style reminiscent of local petroglyphs, it was a horned, hollow figure, sneering, holding a club and a knife. Inside it appeared a human being, upside down, trapped, and helpless. "I doodle sometimes when I think."

"And the food?"

"Lunch? Ah, no. I'm sure it's quite a lovely meal around here, but I think these — things — were potatoes once but not after a century of sitting in grease."

Jack eyed the fries on his plate. "Molecular disintegration."

"How politely framed."

Neither touched their food, especially after a caravan of SUVs appeared, speeding away from the direction of the Mesa. They roared through town and up the road to the highway.

One of the two caravans they had seen earlier.

Just one.

They waited, picking at lunch, and trying to have a conversation without words.

No more cars came.

Finally, Tessa spoke up. "I do believe they've misplaced a good half of the party."

CHAPTER TWENTY-ONE

JACK LEANED AGAINST THE FRONT DESK, watching over the manager's shoulder at her sixty-inch, HD, flat screen TV. An Albuquerque news logo highlighted the lower left-hand corner of the screen while a running tickertape of information slid along the bottom. A blond man stood stoically with his microphone, coolly explaining the scene behind him. The tickertape read: "Los Angeles neighborhood erupts in gunfire. Three children have been shot including a 7-year-old. Escalating gang violence is being blamed ..."

Blue and red lights flashed behind the reporter. Not too far away, a pair of jackets with glow-in-the-dark lettering could be seen — LAPD.

"Mr. de Sombras?"

He instantly recovered his exterior calm and gave her a *Big Jack, Everything-is-Just-Fine* smile.

"Was there something you needed?" The manager snuggled up to the desk.

"Not tonight, ma'am. I guess I saw all that fuss and was reminded why I'm glad I'm from Albuquerque."

"Oh?" She leaned back. "I would have taken you for a Texan."

"You got me! New Mexican by choice — *Texican* by love." He tapped the brim of his hat and winked. The manager melted under his gaze. *She's almost too easy*, he thought.

"I love me a Texas man." Her shoulders wiggled a bit while her arms pushed her breasts closer together, creating a deeper cleavage for his view.

There wasn't anything to be said to that without it reeking rudely of sarcasm, so he simply reached out and touched the top of her hand kindly. "Y'all have the most charming place here. It has yer influence for certain." He tapped his hat again and started toward the front door.

"No, no, Mr. de Sombras." Her voice rang with a song-like delight, but determination to block him.

Jack stopped mid-stride. "Pardon?"

"You shouldn't go out at night."

"I was thinking of a nightcap and …"

"Diner's closed tonight," she warned sharply. "Some sort of private dinner party for Connor and some of his friends. Now if you want a little drinky?"

Ah, shit. "Well, ta' be honest, I'm feelin' a mite restless. Unfamiliar bed an' all that. Maybe I'll take a quick stroll."

"Nope." The song in her voice started to fade.

Think fast, Jack Rabbit. "Y'all worried about night critters? We got 'em in Albuquerque too. Never met a coyote I couldn't scare off."

"I'll bet you haven't, Tex. No," she tried her worn charm again. "It isn't the live ones, it's the ghosties."

Oh Sweet Baby Jesus, not you too. "Ghosts? Now, come on."

"Serious as a heart attack. They're called … uh … *Zaa-huu,* or something. Never got a handle on all that mumbo jumbo, but in this case, even them dumb Indians around here are onto something. Look, I've seen them ghosts. Scared the hell out of me. I've heard they make people sick or push them over cliffs n' such. So, listen up good, Tex. If I let you out there and you so much as twist an ankle, the sheriff will come down on me like the wrath of God." She batted her eyelashes at him. "You wouldn't want that, would you?"

Jack's shoulders slumped. "No, ma'am. I wouldn't want anyone to harm a hair on yer kind head." He grinned at her.

She giggled again. "The drink offer still stands."

"As to that, I think the Boss Lady might disapprove of my takin' up with a lady while in the middle of an assignment. But I do want to thank ya' kindly. A good night to ya', ma'am," he said, and strolled off before he committed to something unnecessary to the mission — and undesired. That had always been the problem with using charm and manners to conduct his work.

Each step up the staircase was a chore until he reached the top to find Tessa leaning against the door frame of her room, smiling with tremendous amusement.

"Learn anything new?" She looked far too pleased.

"From the lady? A little, though mostly nonsense. From her TV set, which is a nice piece of expensive technology? Hell, yeah."

"Mission sensitive?"

"Mission critical. We need to see if one of the missing gang leaders is tied to a new shooting they're reporting in LA."

Her face straightened into wholly professional. "I can get that."

"There's somethin' else I need to update ya' on." While Tessa tried giving him the Eyebrow of Doom, he proceeded to share with her the incident with the cook, the cigarette, and the warning to go home. The subject of the shadow he saw came to mind, but he left that aside, for now. Checking again to see if anyone could be watching, Jack produced the bone object from his pocket. "What the hell is this thing?"

"That's interesting." She took it in her delicate fingers and rolled it back and forth. "A good luck charm?"

Jack could only produce a scowl for her.

"From what you said, he might have thought you needed it."

"Bull."

"It looks like a charm? It's not cheesy, like a tourist trinket. In fact, it feels old — and real. Like an old-fashioned bone sewing needle. Maybe ..."

"Don't make me remind ya' I don't believe any of that kinda' shit," he snarled, realizing he was not sounding assertive.

"Well, it's a nice artifact all the same. You might want to find out about it later. In the meantime," she paused, "it would seem we're not wanted here."

"I've lost count of how many warnings we've gotten to get out of town and more than those to stay away from Mesa de los Muertos. I smell a problem with the fish."

"Fish always begins goes bad after three days, like guests and corpses. I don't know about you, but now I seriously want to take a look at the Mesa."

A squeal of tires and smash of gravel interrupted her comment. No fewer than twelve Lincolns and Cadillacs parked in front of Jenny's Diner and under Tessa's window.

The street below them was full of townsfolk, deputies, a number of over-dressed individuals, and the sheriff. Bergman was in an animated side-bar conversation with Billy-boy the Deputy. Though most of what was being said was inaudible, words such as "This one" and "We agreed" made their way from the deputy below up to Tessa's room.

Jack stepped to the side of the window while Tessa turned off the light.

"Damn," she added with a sigh. "Looks like we're not going exploring, not with all those boys in town and likely headed to the Mesa."

"And the manager is guarding the front door, so no getting out that way," Jack said flatly. "I have an idea, for when we can go."

"Let's get some sleep first. We'll still have time."

"Sounds like a plan to me. Meet ya' after the Witching Hour?"

Tessa's mouth twisted. "I have a bad feeling about that crowd down there. Like half aren't leaving here — ever. Let's aim for 2:00 A.M. That should leave us plenty of time to look around."

Jack knew when he was dreaming. He hated that one dream, and most nights, he knew to expect the same sequence of events during that dream, and the same exact thoughts that followed. Thus, it was no surprise to find himself seated in a semi-fetal position, upright in bed, all the bed sheets kicked off, listening to the pine tree scratching his window, and clutching his revolver.

The same cruel dream, over and over. Chaos. Lies. Sacrifice. Loss. Being taken into a dark room. Forced to kneel down. To lower his eyes. Ordered to put his hands behind his back.

His heart pounding, climbing up into his throat, choking him with the nightmare he couldn't escape. An easy memory.

He'd lived it.

He knew what to expect. Two shots to the back of the skull. They told him that's what was coming.

More Lies. Shouting. Shooting. Blood. Pain.

Guilt.

They didn't get what they expected. They got what they deserved.

Did he?

Sacrifice. An appeasement to … to … something unworthy … profane.

He didn't dare think of it and could never speak of it.

Jack's nightly ordeal, he feared, was exhausting, and tempted him to reveal his secret, if only to relieve the horror. As though the situation wasn't bad enough, a new element had twisted its way into the dreamscape. A six-year-old boy, clutching a toy pony, dirt smeared across both tear-stained cheeks. Terrorized. Waiting to be killed. Waiting for unholy madness to come and steal his life.

The tree scratched at the glass, straining to get into his room. Shadows moved across the bed and floor, dancing around the altar of his unfulfilled promises of self-sacrifice to their gods.

So easy, he heard, as if someone were whispering it inside his head. *No more dreaming. No more pain.* The voice — so soothing. Dark fingers rested on his gun hand. *So easy.* The pull on his arm, lifting the gun toward his head.

So easy.

The Darkness, a figure helping him settle the gun on his temple. *So easy.* Small red eyes stared into him, as if he was its suicidal marionette.

Off balance, he fell across the bed. His left arm landed on the nightstand.

Jack didn't wake. He couldn't.

So easy to be free — no more pain.

His wallet dropped off the nightstand and onto the floor.

Do it. Be free.

Caught between waking, lucid, and deep sleep, he heard the sound of the object, the old bone needle — *needle* — sliding off the nightstand, following the wallet. His brain didn't understand.

His body did.

Jack's disabled hand slapped down on the bone needle, holding it flat against the table surface, preventing it from slipping.

The Darkness jerked back.

No!

Wait! *What the hell?* Where had the mad thoughts come from? In his whole life, Jack had never given substance to taking his own life. He slammed the revolver onto the mattress, declaring his refusal to comply.

The Darkness withdrew further into the corner, pleased with the failure. This one was stronger ... better.

Jack pounded the sides of his head, trying to wake up fully. He had no idea how dangerous lucid dreaming could be. The blur of gloom gave way to clarity. He wasn't at the ranch as before, when having his dream. This time was different and new, and he longed for that difference to free him from the unceasing cycle of that dream. *To hell with that*, he decided. He would free himself.

Awake, with eyes adjusted to the darkness, Jack could see through his partly open door.

Through the tiny hallway.

Through her partially open door.

They kept their doors open to protect each other.

Her figure curled comfortably on the bed, illuminated by various lights from her laptop and the streetlamp outside her window.

He imagined her hair braided. Strands would be draped sweetly across her forehead and cheek. Her violet eyes were possibly fluttering with REM sleep. Tessa was blessed with the ability to sleep damn near anywhere, at any time.

The breath he held prisoner flowed out in a slow and steady sigh. Gently, with exaggerated motion as if to prove to himself that he was making deliberate decisions, both physically and mentally, Jack picked up the gun on the crumpled sheets. There was nothing more to fear from his dream. And, he had a mission.

He wouldn't get back to sleep tonight — this morning — whatever it was. Wallet and whatever that bone thing was were centered safely on the nightstand.

His watch read 12:20A.M. Fine, he wanted to take a look at a couple of spots around town, to gather up intel. They weren't meeting up until 2A.M. He had time.

The manager had to be asleep by now. He was going to do this damn job and do it well.

He'd always done his best for the mission. *For the mission.*

To relieve the pain and guilt. The obligation.

Yeah, *for her too.* He'd do it *for her.*

For one of the only two people in the universe who still believed in him.

They could never know the truth. *For their safety.*

Never.

CHAPTER TWENTY-TWO

12:59 A.M.

SOMETHING WAS BEING SLAUGHTERED. It cried out in the distance, pitiful, terrified …

Is that a coyote?

Tessa bolted upright in bed and listened hard.

The wind blew grit against the window.

She listened, her whole body frozen, waiting for the sound to happen again. See knew the sound, but from where?

Her heart pounded in her ears.

Laughter came from across the street from the diner. Someone was still awake and alive—and human.

With a sigh of relief, Tessa punched her pillow in private embarrassment and rolled over under her covers. Her fingers caressed the grip of her pistol, and she took another deep breath. The light from the diner showed through her window, plastering a shadow of clashing tree limbs on the tacky wallpaper and popcorn ceiling. Plenty of laughter followed as a rowdy few spilled into the road and staggered away.

The light from the diner turned off. Was it the Witching Hour? Or Closing time? 1:00 A.M.? She looked at the clock. Yes. 1:00 A.M.

Not yet time for Jack and her to go exploring. Jack was likely sleeping through all this. Nothing would wake him short of a nuclear explosion.

Silence was not her friend. Tessa waited and waited for the cry in the night to repeat.

Where had she heard that?

Ben.

That had to be wrong. Ben hadn't cried out. But was she remembering correctly? She fell back against her pillows, feeling her body start to shake. Damn it, she couldn't panic

Think. Think!

One, two, three, four, five … breathe …

Ben had died years earlier. The mission had sideways. He'd taken bullets to the stomach and chest. One was a pass-through, the other lodged in his body.

She could see it – fresh in her head – as though she'd seen it the day before. Blood. So much of it.

She'd reached Ben in seconds, but the wounds were fatal. He said nothing. No lingering, prophetic last words. Only shock. Disbelief. Blood – all over her fingers – all over her lap where he lay.

He was gone. Empty. Hollow.

Something came for him. She saw It. It squealed and cried like a wounded coyote — or a nasty vulture. Its shape vague, Its presence solid. No one else saw It.

She smelled something — sweet and spicy, almost like tree sap. Too strange to be a random perfume. The sweetness turned her stomach.

And the sound — beads clashing — fabric and feet scraping along the ground. Dragging.

Tessa clutched Ben, but the Thing grasped and picked at him, catching a part of Ben in Its beak — something ethereal or non-corporeal — something ghoulish.

The thing ripped Ben's essence out of her arms. Shrieking, the two spirit entities tangled, fought, and what had been Ben lost.

Tessa screamed and grasped at the ghost of her partner.

The vulture-like Thing, wrapped in a cloak of decaying black, reached out Its boney hand and stroked Tessa's face delicately. *Death*. The It that terrified all.

Between the cries of the other souls lost and collected, It whispered to her.

We have too much to do, you and me. But not yet. Not now.

It enveloped Ben completely in Its cloak and descended.

Down through the street. Through the asphalt. Through the Earth.

Through the spaces between men and Hell.

Had that sound been the same she'd heard that night so long ago? *Damn it! Do it again! Tell me I'm wrong! I need to be wrong!*

Tessa sat up again and listened with every inch of her body. Hurt pricked at her eyes. All of her will was needed to keep her from puking into the bedsheets.

And she was not **Death**'s partner, *goddamn it!* **Death** could do Its own dirty work.

Tessa kept swallowing an unstoppable flow of saliva that filled her mouth. No. She couldn't panic. Not now.

Finally, her mouth dried and her hands stopped shaking.

A gust of sandy wind pelted her window and she rose to look out. At the front window, she found that the diner was shut for the evening. A cloud of dust rolled down the street, lit by a lonely streetlight. Putting on a soft robe and flat slippers, she checked out the side window.

The window that faced Mesa de los Muertos.

Lights. Flashes of lights. Quick to appear. Quick to disappear. Blue. Green.

Again, the unearthly cry.

The same? Different? She couldn't tell.

Distraction was what she needed. No amount of pills or therapy could keep her from suffering panic attacks so well as the distraction of work.

Tying her robe tightly at her waist and pulling a jacket over her shoulders, she hurried out of the room. Stopping at Jack's door, she knocked softly, desperately. She had to tell Jack.

Nothing.

Opening the door fully, a rush of cold raced through her body. The bed was empty. *Damn it. Where was he?* Had he run … No, she wouldn't think that. No. She would go look.

Her feet were cold in the flat slippers she wore but they were utilitarian and functional if she ended up in a fight. The last thing she needed was to be caught out looking and acting like some idiotic damsel in distress. Then again, it was an option to be played if necessary.

Silence greeted her steps down to the lobby. Watchfully. Quietly.

She shoved out the lobby door, letting it close, and raced into the parking lot.

The wind grabbed the lobby door, flung it open and banged it closed. Tessa spun on her heel to see if someone was there.

No one. Her heart pounded hard enough to escape her chest. Gripping her jacket closed, clinging to it as her robe whipped around her legs, she walked out toward the diner, taking each step as quietly as possible. The gravel crunched lightly.

She noted that none of the cars from earlier were there and deep tire tracks led from the diner out toward the Mesa. *Quelle Surprise.* Far in the distance, the canyon below the Mesa waited in shadow.

"You shouldn't be out here."

Tessa flinched. *Goddamn it.*

Sheriff Bergman stood behind her, feet planted wide, left arm at his side, right arm holding a shotgun — the prying indecency of a leer shaped his features as he noted she was wearing a robe under her coat.

"I heard something and thought someone was hurt." No sense lying when the truth was safe. "Didn't you hear it?"

"Coyotes. We have them all over here."

"It sounds like someone, or something, is hurt. Shouldn't you go look?"

He sighed heavily. "Unfortunately, there aren't a lot of resources around here, for coyotes or people. Can't spare anyone. Coyotes fight. Probably one of them didn't hold up too good. Maybe got killed. Things die around here all the time. That's why it isn't safe to be out alone at night."

Charm. Turn on the charm. Tessa delicately smiled and ran a hand through her hair. "I must seem like an absolute idiot to you. Truth is, I've been behind a computer screen for too long. I really do need to get out more."

"Your friend seems comfortable."

"Rio? He's field savvy. Don't tell him, but I hijacked his assignment so I could get some field time. I think he'd resent it if he knew."

"And you picked Four Corners?" His voice dripped with disbelief.

"Of course! This," she waved her hand for dramatic effect, letting loose of her jacket and robe, allowing a bit of delicate skin to show, "is a geologist's dream. Extreme erosion patterns in oceanic sedimentary rock, volcanic intrusions. If you're into rocks, this place is heaven."

He stood stiff, staring at her with satisfaction. "Maybe you'd like to stay," he ventured, taking a few steps forward. "Or better, maybe you'd prefer staying with someone who could keep things interesting."

"Leave my management post for some of the best geological sampling in America, you mean?"

"I could make it enticing." He was getting closer. Too close. "One of those 'offers you can't refuse?' And I don't think you want to."

CHAPTER TWENTY-THREE

1:00 A.M.

WHAT THE HOLY HELL WAS THAT?

He'd heard a human being brutalized under torture before. Jack knew the sounds a man could make when the pain was unbearable. To his ears, the howl sounded like that.

Terrifying and unearthly.

A wail escaping from deep in the bowels of Hell? That's what its fading echo sounded like to Jack. Gooseflesh pinpricked his arms and back.

Earlier, the two townies in the bar had been talking about the drought. Jack simply listened and pretended to drink. Gas Guy, two townies, the bartender, and Jack — no one else. No waitress, no cooks, no other townies. But thanks to Gas Guy, the discussion *du jour* had turned ghostly.

"They'll steal your soul," someone mocked.

"They'll steal your first born," another added with a lubricated smile.

"They'll scare you to death then eat your flesh!"

"You don't know nuthin' about the *Skin Thief*," Gas Guy slurred over his drink.

Right.

It was hardly surprising to Jack that Gas Guy got hammered every night if he lived in this place. It was Gas Guy who wouldn't stop with the spectral myths of the area, as if he was the great wisdom keeper of the region. Every tall tale was met with another shot. Before he was done telling about how the shadowy *Skin Thief* and other evil spirits, he was soused.

The townies must have been embarrassed by him, in his oily coveralls, old truck company cap, and desperate need for a shower and now his inebriation. Neither of them spoke to him. They interrupted him constantly, and there seemed to be a competition as to who could tell the tallest ghost tale. Jack was starting to feel a little sorry for the guy.

As if Gas Guy had read his mind, he sidled up to Jack and breathed heavily on him. "He wants … it all … to be clean … so the water comes back. That's his purpose." Gas Guy gesticulated dramatically and in slow motion. "Eternal punishment …"

That wasn't the first time he heard the term — *Skin Thief*. Jack wondered where he'd find such a thing. Not in town — probably the Mesa, no surprise.

Gas Guy flipped the townies off and staggered away as more stories were added to the pile. If they were to be believed, this creature was nothing anyone could agree on. No surprise there either.

He wondered where he was going to find out what this Skin Thief was. For all the drunken laughter and wild tales, Jack could sense fear in the small vocal changes when they spoke the words "Skin Thief" – if they spoke it at all. A little hesitation before using the term. A slight quiver in the word "Thief." A hard swallow or fast drink before speaking. The little clues.

He needed to learn more about this fearful thing. Later – at the Mesa. Or outside of town?

Not inside the building he was going to infiltrate.

Maybe Gas Guy was not so drunk he might have some answers. Since Jack didn't want to be known as the guy with all the questions, he quietly followed Gas Guy out of the diner, and prepared to corner him accidentally or some other excuse he'd come up with on the spot. Somewhere away from other ears.

At first, the man in his greasy coveralls, with a cup of coffee Jack didn't see him get, had staggered from the diner, his stories all told, heading home. He'd turned toward a set of stairs that led up to an in-law apartment above his garage. Yeah, that cup-a-joe was gonna' help — *not* — but Gas Guy was going to be a very alert drunk if he managed not to spill it.

At first, he had trouble on the stairs, so he set down the coffee in the business office and used both hands to push and pull himself to the upper floor. Even blasted, Gas Guy appeared to know when to go to bed.

Jack followed him, directing his movements to appear to anyone watching that he was as drunk as any townie. He pulled off his hat and held it down low to his body, keeping out of any direct light as he moved. He counted on his silhouette resembling a generic *everyman* from town.

Once upstairs in the garage, Gas Guy dropped into the deepest shadows.

Shit, where'd he go? Jack moved from one shadow to the next, using his long stride to leave as few footprints as possible. Gas Guy was out of site and Jack swore he hadn't heard a door open or close.

If not out cold upstairs, where the hell was Gas Guy? Perhaps he hadn't heard a door. His first inclination was to storm into the apartment, gun drawn, and to hell with anyone who tried to stop him. Someone in this town knew what was going on and he was in the mood to start issuing threats.

The air was lifeless and stale.

Somebody shut off the lights in the diner, plunging the street into further darkness. Only the weak streetlamps were left.

Quickly, Jack slid inside the garage door and waited, listening. *Patience, Jack Rabbit, patience.*

Nope. Patience had blown away with any hope he might have had for getting a good night's sleep. *Where did Gas Guy go?*

Goddamn it! This place was too weird for his taste, and he was going to be quite happy to leave it to the dust and the grime and hallucinations it dragged up from the not-so-distant past.

Annoyed and sleep deprived, he wanted to pull his gun from its hidden holster, and with more than a couple years' worth of pent-up frustration, beat the truth out of someone. Not practical but he might enjoy it. Where was Gas Guy?

Again that damn howl. That unholy scream.

Was that what a Skin Thief sounded like? Jack didn't believe in ghosts. Not Ghosts, not *Skin Thieves*, not … any of that. It *was a coyote, right?*

Tessa's window was partially visible out the open garage door, Jack checked it and confirmed … nothing. No light. But that didn't mean she hadn't heard it, or that she wasn't awake.

Jack leaned out a bit more and looked in the direction of the Mesa. Lights? He swore he saw lights.

Cool down, Jack Rabbit.

Nothing more followed beyond desert quiet, darkness, a gust of wind blowing the dirt down the street as though it was sneaking out of town before the last gunfight.

Christ, did it have to blow through the sewage dump first?

Silence, that let him hear the sound of his clammy hand squeaking on the grip of his gun and the twist of fabric of his jacket. The buzz from the streetlamp. The distant scratch of the pine trees against the sides of the motel.

Again, the horrible scream exploded into the air. *That's it!*

If that didn't wake Tessa, nothing would. She was a city gal and probably could sleep through anything. But not this. *She's a good agent.*

Gas Guy couldn't pretend to be deaf to that!

A shadowy figure moved past Jack's position. Gas Guy?

He drew back into the garage, grasping his revolver, holding his breath, stopping his thoughts as if the figure could hear those too.

The figure hovered before the open door, glancing over its shoulder to glare into the garage.

Red eyes — shadowed form.

Skin Thief? Christ, it doesn't exist?

Jack's chest tightened, and his lungs begged for air. *No such thing as ghosts.*

The shadow was big. It had an aura of brutality, maybe even malevolence. A Skin Thief?

Jack locked every muscle and took slow measured breaths. He couldn't be discovered by whoever was standing in the shadows outside his hiding place. Or ... by the …

His eyes were all Jack dared to move, searching the garage for a better place to hide. Where? A new limousine, hood open. Two expensive cars. None of them had that tell-tale layer of dust. They hadn't been here long. And if Jack didn't find a safe location fast, he wasn't going to be here long either.

The business office for the garage was behind him and to the right. Door open. Where was Gas Guy? Would he leap out of his own hiding place?

Jack's heartbeat was thrashing in his ears. The shadowy figure outside didn't move an inch. Whoever it was, they weren't concerned about the haunting noises.

Then, the figure slid around the building and disappeared.

There's no such thing as ghosts.

Cautiously, Jack let his breath out, the little he had, and sucked in as much as he could as quietly as he could. Where had the figure gone? Who was it? Damn, *what* was it?

Hadn't he heard of such things before? At summer camp, in the mountains outside of El Paso, in those long, horrible, hot summers. *La Llorona*, *the weeping woman's ghost*, the favorite topic of the camp councilor's tales to keep the boys in their tents at night.

Near the top of the stairs, there was a slight thump.

Turning torturously slow, desperate for pure silence, Jack looked up over the muzzle, his muscles locked so tightly that his fingers, even the phantoms of his missing fingers, began to sting from the lack of blood.

This town needs a shrink.

The bang of the motel's lobby door startled him.

Tessa.

Wearing a jacket, shoes, and a robe underneath, she stood in the parking lot.

Ah hell, what is she doing coming out without ... without ... Jack's heart was working its way up into his throat again. *Without me.* Of course she would have stopped to collect him from his room, to come with her and, well, he wasn't there, was he? She was going to be pissed at him when she got back. Not unwarranted.

The shadow figure reappeared, moving swiftly behind Tessa.

But this time, Jack saw who it was.

Bergman. The sheriff. Not a ghost, only flesh and blood. Arguably worse.

Jack felt a twinge of pride as he watched Tessa maneuver the big creep, keeping him out of reach, sweet-talking him, probably even gleaning information from him. She was poetry in motion when it came to the intelligence game.

Hold on! Bergman was too close. In the space of a split second, the creep's body language significantly changed. Did she see it?

That asshole is threatening her!

"Of course I can refuse." Tessa playfully swatted at the sheriff, moving deliberately so that there was no misunderstanding. "Your nightlife here is quite exuberant, but perhaps too fast paced for my taste."

The humor missed its mark. "This town is dead. But I don't plan to stay here forever. I'm not a poor, uneducated, hick!" He must have heard the fury in his voice and felt the heat rising on his face. Instead of continuing, he took a deep, forced, sour breath which played out on his face.

Crap, that was a big mistake. *No, Sheriff, you are none of the above. Backpedal fast.* "I'm sorry, Sheriff Bergman. I think my midnight joke either needs more sleep or more caffeine. Maybe both. I had no intention of implying anything derogatory about you or your town. I'm genuinely sorry if it came out that way."

Bergman took another slow breath and gave her a sharp, acknowledging nod. "Hell, this town was never alive to begin with, but I have my own plans. I'm very much alive. I'm more than what you think I am. But I'll admit I'm now even more curious about you and what I want from you." He was nearly standing on top of her.

"Like telling you my life story?"

"Depends on which life story you tell me. See, I don't know if I believe you or not. You could be a terrible liar, and someone come to make things bad for me."

"Or I could be someone quite nice, here to make things better for ranchers and farmers."

He sneered, only lit by the streetlight which made him look like a film noir villain. "I'm still leaning towards you telling me the lie. I just haven't decided which one it is yet."

"Now, now." She kept her voice coy and smooth. "It's not nice to sound threatening to a lady. You're supposed to be *enticing* me, remember."

"I'm a hard man. I don't play games well."

"But the game is what it's all about. One doesn't need to be a poet to understand what is romantic. Even old sailors knew about the romance of the sea."

The sheriff seized her arm and pulled her to him.

Tessa locked her stance, fists curling into effective weapons, ready to act.

He tightened his grip and stood leering, waiting for her to do something.

Anything.

"I want to know everything. What thrills you, what frightens you." He touched her hair.

She didn't stop him.

His face was not attractive to her, yet his voice and his touch were exciting. Unlike Jack, Bergman wasn't handsome or charming, but the allure was irresistible. Tessa allowed him to pull her closer.

His touch made her hands unclench. She could escape him but didn't.

His voice, as he kept telling her what he wanted, pulled her deeper.

CHAPTER TWENTY-FOUR

"I'LL TAKE YA' HOME AGAIN, Cathleen!" The loud, melodic bumbling from behind them turned fast into a warbling, off-key song being sung with in an alcohol-loosened slur.

Bergman and Tessa both tensed, parted, and searched for the source of the song. Tessa ripped free from the glue that held her.

"I'll take ya' home again, Cathleen!" Jack tried again as he wandered around the corner with a steaming coffee cup in one hand and his hat in the other. "Oops, sorry Boss Lady." He held up his hat hand, realized he needed to put the hat somewhere, swatted it awkwardly on his head, and saluted her with a faux-British, palm-out salute.

"Rio, there you are," she said sharply while gathering her wits. "Are you drunk?"

"This ain't ma fault." He drew forward, stopped in front of the sheriff, forcing the man to let go of Tessa, "Evening, sir," he said, and showed Tessa his cup. It was indeed coffee, and reasonably hot. "They kep' buyin' me drinks. Nice folks here," he sideways slurred to the sheriff. "Anyways, we got things ta do in the morning, so I stopped at the gas station to get me some coffee. An, poof! There it was. Waitin' fer me. Ain't my uncle's coffee — in fact, it sucks — but it'll do."

"Alright. I won't make a complaint if you're ready to work in the morning. Besides I'm awake at this hour too, so neither of us is going to be too bright and sunny tomorrow." She took Jack by the arm. "God, Rio, don't make me have to explain this."

"Yes, ma'am." He didn't quite slur his words, but they didn't come out exactly clear either. "I'd appreciate it."

"And I sort of owe you one, don't I? No, don't ask." Before Jack could comment, she looked to the sheriff and silently asked him not to tell. "Come on. You don't look that sloshed but those stairs are going to be a challenge. Terrifying in fact."

"So's the meatloaf. Don't," Jack insisted in a loud, sloppy whisper, "Just don't."

Inside the lobby, with the door locked behind them, they peered out the sheer curtain over the door's window. On the street below, the sheriff gripped his gun with both hands, snarled something, and stomped away.

"Well, you certainly have good timing." she straightened up and crept back to the stairs, shaking her hands and arms to get the feeling back into them.

"I didn't interrupt anything, did I?" His whisper was tinged with annoyance. And he was very, very sober.

"I'm not sure."

"He was. He was absolutely sure what he was going to do. Ya' need to be more careful. He's already threatened ya'."

"Why Jack, methinks the gentleman doth care too much." She flicked the brim of his hat and started up the stairs. "I also think our Oh-God-Thirty trip to the Mesa is off. The sheriff is watching."

Jack reached out and snagged her by the hand. The stern glare he gave her was unfamiliar. Sure, old Jack would have given her a warning, but old Jack would have thought she was going to chew up and spit the sheriff out. Probably breaking the sheriff's jaw for good measure.

This was not the old Jack.

"Is that you, Mr. de Sombras?" The manager came out of her room, adjusting her glasses, and sporting a serious frown on her face. "Now what did I tell you about going out at night. That front door is locked for a reason."

Tessa noted a bulge in the pocket of her dated, flannel night robe. Taking Jack by the arm and leaning her head on his shoulder, she called down, "Oh, I'm awfully sorry, but Rio was getting me back in. After that terrible ruckus out there — with the coyotes? I went running out there, all stupid, and Rio came to my rescue." While the manager thought about what to say, Tessa whispered in Jack's ear, "She's packing. Snub nose."

"Oh, well, I'll tell you what I told Mr. de Sombras. No going out after dark. It's dangerous and we can't be held responsible for any injuries."

"Thank you so very much. I'll heed your advice."

"I'll be watching you two," she added, wagging a finger at them, and standing her ground.

Jack turned to face his partner with an expression made up of wide eyes, a twisted mouth, and a jutting chin that pointed toward the second floor.

Tessa continued up to her room with Jack right behind her. Once she was sure no one was waiting in the hall or following, she rounded on Jack. "What is going on with you? You know perfectly well I can handle men like him — you've seen me do it a hundred times. What gives? You're not acting like yourself."

"Me? I'm not the one …" He took in a breath that he held too long. "I'm not the one who's taken a sudden interest in ghosts n' death. Y'all aren't thinking like an operative either."

All the energy in her cells flushed down through her body, down through her knees and feet leaving her dizzy and unbalanced. "What the hell is that supposed to mean?"

"Where's your weapon?" His words came out brutally.

Tessa's lips parted but there was no answer to release through them. *Don't do this, Jack. Think. Think. Shit! Why didn't you take it?*

"No weapon, no plan, and that creep. Ya'll're letting him get to you."

"I am most certainly not."

"Ya' might not see it, but I do. The look in yer eyes. He draws ya' in. And goin' unarmed is a mistake …"

"Jack, I didn't take my gun because I didn't want anyone catching me with it." There, that was a reasonable explanation. Probably what she was thinking of anyway.

"Good thing, maybe," he said, putting too much space between them for a heart-to-heart chat. His eyes were big, and if she hadn't expected otherwise, she would have thought them fearful. "I'm beginning to think he woulda' just taken it from ya'."

"Well, Jack, if it's one thing I've learned, over-thinking can be dangerous."

He whipped off his hat and bit down on the inside of his lower lip, strangling the string of curses he was renowned for. They'd made it as far as his mouth before he pulled them back.

She didn't mean to frustrate him.

He stared at her, and in the pale glow of the night-light in the bathroom, she could read his black eyes. Yes, *they were fearful.* For *her.* They were big, too. Infinitely dark. Enveloping. Something that could swallow up a heart whole and never give it back. But his mouth was turned down, hard. The moustache only made it more obvious.

"I know men like him. I was like him. I did anything and everything for what I wanted. I wanted missions to go my way. I wanted to feel like I was ... I'm just saying, if ya' flirt with him or lead him to think he can get away with mistreating ya', he will take that inch and run a mile with it."

"This isn't my first rodeo. And that's not a pun for your benefit."

"He. Will. Hurt. You."

"And I might hurt him first."

"Not if ya' hesitate."

Her blood froze as her fingers knotted into a fist.

"Ya' did, didn't ya'? You hesitated with Bergman." His eyes widened. "Tess ... you've started hesitating? God woman! That'll get you killed! An agent who hesitates is a dead agent."

"I did what I determined was right to do. I'm outstandingly good at taking care of myself, weapon in hand or not." *Don't get mad*, she rolled around in her head. *Don't get mad at him.* "I need to get some sleep. So do you. I would appreciate it if you'd at least try to trust me. In this business —"

"It's next to impossible."

"It is possible. We did once, didn't we?"

Those gorgeous pools of black were angry and vanished into a shadow cast by the hat he slammed back on his head. "Maybe ya' should ask the fellas who trusted me and wound up betrayed."

"Maybe you should ask my dead partner?" Her voice was only a whisper, but she meant it as a knife to stab his cold-hearted comment dead center.

As he pushed past her to go to his own room, his hand slipped over hers and held it for half of a second before the door shut behind him.

No more discussion. The mission would come first.

The mission always comes first.

Outside her front window, a short parade of vehicles drove up from the direction of the Mesa and out of town. Lincolns and Cadillacs. There had been more to begin with earlier in the evening. *Incomers*, the waitress had called them. Only half ever became *Outgoers* if she was using the right terminology.

The sheriff stood in front of the diner, like a proud statue as they drove past. Not that she ever doubted that he was a part of whatever was going on, but when Billy-boy was dropped off by the motorcade and left standing next to Bergman, her opinion was solidified.

If it looks like an enemy, smells like an enemy, and acts like one ...

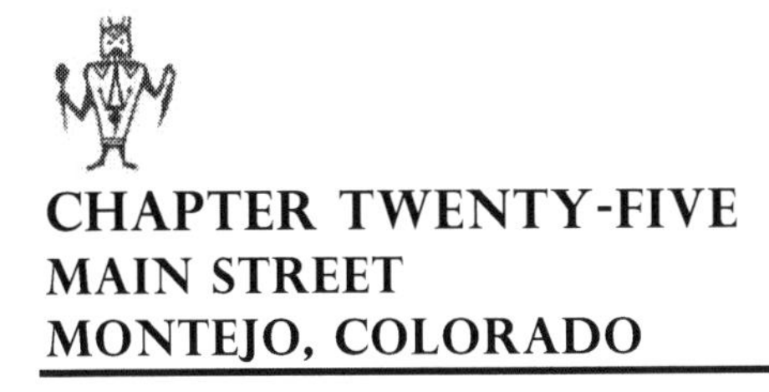

CHAPTER TWENTY-FIVE
MAIN STREET
MONTEJO, COLORADO

MORNING WAS FAR TOO BRIGHT, especially after tossing and turning until sunrise. Jeans, boots, tee shirt, and jacket made sure she was correctly attired for the day. After last night, they would have to play their parts without any deviation. Her disguise might be correct and complete, but her mind was unsettled.

Jack was equally sleep deprived and work-attired, except for the baseball cap that had replaced his cowboy hat. He hadn't shaved yet the scruff made him look presentable if not thoroughly blue collar. But he stood with one leg crossed protectively across the other and his arms wound tightly across his chest covering his vital organs, leaning against the jeep. His chin was set low, and he glowered out toward the Mesa. She couldn't quite tell if that was a pretend hangover, or he was still upset.

"'Morning, Rio."

"'Morning."

Yes, the expression of distance cemented in his narrowed eyes bothered her.

"Where do we start today, Boss Lady?"

"Let's go out as far as the crappy phone signal will let us and work our way back into town. Later, we can go up the hill and see if we can send out our reports."

"Yes, ma'am," he called over the roar of the starting engine.

The side mirror, she adjusted, reflected Billy-Boy, another deputy, and the sheriff talking outside the diner. "No surprise. We're being watched," she commented while pretending to look for something in her backpack.

"More than that," Jack added, swerving around a pothole that could swallow up their jeep whole. "Bergman came by this morning — to see if I was in trouble with ya'."

"Oh?" *How would Bergman know we'd had a fight?*

"At first, I got the feeling he wanted to verify if we were lovers. But seems he only wanted to know if I needed any info that could help, if ya' were going to report me to the office as being drunk on the job."

"Hmm. Taking sides, is he?" Tessa smiled. "What did you tell him?"

"That I might need it. I figure he and I can have ourselves a nice, friendly excuse for a chat later on. Maybe buddy up over a common enemy— *you*. What was it ya' told him?"

"That I wasn't supposed to be in charge of this field trip. That I hijacked your assignment to get some outdoor time."

Jack nodded and for a moment looked a little impressed. The side of his moustache moved up. "Should I be officially upset?"

"I leave that to your judgement." She pulled the phone out of her work bag, unreasonably hopeful, and noticed a cool rush of tension sliding away from between her shoulders. The argument had been forgotten and the mission was foremost in his thoughts. Their jeep lurched hard side to side. "Lovely roads." The tension rushed back. "Did you learn anything earlier last night?"

"Nothin'. Mostly they were drinking, which only made their ghost stories even weirder in the telling. That kind of drinking ya' do when ya' don't want to think about where ya' are or what yer doing." He dodged another pothole. "One thing I found interesting. Our friend, Gas Station Guy? When I followed him home, before he went drinking, and before …"

"… before I interrupted your surveillance …"

"… before some coyote got killed a ways out here, he had been working on one nice piece of tarted up limousine."

"I thought all the limos left yesterday."

"So did I." Another pothole was missed, but a deep rut wasn't. "Just how many limos do ya' think need to stop in this little shit-hole town for a lube job?"

"At least the one you saw. Or maybe it's here for another reason?"

"Must be lucrative work, whatever the reason. And I think he knows what he's doing, so it isn't the first one he's worked on."

"There may be a few sedans soon. Saw a motorcade leave town after we ditched Bergman last night. I do believe it represents only half the *tourists* who went out earlier in the evening. I'm betting they all went to the Mesa. That place is turning into a black hole for criminals. See anything else?"

"Somebody around here owns himself a sweet, classic Cadillac two-door convertible. It was parked in the back, ya' know, where prying eyes like mine shouldn't have seen it."

"Were you looking where you shouldn't, Jack? I'm shocked. Absolutely shocked."

Within ten minutes they were as far away from Montejo as their cell phone signals allowed. They were also covered in dust, and sore from the nerve-jarring ride.

With little explanation, Tessa had the worksite looking organized and authentic. Exactly as one might expect a scientific sampling dig site to look. Jack took the moment to *test* the equipment, including a pair of binoculars.

For the moment, they weren't followed. By the top of the hour and the beginning of the heat, they were deep into their performance, following a checklist of necessary toil that their cover required.

The surveillance began shortly after. Cars would drive by. Never a tourist. Every time either a townie or a deputy.

"Didn't take them long," he grumbled dryly, unscrewing the cap off a second bottle of water. "They're pretty damned determined to know what we're up to." He held the bottle to his face.

"The interest is mutual." The latest vehicle, a rusted-out pickup truck, sped away towards town. Tessa stretched her legs out, aware of the sun pounding down on her scalp. Direct solar radiation on her head or steam cooking underneath her hat — seemed to be her only choices. A droplet of sweat rolled down her temple and cheek.

Yet for all the brutality of the temperature, the wind brought a consistent relief, just to spite it. Tessa used her arm and brimmed hat to protect her eyes and took in the landscape. Sage green bushes punctuated an expanse of pink sandy dirt and dots of gray stone. The land rose gently on a shrub covered hill to one side and fell precariously into a ravine on the other. Patches of ochre, green, rust, and shade climbed desperately up the ravine's side in a last-ditch effort to survive a fall. In the distance, coaxing a few clouds to its own summit, the dome of Ute Mountain slept under a blanket of indigo and gray.

Behind her, Jack stood up, tall, and leaned back to stretch. As he placed his hands on his hips, she had a quick look at the disfigured hand. It was gloved, as always, but the glove was soft, supple leather, and now she could discern how he hid the damage. The little and ring fingers of the glove had been filled with something flexible, like cloth wadding. It stuffed the space and gave the hand a more natural appearance. The flaw in the design was that those digits did not bend as the others did nor did they have the differentiating shapes of a finger.

"It doesn't hurt," he said. "Sometimes I don't even notice it."

"Sometimes?"

"Yeah." He looked around for someone who might be listening in, other than the piñon pines and scrub. "It itches or burns occasionally. I don't mind that. It's the phantom sensations that … don't … I don't know. There are times I forget they're gone. But most of the time, it's okay."

"I'm glad for that," she replied, embarrassed she'd been caught staring. "Sorry, Jack. I guess I was curious. I would have thought they'd do a better job with it at the hospital."

"It wasn't exactly Cedars-Sinai. They did the best they could with what they had. Saved my life. The phantom pains are normal, though I think I can tell if bad weather is comin' now." He wiggled his fingers magically.

"You're here. I'm grateful to them, whoever *they* are."

Jack stared back at her, her strands of hair whipping in the breeze, and smiled, lopsided and all.

Her cheeks warmed as she crouched down near her sample kit. *Must be the heat.*

"Why, *Mrs. Peel.* Methinks the lady doth give a damn." He took a long swig from the water bottle, reminding her of the description, 'a tall cool drink of water'. He crouched down next to her and moved a wayward piece of hair out of her face, tucking it neatly behind her ear.

That familiar touch took the tightness out of her stomach.

"Darlin', I'm sorry about last night. I was tired. And I didn't like the way he was handling ya'. I shoulda' known better."

"You don't need to apologize," she replied, not wanting him to stop.

"Yeah, I do. There are lots of things I should apologize for, and I know I'll never get the chance. I figure the best thing to do is to not make the list any worse."

"New start and all that, eh, *Steed?*"

"Sort of. It's been rough. Lost track of what's important and gotta' get back on target. Recommit to the objective. So far, I've succeeded. Not convinced I always will."

"Sleep helps."

"When ya' can get it." For a second, he looked diminished, hope draining from his face, then he snapped back. "Since it seems we don't have an audience for the moment, I've been wanting to ask something."

"Ask what," she replied, while obsessively crimping the brim of her hat.

He was so close to her. "You've taken an interest in …" he pressed his lips together, his moustache covering his upper lip entirely.

"Ghosts?" She didn't mean for the word to come out so sharply. "It's a … a long story."

Jack stood up and looked around, a bit dramatically she thought. Crouching back down, he grinned. "We appear to have a few private minutes. Tell me all about the ghoulies."

Damn you. His smirk was dismissive. The coy body language. The notion she could explain it — *all of it* — in the few moments until the next car drove by was unexpectedly infuriating. *Let it go, he's only asking.* "It's a long story, Jack, and we shouldn't discuss it out here." She stood up, slapping the dirt off her jeans and shoving her hair under her hat.

His grasp was sudden but tender. "Hey."

Jack immediately let go of her hand and they both separated as a roll of dust approached them on the road.

Sheriff Bergman, and a deputy they almost couldn't see in the passenger seat, pulled up alongside them on the road. The sheriff leaned out his window, and barked, "You two can't go any further out."

His voice. Even outside it grabbed her.

She was drawn to him, unable to resist going over to him at his mere beckoning. "We couldn't even if we wanted to," Tessa replied, dusting off her jeans even more. "Not on our map," she lied without blinking. "We're not allowed to go where we're not given specific permission. As for your Mesa, we'd have to get substantial survey equipment and a full team in there. And that would also require either tribal or other local approvals, environmental reports. You get the idea. I suspect you've seen that sort of red tape a dozen times." Her legs carried her over toward his car, too willing.

The sheriff looked pleased as she approached. "Yeah, that's not going happen anytime soon." He looked at his watch — a nice thing, possibly new. "You might want to take a break midday. There's a reason the Indians and Mexicans around here take a siesta. Hottest part of the day. Your man over there can warn you about it. I suggest a long lunch and a rest."

"Sounds sensible. Meanwhile, we'll be staying within our assigned range. Really," she took a few steps closer and removed her gloves. Maybe he would touch her bare hand? She removed her hat and let all her braided red hair fall down her back. After all, her hair was one of her best assets.

"See that you do," he said, looking hungrily at her hair, then her waist, then working his way up methodically. "Stick to your map and don't go south or west. I don't want to have to go in and get you."

"I think we can agree to that."

His fingers reached out and almost ... almost ... touched her.

The deputy whispered something, and the sheriff withdrew into the air conditioning of his vehicle.

Spitting up a cloud of dust, the car drove away without an acknowledgment of her agreement. They went west, Tessa noted, to where he'd just told them it was too dangerous to go. The impulse to be with Bergman, to listen to his every word — to be touched — vanished in the dust too.

"Nice Rolex Bergman's got." Jack whacked his cap on his thigh, clearing it of dust, before putting it back on his head. The sound jerked her back to the hot desert. It wasn't the only thing heated. Jack looked to be ready to fume.

"Yes. Quite nice," she replied, getting back on target. "Five, maybe six thousand dollars' worth of watch?"

"I was thinking about eight thousand."

"Apparently, they are doing fine." *I'm not*, she worried, *and won't, if I don't get ahold of myself regarding Bergman.*

Jack muttered something and bent down to pick up a trowel.

Danger, It hissed?

Tessa squeezed her eyes shut. *Oh shit.* It was here. Waiting on the edge of the canyon lands.

It's here.

CHAPTER TWENTY-SIX

"I DON'T GIVE A RAT'S ASS what you want! You want to be dead?"

Tessa rolled over on her side, kicking the tangled, sweaty sheet off her legs. Her thoughts slogged forward in an effort to remember where she was. The room felt heavy and caught between moments in time. Tessa shook her head, forcing away the deviled sleep clinging to her.

He could be mine, you know, girlfriend.

Shut up! Go away!

Her lucid dream broke away.

"Look. I left it down there and I need to get it back." The conversation —outside her window — in the parking lot. That was a voice she'd heard before, but where? Her fingers moved under her pillow to the gun.

"Too bad. You should have thought about that before you and your idiot friends went trespassing."

That second voice belonged to the deputy. No mistaking Billy-boy.

"Man, I can't afford to replace expensive equipment."

Equipment? Tessa snagged the bedsheet by the corner, pulling it up over her undressed body as she listened to the male voices.

"Tough shit, asshole."

God, she despised hot weather. Made everyone rude. No matter how much clothing she took off, and she had taken it all off in desperation, she was still hot. Naked, and still there was no relief. The hum of the battery-operated fan provided in her room mocked her by pretending to move the air. Any so-called sleep had been abused by discomfort and lucid waking intrusions.

"Hey, are you supposed to talk like that to taxpayers?"

"I can if they're criminal trespassers."

"How about I call the county and ask them to help me get my stuff?"

Now, he will be mine. Unless you shoot the policeman and save him.

The clack of beads and scent of spicy resin engulfed Tessa's room.

Despite the temperature, which had to be over ninety degrees, a chill ran down Tessa's back. Whipping her legs over the side of the bed, she leaned out of the window as far as she could. This wasn't a heat-driven, lucid dream — It was there. *Death* wanted someone near.

Sid. From the ghost hunting group. Same Bermuda shorts, socks, hiking boots, and now the official *4-Corners Paranormal Research Society* t-shirt. Still needed a shave. Sid … Franklin. That was his name. Sid Franklin. Young, vital, curious Sid Franklin.

No.

Deputy Billy-boy was moving in closer to Sid. "Go ahead. You think the cops over there are going to listen to some outta' work hippie? Think they'll take your side against another cop?" His index finger darted out, slamming Sid in the chest.

Sid was no body builder, but he wasn't the weak kid in those comic book ads getting sand kicked on him. Lifting all that equipment gave him a good pair of shoulders and arms. His hands balled into fists.

"You pack your hippy-shit truck and drive your hippy-shit ass out of here. Got that? The Mesa is off limits and you jerks don't get no sympathy from me if you broke the rules and lost something down there."

Taking a deep, shuddering breath, Sid held his hands out. "I didn't lose it at the Mesa. I lost it on the way over. Okay? I don't want to go to the Mesa. Okay?" His voice was loud and full of fear. "There's not enough money in the world to make me go there again. You and your creepy little town can have it."

Ah, Christ, Sid. Don't tick him off.

"Are you leaving like I ordered you to?"

"It's a public road. I don't have to ..."

The deputy drew his sidearm and put it right up against Sid's head.

Tessa screamed, knowing that both men would hear her. Knowing that she was going to rob Death of ...

Of what? What was she thinking?

"Oh my God! What's going on down there!" *That's right, Billy-boy, there's a witness.* She got the attention of both men, and the deputy backed up a step, desperately looking around for the source of the voice. Finally, he looked up at her window.

Tessa's door burst open, and Jack raced in, gun clutched in both hands, and his unbuttoned jeans barely over his bare hips.

"Hold up," Tessa ordered before he was at the window.

Below them, the deputy's movements were jerky, and he kept muttering something to Sid through a clenched jaw. He ordered Sid to put his hands on the truck, searched him, took Sid's wallet for a quick examination, threw it into the truck, and backed away. The service weapon was reluctantly put away.

Jack watched and waited out of sight, knuckles white in his gun grip.

Tessa checked for every nuance she could memorize about the encounter. Something nagged her about the situation. Had Billy-boy taken anything off Sid during his search? No. The deputy's hands were empty once he'd holstered the weapon. Wait — Billy-boy pocketed something.

Cash. He'd taken money from Sid's wallet. Well, it was better than shooting him.

Inconspicuously, she glanced back into the room. The sounds and smells from earlier had vanished.

It was not there. Death wasn't there.

Maybe she had imagined It.

After what felt like a span of minutes, the deputy ordered Sid out of town again and marched away.

Whether or not Sid could fully see her didn't stop him from looking up toward her window. The breeze drew the old lace curtain out, billowing it much like a sail.

He didn't drive away but put his head in his hands.

Tessa looked at Jack, at first in mutual sympathy for Sid, who'd likely never been on the losing end of a gun muzzle, then in mutual surprise.

Tessa was holding a bedsheet over only the most delicate portions of her body. Both bare legs were wrapped over the bedspread, exposed to his potential gaze, and the sheet's corner was scarcely placed to cover her breasts.

Jack had done little more than pull his jeans over bare skin before rushing into her room. Otherwise, he was no more clothed than she was. Apparently he, too, had stripped down to nothing in order to survive the heat.

She'd forgotten that he had rather beautiful, masculine, strong yet graceful feet. Dancer's feet.

He wasn't known for being squeamish about bodies or sex, yet for a second, Tessa was sure she saw something in his eyes that was amazed, perhaps even caught off guard, by finding her like that.

Standing straighter, gently tugging on his belt loops as though not a thing was amiss and not wanting his jeans to slip down further, he cocked a lopsided smile. "Siesta time over?"

"I daresay." She couldn't move, she didn't dare, and she was staring, too. While his left hand and arm were scarred and disfigured, he was otherwise in remarkably fine condition. He was shiny from sweat and exertion. Life as a rancher had not harmed his physique at all. No, sir, not one bit.

Laughable, and it truly was, her cheeks heated. As close as they had been, they hadn't … well, they *hadn't.* Not a good idea. Never a good opportunity. Now her cheeks were hot, and she could imagine her face to be redder than the maraschino cherry sinking in the cold cocktail she desperately wanted.

Jack began an attempt at nonchalantly leaving the room. "I'm gonna' get dressed and see if I can't chat with … what was his name?"

"Sid Franklin."

"Yeah, uh, Sid. To see what he may know." With that, Jack turned his back on her and swiftly scooted out the door.

Tessa did her best neither to laugh nor to sigh in response to the wave of frustration that flooded her

CHAPTER TWENTY-SEVEN

"AT LEAST YOU GOT TO HEAR about the Skin Thief. Better than what I got." Sid drew in smoke from the cigarette and tried not to cough when he exhaled.

Jack watched in sympathy. He held his cigarette for the visual pretense and to give Sid a sense of camaraderie. So far, it was working.

The booze was helping too.

Jack handed Sid the bottle of cheap whiskey and Sid didn't demur from it. While the man put the bottle to his lips and tilted his head back, Jack had a chance to size him up. Sid seemed a bit older than he'd originally thought. Maybe in his mid-thirties. He had pockmarks on his face —. Some patchy scruff on his cheeks. A couple of interesting scars on his jawbone. Otherwise, Sid could pass as a California tech-geek.

"I thought I was dead," he agonized, clutching the bottle for a moment. He stared bleakly out at Ute Mountain.

"Y'all never had someone pull a gun on ya' before?"

Sid only shook his head. "What is with these people? I mean, come on. It's a three-thousand-dollar piece of equipment. I can't afford to replace it. What do they think, I'm drippin' in cash?" He knocked back another swig and pushed the bottle away. "That deputy should have seen I don't have a lotta money."

"Missing a few dollars post encounter?"

Sid shrugged. "Not the first time. We break the rules a lot. Sometimes you pay *fines* in unusual ways."

"Think he wants your camera too?"

He shrugged again. "It isn't even my camera to lose," he half whispered.

Jack took back the bottle and slammed down what appeared as a big swig. "Geez, I didn't know your hobby cost so much."

While his eyes were starting to look a little unfocused, Sid's response was solid. "Not a hobby, man. This is what I do." Sid glowered at Jack.

The wind was hot, the still air was hot, no escaping the heat. Jack realized that Sid was staring at his gloves. "What, these? I try not to take 'em off." He waggled his fingers at Sid. "Missing a couple of digits."

Sid made the *ah-ha* statement with his mouth but didn't actually say anything. Perhaps he was too polite.

The back door of the motel opened, and Tessa slid through, making an obvious effort of sneaking out to join them. There wasn't much in the way of seating: crumbling cement stairs, a fenced off pool with no water, and a set of swings twisting in the breeze.

"My mother always taught me," she whispered loudly, "that to be the life of the party, bring food." She pulled out a couple of bags of chips, a newly opened jar of something that smelled spicy, and a handful of paper towels. Sitting on the steps above the two men, positioned between them, Tessa set the snacks on her lap. While Jack took the top off the jar, she took a drink from the bottle and handed it to Sid.

"Now, did I hear you right, Sid, you ghost hunt for a living?"

Nodding without removing the bottle from his lips, shaking the contents, Sid sort of grinned. Filling up with a mouthful of chips he continued, "Look, I know you guys … uh, gal … you're like all science. Well, so am I. But this is my science."

The bottle kept moving around, like a permission slip to chat.

"Ghosts," Jack muttered, not quite snarling. Not that he didn't want to mock all of that spectral nonsense, he just needed Sid to think of him as a safe confident. He couldn't afford to lose the man's budding trust.

"You never seen something you can't explain?" Sid glared at him with an ever more stoned gaze.

"I've seen tons of shit I can't explain. I leave it in the file marked, *Not Explained Today.* I don't try to label it as paranormal."

"Today," both Sid and Tessa added.

Tessa laughed a little and started combing the hair off her forehead with her hand, something she did when she pretended to be inebriated. If Jack knew his partner, she'd start gesticulating too. "Rio is just being Rio. He doesn't believe in anything he can't see, touch, drink, or smell."

"Thanks, Boss Lady."

"Jack, I'm simply saying that you are a skeptic."

Sid took another swig. "So am I. But I've seen things …"

"Like what?" Tessa actually batted her eyelashes at him.

Damn, she can drive a fella mad if she wants to. A thought Jack kept to himself.

"Well, there was this case in Ohio …"

"No, no, no. What did you see around here?"

"Over at El Muertos? Man, you wouldn't believe the shit I saw there. Now first when we got there, it was quiet, like, man, way too quiet. But we're out in the middle of nowhere, so of course it's quiet. You know, like when you've been in Los Angeles for most of your life and you've gotten used to constant noise and then all of a sudden, you're in the middle of …"

Jack put some chips on Sid's paper towel. Keeping someone lubricated but not soused was a fine art, even if some of the brushes were cheap imitation BBQ potato chips. "The Mesa? Y'all were telling us about the Mesa de los Muertos."

"Yeah. Ok. So, it was too quiet. But we went in anyway. Bel insisted. She's always insistin'. 'Where's the video' — yeah, like ghosts are willing to repeat for a better take?"

Tessa leaned forward. "Go on. What happened next?" She leaned her chin on her hands and flashed her violet eyes at him.

Throw in the towel, boy, she's going to get ya' by the short hairs if she hasn't already. Jack smiled and motioned Sid to keep going.

"Um, so we go down into the actual cliff dwellings. Man, the National Park Service shouldn't have given up on that place. It's beautiful. I'd say it was in about the same condition as Verde but needs to be made safe for tourists." Just as the two agents were going to encourage him to stay on topic, Sid finally kept going on his own. "There were sounds, like a lot of people moving around. And whispers. Falling rocks, though that could have been the place, being a cliff and all. So I got out my EVP recorder."

"Y'all got out what?"

"Oh, EVP, Electronic Voice Phenomenon. I told you I'm a scientist. I set up recording stations around the area, with cameras. Got to have evidence," he punctuated with the bottle.

Tessa glanced over at Jack, her expression remarkably sober. "Is that the piece of equipment you left behind? One of your recorders or cameras?" Her voice was-hopeful, and Jack was thinking the same. Maybe Sid and his group had recorded what was going on around here.

"Nah. I picked up all of those I set up inside the dwelling."

Jack felt his chest drop. "Say, what did y'all lose out there?"

"Not in the Mesa, man, *on the way to the Mesa*. See, I need a base reading to compare sounds to. You know, scientific method and all. So I set up a camera and recorder *on the way to the Mesa* to get an idea of what were outside sounds."

Tessa lit up. Jack watched her as she leaned back to make certain no one was listening at the door. His settled his elbows on an upper step, feeling the gun hidden inside his work vest push against his spine.

Tessa gave him an All-Clear nod, behind Sid's visual range. "I get it. If you pick up some sort of echo out of, say, somebody playing their car radio too loud, and it all bounces around the canyon until it sounds like odd whispers inside the cliff dwelling, then you can debunk it."

"That's it, yeah. But ... there was something else. Bel says I was just scared, and my head played tricks on me." His chin dropped down to his chest. "Bel never was confident in me, I guess."

"Well, Sid, I'm not Bel. I'm Tessa and I promise you I'm listening." She set both of her hands delicately on his shoulder and rested her chin on top of them.

It took Sid a moment to swallow and work up his courage. "On our way to the Mesa, I noticed something down in one of the side ravines." He took a few deep breaths. "I thought I saw someone moving around. Bel was too hot to get into the ruins, so she wouldn't let me take a better look. I explained about needing to set up my baseline recorder and promised not to do more than that." His face fell in embarrassment.

"Sid, you were doing your job right."

"Yeah." Long breath. "So, I set up everything … and … I stopped to take a look at the ravine with my binoculars and a GH 5-60."

Jack's face screwed up a bit. "There's another term I don't know."

"Oh, Ghost Hunter 5 x 60mm Night Vision Monocular." He pulled out an impressive item, army green in color, single lensed, military looking. Sid leaned back and handed it to Tessa.

She held it in her fingers then handed it over to Jack.

"Okay, so, I didn't see any people or … ghosts ... not yet. But I thought I could make out graves. Rectangular, recently disturbed dirt, or something covered. But my camera couldn't pick it up so far away. Not the same range as the GH 5-60."

Damn, Jack forced his expression to stay neutral. He handed back the impressive tool to Sid.

Sid took it and frowned. "You know Bel — no video, no photo, no evidence."

Tessa nodded. "So, what else after that?"

"The usual, but lots of it. Let's just say we got out of there as fast as we could … once Bel was sure we got something on tape. But even she wanted out of there pretty bad."

"Whyever for?"

"Shadow people." He reached out and took the bottle out of turn from Jack. "Lots of shadow people. They were everywhere. Except on our video tape, of course."

The agents exchanged confused glances as Sid nearly drained the bottle.

"Yeah. I mean, I never believed in them, the Skin Thieves, or the main Skin Thief, but ..." He drank again. "Everyone who spends anytime investigating the para … um … normal knows about Shadow People, but this stuff is … different."

Sid let the bottle descend for a moment and Tessa promptly snatched it away, smiling as she pretended to take a long drink. Jack temped the Ghost Hunter with more chips while his partner poured the remaining contents of liquor quietly down the side of the steps.

"Why are *these* Shadow-*thangs* so different," Jack asked in hopes of refocusing Sid.

"Some of the scariest varieties of ghost, man. They're like the worst of your worst fears."

Tessa wrapped her arms around her legs and pulled them in tighter to her body. "I thought those sorts were *demons* and *devils*."

"Nah. I don't believe in them." Sid started looking around for the bottle but gave up after a moment. "Never seen one of them."

"Are they the same as the … um … *Skin Thieves?*" Tessa shivered with excitement.

Sid shook his head. "Nah. I got a chance to look it up after we got back to Farmington. Not sure if that's a real name for them but that's what people call 'em. They're the spirits of the ancient people who came *before* the Basket Makers who lived in the cliffs, like Mesa Verde. They're like Shadow People except for one nasty trick specific to them. They don't just creep along the walls and go boo! They're rumored to get inside people, and they take them over. They use them. Most of the time, to death."

Tessa's eyes widened and she froze in place.

Darlin', what scared you? Jack watched her closed eyes, forced breathing, blanched face. Something had her spooked bad, though she was trying to hide it.

"Hence the term *skins*?" She blurted out, displaying her formula calm expression.

Sid gave her a fearful side-eye.

"If I believed that Skin Thief was real …"

"If," Jack said, sniffing loudly, for Sid's sake. For Tessa, he'd keep an eye on her. He knew when she was trying to look brave.

"Yes, if, then they could do almost anything they want borrowing anyone they want."

Sid ran his fingers through his hair while his laugh merged with an uncomfortable cough. Pointing at Jack, as if saying he agreed with him, Sid added, "The legends say once they can make other folks do what they want. Kinda like mesmerizing people to do your bidding. Creepy, but if you can't explain why some people act against their own best good, having a legend that blames a charismatic demonic shadow creature," he added with dramatic flair to impress Jack's sense of skepticism, "might be a handy thing to have."

Tessa's face fell into a frown. "Well, isn't that jolly."

"Well, if … and this is a bigger if … we're understanding this pre-Puebloan culture and its stories correctly, then much of the culture's destruction was due to the Skin Thief and his followers. The truth is scholars don't know enough about these ancient people. They're so new to archaeologists, there isn't even an agreed-on name for them. Local tribal folks won't talk about them in much detail. They're the big mystery."

Jack's face screwed up then had an 'ah ha!' expression. "Yer our expert tonight. Tell me what ya' think of this." He scrounged around in his back pocket. What he removed he held out for Sid to examine.

The bone object.

Sid's eyes lit up and he acted remarkably sober all of a sudden. "Where did you get that, man?"

"A gift from someone local. Is it a tourist trinket? Or an ancient sewing needle?"

As though he was touching a fragment of the Dead Sea Scrolls, fearful his fingers might damage it, Sid picked up the object by the thread loop and held it suspended above his other hand. "This is a talisman." He turned to so that he could look at the whole object. "Man, I could have used this."

"Oh?"

"Ok, we're back to *if* again." Tenderly, he handed the needle back to Jack. "That would be on a cord, worn for protection, from … wait for it …"

"—The Skin Thief?"

"Bingo! And not just Skin Thieves, but a whole bunch of crazy cryptoid or spirit monsters."

Jack's skeptical expression came back, and Tessa felt an intervention was in order. "Sid, why would such notably powerful spirits be afraid of a bone needle?"

"Not a needle. An awl. For piercing leather. You know, for stabbing holes in tanned *skin*?"

"Holes captured beings might escape through," Tessa asked. "Or could damage them permanently?"

"That's it. Great thing to have if you don't want to be possessed or jumped."

"Such a concept almost suggests that these spirits are aware of what they are doing when they possess a living body or try to *charm* or *enchant* someone. Now correct me if I'm wrong, but if such entities exist in the ruins out there, don't paranormal researchers call that an *intelligent haunting*."

"We can hardly call it a *residual haunting*, can we?"

Sid looked at Jack, who was trying to hide his annoyance with the weird discussion and even weirder lingo behind a staunch expression and a stern nod.

Sid continued undaunted. "The possession act is also called *jumping*. You know, we don't know whatever happened to the Anasazi or the pre-Puebloans. Places like Chaco Canyon and Mesa Verde appear to have been suddenly abandoned. We may never know. But there tends to be a shit-ton of evidence — okay, mostly conjecture — about spirit activity continuing in places like El Muertos. Deadly activity if you catch my drift. These are people who lived one or two thousand years before the people of Mesa Verde. They had planned cities, organized religion, and complex social systems. I wouldn't put anything past them that required planning and patience."

"Even their ghosts?"

"Especially their ghosts." Sid paused to think for a moment. "Well, the evil ones. Like people, there are good folks and bad, and some in between. Same with the paranormal."

Tessa giggled. "And the bad ones think they're the good guys. Every villain is the hero of his own story, eh?"

"Y'all ought to write this down and sell it. I don't believe in any of it, but ya' sure got my attention," Jack tried not to laugh.

"I hope so." Sid's grin was shy. "That's why Bel is such a slave driver. We're trying to get a cable TV show of our own."

Jack frowned and rolled his eyes.

Sid kept going, "You know, like all those cable channels that used to be about other topics, but now they only have ghost shows because the ratings are huge?"

"I'll take yer word for it."

"You're one of those guys without a TV, aren't you?" Sid looked at him suspiciously.

Tessa bumped Sid playfully with her shoulder. "If it isn't beef, beer, or …" she gesticulated roundly under her bosom.

Jack gave her a raised eyebrow.

"… or babes, Rio doesn't bother with it. Outside of work, that is."

At first, only Tessa and Sid laughed, but Jack soon relented and joined in. And for a good many minutes, they each enjoyed a great belly laugh, leaving her to wonder if it had been so very long since they'd each had one.

Genuine. Unstoppable. Human.

CHAPTER TWENTY-EIGHT

TO GET SID A PLACE TO CRASH for a few hours didn't take a great deal of effort. Jack simply turned on the charm for the motel manager.

As far as Tessa could tell, the manager wasn't happy about the semi-conscious ghost hunter on her lobby couch, but then, she would be paid good money with or without a room provided.

Tessa watched Jack's body language — leaning in, rolling his shoulders a bit, confidently signing paperwork — and she relaxed, knowing that Sid's overnight stay was secure.

Poor Sid.

All he wanted was video of a ghost and a cable TV career. It wasn't a bad lifegoal. A bit niche, but not bad. She laid a blanket over his legs and whispered, "good night," hoping she hadn't inadvertently portrayed a whispering spirit in his dreams.

Jack strolled up and in a gentle voice, asked, "Do y'all see his car keys? I have to move his truck to a proper spot, or the local constabulary will tow it."

The keys were easy enough to find.

Looking over Jack's shoulder, to see where the manager was, watching her TV of course, Tessa grinned and gave a solid nod.

"He's had a rough time. Thought he'd like to find his truck in the morning. Something tells me he's gonna' be feeling the sunrise pretty good."

"I'm not convinced I won't."

Jack drew a circle with his finger, an indication she recognized as meaning he'd take a look around the truck.

Tessa sidled up to the manager and her TV, ready to provide a distraction with some conversation, freeing Jack to use whatever time he needed to search the truck.

The minute the engine turned over, a squeal rose from under the hood. Jack scowled — a new belt was needed. Night vision scopes, digital cameras, electronic detectors, all that cost money, and yet the kid hadn't dropped a single penny on the upkeep of his silver Ford F-150? And the mileage said the owner or owners had driven it nearly one-hundred-thousand miles. Someone was lucky.

Once he'd parked it, nose-in near the front door, Jack double-checked to see if anyone could watch him from the motel lobby. No? Good. Moving casually, he leaned over and opened the glove compartment. Why was it called that — a glove compartment? It would be better and more accurately called a weapons compartment or gun box, wouldn't it?

Sid didn't own a gun.

In fact, based on the paperwork in the truck, he didn't even own the truck himself. Bel McGuire, the leader of the *4 Corners Paranormal Group,* had co-signed for it.. The group had a station wagon, complete with logo stickers. The truck looked like it was more for Sid's personal use.

The left side of Jack's moustache lifted. So, there was more to Sid and Bel than buddies who went out on weekends to pester the dead. She bought him a truck. Used, but nice. And, based on one of the receipts Sid had kept, she'd purchased a set of new tires, too. Practical kind of girlfriend.

There was a calendar on the floor of the passenger side, along with maps of the region. Jack had to respect all those old, colorful, folded, crumpled, and heaped papers. While there was much good to be said of GPS and digital street maps, nothing beat the idea of finding an old-fashioned map, at least not to him.

On the floor was a tightly balled-up paper, pale blue in color. Unfolding it, Jack found a message, written by hand, in black ink. "Sid," it started, brutally plain, and promptly went downhill. *Can't work. Was fun. Too much work. Not your fault.*

Yeah, he'd heard that kind of thing too. Spoken, written, or shouted, it was all the same message: *I'm trying to protect your ego, but you don't cut it anymore.*

So, they were breaking up? Did that matter to their mission? Possibly not, but one never knew what tidbit of information was important. Jack wadded up the *Dear Sid* letter and put it back where he found it.

He and Sid needed to have a nice man to man chat again —in case *it* did matter.

CHAPTER TWENTY-NINE

FOR WHATEVER REASON, Tessa slept fairly well through the night. That was hardly expected, but she welcomed the rest all the same. Not having her nerves on edge made it easier to get ready. She collected her laptop, and her 9MM, and stepped into the hall. In the small space separating their rooms, she stopped and listened to Jack fussing around. A creaking bed frame, a grunt of frustration, a stomp of boots to force each foot into them. It was an array of noises she would have expected from any man. But was it just her, or did Jack sound more aggravated this morning?

He'd had his share of the bottle last night, but nothing like what Sid put away.

The other night when she couldn't find him? Yes, she believed he had abandoned her — and she had been wrong.

He was, after all, doing his job. And what he'd discovered was useful.

"Good morning Rio."

So why didn't he communicate his intentions the other night? Going out on his own that night was a risky move, and it bothered her. He could have been hurt. Or killed.

Taking a deep breath, she counted to five, and took another.

At least she hadn't been paid an annoying visit by Sheriff Bergman. Given his behavior around her so far, it was almost strange that he hadn't made an appearance. By the same token, Tessa thought, Bergman's absence was welcome. The last thing she needed was to have to defend herself from his advances in the cramped quarters of her room, and to deal with Jack's overwhelming need to protect her. *Men*!

Jack was still stomping around in his room, making enough noise that Tessa was grateful they were the only two guests in the motel's registry. She knocked once on his door.

"I'm heading down, Rio. Meet me in the lobby when you're ready."

All she got for her effort was a vague grunt, which could be either acknowledgment or dismissal. *Men*.

The view downstairs hadn't changed, at least. She could see the front desk, and the back of the manager's head. The woman was watching her huge TV screen, as usual. The cleaning equipment she might actually use in their rooms sat in the corner, less entertaining, apparently, than the fight about to erupt between divorced couples on a faux-psychologist's show.

Tessa stopped mid step on the stairs. Sid wasn't on the couch. She was about to head back up and tell Jack when she realized he had caught up with her and nearly run into her back. "Sid left?" he asked over her shoulder.

The couch's pillows were all aligned as they had been the night before Sid was unceremoniously deposited there. The blanket was folded neatly and set on the left-most cushion.

Jack leaned over the rail to look into the parking lot. "Truck's gone too."

The manager heard them and leaned back in her recliner. "Who, the kid? Yeah, I think I heard him leave early this morning."

"That's too bad," Tessa quickly responded. "I was hoping we'd have breakfast with him, to hear more about his work. Oh well. We have enough to do, don't we, Rio?"

"Whatever you say, Boss Lady." He surreptitiously winked at the manager who suppressed a girlish giggle.

What a flirt. There was the Jack she knew.

Jack loaded the jeep with what Tessa considered to be a determined, calm effort. He set down soil kits, unlocked the doors ... every motion nice and slow. Not in a rush for any reason.

He kicked the front tire, moved to the rear, repeated the move with each tire there and ended up at the passenger side.

Tessa looked up, having put away her computer and equipment bag. "Something amiss, *Steed*," she whispered without facing him.

"Sid's truck tires. Left nice deep tracks."

"And?"

"He backed up carefully."

"And?"

"Headed west-southwest." Jack lowered his chin.

"The highway is east."

Jack gave her a lopsided grin she couldn't quite interpret: annoyance or amusement?

"The Mesa is west-southwest."

Yes. The Mesa is west southwest. Was that **Death**'s voice she was hearing? Or her own?

Tessa's blood froze and her hands trembled. She grasped the jeep's door handle and prayed Jack didn't see. *Run? Flee? Go away!* She breathed forcefully. *One. Two. Three…*

When Bergman pulled up, blocking them from leaving the parking lot, Jack was ready to fight. Every sinew was prepped for a fight. He noticed Tessa's sudden discomfort. It had to be Bergman who'd unnerved her. Now, he really hated the man.

And they'd befriended Sid, so he was sure that word of that association had gotten out via the motel manager. Such a connection would work in their favor if he played Bergman right. His lips curled upward. He liked the idea.

The cocky sheriff slammed his patrol car door a bit too hard and strolled around to stand in front of him as he loaded equipment for the day's work.

Looking down at the tracks, Bergman smiled. It wasn't something pretty to look at. "So, where's the kid who stayed here last night?"

"Drove off early. Probably couldn't afford to stay here much longer." Jack sensed Tessa twitching at the remark and the sly reference to Billy-boy's threat. Still, he'd worded it prudently. He wanted to say more but knew that wouldn't help the mission. Instead, he softened and offered a saccharine "good morning."

Tessa put on a perky smile. "Good to see you up and around this early, Sheriff."

Bergman genuinely appeared disappointed. "Did that boy say anything to you, Mr. de Sombras?"

"About what? He was long gone before I got up." Jack shook his head innocently.

"Where was he planning on going?"

"If I had to guess, he was headed home with his tail between his legs. He was pretty upset at losing that expensive piece of equipment. Talked about it most of the evening."

"Shouldn't have been out there."

"So y'all've said, on numerous occasions."

Abruptly, Bergman turned to Tessa. He stepped forward, put one hand on the back of the jeep, and physically cut off Tessa from Jack.

A goddamn challenge.

If he took the bait, he'd blow their covers. If he didn't, his ego was going to be smarting for weeks.

Remember the mission.

As Bergman shifted his body closer to Tessa, she had regained a firm grasp of her wits and dangerously toyed with him verbally.

Jack's ego started counting the punches. Calmly, he moved away, picking up the cases with soil samples, the drill, and bits for small scale coring, and both of their backpacks. Jack had them neatly aligned in the rear of the jeep, efficiently, as he silently observed. And hated what he saw.

He hated the way Bergman loomed over Tessa; he hated the leering advance.

His chest was on fire. He hated Bergman.

Tessa's eyes were on Bergman, only occasionally blinking gently. Her shoulders were square to him, hips slightly forward.

The sheriff was saying something out of Jack's hearing and using the whisper to excuse his bringing his lips up to her ear.

Tessa did nothing to resist.

Jack felt the tire iron near the driver's seat. It was cold against his fingers, even in dampening gloves. It felt smooth, heavy, rounded. Powerful. *I'll give you justice*, he thought, picturing the iron crashing into Bergman's skull.

Tessa smiled at Bergman the way she had smiled at Jack — once. Her lips parted and her eyes began to close. Compelled.

Bergman reached out to hold her face in his hand.

The air was dead. And hot. Suffocating.

The tire iron was cold — ready … *Do it. Do it!*

"That's Billy on the radio," the voice announced behind them. "Ain'tcha' gonna' respond?"

Gas Guy. Cleaning that damn screwdriver or what-the-hell-ever it was. The man in the filthy overalls leaned against the base of the streetlight. He pointed to the patrol car. "Sounds kinda' urgent."

As if slapped awake from a nightmare, Jack pulled his hand back from the tire iron. Tessa stepped around the back of the jeep, adjusting her hat on top of her head. Looking over at Jack, he'd never seen a more confused look on her face.

Confused, she jumped back into the passenger seat. "We'd better get going, Rio."

"Ya' got it, Boss Lady." To the disappointed Bergman, he added, "Sorry to ask, but we need to get around ya'. Y'all mind moving?"

"I'm done for now." The sheriff climbed back into his patrol car and sped away.

At first, Jack didn't even start up the jeep. He sat facing forward. "What the hell just happened."

"I … I have no idea. I promise you, I have no idea. I just …" she sighed heavily. With a catch in her throat, she asked him, "Tell me I didn't do anything that might … endanger us?"

"No." His brain was racing with ideas and chasing after memories insisting on fleeing. "But I almost did. I damn near took him out." With that, he lifted the tire iron enough that she could see it. This was the second time someone had tried to make him do something that was not in his best interests. The first time, though, he'd been asleep — it had all been a dream. That was okay, right?

After staring at each other for a long time, Jack put down the iron beneath the seat. Then, before he could keep the words inside, "I wanted to kill him," slipped out of his mouth on a breath.

"Let's keep an eye on each other whenever possible. *That* was not covered in the procedural manual, whatever the hell *that* was."

CHAPTER THIRTY

TESSA STARED AT THE DINNER MENU in her hand. Specifically the cover of the menu. The image on the cover, underneath the yellowing and cracking plastic, did nothing to support the diner's image. If it were not for the words JENNY'S DINER printed at the top, the menu might well belong to a run-down place outside of Bakersfield. Certainly not an old-school, cool 50s diner.

The type-font was plain, stating the name of the diner, its so-called hours, address, and a phone number Tessa was sure didn't work. She'd spent enough time in the diner so far, and never heard the phone ring.

Gas Guy came in slyly, closing the front door behind him. He made about a second's eye contact with Tessa, then inspected a newspaper lying on the cashier's counter.

Tessa forced her eyes not to roll and dragged her attention back to the menu. She was struck, yet again, by the bizarre choice of decoration on the cover. The ghastly figure with the suggestion of a man inside the figure's chest cavity. Local legend? Cannibalism? That would be a seriously poor choice for a restaurant advertisement. But then, Tessa mused, this was Montejo.

"Afternoon, Doc. Whaddya have?" The waitress, same one, held pencil to paper.

"Burgers, fries, to go, and what," Tessa asked, pointing to the odd figure on the menu, "is that?"

The waitress must have decided Tessa had two heads by the stare she gave, but finally replied, "Burgers, fries, for you and Mr. Rio," she took the menu, "and that's some drawing we see all the time around here.

"And you put it on your menu?"

"Some professor told us it was a Justice Keeper, so the Sheriff said he likes it."

"It looks like it ate someone. And you put it on your menu?"

"Yup. In honor of Sheriff Bergman and all the boys."

"Including Billy-boy," Tessa winked. "Is it Anasazi?"

The waitress turned a bit pink. "You bet. It's just some ... I don't know ... Indian scribble ... but whatever the boys want, they get." On that note, she turned on her heel and left.

"Uh, we don't call them Anasazi anymore." The voice was baritone, smooth, and polite.

Tessa glanced up to find a tall, elegant man, perhaps Navajo, standing at the side of her booth. He wore a dress shirt, tie, and slacks. His tie pin was a beautiful silver-set row of turquoise stones. Over one arm was draped a sports coat with leather elbow patches. The other arm was occupied by a book and a vintage style book bag. An educator? A Professor? The one who told the Sheriff about the drawing?

He smiled softly. "You referred to the local pueblo dwellers as Anasazi."

For several deep breaths, Tessa was fascinated by the man. His face was tanned and hardened, yet the lines had been formed from emotions like smiling, frowning, and laughing. Graying hair lay smoothly under the brown cowboy hat he removed respectfully.

"Actually, I was referring to the image," she said while waving him to sit.

"Image?"

"On the menu, but she took it with her."

"Ah. Well, none the less, the term has gone out of favor."

Never look a gift resource in the mouth, Tessa welcomed. "I stand corrected. Thank you. Are you well-versed in local history?"

"Very well-versed, though I'll warn you, I'm a history professor and you'll get the whole lecture if you ask."

Tessa nodded, more than a little satisfied at her luck. Peeking over his shoulder as he sat in response to her invitation, she wondered where Gas Guy had gone.

"… Pete."

"Eh?"

"Peterson Begay, University of Colorado, Colorado Springs." His hand reached out over the table and his black eyes twinkled, reminding Tessa of Jack. Yes. Just like Jack.

"Tessa Wells, USGS, Virginia most of the time."

Their hands clasped and his fingers, contrary to what she expected for his alluring friendliness, were ice cold. He must have seen her reaction as he quickly pulled away his hand.

"My apologies, Ms. Wells. I have terrible circulation and my hands are always cold."

Cold like a corpse. "I completely understand. My hands and feet are cold all the time too. Please call me Tessa."

He settled into his half of the booth. "Now, where's this image you want to know about?"

Tessa searched around for the waitress, but she seemed to be away. Remembering the first time she'd seen the image, Tessa pulled out her napkin sketch from days earlier. "The waitress says it's a Justice Keeper."

Pete pursed his lips together and shook his head. "I don't know if that's the best term. That image was created by local people for a particular Justice Keeper — an outsider we think — who showed up at the Mesa de los Muertos about the 1300s CE. Current thinking says this person and his followers chased everyone out. Or killed them. Those folks who survived went south with the other people of the Canyons."

"To where?"

He shrugged. "Mesa Verde. Chaco Canyon."

Tessa tapped her drawing. "And this guy and his people?"

"Stayed for a time. We don't see that he or anyone who remained at Muertos lived long beyond the main abandonment."

"They just died out?"

"So it would seem. But then, we learn more every year about the people up here. We also unlearn things at the same time."

"Like ... we shouldn't call them Anasazi anymore."

He folded his arms and looked directly into her eyes. His voice became so very alluring … charming … just like Jack. "It's an old term, meant to call the ancient people the 'Enemy.' Some of their current descendants take offense at being given a negative name by someone else's culture. It's a fair point. It makes people feel like the 'other.' It's so much easier to hate 'others.' Exclude them. Destroy them." He leaned closer. "You don't want to go poking around the Mesa. It's a bad place."

Warmth and comfort rolled across her muscles. "Bad place. Because of *him*," she asked, still pointing to her drawing.

"Good people lived here and *he* pushed them out. *He* wanted to be the 'other.' Good people don't need to be here anymore."

"And the water? There's something about justice, cleansing, and water?" Tessa thinking was fuzzy, as though sleep was going to blanket her at any moment. Dear God, she wanted a nap.

"Droughts are normal here. This one's bad but not for you to worry about. You should probably go home and not worry." His voice was calming. "Justice means different things to different people. You don't need to worry." Soothing. Enveloping. "Outsiders, ancient or modern, don't always understand what a community thinks is just and right." Engulfing. Overwhelming.

She wanted to sleep so badly. The day was hot — isn't siesta time? Taking a nap with Pete would be a delightful thing. With Jack, it might not be so safe but it would be … "That is very true. His idea of right and wrong must have gone against the grain of the existing culture. I can't even begin to think of the type of punishments that …". Pete's eyes were awfully nice. Dark … like Jack's …

She stopped as cold rushed back into every muscle. "Could he be known as the Skin Thief?"

Pete's eyes grew wide. "No … uh … no — Skinwalkers are —"

"Skin *Thief.* Whole different creature I'm told. Completely different."

The professor looked at her strangely, at first concerned, yet oddly pleased. Nodding, he began to smile. "You are a very smart lady. You know your ghosts and spirits. You're different."

"I wouldn't go that far," Tessa replied quickly, chills racing along her arms.

"Tell me Ms. Wells, have you seen a ghost? Really seen a ghost? You of all people should know not to chase down the dead. *You* know that don't you?"

That was a bizarre question. Images rushed through her head of Ben, of people she had to deal with in her job. Of *Death*.

"Yeah. You know," he answered himself.

"Pete. I need to know a lot more. Honestly, I'm very ignorant about this place — its culture past and present."

"You need to leave this crazy place and go home. Quit chasing the Dead."

"I'm here to ... I'm here to do soil sampling so that the USGS can help farmers, ranchers, and others survive this ever-worsening drought. The only dead I'm dealing with are microbes in the dirt." Her hands were freezing. "Professor, who are you and what are you trying to tell me — other than 'go home.'"

Pete began to open his mouth when the waitress approached with two cups of coffee. "Hey Dr. Begay. You want anything?"

"No thank you." Pete stared at Tessa with a coy grin. "You need cream for your coffee, don't you?"

Tessa squeezed her eyes shut and pushed any thoughts of Ben Solomon out of her head. Opening her eyes, she saw that there was neither cream nor sugar on the table. They were over on the counter. "A moment please." Getting up would stretch her legs and clear her head. She slid out of the booth, took three fast strides to the counter, snatched up the condiments, and rested for a second. What the heck was happening?

Spinning around, ready to march back to the booth to question Begay further, she found the booth empty.

The diner was empty.

The waitress was in back, talking to the cook.

Outside, Gas Guy was walking across the main street towards his business.

Jack was never going to believe this.

"Skin Thief?" Jack sneered. "That again?"

"I have a feeling we're going to learn more than we ever want to know about Skin Thieves."

Jack inspected his 10mm Smith & Wesson before firmly setting it into the holster at his back. In the sheath between the holster and the belt, he adjusted a sharp Bowie knife. Dressed in black from neck to foot, he pulled on a deep indigo denim jacket. Regardless of how naked it made him feel, any headwear would stay behind. It only gave him a recognizable silhouette.

His eyes followed every one of Tessa's gestures, with his greatest interest focused on her weaponry. Boot knife. Short nose 9mm. Black leather body suit with hooks and straps to load up equipment as needed. Dark jacket. She'd braided her hair tightly to her head to prevent it catching on sharp objects or falling into her eyes. This was her battle gear. Flexible for fighting, disarming in appearance.

All lights in town were out.

Except …

The manager downstairs.

She was sitting with a glass of something over ice, feet up, watching the big screen TV behind the front desk. Her hand snaked out, took the glass, and dragged it dripping over to her lips.

They couldn't get past her.

Backing up to the hallway between their rooms, Tessa grimaced at Jack. He grinned for her. He had an idea. He wasn't smiling because he had a plan, he was smiling because she wasn't going to enjoy the plan he had.

He gestured for her to follow him into his room. Closing the door, he whispered, "Out the window."

"Through the tree?"

"Precisely, Darlin'. Looks like the spindly old pine Uncle Joe had near his house in El Paso, back in the day. Used to climb that thing every time I got shipped away for summer camp." His smile lifted then fell. "I've got some good memories of falling out of that tree."

"I'd rather not fall out of this one. If I break my leg or sprain my ankle, I think Bergman will shoot me to put me out of my misery."

"Nah. I'll do that, *Mrs. Peel.*"

"Oh, I'm so comforted," she droned as he pushed up the window sash to look out.

The tree was a piñon pine, with thick needles curving up from sparse twigs and branches. Inside the veil of sharps was the trunk, covered in rough and sticky bark.

"Quite doable," Tessa whispered with reluctant authority. "Mind giving me a boost?"

"My pleasure, ma'am." With Tessa facing him and setting her hands on his shoulders, he grasped her waist and lifted her up to the sill.

Without waiting, she wiggled her legs into the greenery, and began her climb to the ground. The tree jerked, slapped the side of the motel, and shivered. He tried his best to block the scraping and bumping, grabbing the violently shaking branches with his hands and hoping the manager's midnight talk show was loud enough to cover their exit.

The tree shook in three quick sets. Tessa had made it to the ground.

His turn. His left hand began to throb with phantom pain. *Not now!* Pins, it felt like pins sticking into his skin, driving into his bones. He pumped his fingers and pounded them on his leg, listening for any indication that the manager was alert to their egress.

The TV burbled with a crowd's laughter, and the manager giggled. The sound was far away — downstairs.

The tree shook three times, again.

Coming, Darlin'.

Ignoring his left hand, he hoisted himself up on the sill, and reached through to the branches. He felt the needles scratching his arms, his legs, his chest. Tucking his chin down, he pushed his head and right arm deeper into the pine, finally touching the thicker inner trunk.

Exactly like the tree at Joe's old house. Almost.

Joe had been too busy to raise a boy. He'd done his best, but he couldn't drag Jack to Langley or on CIA missions. School for eight months of the year in San Antonio, was lonely but survivable. But those summer months were much harder on the overactive, curious, PTSD-suffering boy. Growing up, no one knew what Post Traumatic Stress Disorder was. So all Jack ever heard was, *be a man, toughen up, cowboy up*. Falling out of trees and taking it like a man was simply expected of boys.

His foot struck the split in the trunk, and he swung down to the ground, next to the kneeling Tessa. She was waiting, hand on the grip of her gun, watching the road.

He tapped her lightly on the shoulder, faced the opposite direction, assessed any risk, and indicated they were clear from his viewpoint. Keeping low, they moved, around the side of the motel, down the road opposite the kitchen door of Jenny's Diner, and into the dark desert.

CHAPTER THIRTY-ONE

BEHIND THEM, A HANDFUL OF LIGHTS dotted the horizon, yellow and artificial. Far away and unreachable. Nothing else of humanity made its presence known ... Except the footsteps of the two agents as they walked swiftly down the sides of the dirt road. No sense in leaving tracks in the middle where anyone could find them. The crunch of sand, pulverized rock, and detritus sounded much too loud to her ears.

The horizon before them was black. The sky above was deepest cobalt, lit only by stars and a waning moon chasing after the sun, which had long ago set. That moonlight gave them barely enough illumination to navigate without flashlights but not enough to interpret the detailed reality around them. All was left to their imaginations. Luckily, Tessa's partner wasn't interested in paranormal explanations, thus, she was grateful to know, he wouldn't jump to any ghostly conclusions.

Or would he?

The sky was full of so many stars. Tessa had to fight against the urge to keep her eyes on the sky. It wouldn't do for her to end up a medical casualty with a twisted ankle or worse. She couldn't remember the last time she could make out the Milky Way in such detail. Was it so long ago she was sitting in Kenya with her father?

"Definitely pretty country out here," Jack stated in a soft voice, breaking the silence.

"Reminds me of a sanctuary in Africa. Right down to not knowing what might leap out at you from behind a bush."

"Ah, nature." He said with mock enthusiasm. He activated his cell phone. The light cast a strange glow on his face, rather reminiscent of a camp counselor with a flashlight trying to scare the kids. "We're past the signal limit." He pointed. "There's that big bend up ahead, and based on the map, it loops south a bit, then back to the west again."

"Shall we short cut? Probably nothing on that loop."

He shrugged. "We can always check later, too."

"Yeah, but I also have this, I don't know — feeling — we need to get completely off the road."

Jack stopped. "The only time I ever distrusted yer gut feelin' it nearly cost me a coupla' teeth. Off the road it is. Ladies first." He swept his arm out in a grandiose manner, teasingly bowed, and allowed her to slip past him.

The crunch under their feet was louder, but the brush they had to wade through, sometimes up to their hips, made up for it by padding the sound and hiding their footprints. With each step, Tessa felt the urge to hide. Heaven help them if whoever was behind this situation decided a helicopter was a viable tool. She was rather surprised they hadn't. Without realizing, she'd said so out loud.

"Funds," Jack replied with confidence, pushing a tall grass out of his way.

"From the look of things, this is a highly lucrative operation?"

"To a degree." He stopped to get their bearings. "Y'all figured out the crime bosses are disappearing around here, right?"

"The agency has people planted inside several organizations, including, shall we say, familial ones. We got insider information and put two-and-two together."

"I'd be disappointed to hear otherwise. Add to it, we've seen for ourselves that law enforcement ain't precisely the epitome of chivalry and honor in these particular parts."

"I'd say Montejo is the outlier. We had a different reception up in Cortez."

He nodded sharply. "So, hypothetically speakin', how do y'all keep everyone quiet? You're runnin' an illegal operation in a small town, where everyone knows everyone and everything about everyone. How do you keep secrets?"

"Well, I would ..." She stopped abruptly and seized his arm.

Lights flashed in their direction, and they both dropped down in the dirt.

The lights flashed again. Swept away from them. Disappeared.

Jack leaned in toward her ear and whispered. "Car. Two hundred feet out. We drove that rough patch to work, remember?" He indicated the bouncing and apparent blinking lights with his hand. "They'll be around the curve in a second."

Sure enough, the bounding lights, flashing as the vehicle jumped from rut to rut in the road, came around the other side of them. A powerful search light came on and Tessa pulled Jack down lower in the dirt. The taste of dust and dead grasses seeped into her mouth. He tried to blow the debris away that stuck on his face, but it caught in his moustache.

The search light was much stronger than the headlights. In front of them, she could see the strobe working along the bushes and into the road. Handheld by the driver, she decided. Coming toward them.

Illogically, she held her breath. The dust tickled her nose, and she stifled a sneeze.

Equally illogically, Jack reached over and clutched her hand.

The search light kept coming, sweeping back and forth over them like a scythe.

Tessa turned her face, pale in any light as it was, into his shoulder to hide her reflective skin. He tucked his nose into the crook of his elbow and pressed tightly to her, accomplishing the same.

The vehicle rumbled past, no more than seven and a half feet away. She could see the tires over Jack's back. Her head dropped below him as the light swept over their heads. Warily, she lifted her head enough to see the undercarriage of the car and the lower half of the door. White car. Bottom of an official logo.

The sheriff or one of his men.

The vehicle screeched to a stop.

The light whisked back and forth behind them. Above them.

A rabbit dashed out from the bushes and disappeared a few shrubs away.

It was followed by the search light.

To a barrage of muttered curses, the police car moved again, unhurriedly down the road. Maddeningly and unhurriedly down the road.

Waiting for an extra minute, Tessa finally sat up.

"We might as well stay comfortable, Darlin'. Unless they're campin' out at the Mesa, they'll have to come back to get home."

She folded her arms, a bit testily, and turned her chin in his direction. "Are they onto us? If so, our plans will have change significantly."

For a long time, Jack lay still, lost in his thoughts. Finally, shaking his head with confidence, he told her, "Nah. They're not onto us. We didn't leave any signs, we got out of the motel without alerting the manager. I don't think this is about us."

"Hmm. Probably serves us right for thinking everything is all about us."

"My gut is telling me to take a little look-see out there. They weren't lookin' into the bushes, they were mostly focused down on the road." He climbed inelegantly to his feet and automatically offered Tessa his hand to get up with.

Suspiciously, hyper-aware of any lights, they crept out to the edge of the road.

Jack took out a small flashlight and began an examination within a very narrow portion of the area.

"Why, my dear *Mr. Steed*, are you going to show off your amazing tracking skills?"

"Of course, *Mrs. Peel.* Especially if I can figure out which are those belongin' to the officer's car and which belong to …" He hesitated, resting the flashlight on a particular track.

"You holding back on me?"

"Don't like talkin' in maybes too much, but I think this time, yup, this time I've got an idea that's a bit more solid." In the left-over light, Tessa could see his lopsided grin forming.

"See that? After I parked Sid's truck, I noticed he had new tires. They'd leave nice clean tracks in the sand. And there they are."

Jack was quite right. "A brilliant observation."

"Thank ya', ma'am."

"Conclusion?"

"Sid went to go get his equipment, bright and early this morning, hoping he wouldn't run into anyone official. They're lookin' for Sid, not us."

"I think you've hit the nail on the proverbial head. I sure would love to see what he recorded with that expensive camera of his."

"Might not have filmed much more than that rabbit making little rabbits."

"True."

"Clearly he didn't go for a Sunday drive after his confrontation with Billy-boy. There's the proof," he noted, indicating the distinctive, deep wheel indentations.

"Clearly," she remarked. "He came out *after* our little cocktail party. He wouldn't have been in town to fight with Billy-boy if he'd come out here and found what he was looking for. No point."

"Agreed."

"I think we need to go see if we can find Sid, don't you think? Rather than heading immediately to the Mesa?"

Lights in the distance appeared. Jack had been correct. The police car was on its way back.

The engine roared as it pushed up and over the hill. The echo, Tessa noticed, created a fascinating if frightening sound. The insane shapes of the rocks and sandy outcroppings created such variation that the collision of sound was horrible. The vehicle moved at a faster pace than before, and the search light only whipped over their heads as it sped past.

"That was a bit cursory, don't ya' think," he whispered, his breath warm against her ear.

"Quite." She wasn't entirely paying attention to the vehicle. As it raced back to the town, it was clear that they had done their job well enough and hadn't found anything. What was holding her attention was what was keeping *her* firmly in place — the overprotective Jack, who lay partially over her body.

Jack allowed her to wiggle out from under him.

"Why thank you, sir."

"Entirely my pleasure, I assure ya'."

"I never know if I should take you seriously. Never knew back in the day either." She moved into a crouch, then stood once she felt assured that the coast was truly clear. Jack remained hunkered down, giving him a unique vantage point she was all too aware of.

"I'm assumin' ya' must take a bit of me seriously or I wouldn't be here."

"Oh, my dear fellow, I've never doubted the seriousness of your skills and intelligence. It's that Cowboy Charm of yours. Mother never warned me about men like you."

"As long as I keep surprising you, Darlin' — as long as I do."

For a careful moment Jack looked up and down the road. She couldn't see the expression on his face, but she could guess. The flirtation and charm had ceased. Back to business.

He was right, she decided. Mission first. "I think we're clear for the moment. Can you pick out Sid's tracks from the others, despite all the traffic?"

"Pretty sure." He pointed with his flashlight at different angles.

And for one very long hour they followed the trail. Every few yards the distinct tracks of Sid's new tires showed up cleanly.

Then — they didn't. They were gone. He'd lost them.

Jack was more than a bit angry at himself. "We need to backtrack. If those treads ain't here, then they're back there."

"Did he pull off road? We didn't see any sign of that."

"I've got no idea," he snarled. Closing his eyes, he took a deep breath.

She watched his face for a time. From the tight, downturned mouth to the sudden, gleeful spark in his eyes, she watched. Encouraged by the tapping rhythm of his chin, his lopsided smile turned into a satisfied grin. He winked.

"Damn wind — covered it up. Wouldn't surprise me if it was on purpose." He pointed to a break in the side of the road, back about forty feet.

"Sid? What did he do?"

"Made a smart move. He got off the main road and did a little four-wheel road trip down that way." A good gust blew sand at them both, obligating them to shield their eyes. Tessa batted at her hair and face. "And that damn wind's wiping out the trail, grain by grain."

"We better hurry if we're going to find Sid before someone else does."

CHAPTER THIRTY-TWO

THE MOON HAD FINISHED ITS SHIFT for the evening and left them hunting by the limits of their flashlights. Overhead, the sky was a post-midnight blue with a blaze of milky stars streaked across the uneven horizon. Behind the silhouette of a squat, weather-worn pinnacle in the distance, a slight glow was forming. Sunrise was waking for the day; a cup of coffee and toast, and the yellow star would head to work. That meant the agents were getting precariously close to running out of search time.

Salty sweat coated his upper lip and absorbed into his moustache. Jack wiped it away with the sleeve of his jacket, smearing grit and dust across his face. The tire tracks were at his fingertips, half faded in large swaths, and the constant wind was indeed tearing away at them. By morning, not much would be left of the tracks. That any part of them still existed was more proof that Sid had come through here recently. Poor kid, what had he been thinking? Hadn't Billy-boy scared him enough? Someone like that needed a manly talking to. Actually, both of them did, but Billy-boy needed a follow-up discussion regarding law enforcement and other people's money.

Tracks, he remembered, as he felt the dryness of his mouth and focused on the work at hand.

Tessa stopped to take a few deep breaths and wipe the dirt deeper onto her cheek, causing a dark smear above a dimple forming from her exhausted grin. In what had to be restraint from laughing at him, she took a quick drink of water, handing him the bottle.

His face tightened into worry. Jack stood for a long time, staring ahead. *Damn.* He wasn't seeing things right, at least he hoped he wasn't.

"Jack?"

"See that spot down there, on the other side of the boulder?"

She peeked through a pair of small binoculars and a hiss slipped out from between her lips. "Sid's truck."

He didn't bother to agree. His stomach told him how right they were. He hurried down the rocky hill, careful that the peeling layers of stone didn't break under his weight and send him flopping wildly ass over teakettle, down to Sid's vehicle. Tessa stayed right behind him, sometimes kicking aside rocks that scattered in his wake.

This discovery was not necessarily good.

Sid had left his truck parked next to a large, pink, and orange boulder, both trapped in deep accumulated sand. Pale shoots of weeds and dead twigs stuck straight up out of the ground, grasping desperately for air.

His first thought was to check the cab of the truck. Yup, Sid hadn't locked his doors. What did that mean? "Well," Jack answered his unspoken question, "he either got out in a hurry and didn't think to lock 'em, or he didn't think he needed to."

"What do the footprints suggest?"

He kept the flashlight beam low, in case someone else was still out looking, and checked at the stride of the steps away from the truck. He noticed that Tessa wasn't watching him. She had her own search off to the other side of the truck.

"Here, in the deeper sand, it looks like he just walked. The back of his print isn't pushed out as y'all might expect with exertion from runnin.' My first guess — he wasn't bein' chased." He stepped observantly around Sid's prints, taking measure of where they were going. "Or he didn't know he was."

"Jack?" Her voice was hesitant.

"Darlin'?"

"I think he had company." She crouched down and held her light on another sandy point, ten or twelve feet from the passenger side of the truck.

Tingling ran up his arms. Fact was, he sort of liked Sid. No, he didn't know the kid, but he was a nice guy, breaking up with a girlfriend, passionate about a crazy bunch of ideas, trying to get along in the world. In so many ways, Sid was one of the innocents they were on a mission to protect. If they had failed him …

"Whatcha' got?"

"I'd say at least two different sets of footprints." She looked up to him as he approached. "I will, however, defer to the expert."

"Yer not wrong, Darlin'." He reached over to her hand and guided it along the prints, gauging their direction. "A little off from Sid's path. Not his shoes. Boots. Military style. Let's follow those for a bit."

"Are you being hopeful?"

"Yeah. Maybe these belong to the fellas' that passed us earlier. If they didn't find Sid, maybe that's why they turned around and left."

She nodded at him, lightly touching his shoulder. "I like Sid too."

Pointing their lights, they followed the footprints to a wide space near the rim of a small ravine to the northeast and an impressive pile of ruins not yet excavated.

She pointed to a beautiful above-ground set of rooms, with walls still standing, some with only the outline left imprinted in the red soil. Their flashlights changed the building blocks from black to glorious orange red. Even at night, the colors were dazzling, the architecture stunning. "This can't be Mesa de los Muertos? I thought it was a cliff dwelling, not a free-standing structure."

Pragmatically chosen stones of the same size had been used like bricks to create buildings that had lasted longer than the skyscrapers of modern man. So few windows, Jack noted. Made of the same desert tones to blend in, that an enemy's eye might miss it. Geometric. Planned. Designed. Mysterious. *Los Muertos*? No, those dwellings were in a cliff. Tessa was right.

He risked the light being seen and scanned the whole area. "I don't see any signs of a fight."

"Then, they didn't find Sid?" Her voice sounded so optimistic.

"Not here. But their prints continue over to the rim." He pointed with his light. "Still a walking stride."

They both waited, listening to the emptiness, and while he couldn't confidently speak for her state of mind, he was afraid of what he might find and suspected she did too. After a moment his legs moved, his knees bent, and he was walking toward the rim.

A low hum greeted him as Tessa caught up. "What the hell is that" he let come out of his mouth in a whisper.

"It might be the wind through the ruins?"

"Y'all just keep saying that." He swallowed hard. "Keep tellin' me too."

"Sure thing," her voice warbled a bit.

Finally, the wind began whistling as it crossed the varying shapes of stones. His relief was almost audible. Glancing over to Tessa, his muscles stiffened again — she was not relieved. She was as tense as ever.

Moving forward, watching for tracks or tire ruts, he couldn't miss the fact that she had one hand on her flashlight and the other on the grip of her 9mm.

A powerful gust of wind sprayed grit in their faces and for a moment they had to stop and cover. Silence followed. The odor of dry or dead grass, juniper perfume, his own sweat — it all combined into a scent that would normally be natural. All he could think was how lucky he was the odor of decaying flesh was not in the air.

Or was it?

Something lingered around them that wasn't easily dismissed or identified. Foul? Moldy? Unnatural? It prodded his most primitive instincts with fear of the unknown. It also grew stronger.

Putrid reeking air overwhelmed them. Tessa turned her head to cough, covering her nose and mouth. Jack pressed his face into the crook of his arm.

The hum returned and his limbs froze.

The stars above their heads looked unfriendly. Though that made no logical sense, it felt in his gut to be the truth. Sage bushes and weeds swayed, and he swore all of them snarled, *go the hell away!* Sickness was bubbling in his stomach.

The humming stopped.

The sickness remained.

Rocks scattered behind them.

Kneeling and turning, Jack pointed both his light and gun at the sound.

A patch of shadow shifted and disappeared into the ruins.

Tessa, gun drawn, moved out to give them better coverage.

Absolute silence.

This far out from everything, even the highway couldn't be heard. Just the wind. Scattering sands and shaking bushes. His nerves were on fire.

Tessa's light slashed along the wall of the closest building. He watched intensely, sucking in as much dry air as his lungs would take.

At the far corner, a dark body shape appeared and vanished.

"Did you see that!"

"What the ..."

Tessa ran forward before he could give a better option. Circling wide of the building, she kept the light and her weapon on the structure. Duplicating her plan, in reverse, Jack swung around the back of the building to catch anyone trying to escape.

Nothing.

Their lights met on a blank, broken wall.

No one was there. Nowhere someone could hide. Nowhere for someone to have gone.

The loudest thump, or bang, or — something echoed up from the canyon.

The agents raced back toward the rim.

Again, the wind gusted and sprayed them with sand, pebbles, dead juniper needles, and other abrasive debris, blowing into their faces, blocking their movement. *Hell no*, nothing was stopping them from getting to the rim.

"Hold on!" he heard her cry out.

Turning, he saw her bent over, picking up an object.

She picked up Sid's monocular, the GH-5-60 and held it out as though she'd found her grandmother's lost wedding ring: too late.

Fear ripping at his insides, Jack pointed his light down and interpreted what he saw laid out in the sand. Prints. Sid's to be sure. But no one else's. Sid's. Facing the ruins. Shuffling backward. Toward the rim.

Jack, too aware of every muscle moving him forward, approached the rim.

It was the nature of the canyon lands that runoff from streams and semi-regular flash floods had carved smaller ravines and gorges beside the greater canyons. Sedimentary rocks behaved differently at different elevations, and thus a sharp ledge could be followed by a sloping shelf of soft stone, followed by a hundred-foot drop to the bottom of the cut.

Sid had backed away from something. Something that scared him so much that he didn't care where he was stepping. Maybe he hadn't seen how close he'd been. Or the terrifying fall was better than what he faced.

The young man of their mutual acquaintance and admiration lay on the slope sprawled on his back, head broken open and turned in an unnatural position.

Sid stared at the sky, eyes wide in horror.

And very dead.

CHAPTER THIRTY-THREE

EXHAUSTION DRAGGED THEM as low as they'd ever been. They argued over what to do with Sid. If they moved him, whoever or whatever had killed him — Jack finally accepting that something non-human was a possible explanation — would know he had been found. Suspicion would fall on them.

That same exhaustion drove her to mumble and snarl about death, as if it was an individual she held personally responsible for Sid's demise. Ah hell, maybe he was reading her wrong.

What happened to Sid? Neither agent could agree. Tessa, being Tessa, leaned toward actual or perceived ghost. She emphasized *perceived* knowing full well his distaste for spectral evidence. Jack believed it to be human or animal. After all, coyotes could be terrifying to people who'd never seen them before.

It was almost full sunrise before they got back to their rooms. Back up the damn tree, which was unpleasant at best and excruciating at worst. Desperate to get a little sleep before they had to rise and go about their cover tasks, as though nothing was found or happened, they collapsed onto the same mattress, still dressed, clutching each other out of exhausted despair and mutual protection. All Jack could do was obsess about Sid's death and the shadow both agents thought they might have seen, until unconsciousness conquered his brain.

Things weren't helped by the fact that he woke to find Tessa repeatedly swearing at her computer, in a whisper of course, while trying to report back to her HQ. Maybe they could recover Sid's body. That might give him something to hold onto. The mission was going sideways. He knew Tessa felt the same.

Added to it all was the vicious weather. The Four Corners region was locked in that damned drought that showed no sign of letting up. It was out to get them.

It was not a good day in the making.

The expression on Sid's face — it bothered him too much. He couldn't let her know. Everything needed to be work as usual. Sid was collateral damage. He'd seen plenty of dead bodies in the past. So had she. They'd both seen friends and colleagues die. What was it about Sid that crawled under his skin? He needed a distraction badly.

If Tessa had cried or expressed any emotion beyond raging frustration, which she kept boiling beneath her skin all the way back from the scene of the crime, she hid it from him now. He couldn't blame her. One didn't emote in the Business.

At dinnertime, instead of trying to relax, they tried eating their uninspired leftover lunch and staying close to one another.

Jack watched Tessa, who was picking apart her lukewarm burger and still eyeing the fries with skepticism. *Once burned*, he thought, drowning his fries in brown mustard to hide the taste of stale potato.

They'd both changed out of their filthy work clothes into anything they had that was cooler and cleaner. Their luggage was relatively light, but it had to contain whatever might be needed in spare parts. His turned out to be a better t-shirt, jeans, and what Uncle Joe would call a *go-to-meetin' hat.* He even had a tie somewhere in his luggage, but he'd grown unaccustomed to those. Tessa had slipped on a fresh blouse and skirt, something folksy that he'd never seen on her before, and frankly wouldn't have imagined.

Pins and needles shot through his left fingers, and if he hadn't known better, he would have sworn on his life that they'd gone through *five* fingers, not three and a half. *Damn phantom pain.* He dropped his hand down below her line of sight and began the pumping, stretching exercises his physical therapist had given him.

The less she saw of it, the better.

The laptop on the desk behind him pinged.

At last!

Finally the call signal started. They wouldn't have to fight the heat and go up the hill to try to make contact. The Home Office was reaching them successfully this time. Perhaps something new had happened? Or new data? They'd reported about Sid and maybe someone would care enough to come get his body?

While Tessa opened the laptop, Jack moved to a spot where he could not be seen via the camera. He could observe some of what was happening, so long as he didn't lean forward too much.

A man's face appeared on the screen. Jack assumed it was Kýrios. Some other agent added his mug to the view.

"Good afternoon, Kýrios," Tessa offered sweetly.

"Dr. Wells," Kýrios hissed with a touch of annoyance in his saccharin response. "I was sorry to hear about your student. We cannot currently reach his family but in due time, an effort will be made. I'm sure you understand."

Jack's stomach turned. Kýrios was speaking in code in case someone was listening. And he was saying that Sid was being left to rot. Not the first time, not the last, in the Business. Didn't mean he liked the notion, especially for a civilian.

Tessa's soured expression said she was thinking the same thing. She quickly recovered her composure.

Kýrios continued, "As your original assignee is here with me, and your earlier attempts to reach me indicated that you are not alone, I should like very much to verify which *surveyor* went into the field with you. And I should point out that the original assignee is making a formal complaint. You know how much I loathe extra paperwork. I wouldn't be bothered with any of it, but he is … well, connected … and feels this unauthorized personnel change may reflect badly on *his record* as well as his connection's."

Tessa's face remained locked in a rehearsed smile, but Jack swore he could hear a stream of curses coming from inside her head. Well, he would be cussing right about now, too, if he'd been snitched on by a fellow agent. It was unprofessional, especially under the circumstances Tessa had told him about.

The guy hurt his own career, the sniveling little asshole. Getting Daddy, Mommy, or Uncle to save him was low. Jack could have had a fine CIA career handed to him by Uncle Joe, but Jack wanted to follow his own path.

Tessa had every right to take her revenge if she wanted it. Slowly, though, her face softened a bit, as if she might be more forgiving than he was. Ever the professional. "As you know, sir, we're in a rush to get caught up on all the testing. And, being so very behind on all of it, time was of the essence. When the original appointee turned out to be unprepared for this assignment, I snagged a senior field surveyor. One of exceptional quality and one who was immediately prepared to get his hands dirty with the necessary tasks. We left on time and are in the midst of completing the assignment."

Kýrios quieted for a moment. "I should like to know —"

Tessa interrupted him. "I snagged the best man out of the Albuquerque office, though he may be too senior for the assignment. We were both in need of some field time. He was exceptionally well suited when it came to that … highly irregular formation we found yesterday. I hope that experts in the office will be able to settle matters regarding the uniqueness of the formation and my current assignee's suitability?" She waited while Kýrios digested the sideways references. Apparently satisfied, she continued. "I'm sure with more guidance and maturity, *Manny* will be better suited to field operations. I have no doubt regarding his skills with analysis, but when it comes to being field ready? I'm sorry to say that he needs more training, specifically in hand-to-hand combat techniques."

"Goddamn it!" The young man, Jack presumed was Manny, shouted.

"That's enough," Kýrios snapped. "Dr. Wells, any other time, I would very much approve of your decision. Indeed, I hate snitches as much as I hate paperwork. However, *Manny* has told me some disturbing news about your man's home life that needs to be addressed. This could be disastrous, and the fallout will be on you, Doctor. I am perfectly happy to allow consequences to land on those who earned them, including consequences regarding the *geological formation* you found and how it got to be in such a sorry state. Your ham-handed approach places you alone at the center of what is becoming a disaster."

He couldn't let her defend him, alone. He had agreed to this and at any moment this actual situation had been possible. What shocked him more than anything else was this Manny's willingness to rat out a fellow agent. It simply wasn't done. Not only was it not gentlemanly, but it was also downright cowardly, in his opinion. And blaming her for Sid's death? *Screw this! Screw it all!*

Before she could try to make the situation better, as was her wont, he stepped around to the front of the laptop, folded his arms, and dared *Manny* to say something.

Tessa opened her mouth, to tell him to stay back. The words were never spoken. Instead, glares were exchanged and she said nothing against his decision.

Jack had plenty he wanted to say, out loud, to the men on the screen. The weasel, half protected bodily by Tessa's boss, moved until he was almost completely behind Kýrios, as if Jack could reach through the screen and choke him. That wasn't a half bad idea if the physics weren't so impossible.

Kýrios and the young man looked at Jack, then a tablet with a report, then at Jack, then the report. That went on for a minute or two. Jack declined to say anything, a habit both men on the other end ironically didn't understand.

After the tension was strained to a proverbial snapping point, Kýrios handed the tablet to Manny and sat back. "Well, it seems we *do* have a problem."

"No," Tessa countered, "we don't. We have a full report. Sending now while we still have some sort of signal."

A car door banged shut outside, followed by a series of curses. Jack moved to the front window of Tessa's room. "It's my friend, Billy-boy. Looks like he may have started Happy Hour a little early." Jack squinted. "Looks like he took quite a fall too. Uniform's all messed up."

He stood, weighing his options, then picked up his *go-to-meetin'* Stetson and suede jacket. "Maybe my friend could use a kind ear to pour his woe into."

"Is he leaving?" Kýrios demanded.

"What is it, sir?" Tessa's voice betrayed her growing frustration.

"Tell your man to wait. I want you both to look at these. Is this the man you saw two days ago?"

An image appeared on the monitor. Big and distinctively ugly. "No, sir."

"Yeltsin Dramelov. An enforcer. Russian mafia operating in the U.S. And this one?" It was the man from the limo, on the first day they'd arrived.

"Yup, that's him. Carrot-top and all," Jack volunteered.

"Vladimir Polanski. Former Moscow insider now set up in America."

"And he's gone missing, like the others, hasn't he?"

"Yes."

After an uncomfortable pause, Jack blurted out, "Am I dismissed? Can I go to recess now?"

"Yes. Oh, for God's sake, T301 get onto headset. Now!"

"I apologize for his rudeness. It seems I need to take this call, privately," she said flatly, patting the motorcycle helmet.

"I'll see what Billy-boy can tell us."

"Thank you." Her smile was weak. She mouthed the words, "I'll be okay."

Jack nodded to Kýrios on the computer screen. "Kýrios. That's Greek for 'master' isn't it?" he asked to no one and yet everyone. "If y'all will excuse me, there's an opportunity I need to seize before it disappears. That is the job, isn't it?"

Tessa slowly nodded. "See what you can learn."

"I won't be far." Once he reached the door, he gave her a look that read, *I'm sorry you had to tell them about me*. He wanted to say something more … intimately supportive. But that was not the job. Nor the best situation. Nor the future, he was damn sure now.

CHAPTER THIRTY-FOUR

BETTER TO ASK FORGIVENESS than permission, she thought as he closed her door.

"Is he gone?" The voice came thru the helmet.

Tessa went over to the window facing the diner and waited until she saw Jack stroll across the street. A dust devil followed him.

"Get onto headset." She heard. *People in Oxnard heard you.*

Tessa did as she was told. The headset was contained in the motorcycle helmet that completely engulfed her head. Kýrios disappeared from the computer screen and appeared to Tessa only via a heads-up display on the helmet visor. To have worn this with Jack in the room would not only have been rude but would have made him extremely uncomfortable. "I'm on," Tessa said. "He is across the street, interrogating a local. And no, I didn't make a mistake bringing him onboard."

"Do you have any idea what you've done?"

"I've brought in a skilled, retired agent who is off the books. As long as he stays off the books, we don't have a problem. Do we have a problem, Kýrios?"

"I don't like your attitude or your tone."

"You don't like a good many things. But you hired me because of my experience and judgment. You need to trust that now. M021 was going to stick out like a sore thumb in the field. He would have gotten us killed before we even started. This situation here is extremely volatile as I've described and of the two of us, it is my associate who is blending in better. He is holding his cover and being highly effective."

Ký́rios sighed, so Tessa kept going. "I believe I've sent enough information that M021 will be able to do a full financial analysis from the safety of HQ. I have no doubt that if there is anything monetary to be found, he will find it."

"Oh, you don't have to be so damned professional about it. Call him whatever you want to: he ratted you out and he is going to hear about it from me." Ký́rios clenched his jaw. "But you don't think this is about international money laundering?"

"No. This is something … homegrown. Tessa nodded. "For now, unless M021 finds otherwise, my gut says no money laundering."

"Was it your *gut* that brought *him* into this? Please tell me a Ouija board was not involved."

"No." She bit her tongue. "That was plain and simple logic."

"Based on him being off the books. If that were still true, I would not be entirely peeved. I might even be understanding." Ký́rios sighed heavily if not dramatically. "Well, time for the bad news. There have been multiple inquiries about your man. M021 may or may not have initially triggered something by nosing around after him, but he certainly finished the job. He didn't find every detail, but enough to prove that you may have a liability on your hands. And I cannot fix this for you if things go worse."

"I have a first-rate agent on my hands, who can go dark when he needs to. He's certainly proved that already."

For a moment, Ký́rios looked a bit satisfied.

"Now, can we discuss the mission? Some scheme is funding this town. They're not starving. Yet no one here gives a damn about tourists or commerce. And —"

"And what?"

"The sheriff has a … skill. One you need to know about. He is charming. Not in a usual way, but in an irresistible way. I can't explain it yet. It isn't something average or normal. It's almost, I don't know — compelling. Seductive. I think he's the one talking the crime bosses into coming here. To what end, we still need to discover. But he appears to be your source of power over the criminals."

Kýrios nodded, while receiving a note and a flash drive, from M021. Kýrios's resting face was indignant, and now he looked angrier than ever.

A phone in the Seattle room rang. With an angry gesture, Kýrios ordered M021 to answer it while he continued talking to Tessa. "I don't like risking our agency's reputation on someone said to be a traitor."

Tessa's whole body tensed. "He is not a traitor. I stand by my decision. And once this is over, he can go dark again. But if I hadn't brought him in, we would be sending agent after agent to their death, never once understanding what went wrong. And all the while innocent people would continue to be caught in the crossfire, in ever increasing numbers."

"Traitor. Not a traitor. *Tomay-to – tomah-to.* I am not arguing entirely with you. But you must be aware that someone has noticed the questions being asked about a man who should be dead."

"And will be again. No one in this business is ever allowed to simply die."

A note was handed to Kýrios, delivered with a smirk on M021's face. Kýrios snatched it up. "What, are we back in primary school? Notes passed in class?" He nearly destroyed the paper the note was on when he ripped it open. His face fell.

M021 backed up and stood, his smirk not changing.

"I'm afraid things have changed." Kýrios held up the new note. "The mission has been taken out of my control." Kýrios put his chin in his hands and took long, angry breaths. "T301, the *Meister Committee* has ordered this assignment to be coded *Blue* if it is not successfully resolved in two days."

Tessa's heart skipped a beat and began pounding hard.

Blue. No witnesses. Only the primary agent or agents walk away.

"Agent, you have a very limited window of opportunity to complete this mission before we send in specialists who will eliminate any and all threats, suspects, and others we consider a risk. We can no longer allow the situation to escalate. This is a code *Blue*."

Blue. What the hell changed?

It was an agent's worst nightmare. A whole clean slate — everything and everyone involved in the mission wiped off the face of the earth. All, except the agent … or agents.

It had happened only twice before that she knew of. And only when the international stakes were too high. "*Code Blue*? Isn't that too much too soon? We *are* on the verge of solving …"

M021 looked horrified, no doubt shocked at Tessa's willingness to challenge not only Kýrios but the *Committee* as well.

Kýrios was unreadable, which in itself was odd. Perhaps that twitch in his mouth was a prideful smile he was allowing to show. "The decision isn't mine, Tessa, and I agree that it is reactionary. I will confess I feel it is like using a fire hose to put out the match before it touches the pyre. But you and I are not the *Meisters*."

"No, we're not, but I suspect they know some of us too well." She watched the comment sink into M021's comprehension. His smirk slowly drowned in her remark.

"We do not have access to the intimate global information they have. We cannot simply second guess them." Kýrios leaned closer to the camera while holding a stern finger up in front of M021, cutting off any unnecessary commentary on his part. "You have *two days before* the code is to be executed."

Two days. She had only two days. The stakes *were* important, but, enough for a *Code Blue*? Yes, the casualty numbers were getting worse with every incident. But, enough to terminate every suspect with extreme prejudice? That part, she easily convinced herself, was M021's doing — he was just the type to do it. What did he convince the *Committee* to believe was next, a whole neighborhood being bombed? A city?

She would have to save further inquiry until later. Tessa had no time to waste on M021's back-office shit.

Two days.

"And T301. You must personally see to it that a primary threat is eliminated once the code is in place. *You* must do this. I'm sure you understand why." Kýrios pointed. "You will terminate this associate of yours and present evidence of his elimination to the *Committee*. There must be proof that you have assumed responsibility for your error in judgment and corrected it. Once we are *Code Blue,* that becomes mission critical. Do you understand?"

Tessa's couldn't feel her hands. "I do not."

She did.

"Once in a state of *Code Blue*, everything we do from that moment on will be scrutinized, surreptitiously of course, by every global intelligence agency. That is the nature of a *Code Blue*. It allows all parties to know we have done everything necessary to remove the threat permanently. That we have taken ownership and that no more trouble will occur from this particular situation. As for your associate, he will be found out with everyone inspecting our every move, and the Athenaeum can never say we had ever heard of *him*. The Athenaeum can never say we approved *him*.

"This was your private decision, T301, outside of Athenaeum authority. If this situation goes as far as *Blue*, then *you* will fix it: you will personally eliminate your associate and prove your loyalty to the Athenaeum. You cannot hesitate this time. I cannot detour your career from a Department 44 reassignment if you fail. Do you understand?" Kýrios completed his statement, particularly loudly, and cut the comms line.

She did.

Panic overwhelmed her, yet she sat stone still.

CHAPTER THIRTY-FIVE

JACK ONLY KNEW TWO WAYS to walk into a bar, and either of them would pass as the opening line of a joke. If only he was in the mood.

The fact that his true identity was no longer a secret to Tessa's employer wasn't just troubling, it was frightening. What had he done? To hell with what he had done. What had he blindly done to Tessa and Joe, people who had placed their trust blindly in him? He might deserve whatever happened, but *they didn't.*

Jack stopped, pumping his fists to release the frustration that heated his face and caused his hands to tingle.

Was he an innocent? He tried not to laugh and felt thickness in his throat he couldn't clear. Sure, on the one hand, he didn't want to be caught and executed – again. He didn't want to get shoved in a dark hole he'd never emerge from. On the other hand, he had died already, in a manner of speaking, and it was proving bizarrely liberating. No more hiding the fact that he was aging out of the business by doing things his body wasn't able to do anymore.

Looking up at the twilight sky, at clouds far, far on the horizon, and back at her window, he decided such decisions were better made at a later time — when he'd had more rest and the mission was complete — although he knew what that decision would be. He'd long ago made it.

His face began to cool.

Two ways to walk into a bar, eh?

He swaggered into the diner, through the dining room. A busboy, one of the townies, shuffled past him, balancing cups and plates in a small tub. Another local, this one a patron, filled his hands with freshly opened bottles, turned away from the bar, and focused on a table near the dark corner. Jack stepped aside to let the man by and sauntered up to the bar. A big bartender, younger than the man normally tending bar during the day, gave him a once over and asked what he wanted. Toby, yeah, that was the guy's name.

"Cuervo." Tequila was cheap and popular. The big bartender nodded and poured a shot. Jack picked it up and rolled the glass between his fingers. He'd nurse it, make it last. Truth was, he hated most brands of Tequila. The only way he liked it was in a margarita, with a chaser, and several ladies cheering him on.

Now his left hand was brutally itching. Dropping his hand down by his side, he blocked any view of his fist, clenching and unclenching.

Billy-boy called out to him from the Men's Room door and wandered up. Despite wearing a uniform, the man was well on his way to being soused. "Hey there, my man." He slapped Jack on the shoulder. "A Stetson, man? You lookin' dangerous tonight," he laughed.

"Leftover of my bad-boy days." Jack jammed his gloved hand into his pocket, hoping he looked casual. "I figure if I wear it maybe I'll at least look like I had bad-boy days. Ya' look like ya' had one hell of time today. What's all this?" Jack swept his hand up and down, indicating the state of Billy-boy's uniform.

The deputy looked down to what Jack was staring at: a pocket torn on his shirt, dirt rubbed in, and what appeared to be the better part of the Four Corner's farmland ground into his pants. "Took a fall."

"Not over at that Mesa? Y'all told us not to go there. Is it that bad?"

Snorting a harrumph, Billy-boy shook his head. "If ya' know what'cher doin'," he cleared his throat, tried enunciating better, and nearly failed. "If you know what you are doing, it's not so bad." He knocked back what was left in his glass and shoved it toward the bartender.

"If that's what y'all call 'not so bad,' ya' don't have to tell me twice to stay away. Christ almighty, ya' could have done yourself a permanent injury."

The throaty laugh that followed a wink sent shivers down Jack's spine and he covered his expression with a sip of the booze.

"A permanent injury. Yeah, someone got permanent injured. Was poking around where he shouldna' been." Billy-boy held his left hand out and used his right hand to mimic someone running off the edge, making a falling whistle as the hapless creature plummeted toward the bottom. He made much of the splattering at the bottom and laughed at his own cleverness.

Jack saluted him. "Glad it wasn't one of y'all."

Wrapping his arm around Jack's shoulder, Billy-boy pulled him along to the table where two other officers and a fellow in standard flannel were all making themselves comfortable. Billy-boy's usual drinking companions. Jack never had been told flannel man's name.

Jack looked at them and allowed two thoughts to cross his mind, behind his friendliest smile. *Oh look, a drunken data base to tap and potential target practice if necessary*. Handshakes were exchanged.

It was perhaps only twenty minutes later when flannel man was sitting perfectly still, clutching his drink and grinning like an incoherent idiot. The other three men were much more vocal and rowdier. Jack chose the *I-get-slower-and-happier-when-I'm-drunk* style. He lifted his glass of Cuervo and used it like a pointer. "What's wrong out there? Why not make it better than the National Park place? Charge for tickets —"

"Oh no, no, no," one officer slurred. "See, the place is haunted."

"Bullshit!" Jack snarled.

"Nah. I ain't kiddin'. I've seen the ghosts. And something that howls in the night. People go out and never come back." The officer looked desperate for someone to believe him. "Local natives don't know what it is 'cause it's older than they are. Pre-pre-ancient people, you know?"

Billy-boy scowled. "Yeah, spooks and ghosts and demons."

Jack shook his head and glared at everyone. "I call bullshit. So, maybe all y'all have ghosts. What harm can a ghost do? Sell tickets to that, too. There were these here ghost hunting type kids when me and the Boss Lady got here. All y'all could milk 'em dry. People like that always got money."

"We'd have to repair the place. An' the ghosts, they don't jus' scare folks." Billy-boy got big and dramatic, standing up and waving his arms. "The angry spirits have been known to throw people off the cliff side." He grinned evilly again. "Remember?" He duplicated his hand-puppet show of a man going over the side to his death. This time the splat at the bottom was marked with a huge, expressive *boom*. "People who don' belong here, and go to the Mesa? They. Don't. Come. Out."

Jack let his lopsided smile lift the side of his face. "What if I don't believe in ghosts?"

The sheriff answered for Billy-boy. "Still kill you even if you don't believe."

Everyone jumped, even Jack. Where had Bergman been that whole time? Had he been waiting around the other side of the bar, listening to them? For that matter, how did a man that big move so quietly? He arrived behind Billy-boy, like a shadow. Unlike his deputies, Bergman was sober, and armed, as usual.

Jack knew he appeared to be the disbeliever, but he wanted to know more. "Seriously, ghosts? No shit?"

Again, the sheriff provided the response. "I for one haven't decided. There are things I didn't believe in before. Not so sure now. As for your notion of making it a tourist spot, that's unlikely to happen. Besides, it's not our responsibility to repair the place. BLM or the Park Service, or some Federal department, should put up the cash. Every time we ask, all they do is whine about budgets and other priorities. Meanwhile, anyone foolish enough to go down there, well, if the spirits of angry cliff dwellers don't kill them, the crumbling ruins will."

Billy, the deputies, and bartender Toby all chuckled awkwardly.

Jack yawned, saluted with his drink, and replied with a modicum of slurring, "And me and the Boss Lady said we wouldn't go, and we won't. Cross my heart. She ain't so fond of ghost stories, so I suspect she won't want to go looking for one. I doubt she'll want to go even more when I tell her what y'all'ave told me tonight." Jack drank from his glass, for the first time in a while. "Spooks? Ha!" He yawned again. Stretching his arms wide, he looked at his drinking companions. "Don't know how y'all do it. I feel like a ploughed field after a dust devil."

"My boys are made of stern stuff, or they aren't my boys," the sheriff announced.

Billy-boy and his two deputy-companions were remarkably sober all of a sudden. Jack didn't let his mask slip. "Ah, ya' ain't taking 'em off to work now, are ya', Sheriff? Damn, and I thought my Boss Lady was a slave driver." He saluted with his drink again.

The sheriff looked at Billy-boy, who shrugged at Jack. Good. They thought he was smashed. What might he learn while they thought he was insensible? Then again, what might they do, or try to do, to him?

For a few moments, he waited, looking at his cell phone and pretending not to care what was going on in the other room. Sure, he was getting older, but his hearing was just fine for now. That's when he heard the strangest word ...

"... Duel."

She'd shrewdly hidden the coded note telling Jack where she was going. He knew the routine, all the signals and where to look. She had to trust in that.

He was still out, possibly with Billy-boy the deputy, maybe with some of the others. Out, but working the mission in his own way. Fine. She needed to give him space to do the job; interfering would jeopardize the mission and set them up to be killed if her suspicions were correct.

For safety, she took the laptops and the communication helmet out of the room. If Jack was busy, and she wasn't around, and the sheriff was overly suspicious … well, no sense leaving anything incriminating. She knew where to hide the equipment in the jeep, which she was taking with her anyway. When Jack got the note, he'd understand. She had to trust that much.

Besides, what would she say if she walked in on him now? *Hi Jack, can you hurry up? We need to solve this mission before the Athenaeum sweeps in with an elimination squad that will wipe out every unfortunate witness in this town, along with all evidence of wrongdoing. Oh, and yes, I'll need to take you out to the desert to put a bullet in the back of your skull, all because the rumors about you are true.*

It must be done, echoed in the back of her mind as Tessa gingerly, quietly opened the jeep's door. *No weakness*, hissed inside her brain. *Lovers are only ever liabilities …*

That wasn't the voice of **Death**.

She closed her eyes and felt with her mind and body.

Death was not there. She peeked out to see. *Please, not* **Death**.

No **Death**.

Movement. Seen out of the corner of her eye. A shape sliding across the front of the motel.

Tessa pushed the door open to step out.

The streetlight cast a moving shadow of a tree onto the lobby door and side of the motel. That was all she must have seen. Sid's loss was hitting her harder than she knew, and her new orders for Jack were nothing short of soul-crushing.

A moment of horror and desolation rushed up her spine. Tears didn't prick at her eyes, they hammered at them with pickaxes and shovels. This was her worst nightmare.

Forgoing headlights, she guardedly crept the jeep past the diner and out to the main road before turning them on.

Oh, for the love of God …

The jeep threw out a cloud of dust behind it as she powered up the road, gunning the engine too much.

A group of well-appointed cars drove past her as she left Montejo. She leaned her head on her hand, against the jeep's window, blocking her face from view. It was an old trick. Not that it would help much. She and Jack were the only other strangers in town. So much for sneaking out.

At the onramp, she braked hard before entering the highway and looked back through the cloud of dust. Jack was alone and might *not* read her message for a while. Should she go back? No. She had to catch the plane she'd arranged for in Cortez. *Damn it.* She would only be gone a few hours. Back before midnight. Jack could manage that long. Frankly, he could probably do better than she could.

Right now, she needed to get to Denver, to talk to *The Sicilian.* Certain questions had answers that only someone like The Sicilian could provide. With a two-day clock hounding Tessa's every step, it would have been easier to pick up the phone. Of course, The Sicilian didn't take calls about business. Face to face only. Inconvenient, but necessary.

Her gut — the same gut that told her to find Jack in the first place — was telling her something was wrong about leaving. But, if she was going to confirm her hypothesis, she needed information only the *Sicilian* could give her.

Trust Jack. He was fine. *Trust him.*

Less than two days to resolve this.

She pulled onto the highway too fast, squealed the tires, and raced to Cortez.

Duel?

Had he heard that correctly? Billy-boy muttered something about a duel, before Yeltsin Dramelov stamped into the diner, demanding where everyone was.

Jack listened so intently, he thought he might shatter the glass he gripped in his fingers. He recognized the Russian from the mug shot shown by Kýrios. Ugly as sin and standing twenty feet away from him. Whatever was happening to these crime bosses, it was happening right now and right here.

The sheriff began a formal, professional welcome, and sent his primary deputy to go check on the out-of-towner and the stupefied townie. With a stern, "Wait here a moment," in Jack's direction, Bergman headed out to the parking lot as Billy-boy sauntered over towards Jack.

Jack dropped his head down on top of his cell phone and moaned a little for extra effect. The townie, still sitting at Jack's table, had leaned back, and was soon snoring.

Billy-boy leaned over him and laughed a little. "Come on, de Sombras. Cain't be all that bad."

"Hell, yeah. Who told all y'all I could out drink ya' boys? Man! My boss is gonna' fire my ass. Bye, bye promotion. Bye Denver."

"Where *is* that pretty little lady. Don't know how you keep your hands to yourself."

"Temptin' ain't she. Knowing her, she's working on some sorta report up in 'er room." Jack let out a stifled belch. "Hey, think they'd mind much if I stayed here for a bit? Jus' till I can walk straight?"

"Sure. Toby don't mind, do ya', Toby?"

The bartender rolled his eyes but agreed. Billy-boy plopped the Stetson back on Jack's head, leaving him in the corner to sleep it off with the townie, who had since curled up in a ball. Taking his own trooper hat, Billy-boy nodded in Dramelov's direction.

Holding up a finger, the deputy tucked in his shirt, adjusted his belt, and wiped away the grime on his face. His posture straightened deliberately.

"Disguise," Dramelov asked.

"Nah. We had a little incident I needed to take care of. Some of our neighbors forget where the borders are." Billy-boy winked. "It's not a problem no more."

"Dis right place ver ve come?"

"Yes, sir. Everything is all set up for you and your employer. If you'll follow me."

"Ah. Ver is sheriff Berk-man?"

"Already out there, sir," Billy-boy replied, pointing toward the parking lot. "We'll escort your party to the location and make certain that you have any questions answered. The sheriff is overseeing every detail, and we'll make sure you are a satisfied customer."

One thing was certain, ole Billy-boy Halprin knew when to sound like a sheriff's deputy and when to sound like a hick. When to play it drunk and when to play it sober. Jack had to admire that. It was a good technique. One Jack knew all too well.

He listened for shuffling feet. Those folks going out. Those who stayed back to watch him. Yup. The bartender came down to the end of the bar to look over at him. Jack didn't move.

Outside, several cars started up. One at a time, they pulled out from the diner parking spaces and headed down the Mesa de los Muertos road. The bartender mumbled something, but Jack didn't catch it. He listened as Bartender Toby stomped off to the back room. Before he reached it, he turned off the light in Jack's end of the bar. Convenient. The kitchen door opened and closed.

Taking off his jacket and hat, Jack piled them to look like he might still be sleeping away the drink he didn't have. The soused townie mumbled something but otherwise was out for the rest of the afternoon. Watchfully, Jack walked out toward the front door. No cars were in the lot. He made it about six more steps.

"You ain't sleepin'."

Think fast, Jack Rabbit. "I need me some coffee."

"You can't sleep with coffee in you."

"Can't apologize to the Boss Lady without it. I don't think I'm sleeping this one off like the other guy. I'm gonna' come clean and —"

"You ain't drunk, are ya'?"

"Come again?" Jack tried a little wobbling.

"You. Ain't. Drunk. I got drunks in here all day. I know 'em when I see 'em. You're just acting drunk."

Jack stood up straight. "Seriously? What was I missing? I thought I was doin' a perfect drunk."

"You ain't slurring enough." Toby said, his face screwed up in irritation.

Jack thought about it for a moment. "Now, see, I always thought that slurring yer words when playing drunk was way overdone. So, yer sayin' I wasn't doing it *enough*?"

Toby charged, kitchen knife in hand.

"Apparently not."

Only a couple of years ago, Jack would have pulled out an array of weapons chosen for his personal use.

Not today. A boot knife was all he had on him, and it was out of reach for the moment. Jack twisted, dropped to one knee, and grabbed Toby by his knife hand. Momentum and Jack's bent arm flung the bartender up and over. The air burst out of Toby's lungs as he slammed against the floor. Another bone-cracking wrench, and Jack tore the knife from Toby's hand in a jerked motion. Even lacking a finger and a half, Jack maintained a powerful grip.

Someone sweaty and smelling to high heaven tackled Jack and stayed on top of him, pinning him face up. One knee was slammed down on Jack's left arm, with the disabled hand still gripping the knife.

Whoever Stinky was, he seized Jack's left hand by the little finger and prepared to break it outward. The guy was taking too much glee in the pain he was planning to inflict.

The gloved digit bent out, and out. And out.

Stinky stared at Jack, Jack's hand, Jack, then at the knife Jack still held.

Jack only glowered and grabbed Stinky by the nostrils, wrenching his head back until he tumbled off Jack's chest, bowled over, and crawled a few feet, whimpering as he went away.

Shock ruled the day: Stinky's nose was bleeding, and he kept falling over and hurting himself more than Jack had. Toby was too busy catching his breath and rubbing his ribs to help his colleague.

Jack swept his leg under Stinky and tossed the man on his back. Jack landed a punch square into his abdomen and Stinky curled into a fetal position, clutching his torso and crying about something broken.

Toby had recovered enough to seize a bar stool and try to hammer Jack with it. But he moved too slow and hadn't realized how much those ribs of his were going to hurt.

Slipping under Toby's reach, Jack slashed deeply across the bartender's ribs with the knife.

When Toby screamed and bent over, Jack sliced across his forehead, starting a gush that blinded the bartender. Toby collapsed to his knees, wiping blood out of his eyes, and crawled over to Stinky.

In the old days, Jack would have killed them both. They were the bad guys, he was the good guy. If bad guys come to get you or others, you take them out. That's how things were done.

Stinky and Toby were whining and begging and trying to be a small as possible. Christ, he couldn't kill them. They were pathetic. He didn't even have to try hard to beat them. Bad guys were losing their touch. These two were nothing but fish in a barrel, not even real bad boys.

The fellow moronically demanding, "What the hell?" right behind him? Well, all bets were off with him. That fellow was a bit too close and closing. Jack could imagine flattening him right fast. He balled up his fist, ready to spring forward.

The hard prodding from a shotgun against his back, however, dissuaded Jack from being too rash.

CHAPTER THIRTY-SIX
Signuri Cucina — *FINE SICILIAN CUISINE,* DENVER, COLORADO

THE ROOM WAS ARRANGED like a television sound stage. Two huge cameras waited in the dark half of the set, pointed toward a fake kitchen. Men with shouldered cameras moved around trying out angles. A boom-mic lingered over the preparation counter. Something was boiling in one pot while another waited for the gas-flame to be lit. A director, two producers, and a Sicilian mob boss argued briefly about the best approach to describing why anyone would ever bother to touch, let alone eat, an artichoke.

The Sicilian looked up to find Tessa standing near one of the big cameras. He'd known something was up. She was not dressed to 'visit' him for dinner or tea. She was in her black, V-neck, jumper suit and dark turtleneck. Black boots, tan coat, black gloves, serious expression.

Ready for a fight.

Mario Amato, The Sicilian, was a big man. Muscular, tall, and only showing the slightest signs that his cooking had affected his torso. Amato spread his arms wide, let a huge grin take over his bearded face, and called out to his favorite *niece*. Other than Amato and Tessa, no one in their families had ever met, let alone claimed each other as kin. It was his way of telling his colleagues and subordinates that Tessa Wells-Lancing was off limits to them. When dealing with a Sicilian, one did not pester family.

He swooped over to her like a condor and picked her up in his arms. She was a rag doll to his strength, and she didn't mind it too much.

When her breath could get back into her lungs, Tessa smelled oregano and pepper on him. If only her real uncle had been so stylish.

Amato held her at arm's length, intently looking her up and down. "You know, I was so surprised when you called me. Out of the blue! I was so happy. Then, I thought to myself, maybe she also needs something." He opened his arms again. "Tell me what you need, little one, and I will see what can be done."

"First you have to tell me how all this is going."

He puffed up proudly. "Well, considering the niche audience. Still, people like to learn how to cook, whether a secret agent," he winked at her, "or decidedly not." Amato was decidedly not. "I film one recipe every other week and broadcast them to my offices around the world. Anyone who wants an *in* with the boss had best be watching. Keeps me busy and confuses the FBI. Come, you can talk to me in the kitchen. The microphones aren't on, and no one will dare to bother us."

Holding her hand in a fatherly way, he led Tessa past a curious film crew and mafia associates. His salt-n-pepper hair was still thick for a man in his sixties, and his smile was infectious. "So, what can your *Ziu Mario* do for you?"

She let him tie an apron around her waist. "First, Mario, I am sorry that the first time in ages I call, it's to ask a favor. I don't like it when others do that to me, so I can't imagine it is what you would like."

"You wouldn't do it if it wasn't important."

Her voice dropped to a whisper as she began cutting onions per his direction. "*Ziu.* I'm actually … working."

"So I suspected."

"I've worked up a hypothesis and you might have a piece of information that could make or break it."

"Go on. Oh, thinner. Cut the onions just a little thinner."

Tessa leaned back, to be clear of the onion fumes to take her deep breath. "I've been observing groups of *family*, in sets of two, going into a certain location at the behest of the locals. They disappear together out in a remote location, one that is heavily protected."

"That already does not sound good."

"Correct. Only one *family* emerges — the other is never heard from again. The locals suddenly have wealth they shouldn't and also suddenly there's a vacuum of power where the other *family* had been in charge."

"Ah. Sounds not only not good but a perfect set up for violence." He kept his eyes on the work his hands were doing but she could tell his brain was active.

"Have you gotten up wind of a new, shall we call it, service? A means to rid yourself of *family* competition?"

Amato's knife stopped in the middle of a chicken breast for a moment, then started again, slower. "I have. An expensive service too. One I won't waste my time or money on."

"I'm glad to hear that." She leaned forward and looked at his face. He was not grinning like a celebrity anymore. "I really am glad. Part of my visit is to warn you off and the other part is to ask you what you can tell me about it."

He kept cutting the chicken meat into cubes while his smile returned. "You were worried? About me? Ah, little one, I may be in the family business, and you've never been sure how smart that is, but I assure you, you never need worry about me. I've been around too long to fall for a scheme like that."

"That too makes me glad. Still, it may seem like a crazy scheme, but I can tell you it is a successful enterprise. What I know, what I've seen."

"And the consequences of the sudden removal of leadership spills out into the streets. I too have been watching the news." He stopped cutting and straightened up. "You said you've seen this firsthand?"

Tessa only nodded.

"What is that idiot doing? Eh? This *Kir-ee-oos*? Sending you into a mess like that. Has your Controller no more brains than this?" he demanded, holding up the carcass of the chicken with his knife.

"I can handle him myself."

"This service being offered, from what I am hearing, this is different." Grudgingly, he set down the chicken. "Four Corners, yes?"

"*Sì.*"

"Nasty business. I'm hearing it is some sort of dueling for a price."

"Dueling?"

That was it. The lynchpin. How did Bergman get criminal businessmen to duel? The answer came immediately. The same way he got her to practically fall into his arms. "Thank you, *Ziu* Mario. That's the missing part for my hypothesis. That's what I needed."

"I am always here for you." He nodded and put down any pretense that he was going to cook. "It's a pure business venture. Getting rid of, or even managing the presence of a competitor, is extremely pricy in normal circumstances. Someone figured out that if you make getting rid of the competition easy, clean, and cheap, then you have something that the whole of … *unconventional business* has need of."

Tessa bit her tongue, figuratively and literally.

Amato continued, "Of course, they don't care about the fall out in the streets. The grasping for vacated power, territory, cash flow ... that is not how a proper business is run. But these boys and girls who think they know everything? Of course, they do not think beyond their own needs."

"If they win, it's not their people or neighborhoods. If they die, well, they can't care anyway."

He shook his head and frowned hard. This was not his usual expression and it caused him to look his age. "Experience teaches us that a good businessman does not abuse those who depend on him, even if they do not know they depend on him. Operations need to be smooth, elegant, organized. Handshakes and signatures must be honored. Products purchased must be delivered at the price and time agreed upon. When you betray your associates, they do not trust you. No trust? No more deals. Everything — and I mean everything — must have a sense of honor or it is not worth the time and blood."

She didn't have any comeback or witty retort for that. While she didn't like his family business, that code of honor he lived by made it all sound reasonable. That, and she proudly looked at the face of a man who laundered money and sold black market goods, but didn't indulge in sex trafficking, drugs, or weapons, at least not that she knew of. And for the record, she recalled with some self-directed pride, they'd had a few heated words on the topic of smuggled antiquities.

Perhaps there was honor among thieves.

"You should not go back."

"I have to. I left a partner holding the fort. If he got my cryptic note, he knows I'll be back soon and will count on that."

The knife was in his hand again, grasped dangerously. "I am going to have a chat someday with this *Kir-ee-oos*. I do not like this assignment."

Tessa sighed, sliding the diced onions into a bowl, and removing her apron. "I have to prove myself."

"You've been with them three years."

"I will always have to prove myself."

"Does you partner have to prove himself all the time, too?" He looked at her kindly as ever. "Did Ben have to?"

Tessa paused before answering. Of course he knew about Ben. She'd stopped trying to hide anything from him, though she prided herself on not necessarily telling him everything. "My current partner is a bit of a, how should I say this? He's an outlier. He's a secret. And he'll likely fade into the sunset when we're done. He had some *specific skills* I needed, and the man assigned to me wasn't going to cut it. My partner … he doesn't need to prove anything to anyone."

The knife jammed into the cutting board, shocking Tessa from her thoughts about Jack. "You will call me. Anything goes wrong, you will call me. That is not open for discussion. It is a fact." As if Amato needed her to inform him — he might even know before she did.

His raised voice and the knife sticking out of the cutting board brought two nicely dressed brunos to his aid. Amato flashed his signature smile and held up his hand. They stopped. He turned his attention back to Tessa. "Secret partner. Dangerous mission. Poor personnel assignment? This *Kir-ee-oos* is not impressing me."

Tessa's hand reached out to Amato's cheek. She touched the assiduously manicured beard and the age-textured skin. She kissed his other cheek, smiled, and strolled past the nicely dressed, and now confused looking, button men.

Once beyond the studio doors, Tessa was glad she didn't need to tell Uncle Mario that her partner's fade into oblivion might well be at her own hand. Now the smells of the staged kitchen twisted her stomach.

Jack.

This was her fault. If she hadn't brought Jack in ...

She accepted that this sort of thing could happen. Agents had turned or compromised their agencies before, always for stupid reasons. *Stupid has consequences*, as Jack would say.

But Jack wasn't an agent anymore. He wasn't supposed to be there.

And it was Jack.

Kýrios, and perhaps even Amato, would tell her to toughen up. The business wasn't for sissies. If she couldn't handle a problem with lethal response, she had no excuse for being involved. Jack knew this. He knew it before. He knew it when she asked him to join her. He was a big boy who could make his own decisions, right or wrong. If wrong, he knew she would ...

But it was Jack.

This was why agents were told to stay out of emotional entanglements. It was weak. Her gut didn't know anything, it was an intestine prone to disliking spicy food. What did it expect her to do, give in to her emotions, and betray the Athenaeum? Or perhaps quit her job so they could run off and start a normal life together? Impossible.

She was expected to use her head to make decisions, based on raw, cold facts.

One and a half days to resolve the mission.

And to find some way to resolve her Jack-problem before she had to risk everything she'd worked for. Or kill him.

You can kill him if you need to. You know how.
And you won't hesitate.

CHAPTER THIRTY-SEVEN

TESSA STOPPED MIDSTRIDE.

She saw It. It wasn't squealing like a nasty vulture — not at all as she remembered. Its shape was still vague, Its presence still solid. No one was there in the parking lot to see It.

The vulture-like Thing, wrapped in a cloak of decaying black, reached out Its boney hand and beckoned to Tessa. It must have left the other souls it collected at home — Hell — wherever It came from It whispered to her.

Right there, in front of her. *Death.*

A figure in black, but nothing like the shadows they'd seen in Montejo. The shape became distinctive. Tattered robe. Scythe. Expected.

The acidic contents of her stomach began to rise – she could feel the panic attack coming.

Oh God, was it her time? Now? Tessa began looking frantically for her killer. One of Mario's men? Had Bergman followed her? Someone from the agency …

None of the above.

Not It — *She. Death* was *She.*

Oh Sweetheart, you don't understand me, do you? The bleak figure moved forward. Ever changing. Adjusting. The robe scraped along the asphalt.

Tessa reached under her coat and grasped her gun in its holster — as if that would do any good.

You can't kill Death. From the depth of the blackened figure emerged a dark-skinned woman. Decorated braids fell from the base of a round hat made of grass, their wooden beads clacking together. Tessa recognized the sound. Colorful stones formed its base and it spread out in a protective halo. A necklace sparkled at *Her* throat and chest, and *Her* motherly ample body was covered in an intricately printed cloth knotted at the right shoulder and left to flow to the ground. A breeze filled with that spicy scent wafted away from *Her* in a cloud.

You can't kill what has always been and always will be. I've been where life has been and always will be. *Her* lips moved and Tessa could hear *Her* voice inside her head, which alternated between a South African accent to a New Orleans drawl with ease. *Do you like the scent of myrrh? It is as ancient as I am.*

"Why … are you here?" Her mouth was bone dry.

I'm Death.

"I'm going to die." She swallowed and stiffened.

Don't be so stoic, everything dies.

"I'm going to die — now?"

Death used *Her* elegant hand to smooth *Her* dress. *Not now.*

"Then …"

Death let out an exasperated sigh. *You are one big mess, aren't you, Honey? You keep looking for why. Why you? Why him? Why now?*

"Yes!"

Death began strolling over toward the sidewalk, where a bench waited near Tessa's car. *You've got yourself trust issues. Because you don't trust, you don't ask the right questions. You assume the wrong things.*

"Who don't I trust? I just talked to a man …"

Death had a surprisingly beautiful laugh — musical and mirthful. *Him? Just how long did it take before you trusted him, your so-called uncle? Years, girlfriend.* *She* sat down and patted the open side of the bench.

Tessa shook her head and realized how tight all her muscles were. "Why did you kill Sid Franklin? He didn't deserve to die?"

Death laughed delightfully. *All deserve to die. Not because of sin or dishonor or some such nonsense, but because you are born. I am the natural consequence of birth.*

"Sid was so …"

Young? So many are. I take babies an hour old to elders over one hundred. It isn't personal.

"But why?"

That is the wrong question. If you die, it was your time and you had accepted it. You really aren't understanding are you? Did I mis-interpret your potential? That would be disappointing. I picked you before others. And no, don't ask me 'why you?' Ask differently. Ask something else. Your future depends on it.

Fight. Flight. Freeze. Definitely frozen. *Death's* perfume — intoxicating. The threat — icy.

"Who?"

Almost. You're asking 'who?' That's better but you should be asking 'what?'

"I should trust you?"

Ah, that is a good question. Death is neutral. Trust. Don't Trust. It doesn't matter. The only thing you can trust is that I exist and that seems obvious, doesn't it?

That was true. "I don't get it," she said through clenched teeth.

So? What does a Fixer do when she doesn't get it?

"Ask. Would you help me understand?"

It's been a long time since I've had a student.

She needed to be careful. "I'm not agreeing, but what does it mean to be a student of *Death*?"

You're all my students, every day. But I don't normally take a personal interest in everyone. *Death* rose and came to stand eye to eye with Tessa.

Fear gripped Tessa by the throat. It grasped her intestines and pulled. Her limbs weakened and the world around her slid into a bleak slurry of dark paint sliding to the bottom of a canvas.

Death held her up by her chin with two elegant fingers. The lines of *Her* face narrowed, growing more feline. *She* shifted to fuller cheeks, a more prominent chin. Changing. Constantly changing. *You are a very talented woman, and you know nothing about it. You think you do, but you don't. You need to spend your time with people of equal power. Ben Solomon wasn't one of them.*

"Ben?"

Imagine my surprise when I came to collect him, and you saw me. You actually saw me. That was a delight I didn't foresee. Not a delight for you, obviously, but I was so ... how should I say it ... amused?

"Are you amused by trying to talk me into killing people, like the man in Seattle?"

I'm trying to keep you alive, so you can reach your potential. You are so far off your path you have no idea. Funny thing for Death to be doing, don't you think? But I loathe the boring and straight forward. Besides, it was his time. You merely postponed it.

Tessa's body was heating, out of anger, or perhaps the reduction of fear? Tessa's world was a clear picture again, distinct, and real, something she could grab hold of like an anchor. Was she grabbing back the control? Could she do that — against the power of *Death*?

I'm still Eternal Death, don't ever forget that. I may appear to you in whatever form you need to see but don't let that distract you from proper respect. I am Death. I am the ultimate conclusion. I am held to no Laws of Physics or Morals. And I am not the only one who appears to you in ways you want to see just to trick you.

Death began *Her* transformation back to the dark, cloaked figure, fading from the physical realm. *Still, I like you. Go finish your mission. Survive it if you can. Then we'll talk more.*

"You don't know the outcome?"

Free will — annoying but necessary. And who wants to know the ending before the beginning anyway?

A car door slammed on the far side of the parking lot. Tessa looked away and immediately regretted it. When she looked back she knew — *Death* wouldn't be there.

Angel of Death. Ghost. Schizophrenic mental figment.

Of course, *She* was gone. And with *Her* all the sensations Tessa would recognize from now on.

Of course, *She* was gone. Of course, *Death* wanted a clean, dramatic exist.

She had made friends with *Death*. Student? "What have I done," she whispered through her own hand clamped across her mouth.

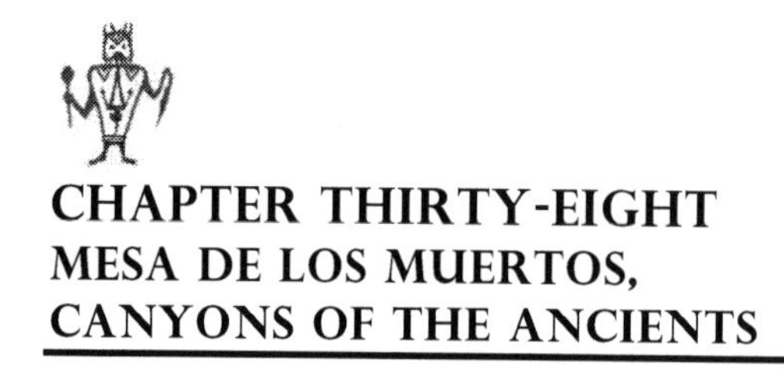

CHAPTER THIRTY-EIGHT
MESA DE LOS MUERTOS, CANYONS OF THE ANCIENTS

TEN STEPS, TURN, AND FIRE. Wasn't that the classic duel?

Jack shifted uncomfortably. The cold stone was ice under his legs, and both his warm jacket and hat were back at the diner. The wind cut through his shirt sleeves, racing gooseflesh up and down his arms, but even that wasn't what made him shudder. Coarse rope tore into his skin, and try as he might, he couldn't free himself. Helplessness was not something he accepted with grace.

Thank God Tessa wasn't there.

He was on his own. Alone. Except for the gangsters.

A few feet away, an expat-Russian mobster argued protocol with a New York waterfront boss. Who got to shoot first, when, and with what? From the sound of things, a barroom brawl was more probable than the civilized duel promised for Jack's amusement.

Jack was not amused.

The gangs had circled around the compacted remains of a former kiva. What had once been a place of gathering and ritual for the people who built them had fallen to the lowest point possible: a dueling ground for criminal scum bent on ruling their own little corners the world. Even ugly Dramelov was present, scowling so hard his face might fall into the dust. The stone walls encircling the space had long since toppled over, creating a miniature Colosseum. Shouts, insults, and accusations flew back and forth across the open ground.

All were waiting for the two bosses to begin.

Townsfolk provided an audience for the spectacle. Everyone had turned out it seemed, including a couple of the usually inebriated townies he'd met. Toby the bartender was here, along with the waitress and her fiancé, Billy-boy. They had all gathered to watch, though none too closely. Obviously, this was not their first time. They knew the rules better than the players.

Gas Guy stood at the back of the crowd, arms folded, face twisted into anger and dissatisfaction.

The arena was twenty-five feet in diameter. Stained dirt was compacted by wear. A Greek style tragedy was set to be performed and Sheriff Bergman was the host of the gruesome play. And by his smile he was proud of it.

How had he arranged it? How had he gotten two men, smart enough to create and control illegal businesses, to take a monumental risk like this? That was the minute Jack remembered the dream, the one that nearly drove him to blow his own brains out. The morning by the jeep, where Tessa was ready to throw herself into Bergman's arms and he, Jack, was ready to beat Bergman into a bloody, unrecognizable mess.

Facing one another were the mobster and the waterfront boss, two men of similar height. Where the waterfront boss was heavier without being fat, he was also a good decade older. The mobster was lean and young, hungry to get the action going.

The officer standing near Jack gave him a sharp kick. "Younger guy always wins."

From where he was sitting, Jack looked up, half-smiled, and couldn't help saying, "Never underestimate hard earned experience. Youth 'n Lechery ain't nothing on Age 'n Treachery." His wit only earned him another kick.

Was he sitting in water? Couldn't be. Wasn't any water. Just the cold rock. And he was seated uncomfortably on a three-foot line of rope that stretched tightly between his bound wrists and his ankles. Damn it! He'd been trussed up like a calf to be branded and he now knew the terror that a calf must feel. For all his skills, there were limits to what he could humanly do, so he sat still, waiting to seize an opportunity. Tessa was so much better at the patience game.

Thank God, Tessa wasn't there.

Earlier, he'd nearly squirmed out of the rope around his wrists, but the sheriff had enough brains to remove the glove, notice the missing flesh of his left hand, and how that could help him to twist his hand free. They had compensated by using carefully placed knots and the remaining length of rope to immobilize his upper body. It worked all too well. Jack leaned back against the metal pipe that was used to brace up a weak section of the roof above them. He was perfectly trapped. Encased. Mummified.

One small consolation: that nasty, greasy rag wasn't in his mouth anymore. One check in the Plus Column. In the Minus Column? It meant they needed and expected him to talk in the near future. He needed to figure out what they wanted to hear.

A fine time for him to be feeling pins jabbing him in the ends of his amputated fingers. The cold did this. Without the warmth of his gloves, those phantom pains were making their unwanted appearance.

The quarrel in the arena ended with a weak but agreeable compromise on the style of the fight and the weapons. The mobster and the boss squared off, about three feet apart. Each man was handcuffed by his left hand to a small chain. In their right hands, each man held a terrible looking knife —Bowie knives, if Jack weren't mistaken — and the two men parted as far as the chain would allow. If they were listening to the actual words the sheriff was speaking, they did nothing to indicate it. Only one word mattered.

The air howled through the broken buildings and carried with it that hideous stench Jack had learned to hate.

"Now!" Bergman backed out of the arena hastily, waving a green-colored lantern.

The mobster made the first attack, yanking hard on the chain and pulling the waterfront boss into closer range.

A slash. The boss's shirt and jacket was sliced. Blood appeared.

The boss stabbed upward, forcing the mobster back out of range.

The mobster tried to use sudden, brute force again, but the boss didn't cooperate.

He rushed the younger man, whipping the chain around until it wrapped around his opponent's arm.

Putting his weight into the pull, the boss rolled the mobster onto his back. So fast.

The boss was on him in a second, burying his big knife in the younger man's back.

Again, into his upper back. Again, into the back of his neck.

For a couple of seconds, the mobster moved. Then he didn't.

The waterfront boss stood up, his hand and shirt soaked with blood. He raised his fist in triumph.

Townsfolk retreated, away from the warring factions, watching like hyenas near a carcass. In creepy silence, they waited, poised on their seats or toes, ready and excited.

Behind them, shadows danced on the walls.

Shadows. Moving on their own. None matching the motions of the humans they supposedly mimicked.

That stench — the one that clung to the whole town — the one that rode on the wind — it arrived with the shadows.

Jack wanted to shout out a warning as the shadows leapt off the walls and slammed into the townsfolk, just as the rival gangs attacked each other.

This isn't real! Had he imagined something that wasn't there? He'd been knocked around too many times that night …

The townsfolk bayed like primeval dogs, a practiced, ritual cry to summon the carnage. The howls and snarls of animals tearing each other apart rose from the arena. Human screams mixed into the massacre, twisting into crevasses, becoming a shriek. Jack wished he could block from his ears. He pressed his head to the cold stone, desperate to stop the onslaught.

He needed time to think. The gangs were still fighting? If the brawl went on longer, he might have time to do something … to get away.

The sheriff changed that. Raising his service pistol, he gunned down the last three from the losing side, facing the winning gang. "Gentlemen! Your leader won, so you have the right to obliterate the opposition. Total victory. Your obligation to bring justice against the weak and sacrilegious."

What the hell was the Sheriff talking about?

Wild dogs of men fell on their weakened enemy and satisfied their every lethal desire.

A memory loosened from its burial place in Jack's brain. The sound was unholy yet familiar. The shrieks, begging for life. He'd heard them before. The concoction of sound, pitched against the ancient red rock, thrust out into the dark air? This was the howl that woke him in the night.

This was the pleading of his brother, begging for his twelve-year-old life.

Suddenly he was nothing but a six-year-old boy, *a six-year-old Jack*, clutching a toy pony, shivering in the muck of a horse stall, hidden away, squeezing his eyes closed, hoping that in not seeing the horror there could be bliss in not knowing. Yet the cries. The begging. The shouts. Rage. Madness. He couldn't get any smaller. They would find him too. They would find him …

Jack forced his eyes open to the semi-darkness of the cave dwellings and the danger he faced. He kept swallowing hard, until his mouth was dry, and his throat burned.

Focus or die.

The howl was louder this time. Knives and fists, the weapons of choice. The victor slashed and pounded the mobster's gang into oblivion. Then came a primitive bellow from victors' throats worn raw from screaming. The sacrificial bloodletting was complete; the waterfront gang cheered their total victory.

Next in the ritual was the humiliation: the Evisceration.

The townsfolk descended on the dead, possessed. Clothing was ripped away, bodies twisted unnaturally. Nothing was sacred. Jack had to look away to make any sense of what he saw. He couldn't. Bad men being bad, that was his morning breakfast. Seeing good people turn ugly, vicious ... insane? There was no word that fit. Was it the Shadows? Or were the people crazy? Were they trapped in *Skins*? Horrible, suffocating, controlling *Skin Thieves*.

Jack had killed many times, during his service. Never like this.

In front of him, the bones of the newly dead were picked for any object of value, without compassion or humanity. Even gold teeth were sought competitively, with a pair of pliers held by hands that had so recently been lifting a cold brew.

Twenty years Jack had served as a field agent and truly this was the most horrifying thing he could remember. For a shameful second, he felt overwhelming relief that the crowd was gleaning its pleasure off the dead and not looking for satisfaction from his living flesh. Just as fast he cursed himself a coward for even thinking that. Survivor's guilt, nothing more.

Gas Guy stood back and secretively shook his head. His expression hadn't changed.

Even the pretty waitress and the aged B&B manager were stripping the dead of money, rings, gold chains, watches, phones. Nothing was left except shredded cloth and torn flesh. The waitress pranced over to Billy-boy and showed him a gold chain. They were far enough away from Jack that he couldn't discern what the pendant was, but something told him it was a cross. Billy-boy helped her put it on as if he'd given it to her on Valentine's Day.

As if nothing at all had happened. As though it were just another Saturday night in small town America. Normal people, simple lives. The *Skin Thieves* slithered back onto their wall and into their shadows. Emptied of the living. Sated with the death and horror.

Had he seen them in the nightmare before him? He was losing it. He had to keep sane and calm.

As if nothing had happened at all.

As if …

Bergman didn't partake. Instead, he relieved the officer watching Jack, and let the man go join in with the townsfolk.

All the while, the waterfront boss and his associates were nodding in reluctant approval. No doubt they were counting the riches they'd control when they took over the mobster's territory. It was a good plan, Jack thought, wondering if the boss was as disgusted as he was, but placated by the payout?

In the distance, the sky lit up. Great. The area would finally get some rain. Or it would be the worst dry-lightning fire in the region for over two decades. Maybe the rain gods had been appeased with blood? Jack's flesh pricked, and he tried to pass it off on the incoming storm instead of Bergman, looming over him.

"You see, de Sombras — if that's actually your name — it works out nicely. Entertainment. Reward. Satisfaction. A gentlemanly duel. One winner takes all. We get paid. Another criminal enterprise goes to Hell."

"Primitive and at very little expense to y'all, I guess," he replied around the bitter tang that filled his mouth. He couldn't let his disgust show. His life now depended on it. Jack was sickened and yet amazed. "Yeah, it ain't pretty but it sure is organized and effective. News of your *Conflict Resolution Opportunity* spreads by word-of-mouth only. Interested parties reach out to make contact, and y'all set it up." How Bergman achieved so much success was still a question. "How am I doing?" Jack asked.

Bergman nodded for him to go on.

"Yer townies keep quiet out of fear and greed. Some even provide a few services to the enterprise. The town is small and unwelcoming, so y'all don't have too many gossiping mouths to worry about, like tourists. Impressive, risky, but lucrative," Jack declared as the tightness in his chest increased.

"Not bad."

"I try not to be too stupid. Stupid has consequences."

"Now we come to an interesting topic, Mr. de Sombras. You."

Shit. "Boring, Boss. I can tell ya' that."

"I only wish I could believe you. That injury of yours — your *gimpy hand*?" Bergman clearly liked describing it that way.

Jack's teeth clenched together while he forced his face to stay calm — his face still heated.

"That there is some injury. Maybe industrial? Maybe a strange mishap. But a thing like that will make a background check more precise. I wish I'd known about it sooner. See, I have done my checking already," Bergman hissed, crouching down to Jack's level and talking with his gun instead of his hands. "USGS knows who you and that lovely lady are. They even have great, brilliantly crafted dossiers on you both. But — "

"But what?" he tried to loosen his jaw, to speak normally.

"I know you from somewhere."

"I doubt that, unless ya' spend your free time down in Albuquerque."

Bergman only smiled bitterly. "You probably think I'm some dumb, worthless, country hick, who never gets out."

"Not with that thing in yer hands, I don't," Jack replied, allowing the implied insult to be noticed or not.

Shifting the pistol forward, teasing Jack to take it from him if only he could, Bergman grinned, "I've made some calls. Looking for a fellow, perhaps a good-ole-boy, your description, maybe a geologist or maybe not, who might have cause to go snooping around other people's business. Might surprise you, but I have good contacts outside." He looked over Jack with an expression that was nearly as satisfied as the ones worn by the winning gang. "I'm thinking you're some sort of P.I. Or an independent contractor working for an employer who wants to use my service. Or maybe, you work for a boss who wants to *take over* my service. Still, the USGS gig didn't back those theories. But then, I'm not buying the USGS bullshit. Now that I have this little extra description of your gimpy hand, and real up-close look at you, I'm betting I can find much, much more on you. Gimp. Mexican. A little older than I originally thought."

The muzzle of his gun settled just under Jack's Adam's Apple.

Jack's internal alarms were all blaring long before the gun rested on his skin. This murdering asshole in front of him had started a public search, *on him.* Would that make anyone else's ears perk up? Would his injured hand give him away to those who thought he was dead?

"I think we need to have a good, friendly talk, *Mr. de Sombras.* It can be a nice long one you'll regret or something much shorter and to the point? What do you say?"

"Buy me a beer, we can talk all night."

The knuckles of Bergman's big fist was all he got instead.

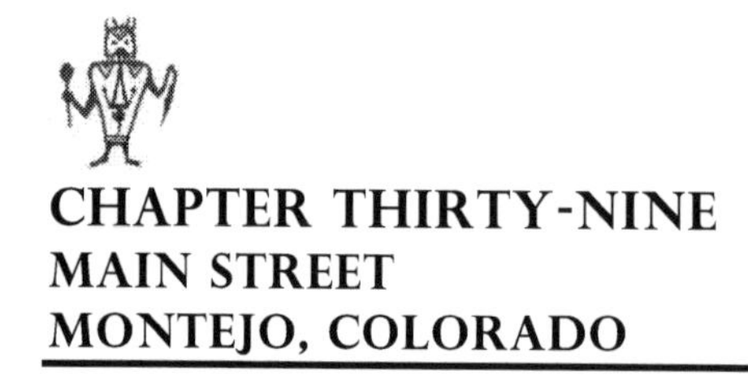

CHAPTER THIRTY-NINE
MAIN STREET
MONTEJO, COLORADO

WHERE THE HELL HAS EVERYONE GONE?

Tessa stepped out of the jeep, hearing the gravel crunch under her feet as if her arrival were announced on a speaker system. Waiting, motionless, she listened. A swirl of dust answered her silent question. Tessa's only companion in town was the damn wind, and it was laughing at her, she was sure of it. Her heart attempted to escape her chest via her throat while her hair shivered on the back of her neck.

No local porch lights. No sounds. Even the gas station was locked up. The diner was shut. Proverbial rolled up sidewalks everywhere.

Inside the B&B motel, she took the stairs two at a time.

To Jack's room.

It was exactly as she'd seen it before. She found his silver flask, just where it should be on the dresser. The bottom half of it was covered in a tooled leather holder. She'd left the top unscrewed and open, the signal that he needed to look for her message. She pulled the leather holder away from the flask and her note fell out. He hadn't seen it. He knew to look for a communication. And while it appeared to be a love note, it was a coded message that included a reminder to destroy it once read. Not destroyed … not unfolded … not read.

Not again.

Where the hell is he?

Two and a half damn hours to get back from Denver! Rough headwinds had slowed her flight. Electrical and radio issues plagued the plane. The Universe was against her.

Too long. *Too damn long.*

The howl. That cry from the distance. It was there again.

Her mouth was beginning to over-salivate and her gut to twist. Had Jack gone to the Mesa? Of course he had. Was the pathetic cry his? She had to get there, fast.

In the lobby, the TV was dead cold — long since powered off. Even the manager was gone.

The front door slammed behind her.

Swallowing, she *felt* with her senses as a deep breath released slowly from her lungs. **Death** was not present. Nothing at all was present — not that she could *feel, hear, or smell* — if she wasn't fooling herself that she had such a skill. She *felt* again, paying attention to her gut. She knew she could trust her gut.

She got the same, empty answer.

Suddenly, an unwelcome series of *what-ifs* ran through her mind, from improbabilities to the cold possibility of Jack's death, alone, disposed of in the dirt, lost to time.

Why did she visualize that? Why so clear?

Strands of his hair moving in the frigid wind. His wide black eyes open, no longer seeing, fogging over, and losing their color. Brown dust coating him. Desert creatures hesitantly approaching to choose which morsel of decaying flesh to savor.

Stay away. You're too late.

His skin, she could clearly see his skin, bruised, bluing ...

You killed him.

The sound of skittering rats and insects surrounding the road made her want to scream. Her legs weakened and she stopped to regain her footing.

You killed yourself.

Department 44. Disgraced and eliminated. Everything she had ever done – all the good things and yes, all the bad. What would they tell her father? He was an intelligence man himself. Would they tell him how she became weak — hesitating — failed because she let her heart get in the way ...

The crushing weight raged with the noise inside her mind. Voices on voices shouted now — you can't — you won't — do as you are told — don't believe! Tessa sank to one knee on the ground, clutching her ears, but the cacophony of angry dissenters weren't crying to get in. They were already inside.

Her world had been a ball of glass — she could see out but never get out. Normal lived outside. She heard voices — believed in ghosts — envisioned and prepared to kill —

Snap out of it! Get a grip.

The glass shattered. The sensation of her skin splintering with it was … was …

Illuminating.

As the prison fell away from her, freedom swept into the vacuum. The wind stopped blowing and spitting dirt at her.

The voice in her head, telling her to give up, to run away, was not *Death*. It never had been.

Stop.

Silence. Clarity. Had stress cleared her path of all the other distractions? The vision of dead Jack? Just her fears rushing to the surface. The idea that something else might be talking to her, getting inside her head unraveled her nerves. And the Athenaeum had used its own mind-screwing to keep her obedient.

And *Death*? Why not?

Why the hell not? Definitely her own voice. Her own thoughts. *Trust my gut. Trust. Myself.* First person thoughts. Now those were hers.

With a strong, calming breath she shifted from unbalanced to crouched and ready to strike. Listening, she cut out the sounds of the desert, seeking any unnatural noises. None – for the moment.

Stay on Mission. My mission. No more toddlers dying because of the games these assholes are playing.

If it was the human enemy she anticipated, she couldn't drive to the Mesa. Too risky, she'd be seen. On foot she'd be slower but quieter. She could take shortcuts, hide, wreak havoc commando style if she needed to. Despite the ticking clock, the pluses edged out the minuses for leaving the jeep behind.

Tessa took out a cross-draw holster for her shorter *Walther PPQ M2-4"* that hooked in front. For the longer muzzle *Q5 Match M2*, she had a holster that sat behind her back. Loaded magazines were balanced equally in the pockets of her coat. Finally, she slid a knife into a sheath in her boot. As she walked away from the motel, she re-braided her long hair and tucked it down the inside of her coat's collar.

Kýrios be damned, it was too late to call for help. No one could get to them to stop this madness in motion. And her allotted time was diminishing fast. The Athenaeum was coming.

But what if it wasn't a human enemy she was headed toward? Unless she was mad — imagining that she had seen or spoken to Death — what could be worse? Right?

Plenty of things. Tessa now knew for a fact that the Mesa de los Muertos held things far worse than death.

She was nearly at a jog as she moved down the side of the access road, kicking up stones nobody was around to hear. If a vehicle came along, she could hide, but it was better by far not to take a chance of getting lost or injured by going off-road until she had to.

A rock skipped passed her. Tessa spun around, gun in both hands.

No one was behind her.

She moved out into the road, to see her surroundings from different angles. No one.

By a piñon pine several feet away, she saw it. What looked like a human? No. It wasn't. But her heart was thumping enough to make her body jerk. Turning, she began walking ... jogging ... running.

She was at a full sprint, starting down a slight slope and bend, curving toward the Mesa. Sweat coated her neck and back. Lightning flashed on the horizon to the west.

Scrub brush and cactus scratched her leather boots and cut nearly to her skin right through the fabric of her clothes. Leaving the safety of the road where it ended in a makeshift parking lot, she moved toward the canyon and, down its length, toward Mesa de los Muertos. Piñon pine trees and sage hid the edge of the steep sides of the ravine. Moving slower and slower,

Tessa crept forward, unsure if a dark shape was simply another shadow, or if it was a deadly drop to the bottom.

No one from the National Park Service had installed proper, modern railings, and what existed was fragile and rusted to the point of shattering.

Three loud bangs echoed from deep inside the canyon. The sound ricocheted around the walls of every stone formation. Gunfire? Ancient drums? The imagination could easily confuse the truth. She chose gunfire. It was logical. It made sense. Anything else was impossible. No, *improbable*, but *not impossible.*

The howling started again, loud, broken into smaller shouts and cries. Fighting. Screaming. Terrors. Ghostly echoes of an ancient battle or the horrific evidence of a fresh, new one.

The shape of the canyon and ravines distorted everything — sound, sight, sensation.

Was her partner in the middle of that? Was he part of that?

She needed to move fast: a thunderstorm was imminent. Flash flooding, slick rocks, and lightning were all going to make things worse.

Tessa probed with her foot, defining the sides of what must be the descending path. It would take her to the left and down at first. Then it must swing over to the right, along the draw at one end of the canyon, below the parking lot. From there, it would lead to the mesa dwellings.

The edge of the path gave way, the sole of her boot finding no purchase.

Loose gravel swept down the canyon wall.

And Tessa was swept along with it.

CHAPTER FORTY
CANYONS OF THE ANCIENTS

IT WASN'T HEIGHTS SHE FEARED, it was falling, and the deadly landing at the bottom.

Ice rushed through her body, and she sat down hard to control her fall. Gasping for a moment, she reoriented herself to the path and rose to a crouch. Shuffling sideways, she worked her way down until trees forced her to turn and start across a precarious stretch around the base of the canyon wall. She only felt the tripwire as it snapped across her shin.

The apparition leaped out and snapped like a whip.

Tessa fell back, gun clenched in both hands. The muzzle shook. Her body quivered. Wide-eyed she waited for it to attack again.

It kept lashing the wind, snapping, and waving back and forth.

Tessa lowered her weapon, but her hands still shook.

A sheet of cloth.

A cheap but effective tourist deterrent. Thrashing and cracking, the primitive device produced a sound that struck deep at a primal human survival instinct. Silence. Her blood rushed in her ears. Her breath came in fits and starts, as though she exhaled far more often than she inhaled.

The cloth caught enough light to look spectral. The snapping of its frayed ends gave it that sickening sound of hardness on soft flesh.

She approached and caught a corner of the cloth, holding it from flapping too violently while she examined the mechanism that put her heart into overdrive. Just a spring-loaded bogeyman on a pole. She'd tripped a man-made scare effect. The heavy sigh that escaped her lips said everything about her disappointment. Chewing her lip for a moment, she kept thinking about each strange occurrence — could all of it have been man-made? Maybe? She released the cloth and let it flap away again.

Why a fake ghost if there were real specters?

Had Jack been right — no such thing as ghosts? Or was this a brilliant diversion from the truth, meant to weed out the easily dissuaded?

Ducking under the scarecrow, brutally conscious of other potential tripwires, Tessa moved forward, down the draw, gun now grasped in both hands.

Along the path, ahead and above, she saw the cliff dwellings lit from within. A glow came from inside, green and wavering. Cut back into a cave of enormous proportion, the cliff dwellings were a tangle of buildings, towers, and fallen ruins. Lights swirled around the cave ceiling. Flashlights?

Tessa stopped and pressed her back against the canyon wall. How many threats were up here?

And how was she to get up to the dwellings? The ancient people who lived here and used the path must have devised a method or two. They were astronomers and architects after all.

The wind began blasting across the top of the canyon ahead of the storm. It would arrive fast. It was cold too.

She held her weapon in her left hand and groped along the wall with her right, as she moved below the cave, perhaps sixty feet below, hoping the mechanics of getting up to the dwellings didn't require a set of long-disintegrated wooden ladders. That would be her luck, wouldn't it? Thousand-year-old wood wasn't likely to last.

Her foot caught on something, and she stumbled forward, scraping her knee. Gun in both hands she pointed it at a dark mound, lying partially across the path. Flies met her and she tried waving them away.

The stink of rot rushed up her nose and she turned her face, burying it in the crook of her arm. Decay.

The mound didn't move.

She poked it in case it wasn't the source of the stink.

Cold and stiff. And it was covered in an old, woolen blanket.

Taking her phone out and hiding the light under the blanket, Tessa peered in, quite dreadful she had already guessed what she would see.

She knew the corpse. Even in this state, she knew him.

The mound had been, at one time, a handsome fellow. X138 - Agent. She'd seen bodies before and had even known some of them in life. Decomposition was natural, though she was holding back her stomach's opinion on the subject. Had the agent not died in the arid, drought-stricken desert, he would have looked worse for a man dead a week. But he looked bad enough.

Not wanting to betray her location, she turned off the phone light and covered him. A moment later, when her eyes adjusted to the darkness again, she noted other potential mounds. Was this where they disposed of the bodies? Some of the mounds might be dirt-covered graves? Some might be bodies decomposing. The smell was strong when the wind shifted.

No one here was going anywhere and she needed to know where all those lights and sounds were coming from. The living needed tending to first. There were no ghosts in this place, only monsters of the human variety.

Tessa was back to square one: How to get up to the dwellings? She must have missed something. The path was descending further, and she had the impression it was going away from the cave along a new spur. Her hand hit on an old chain, which was damaged and felt weak against her fingers. Had it been a ladder from when the Mesa had once been a tourist spot? Maybe. She couldn't count on it now.

Tessa retraced her steps, back to below the far side of the cave. She kept groping the rock in the hope of finding something, anything. Sandstone crumbled against her fingers. Occasionally there was something smooth — it played on her worst guesses, still she kept groping her way.

There it was!

A deep groove in the rock. Another, just within reach, just above it. That's what the ancient people did. They built hand and foot holds, a rockface ladder.

Reluctantly, Tessa put her PPQ back into its holster. Step by uncomfortable step, she climbed.

Nearer the base of the cave, she pushed up and into the dwellings area. Rather than stand or crouch, Tessa chose to lie quietly on her stomach, aligned lengthwise with the cave front. Her holster and gun were painfully pressed under her, but she stayed prone until she could discern what was going on around her.

Several east coast sounding men were cheering each other and making various crude comments. They were deep inside the cavern, behind her. Immediately to her right were other voices, more rural or unidentifiable by any particular accent. A couple of women's voices were among them. Townies? Fine. They were all too busy with whatever was entertaining them.

She got up carefully.

The East Coasters turned to the shouts of one man. Tessa froze in place. Had he spotted her? Was he saying something she needed to know about?

"Come on boys, I've got drinks for all of us in the car."

Her heart started again. Rising only to a crouching position, she crawled in behind a large building stone.

The gang followed the man offering the drinks. Out of curiosity, Tessa waited, watching, hoping to learn how it was that they left the dwellings cavern. Sure enough, a pair of lanterns lit the path to a set of stairs at the back, far end of the cave. *Good.* More than one way out.

Peering around the side of a tall structure, Tessa drew her gun again, and took note of what she could see. Bodies and the townies stripping them on her left. The disgust lasted for a second. Shadows of departing mobsters, for lack of a better term, were on her right. Using those shadows to conceal her, she inched past the brief opening between structures and over to the back of the cavern.

She was safer with a wall behind her. No one to creep up on her that way.

A hard slap against flesh echoed loudly. *That must have left a mark.*

Outside the cavern, the sky burst into bright blue light.

She leaned out from her hiding place. None of the townies were doing anything different. Made no difference to them, storm, or no storm.

"Rio de Sombras!" she heard a man shout, a thick blanket of terror on his voice. "I told you, Rio de Sombras!"

The cold washed over her body as she felt someone walk over her grave.

Thunder boomed and shook the canyon.

She knew that voice, but it was the first time she had ever heard it laced with fear.

CHAPTER FORTY-ONE
CLIFF DWELLINGS
MESA DE LOS MUERTOS

BERGMAN ONLY MOVED HIS FINGERS as a signal, having sat down again. Billy-boy struck Jack across the face, splitting his lip. Jack bit the inside of his mouth and could taste hot, coppery blood- mixed saliva. His face burned at the point of impact and his lip throbbed. Billy-boy was pissed off, having been fooled by an outsider, or so Jack guessed reasonably. "What the hell was that for? What are y'all doing?"

"Who are you?" the sheriff asked again, not bothering to move except to make himself more comfortable on a short, stone wall.

"Rio de Sombras!" He swallowed hard, pushing back as best he could. "I told you, Rio de Sombras!"

Billy-boy moved again, his punch jolting Jack's head back.

Jack spit out the mouthful of blood from biting through the inside of his lip. A trickle descending from his nose only made things worse. "I told y'all already, my name is Rio de Sombras." At least his front teeth were in place. That might not last.

Bergman shook his head. "You keep telling us that, but I don't believe you. Convince me." He nodded to Billy-boy.

"Come on, Gimpy." The deputy seized Jack by his collar and one arm and dragged him until half of his restrained body was teetering on the precipice of the cliff dwelling. Dirt slid from under Jack and hammered down the cliff-face, down into a dark unknown tangle of dead trees, rocks, and scrub. Staring at the debris as it fell out of the lantern light into a black void, Jack struggled against his bound wrists and ankles. Billy-boy chuckled with a sick delight.

"Jesus! What is wrong with y'all? My name *is* Rio de Sombras!"

"Who do you work for?"

"USGS."

"Then you're worthless to me. Billy, throw him over the side with the others." The order was met with a clap of thunder.

The deputy kept hold of Jack, holding more of him out over the cliff edge. "Bye-bye, Gimpy."

""Okay, okay!" Jack stared down into the void below him. "I am USGS, I'm not lyin' about that, but I came here for a second reason." Billy-boy looked over at his boss, then yanked Jack back onto solid ground. Jack swallowed hard and took a moment to regain his breath and composure.

"What other purpose?"

"No one gets rich working for the government. I want more. I *need* more. I heard something was going on here. Something ... lucrative. Jack looked over to the sheriff, his black eyes big and pleading. He bit on his lip, hoping it had stopped bleeding.

Bergman took his sweet time deciding what should be done. Two fingers twitched, all he needed to signal Billy-boy to pull Jack away from the edge and drop him once more onto the ground.

"Proceed, Mr. de Sombras. What did you think was happening here?"

Still hog-tied, Jack pushed away from the deputy and gave the man a deadly glare. His wrists hurt. His mangled hand burned; phantom fingers shot pain up into his arm. His legs cramped from being bound half-bent for so long.

The stormy weather made it colder in the confines of the cliff dwelling. So cold that the townsfolk had headed home, with the exception of the waitress. She sat quietly, probably dreaming of her wedding to Billy-boy and playing with her new necklace. He watched her, trying to tell if one of the shadows still held sway over her.

"Speak up, de Sombras. I can't hear you."

Jack swallowed and stared wide eyed at the sheriff. "I heard something about the town doing *real* good. Too good for some back-water shithole. Y'all don't even get tourists here anymore. But all y'all are doing damn good. As in, who-gives-a-shit-about-the-soil kind of good. My job gave me an excuse to come look."

"What do you think you've seen?" The sheriff took his service pistol out of its holster and checked it over.

Jack kept pushing back. "A well-oiled machine. A business that works. I'm guessing y'all sell a chance, and a place, for gangs to solve their issues with one another — far away from everything and everyone. It's brilliant," he added, hoping Bergman would like the compliment. "What, all y'all have had maybe five of these gangs duke it out?"

Shaking his head, and smiling as if Jack's compliment had worked, Bergman corrected him, "At least twenty. And only the leaders fight the duel."

"Twenty? All y'all folks must be rich as Croesus. And nobody outside knows unless they hear a rumor." Jack tried to laugh. "Not sure where I heard it, but I swear it was only in passing. But I gotta' terrible need, so I'm listening for this stuff."

"I'm supposed to believe that you heard a rumor and on a whim of potential riches you came all the way up here?"

"I got my own reasons."

"You're that desperate?"

Heat rushed up Jack's face. After a long pause and several gulps of air, he confessed, "Yeah. I need money. I need to be able to … y'all know … vanish. There are folks who would like to make that happen for me ..." He let the sentence go unfinished.

"Gambling debts?"

"Somethin' like that." His face was burning without Billy-boy's assistance. His voice dropped. "I need money. More than I'll ever get pulling a government paycheck. I need to disappear … bad."

Bergman stood up and walked closer, towering over Jack, pistol in hand. "Maybe I kill you and the problem is solved." He pointed the muzzle at Jack's head.

"Wait, I know I can be worth keeping around. All y'all need someone to keep the government out of here. Why not someone in the government? Your own inside man? My report to Albuquerque alone could help with that." No one looked impressed. "And I know people … who know folks— who might want to use your service." He began breathing hard again and looking around wildly. They weren't believing him … yet. "I can bring all y'all better clients than those common creeps. Mine? I'm talking about politicians and leaders that go to war with each other all the time. I know about them. I used to be a part of them, and they have some mighty deep pockets." Jack began to calm his voice. He needed to upgrade his vocabulary too — a subliminal manipulation of their perception of him.

"Tell me more." Bergman's voice sharpened.

Success. Now he had a chance. Sly and smiling, Jack looked up, but it wasn't Bergman who towered over him. Bergman's body, yes it was — but no, not him. The eyes. Berman's eyes were shadowed though his face was in lantern light. Something about his skin — it moved even when Bergman didn't. A Skin Thief was still wearing the sheriff. Jack's smile dropped.

Biting down on his lower lip, to stop the throbbing pain, he steadied his voice. "I want to work out an agreement. I don't want to take cash flow away from the town."

"They get the leftovers and they're happy." Bergman looked up at the ceiling of the cave, extending a hand of acknowledgement to the moving shadows above him.

Jack stopped squirming. "Y'all get the cash, they get the spoils of war. That's very smart." *Keep talkin' like you're talkin' to the sheriff.*

"It is. So, why should I trust you to give me better customers? Why should I give up my hard-earned payments? And what makes you think I want to make any agreements with you? You're the one rope-tied, not me."

Jack tried to smile. Maybe it was too soon, but he didn't plan to grin like an idiot. "Because I am willing … to earn yer trust. I didn't fool ya', maybe I shouldn't have tried, so I don't want to waste any more time with that. Look, y'all are a smart, educated man," he watched the Sheriff stiffen with pride, "so, here's my proposal. Y'all hire me. I'll show my cards. All my cards. Straight up. I'll earn that trust. And y'all can get more money and I can get a new chance at life."

Seeing Billy-boy's angry eyes and balled-up fists, Jack kept going. "Better goods coming into town with the … improved clientele. More money to go around. It's only y'all and Billy here collecting actual cash payment. All I want is to restart my life, far from people who want to kill me. Y'all are my only ticket out. Y'all got the leverage, the firepower, control. What I got is a product y'all can use. Can we act like businessmen and make an agreement? Handshake deal. Yer word being valuable, mine being desperate? You, me, and Billy-boy here."

"I dunno. There's a couple more of us involved. Did you consider that?"

Jack was thoughtful for a moment. "That makes sense," he lied with a slight grin. "Y'all have to have people in the gangs or near them, to get the word out. Sure. That makes sense. But they're not my problem. I don't wanna' know. Y'all can handle them. Yer the man in charge — y'all call the shots or this business would be a serious mess, wouldn't it?"

"It's not always advantageous to have too many partners. Too many mouths that can talk." Bergman strolled back to where he'd been leaning, re-holstering his service weapon. "Too many want to be in charge," Bergman's shadowed eyes glared sideways to where Billy-boy stood.

Jack tried to sit up, slowly. "Sure. Slip of the tongue an' all that."

Billy-boy stalked nearer to Jack withdrawing his pistol. "Boss, we don't need some gimpy looser." Pointing to the arena, he added, "We get what we need: fewer gangs, fewer drug dealers — justice. We get what we need to survive. You want too much. We can't handle more than this — we ain't got the resources, the fire power …"

"Perhaps," Bergman sneered, with almost two voices. Jack swallowed hard, telling himself that it was an illusion caused by fear, but Bergman kept talking. "Perhaps I think my form of justice needs to spread, needs, what should I call it? Enhancement? Is it enough to wipe out a few gangs? Is it really good enough? Is what is being done truly justice on this tiny scale?"

Justice, eh? Jack watched Bergman, looking for absolute signs that he was still being worn by the grotesque Skin Thief — after all, ghosts and ghouls weren't real. He needed absolute proof. *Ghosts and ghouls aren't real. Not real.*

Bergman kept talking, and occasionally looking down at Jack. "Yes, Justice, Mr. de Sombras. Aren't you sick and tired of hearing … hearing about these unclean gangs terrorizing villages?"

Villages? Wait, what?

"We need more reach. Justice can't be contained in a small vessel. It needs bigger. It must have more. Justice is an insatiable hunger, that mankind has always fed. A greater scale, a greater scope," the paired voices spoke in unison. Bergman smiled voraciously at Jack. "Improvement."

Jack's body froze. *What the hell?*

Billy-boy was either used to seeing Bergman like that or oblivious to it. "That's not what we need. *He's* not what we need. We need water. This is a good thing we've got going. We can wipe out those sons-of-bitches and get rich at the same time. Ain't none of it any good if we're all thirsty." Billy-boy pointed his gun directly at Jack's face. "Keep things small and contained. Eliminate trouble like intruders — like *him*. We make things here nice and clean, and the water — like the money — will come."

"Everybody's wavin' guns today." Jack twisted to better face Bergman. "Yeah, all y'all do need me. I can help yer business and it's in my best interest to …"

"Bullshit!" Billy-boy put the gun under Jack's chin.

Shit! Jack's voice raised, his wide-eyed gaze darting back and forth between his captors. "Y'all need me. Who else can get ya' in with the largest governmental spy organization in the U.S.? Not *that* one … I'm talking about the one nobody else talks about. The one that *doesn't* answer to Congress. The one with deeper pockets than God. All y'all want more money, more power, and the protection ya' need to keep in operation? To stay safe when the Mob turns ugly or tries to take over yer lucrative business? I can get ya' that! Best high-class, high-paying customers. Not this filth y'all're dealing with now." *I'm scrambling, not making enough sense— keep talking Jack Rabbit — you'll get through this. Give them everything.*

Bergman's face changed. His mouth curled upward only at the end and his eyes widened; he was ready to believe. His shadowed eyes turned black.

No such thing as ghosts or Skin Thieves, was all that Jack could think. He too was ready to believe. In something altogether stranger — and he couldn't afford to let the irrational take over.

Billy-boy was not ready to believe.

Jack knew this was it. *One last chance.* "No more small-time, small-town bullshit. I know these Black Ops people. Top level decision makers. Arms dealers who want to narrow competition. If y'all've got any talent, brains, experience ..."

Tessa closed her eyes. *No, no, no.* This was exactly what Kýrios feared. That Jack was a traitor to their former employer, and worse. *Please no. It can't be true.*

Gripping the gun tighter, she crept closer to the three men.

Lanterns spaced out around the area provided enough light to see what was happening.

As close as she could get, she leaned out, confident in the shadows that protected her, and noted where each man was. And if Jack kept talking the way he was, her first shot would have to — *have to* — take him out. The success of the mission, the safety of the innocent bystanders, was first. It had to be. *She had no other choice.*

If her heart truly embraced him, she would be doing him a favor by easing him out of life of treachery before he did anything worse. A dead man didn't have to suffer the horrors of accusation, judgment, and punishment. One clean shot. He'd never know.

Something pricked behind her eyes: better he dies than be dragged through ...

She had a clean shot on Jack.

Shoot, girlfriend. It's his time.

No. I'm not listening to you.

Shoot. You know you have to.

She lined up her target.

One clean shot. He'll never know. He'll never feel it.

Tessa felt the trigger against her finger. He would never feel it.

CHAPTER FORTY-TWO

BERGMAN BURST OUT LAUGHING, the twin voices echoing against the bleak cavern ceiling. "I knew it. You didn't come here for dirt samples. You have too much mystery about you just for dirt sniffing. I was so sure you were a private investigator or something more exotic. I like being right. You don't move like a yokel. You got military or some sort of specialist training. You watch too much and ask too many questions for an average guy."

Billy-boy looked skeptical and glared again at Jack.

Jack let the panicked expression fade to that of a man with a good hand to play and who'd proudly laid out his royal flush. His smile moved up one side of his face, and he relaxed his shoulders a bit. "I've got nothin' left to lose, but everything to gain. And you, sir, well," he watched Bergman's eyes further blackened with every word, "y'all'll never be poor or unimportant again. Yer form of justice — it could go international if y'all want it to. The whole world. Clean, like you want it."

When Bergman all but leapt to his feet, Jack knew he'd hit the right button. He had the sheriff — and maybe whatever else he was dealing with — in his hands. "I can make ya' the man that every Black Ops team, every private intel agency, every independent operator comes to. They'll want data on which criminal is still alive, who is running what organization. And y'all'll be the one to give it to them, or y'all offer up the ultimate means to eliminate problems ... for the right compensation." He let the sentence drop off while allowing Bergman's imagination to run with the concept. "I can help ya' get a level of 'client' that will bring y'all wealth, power, and the chance to change the criminal world in one night. There's just one thing I don't get, and if this is gonna' work, I need to know — how the hell do y'all get perfectly smart men to agree to risk everything on a duel? A freakin' duel?"

"I charm them." Bergman growled out a burst of laughter. "I know what to say and I can talk anyone into anything. I know how those bastards think, what turns them on. I just push all the right buttons and they show up. Mesmerized to death, as it were. I bet I could even talk *you* into blowin' your own brains out, for no good reason at all. That's how good I am."

Ice ran down Jack's body again. The dream? Had Bergman had something to do with his suicidal, *almost suicidal*, dream?

No such thing as Ghosts. Bad men — that's different, Jack produced a satisfied grin.

Folding his arms across his broad chest, the sheriff smiled as his eyes returned to their normal blue. "What do you want? How much are you going to cost me?"

"You're not gonna' trust him," the deputy whined. "What's he doing here if he's so damn well connected ..."

The sheriff cut him off, a glint of victory in his eyes. "You say you want an agreement. Name your terms, de Sombras. Let's see if I like them."

"Fifty thousand. And ..."

"And?"

"I want the woman. My boss."

Bergman looked more than a little intrigued. "Revenge? I thought she was one of you. Cop or intelligence or something."

Jack shook his head. "No. She hasn't got a clue about me. She's exactly what she appears. An intellectual snob with a bad case of boredom and a need to be in charge."

"And you want her?" Bergman snorted a little.

"Christ. You've seen her. She's the prettiest thing I've ever laid eyes on — y'all think that too."

"True. But she set off all my alarms. I didn't buy her story, just like I didn't buy yours. And since I was right about you . . ."

Jack sighed heavily. "That there was my fault. I'm the one with the weak story. Y'all applied it to the both of us. No, she isn't that worldly despite what she says. She's got all the style and culture, but not a lick of common sense."

Bergman huffed out a laugh. "And you want her? Do I dare ask, for what?"

"I ain't giving it all away, but let's say she's what got me in trouble in the first place. So yeah. I want to spend a little time *in the Manager's Office* before I move along to quiet retirement, if you know what I mean."

"So, it is a little bit of revenge."

"Maybe. USGS had been a safe place for me to hold up, nice and invisible, until she ratted me out. Not on purpose of course. She hasn't got the nerve to do that sort of thing. Still … *handling* her will be good for my reputation, might make folks think twice before coming after me, and it might give me some extra time to … ah … enjoy my self-promotion to her supervisor." Jack shrugged. "I just gave ya' a little information for free. How about a good faith gesture? My arms hurt like hell."

Bergman must have thought about things for a full minute, then nodded at Billy-boy, who reluctantly cut away the rope around Jack's upper body, letting him roll his shoulders, even if his hands were still bound.

"That's it?" Jack asked with annoyance.

"Give me something more than what I almost figured out on my own and maybe I'll let Billy-boy cut you all the way loose instead of just cutting you."

Thank God for hesitation.

Tessa lowered her weapon. *Oh Jack, damn it. You fooled me: shame on me. You son-of-a-bitch! Damn good job.* Was Bergman going to buy it? It was a wild request. Money, sure, but asking for a living being as part and parcel of the deal? It was crazy, maybe crazy enough to make his story the more believable.

That moment, she realized her legs were numb. Everything was focused on her arms, on the gun. A wash of warmth flushed over her. She'd been holding her breath too.

Dark movement caught her eye. Near the sheriff and Jack.

A misplaced shadow, free traveling, skittering off to the far end of the cavern.

Tessa watched for a moment, to make sure it wasn't circling back on her.

"I like that you want revenge. Can't trust a man who doesn't want a little payback now and then. I'm willing to give her to you, but she can't leave here alive. You do understand me? She's seen and heard too much."

The cavern lit up and thunder followed five seconds later.

Jack bobbed his head, perhaps too enthusiastically. "I know. But all I need is a little bit of time."

"Mind if I watch?"

Jack's face flushed boiling hot again, but not due to embarrassment.

"Just kidding," Bergman sneered. "Or maybe not. Just make sure she doesn't last the week. And if you happen to mention how and when you're going to dispatch the lady, I will take that as a kindness."

Jack scowled. "I'd take it as a kindness if y'all would cut me loose. Seriously. Being hog-tied is more than a little uncomfortable."

Berman was laughing again. "Why not? Billy-boy, cut his legs free. You, Mr. de Sombras, need to earn more of my trust before I'll let the rest go. I have a bad feeling you aren't to be fully trusted just yet. You might be plenty lethal in combat, even with that gimpy hand of yours. Billy-boy seems to think you are."

Damn. Almost.

The deputy snarled something barely audible, put away his gun, drew out a knife and cut the rope holding Jack's legs together. He didn't move away and kept the knife close to Jack.

"Much obliged." Jack stretched each leg out with knee-popping noises, while standing up, unsteady. "Sure, I can't talk y'all into freeing my hands? Go all the rest of the way? I swear I'm far more interested in making a deal than gettin' into a fight." As proof he wasn't in fighting trim, he stretched his back and screwed up his face.

"Drop your price to twenty thousand and maybe we'll see," Billy-boy said with absolutely no indication of sarcasm.

"Relax, buddy. Why don't y'all leave negotiation to the Boss?"

"Or maybe we don't give you nothin' and I just beat the information out of you." He balled up his fists, lifted his chin, and leaned in like he was ready to bully into Jack's space. Bergman wasn't going to be able to call him off this time.

"If that's yer stance," Jack replied, noting the waitress was deeply focused on something, none of the gang members were in range, and that the sheriff was relatively calm — almost too relaxed.

It's on.

Jack's heel struck out, catching the deputy in the front of his knee, and distending it unnaturally backward.

A sharp crack was followed by a scream as the deputy collapsed onto the hard ground. He lay on his side grasping his shattered knee.

Bergman was on his feet and pulled his revolver.

Jack closed the distance, throwing his weight into the big man, aiming the brunt of impact on the sheriff's gun arm.

Bergman's shot went wild.

The revolver struck the floor and skittered out of reach.

The sheriff crashed into the stone wall he'd sat on and fell onto all fours.

Jack shoved away from Bergman, staggering until he found his footing and bearings again.

The gun?

Both men spotted it.

They scrambled toward the revolver, but Jack kicked it blindly into the darkness, stomping on Bergman's hand for good measure.

Billy-boy's waitress screamed bloody murder and ran in the direction of her man, skidded to a stop, turned on her heel, and raced out of the area, screaming at the top of her lungs for someone to come and help.

Nobody left to help y'all, Jack dismissed, giving Billy-boy a hard punt to his ribs, grateful Billy's woman hadn't joined in. Women could be nasty fighters, and he needed to concentrate on Bergman.

Struggling to his feet, Bergman awkwardly leaped forward, reaching out to grab the Agent.

Jack dropped to the ground in front of the sheriff, braced and kicked up, hard.

Both feet rammed into Bergman's stomach and tossed the big man over

Jack was up again, headed toward the deputy.

Bergman was on the move, too. He head-rushed Jack, sending the cowboy sprawling onto his back.

Momentum kept them both sliding. Bergman skidded over a short ledge.

Jack slid on the level floor. Forcing his feet under him, he recovered into a half-kneeling stance. He pushed back, drawing his bound wrists under his butt and up behind his knees. One leg drawn to his chest allowed him to get one arm around his knee. The other leg bent down, and Jack rolled while pulling his hands up in front.

Billy-boy, clutching his ribs, limped toward the Agent, dragging his bad leg.

Jesus. Not out of the fight? Jack swung both fists hard, knocking Billy-boy off balance, grasped the dazed deputy's arm and used the momentum to toss the man almost over the edge of the cliff dwelling.

Billy-boy landed with a thump, almost over the ledge. He lay motionless.

Bergman came up behind Jack, wrapped a thick arm around his neck and squeezed.

Shoving back hard, Jack tried to free himself. His vision tunneled. He dropped on one knee, hoping his weight would pull the sheriff down.

It didn't work.

Bergman held Jack locked into the choke hold. He wouldn't let go.

Jack's lungs strained against the desperate need for air and panic sent his heart rate racing. He grasped at Bergman's arm, his mangled hand unable to maintain a tight grip.

His ears ringing, his head spinning, the edges of his vision were fading fast.

His legs gave in beneath him ...

CHAPTER FORTY-THREE

TESSA BROUGHT HER WALTHER DOWN HARD on the sheriff's head. That loosened him from Jack, who struggled forward, gasping for air.

The sheriff collapsed on his knees, staggered back to his feet, with too much fight left in him.

Tessa swept the weapon up in an arc, crashing into the side of Bergman's head. That dropped him. He slumped sideways and lay groaning on the stone-cold ground.

Down, but still not out. That would have to do for now. Jack was foremost in her mind. Pulling out her knife, she freed Jack's hands, and fighting the urge to wrap her arms around him and tell him it was all okay.

Landing on his knees, bent forward, he first rubbed his right wrist, then, his left wrist and hand. He held his three and a half fingers it as if they were on fire, or that he might want to tear the whole hand off. Even in the surreal lighting, or maybe because of it, the disfigurement looked nasty.

She kept her eyes on Bergman and the floor of the cliffside arena. So this is where Bergman had arranged for the *services* he provided to crime lords.

Lightning stretched across the horizon in jagged flashes.

Jack had nearly caught his breath, and neither the sheriff nor deputy were immediately threatening. She let herself look at him now, fully, taking him in from head to toe. Battered, bruised, but not broken. Her chest tightened. She'd brought him here — to this — Her Cowboy. So broken, yet so strong. He'd come back swinging no matter what they dished out at him, wouldn't he. Her Cowboy.

Jack turned his head to her. "Why the hell didn't ya' take the shot?" His voice was raspy, and he tried swallowing several times. Now he held his left hand protectively, hiding it from her. Hiding it from everything.

"Bergman and Billy-boy were in motion."

Jack shook his head. "No, Darlin'. Why didn't ya' take the shot … at me? Earlier. When ya' had a clear line up? Ya' had to have heard me."

She re-holstered her gun, worried if he needed immediate medical attention … or what she might say in thoughtless haste. "Maybe I have faith in you, even when I don't."

His eyes narrowed at her comment. The light reflected in those dark slits.

The sheriff coughed and cussed, unable to stand. Billy-boy was face down, unmoving.

Jack was standing, much to his own surprise. "Y'all gonna' take that shot anytime soon? Yer boss had to have ordered ya' to. I kinda half expected it."

"No faith in me?" she whispered.

"I always have faith in ya', even when I don't. But then, I don't have a boss —"

"I don't always do what Kýrios tells me to."

"A renegade?"

"Discretion is always advantageous."

"Then I owe ya'. I want to … I need to tell ya' —

"Hey!" The waterfront boss shouted at the agents from the far side of the cliff city. The waitress pointed them out and the boss's gang followed at her direction.

"Well, shit," Jack spit out, wiping at the dried blood under his nose. "Prepare to repel boarders, *Mrs. Peel.*"

Jack pointed to the lanterns, indicated three near them and two over by the arena. He held out a hand for her to give him one of her guns.

Arm the very man she was ordered to terminate?

Tessa shoved her Q5 into Jack's hands and drew the second, smaller M2. Never before had her gut intuition been so clear and so satisfied that she was doing the right thing.

He didn't fumble with the unfamiliar gun, but it took him an extra moment to hold it comfortably.

She knew he had no muscle memory with that model but then, she remembered with pride, this was *Her Cowboy* — he could handle any weapon she handed him.

To hell with Kýrios. To hell with the Athenaeum.

They fired five shots between them. Five lanterns shattered, plunging the whole site into further darkness.

"Back wall," Tessa whispered directly into his ear.

Crouching low, they moved as fast as they could to the interior of the dwellings, stumbling and groping in the dark. Halfway, she heard Jack gather up a handful of loose stones at his feet and pitch it away from them.

The scattering rocks echoed and distracted. The sound, bouncing around the high cliff ceiling and ruined buildings, covered their steps. *Nice move.*

They paused behind a fairly complete kiva wall that continued past her highest reach, pressed their backs against the old, stacked rocks, and pushed their feet against the back of the cavern. Tessa dug into her coat and withdrew a magazine for the gun she'd given Jack. They would need to reload soon, and fast.

"What the hell have you got against Smith & Wesson," Jack mumbled, barely audible. He kept moving his hands over the Q5. Feeling it, memorizing it.

All she heard were "hell" and "Smith & Wesson;" the rest she filled in from experience. She couldn't tell if he was teasing or genuinely criticizing her weaponry choices.

Shuffling steps and voices approached.

Tessa closed her eyes, focusing on the M2's grip in her hand, the heat of her other fingers wrapped around that hand.

"Go along the back! We'll flush 'em to you!" Someone thought they were being clever. Someone was wrong.

"There's only two of them," Bergman choked out.

They were still undiscovered. *Good.* And Bergman was with the gang, from the sound of it.

She tried not to jump when Jack's hand touched her cheek. He drew a finger across her skin so that she could feel him pointing to their right. She responded with a grip on his upper arm, squeezing twice to indicate agreement. No words, just touch and trust.

They proceeded meticulously, purposely.

Each time the Waterfront gang was loud, they took more risks under the cover the broken dwellings temporarily offered.

It wasn't enough, and she knew it. Any minute, her *new friend* might show up and demand she do something she was no longer prepared to do. If *Death* expected to claim Jack tonight, it would happen without Tessa's help, and maybe over her own dead body.

They weren't getting very far, groping through a forest of stone. Lightning wasn't predictable enough to be useful to anyone but could reveal them by accident. Morning light was coming, and that was not good. If sunrise lit up the cliff dwelling, there'd be no place to hide. Shit, they were running out of time.

A hand reached over and touched Tessa.

That's not Jack.

"Hey, I found one —"

She slammed her hand into the man's throat, grabbed his collar, and yanked him toward her. His face crashed into the kiva wall.

Their hiding spot was almost revealed.

Flashlights turned on, searching for the pair. Both agents crouched down. Their exact location wasn't known … yet. But it would be in seconds.

Jack readied himself, working over to the left.

Tessa went right.

They stepped out and aimed for the flashlights. A couple of lights hit the ground and rolled over to the ruins, casting light on the area that was haunting and deceptive.

"Take cover, you idiots!" Bergman was near the back of the gang.

Nice and safe, she thought, taking an extra shot in the direction of his voice, and hearing him cuss in response.

The waterfront boss was leading his troops like a general of old.

Tessa felled him with two shots to the chest. It was rare to see a gang boss lead, and as the man fell, a vision of the *Sicilian* flashed across her mind. She had done what was needed. Uncle Mario would understand.

She sure as Hell wasn't hesitating.

Jack worked his way forward, close to the gang members.

Some were fleeing. Some thought they could beat him.

Stupid has consequences, she thought, staying close to her partner.

Jack's weapon clattered on the stone. No more ammo in the Q5, and three men rushing him left him no time to reload.

Tessa dropped the man closest to Jack, but the remaining two had Jack in between them. No clean shot.

Bergman worked his way around the other side of the gang and climbed back up to a higher position.

Tessa got him lined up and prepared to fire twice. Only one shot happened before her weapon locked open on an empty magazine.

The shot kept Bergman moving into the shadows until he was gone. No fool, Bergman ran away. Footsteps sounded from his direction, fading with each second. Apparently, he wasn't staying for the fight. *Coward.*

Jack head-butted the first man who came at him, kicked the second, and punched the first. He took a hit to the ribs and fell back against a half-broken wall.

Tessa pulled a magazine out of her coat pocket and slid the new one in, just as Billy-boy emerged from the deep shadows, brandishing his service gun, half-dragging and half-held up by the waitress.

Tessa only saw the gun in Billy-boy's hand, before she dropped to one knee, aimed, and fired two shots. A roar of thunder rolled over the cavern.

The waitress screamed.

Billy-boy's body took the impact of both bullets. His shirt turned wet, and a dark stain spread above his heart. Falling backward, he pulled his waitress down with him.

"Jack, quit playing with your food, we have to go. Now!"

Catching the first guy by his hair, Jack slammed the man's face into his raised knee. The sound of breaking cheek bones and teeth was satisfying. The second guy wasn't so foolish, trying to move in and out of Jack's reach. At last, he swung too hard.

Jack met the twisting body with his fist, straight to the side of the man's head, then another punch to the neck. The man went limp mid-motion, collapsing lifeless on the ground.

The agents stood, looking for anyone still standing, gasping for air, and Tessa wondered out loud, "What next?"

"Hell, woman, don't ever ask that."

Incoming voices met her question with a violent answer.

"Y'all just had to ask. Time to flee for our lives?"

"Over the side?" She tried to smile.

"Of the cliff?"

"Don't you live for excitement?" She said, pushing past him, headed for the open face of the cavern.

"Ah, shit, not tonight, Darlin', I got a headache."

"Oh, cowgirl up."

He didn't bother with a clever quip in response. Jack snagged up a flashlight, using it to find his weapon. He picked up the Q5 and reloaded on the move. The gun joined the flashlight in his belt.

Tessa kept her flashlight on until they found the edge of the cliff. Their search led them to a chain that might have been used to keep tourists from traipsing over the side, one that was now quite old, of questionable quality, disconnected on one end, and didn't make it all the way down to the bushes below.

"Close enough for hand grenades and A-bombs," Jack grasped the chain with his bad hand, balancing his weight on either side of the metal links, and holding out one arm to Tessa.

"Get moving, Jack. I'll be right above you."

"No — y'all'll be right here," he indicated his outstretched arm.

"Jack, your hand ..."

"Someone's gotta' climb, and someone's gotta' shoot." He nodded over at the Mesa. More lights bounced in the darkness, over by the parking lot, and moving toward the dwellings. "Trust me to do my part — I'll trust ya' to do yer's."

"Well, shit," she cursed. She belted her light and sent out a silent prayer to the universe.

Tessa half sat on his right hip, held in place by his arm, which reached around her, letting him grip the chain with his right hand above his damaged left one. Her feet touched the rock face so that she could participate in controlling their descent and bear much of her own weight. Her right arm was free to aim, and her left hand gripped the chain above Jack's.

Haltingly, they started down toward hopeful safety. The rock face was dry thanks to the drought, but sandstone was rarely ideal for repelling, even in daylight, and in monitored conditions.

Raindrops the size of olives began hitting the side of the cliff wall. Just their luck.

Above them, they could hear the waitress screaming that the agents had escaped toward the far end of the dwelling. "I should have shot her too," Tessa muttered from behind clenched teeth.

Downward they climbed. Painfully. Hands trading places with one another, shifting weight, they passed the first twenty feet below the edge.

The few drops of rain turned into a steady shower.

A flash of lightning filled the whole sky, its tentacles reaching out from cloud to cloud. Just before the clap of thunder stunned Tessa's ears, she heard Jack grumble about metal and lightning and bad luck.

Someone above noticed the chain over the edge was moving. Probably heard it scraping the rock.

Feet scrambled and echoed on the dwelling floor. A small avalanche of pebbles fell on them. They passed the forty-foot mark — she hoped.

How much further down? How far from the ground did the chain end?

Two lights approached from the vegetation below.

The chain was yanked upward, and Jack almost lost his grip with the bad hand.

Aiming toward the top of the cliff, Tessa took two shots. *Fifteen, fourteen. Keep track.* Someone cursed and they let go of the chain.

Tessa kept her focus on the ledge above. A sound of motion scraped along the edge.

Tessa let go of the chain, depending wholly on Jack, flicked on the flashlight and aimed again.

Townie or gangster, she didn't care at this point. The figure and the one behind him each had a gun. She temporarily blinded them, then fired her own shots. *Thirteen, twelve, eleven, ten.* Shots paired up. Hitting close to her mark. This wasn't a steady gun range, she snarled half under her breath.

Jack clutched her tightly to his body, but his grip on the chain was starting to fail. He said nothing.

She flicked the flashlight off again. No sense giving them something easier to aim at. Grasping the chain above his hand, again, they began moving.

Two lights below them, Tessa saw them moving down the path. She twisted against his shoulder, followed his two steps toward the ground, and shot down into the brush. *Nine, eight. Seven, six.*

Shots were returned with no more accuracy than hers.

Five. Four. Three. Two. One.

The Walther was empty.

Tessa shoved it into her belt holster, reached around Jack, and took back the reloaded Q5. The bullet count began again. She hit someone with unlucky number *thirteen.*

They took two huge repelling steps down. Fifty-five feet from the upper ledge.

A flashlight moved. Bullet *ten* hit its mark.

Thirty feet down? More? Rain was running down the rock face. Jack was holding on by force of will alone.

Bullet *four* found the fellow who thought his lack of a flashlight would do him good.

They repelled further down, not far. "We're out of climbing gear," Jack announced to her.

"I'm out of —"

Voices above them began crying out — some in terror, some in anger.

"Jack? What the hell is that?"

He had no answer.

Tessa felt his body stiffen.

He knew what was going on up there, she was sure of that. Now was not the time to …

The chain went slack in Jack's hand and rattled against the cliff wall as it and both Agents plunged into the brush below.

Tessa's scream bounced off the ravine walls.

An equally horrified sound escaped from Jack's lips, echoing.

CHAPTER FORTY-FOUR

FOR THAT PROVERBIAL, ETERNAL MOMENT, they both lay on the path, on top of a pile of freshly dug dirt, staring up at a storming sky, rainwater pouring down on them in a baptismal bath given for their survival.

No bullets rained down from above. No voices called out from the path to indicate they were being pursued. Did they all think she and Jack had died in the fall?

Nothing moved for a full five minutes. Or at least she thought it had been five minutes. After counting shots, guessing distances, gauging gang membership, and clocking her own heart rate, she'd had enough with math.

"You hear anything?" Tessa turned her head to see her partner squeezing his eyes open and shut.

"Not a damn thing, now," Jack whispered back. "Where the hell did they go? They sure as shit were makin' a ton a' noise before."

"And now nothing."

Nearly in shock, disbelieving that they were still alive, they both sat up. The path was little more than a few feet away. She was guessing, but from the lack of shattered bones, their fall couldn't have been far at all. They must have been close to ground level.

Discreetly whispering, she touched Jack, to make sure he wasn't a spirit. "Do you know how lucky we are not to have piñon pine limbs stabbing through our bodies?"

"Ya' call this lucky?"

"Oh yeah. We're lucky people, Jack. Very, very lucky."

"Tell me that when we get back to town and we don't manage to get dead along the way."

"Deal."

"And when we get back," he coughed out, stifling the noise and trying to stand, "I want to have that delayed chat with Gas Guy. He knows more than anyone else besides Bergman and his deputies. He stands back and watches everything. I want to know what he knows."

Accepting Jack's hand, pushing to her feet, Tessa surveyed the area as best she could. "If we … when … when we get out of this shithole alive," she knew she was cursing more than ever, but she didn't care. "We're alive for now"

Tessa pointed to the path and mentioned that she knew the way.

Jack just nodded with whatever energy he had left and mumbled about being too old for this.

"We'll have to go around."

"Around what?"

Tessa swallowed. "Some earlier victims. The smell's pretty bad."

"Compared to what? This place has stunk to high heaven since we got here."

Tessa held back a chuckle. "Some of those bodies have been there a while."

Jack shook his head, mumbling about the unlucky.

"Parapsychologically speaking, creatures tied directly to murder, unnatural death —"

"Bullshit, Darlin'"

"— tend to present with an odor that is reminiscent of raw sewage."

"Bullshit."

"No, no. Sewage."

"Bull—"

Above them, near the top of the draw, car doors slammed.

Jack and Tessa dropped down and waited, searching in opposite directions for any signs of being followed or found. "I thought they were gone. Or dead. Or something."

Headlights burst on as the engines started, and in seconds, the cars in the parking lot sped away.

Silence filled the ravine again, between thunderclaps from the distance.

"Maybe we should wait a moment, to see if anyone else is leaving?"

With empty weapons, it was a smart thing to do, though her gut begged her to get out.

"I want to find Surfer Teen and thank him for trying to warn us. At least someone was trying to be a decent human being. Oh, and that Professor … Begay."

She groped forward, leaning a hand on the cliff wall, constantly checking above in case one of the baddies was watching, before noticing Jack wasn't with her. Jack had stopped.

So had the rain.

He leaned against the rock next to her but looked confused. "Who's Surfer Teen?"

"The kid at the top of the hill when we first came into town. He warned us that the town was terrible. Remember? 'Man, like, that place sucks,'" she mimicked.

He paused again. "Why call him Surfer Teen?"

"Long blond hair. T-shirt. Baggy jeans. That, sort of, typical Dude look. I see them all the time when they come up to Seattle during the summer."

Jack took a while to respond. "That's not what he looked like. He was a dark-haired kid in an old cowboy hat." He stepped in front of her, checked above and behind for danger, then held her close. "He looked like the kids that I used to see around in Texas, especially El Paso."

They stood there as the rain began falling again, each other's presence the only comfort.

"Jack, didn't you say the cook you met and bummed a cigarette off of reminded you of someone you knew?"

He nodded. "He looked much like the cook my dad hired for every round up. Damn good guy." After a long pause, he asked, "Tell me, what do you think Gas Guy looks like?"

"No one *you* need to worry about," she replied, tapping his nose. "Reddish hair, medium height, a little thick in the waist, coveralls. Clean shaven. Right shoulder higher than the left," she paused waiting for Jack to give her the *go-on* gesture. "Five feet, eleven inches. Definitely had the look of a con man. Working class hands. Sly features."

"Someone you know?"

"Now that you mention it, he does remind me of a fellow who cheated me on a car repair. What do you see?"

"Balding, scrawny, in need of a shower. Goatee. About my height."

"How do two well educated, experienced operatives see the same person so differently? This isn't a matter of casual witnesses to an accident."

A roll of thunder further out in the canyonlands rumbled along, fading gradually, until nothing more of it could be heard. The remaining silence was suffocating. Flashes of lightning moved away in the clouds, but the rain kept falling.

"'Water won't come 'til it's clean' he stated."

"So I've heard." Tessa put out her hand, letting the drops pool for a moment in her palm. She spoke out loud. Not shouting. Just saying, for *someone* to hear. She had no idea why she said it — not entirely. Nor did she know exactly to whom she said it, but she did. "We're leaving now. We're not staying."

Instinctively, she knew Jack approved, even if he'd never admit it.

Jenny's Diner, she suspected, wasn't likely to open again in the near future.

The far end of the diner's parking lot was dark. Jack checked for movement before moving closer to the collection of nice cars he'd pointed out a day or so earlier. Tessa, watching the road to the Mesa, followed him.

Seeing him holding his damaged hand and gingerly touching his nose, she hurried to get closer to him. "How is everything holding up?" She wiped the water out of her eyes and pushed back her dripping hair.

Jack sighed. "I am gettin' too old for this." He looked at his hand, almost visible from the distant streetlight. "I thought I was going to lose the last three fingers, comin' down that cliff." He stopped, stretched his back, and planted his hands on his hips. "Think anyone is still home, in town?" He ran his good hand through his hair. With the rain still pouring down, all he managed to do was to look slightly less like a drowned puppy.

"Possibly. By my count, we likely took out the majority of the gangs, the deputy, and left the sheriff with some officers back at the Mesa. Since we didn't see anyone on the main road nor are we being followed," she still peeked over her shoulder out of habit, "I think we only have a few townsfolk to deal with."

"Don't forget we heard some cars speedin' off," Jack added.

"Gang leftovers. That could screw things up a bit, if they didn't decide to run all the way to the next big town."

"Assume the worst."

"Hope for the best."

"Can't go back to the motel." He held up his phone, covering over the illumination. "Weak signal. Back here, at least. We need to call for back up," he added solemnly, "and clean up any injuries."

"I say we get into the diner. If we need to, we can defend that position. We'll have food and water too."

Jack nodded to her and edged forward.

She wiped away the rain streaming down her forehead. "I hope you didn't mind my interrupting your interrogation. You looked like you were having a fine time with Bergman."

"I was. He was telling me all sorts of things. For instance, this operation has been going on longer than Kýrios thinks. Townsfolk don't get money, but if they keep their mouths shut, they get richly rewarded with anything left by the losing side. It's kinda' sick if ya' ask me. Picking the pockets of the dead is grotesque at best."

"Did you get the impression they're laundering money too? That was one idea floating around at HQ."

Jack shook his head. "That would require too much outside contact. The way they work this is by playing their hand close to the vest."

She was pleased with the information he'd obtained, all while in immediate danger of being killed. In her estimation, it was classic Jack: thorough, reckless, and not just a little suicidally courageous. It was damn good work. She explained what she'd learned via her *contact* — adding at the start that she preferred to keep the contact a secret for everyone's safety.

Jack nodded and grinned his lopsided grin, leading her to wonder if he already knew about the *Sicilian*. Or if he appreciated the irony of her many dangerous secret contacts, himself included.

They crouched down and approached the diner's kitchen door.

While Jack had initially been along more for the ride, this sort of action had been his daily bread and butter, sneaking into fortresses, taking on enemy security, infiltrating the bad guys.

He drew his empty gun. He knew it was empty, but would someone else?

She copied him.

He pointed her toward the kitchen while he headed to the side door. She nodded in agreement and slipped away into the shadows at the rear of the building.

Tessa checked the door. Unlocked. Lucky her. Opening it, she listened for the sound the door might make, lights coming from inside, and any other signs of life within. Quietly, she slipped inside the kitchen and worked her way forward.

All the lights in the diner were on, except for one section of the bar. It appeared no one was there.

A slight motion caught her eye and Jack moved past the counter, gun held in both hands. They nodded to each other and began to stand up, to move more naturally.

Jack joined her in the darkened portion of the bar. He surprised her a bit by picking up his hat and jacket. "Coulda' used these." Swinging his arms into the sleeves and wincing while doing so, he asked, "So, while ya' were in Denver, think they gave our rooms a going through?"

"Of course. That's why I took everything vital with me. Except the hot spot, our samples, and charts in case they hadn't figured us out." She crept to the window by the front door. "I need to get to the jeep. My computer is there. I found a good place to hide it, inside the seat padding, but if we are going to contact Kýrios, we need to use it and not our cell phones."

"Got any ammo hidden in there too?" He looked out over her.

"But of course. Not much, only enough to make a difference."

"Okay. Be careful, Darlin'. Ya' hear me?"

"Why *Mr. Steed*, I do believe you care."

"I don't. I've gotten used to ya', *Mrs. Peel*, that's all."

Ha! "Prepare to repel boarders."

His moustache curled up at the sides. "Ya' love sayin' that."

He opened the door for her, holding the bell hanging off the back of it, and she eased out onto the shadows of the street. Jack stayed in place for a few moments, ready to do ... God knows what ... but he was ready.

Tessa sprinted from her hiding place, evading the pool cast by the streetlight. She kept her gun clutched in both hands and her body crouched low. As she reached the jeep, she signaled to him, and he closed the diner door.

Tessa crept low to the road, moving fast, approaching her target in stealth. At the jeep, she strained to hear any sounds of movement beyond those she or the wind made. Even the wind had given up on Montejo. Working her way around the jeep, she kept painfully alert.

Twice she found her hands were knotted around the gun and she shook them one at a time to loosen the muscles. Eyes forward, gun prepared, ears sharp, she reached out and touched the door with her fingertips until she found the handle.

The door opened too loudly, and she tensed and froze.

Waiting for any response to the noise, she opened the door … cautiously … praying for silence.

Sandwiched between the layers of padding on the passenger seat waited two laptops and cords, side by side. Inside the back of the seat, three boxes of 9mm and 10mm ammo rested. Not enough for a long siege, she determined, but enough for now.

Pebbles scattered.

But no wind blew anything.

Tessa turned toward the sound gun ready, anger primed.

It hovered. Darker than anything around her.

Human shaped.

It hissed.

A hand reached through its void.

Nothing had a chance to come out of her mouth …

… or her gun.

CHAPTER FORTY-FIVE

THE DINER'S KITCHEN HADN'T BEEN CLEANED for the night. That bothered Jack. It meant someone might be planning to return — and soon. Then again, for all he knew, he might have shot the cook back at Mesa de los Muertos. Stepping fully into the galley, gun at the ready, his back to the closed meat locker, Jack scanned the room over the tip of the muzzle. Confirmed. No one present — for now.

Jack slid his weapon into his belt and found an empty sack and a couple of bottles of water. If they had to hold out in a siege or were forced back outside to wait for support, water was the most important item beyond ammo. He located some small bread rolls too. Carbohydrates for quick energy. Protein might be a problem, but there was some deli-style meat that didn't look horrible.

Last stop was the bar. Tempting, but the booze was good for plenty more than swilling. Jack snagged a half-filled bottle of Tanqueray gin and slipped it into the sack. Clear. Clean. Good for sanitizing. But that was the only clear booze he could find. No vodka.

He went back into the kitchen hoping there was an actual first aid kit. That would be some welcome good luck. There was, but it was embarrassingly maintained. Still, better than nothing. And God, he needed a pain killer, if only cheap generic aspirin.

Oh good, the sewage was backed up too.

He thought about Tessa's words concerning the stink and the ghosts. Jack shook his head. The whole town smelled bad.

Once Tessa returned with their laptops and ammo, they could hold out for a good amount of time. The diner had only a few exits and a front set of windows. They would need to plan for things like teargas. No doubt the sheriff had such things at his disposal. Kitchen rags and water would be effective to dampen anything flammable or to cover their faces. Maybe they could just use the rags to keep the Montejo stench out?

Please, let none of this be needed, he prayed to no one in particular. Moving swiftly through the kitchen door to the main restaurant, Jack stopped mid-step.

Bergman had Jack's Smith & Wesson shoved rudely into Tessa's temple, and her arm wrenched up behind her.

Neither looked good for wear.

She had hot, red contusions on her cheek and eyebrow. He had a split lip, the start of a deeply bruised eye, and, judging by the way he kept feeling around his mouth with his tongue, a loose or broken tooth.

"Put it down, de Sombras. Put your hands where I can see them."

Jack set the sack of goods down. Standing up, he raised his hands as directed.

"Lose the piece. Use your gimpy hand."

Two fingers and a thumb sufficed to pull the gun out of his belt, but Jack's jaw tightened, and his muscles locked as he heard it hit the floor.

"Who the hell are you two! If you say USGS, I'll shoot you both."

"Goddamn it, Bergman," Jack spit the words out between his teeth. "I told y'all. And what I told ya' was true. I'm a man with a need to disappear."

Bergman's eyes narrowed.

Jack's eyes widened. *Damn it*, Bergman's eyes were black. Just like they were at the Mesa.

"Son-of-a-bitch liar. You've got skills I ain't seen on nobody for a freakin' long time." Bergman's speech was changing — splitting into two voices in unison. "Ain't nobody's got themselves talent like that from bein' dirt sniffin' scum."

An expression of confusion flashed across Tessa's face as her eyes glanced upwards towards Bergman. She heard it too — *the dual voices.*

Jack slowed his words, licked his lips, made his voice smooth. "I told ya' about that too. Y'all weren't listening."

"Listening to lies? You ain't got nothin' but lies." The pair of voices shouted — the sheriff and whatever else — it was unmistakable now. Bergman was sweating and bouncing on his toes, quite literally trying to hold himself together. His skin was gray, like smoke, and his eyes black beyond the irises.

It had to be the lighting in the diner, *that's it.* There was no such thing as *Skin Thieves* or ghosts. Jack hadn't seen what he thought he'd seen at the Mesa. Those weren't shadows or ghouls — just sick greedy people.

Okay, Jack Rabbit. Think fast and cool. "I can't help it if ya' don't want to believe me. I'm havin' some trouble believing y'all, since I thought ya' were more of an educated man. Maybe y'all are just a dumb yokel and can't keep yer head cool or listen to reason."

Bergman tensed up. His natural coloring returned, his cheeks sucked in, and his blue eyes glanced around the room.

That struck a chord. *Nice shootin' Tex.*

If Jack was right, Bergman was looking to see if anyone else had heard him slip up, showing his lower-class background. Bergman the yokel was the real man. Who was the other guy Bergman appeared to be? Split personality — such disorders did exist, unlike ghosts. Didn't matter, the yokel was the one who could be manipulated.

Jack continued, "But if I'm wrong, and y'all are a cool-headed man, smart and reasonable, we have plenty to talk about." Jack waited, sucking in breath through a small break between his lips, forcing his body to be still. Bergman would need a moment or two to collect himself.

Jack took each breath deliberately. His ribcage protested against the bruises he'd collected.

Bergman's face smoothed out, turned gray again. He even smiled slightly. Black eyes, fully encompassing his eyeballs, considered the situation calmly.

Shit. What the hell … eye color doesn't change …

Bergman was intensely focused on Jack now. "It's been an evening, hasn't it," Bergman hissed, but the other voice was stronger, louder than the one Jack knew belonged to the sheriff. And his eyes stayed that deep, haunting black.

Had the grayed-out version of the man taken over?

This isn't happening. "It sure has been. Now that I see I was wrong about you, perhaps we can talk about our situation. Like gentlemen." Oh, Tessa was likely seething about being ignored, but she showed nothing in her expression.

The gray man shrugged, forcing the body he was borrowing to comply with the movement.

There's no such thing as Skin Thieves or ghosts, Jack told himself over and over, while watching Bergman carefully. The man moved like a puppet under the control of someone—something.

"... like, how you're in love with your boss, though you didn't mention that." The sheriff, or whatever he was now, smelled Tessa's hair.

Jack's face fell. "W-What?"

Bergman kept grinning and sniffing. "You are, aren't you? Well, maybe only in lust, but I'm betting it's love. There are things a man does, a way he looks, a way he acts, that says he's doing it all for her. And *you are* that man. I've seen it over the centuries. You killed for her tonight. You've lied for her. But will you die for her? Will you?" Bergman's mouth moved around the words like he was chewing on glass or fighting to regain control of his body. He gripped Jack's gun tight and pushed the muzzle into Tessa's head even harder and wiggled his trigger finger.

Jack pursed his lips for a moment. Any quip he could have offered disappeared from his brain. He couldn't look Tessa in those beautiful violet eyes and say he didn't love her, that he wouldn't gladly give his life for hers — he'd been played. "Yeah. I would."

There. It was spoken. Out loud. No taking it back.

The truth was easier to tell than Jack thought it would. The gray man would know anyway, wouldn't he?

The sheriff snorted a cruel laugh. "Not so sure I believe you about her so-called innocence, but then, what you told me about yourself was only mostly true, not. . ."

Again, the man's mouth moved like it was trying to form different words, when the monster inside him fully gained control. His jaw snapped shut, and he ground his teeth together before he continued, in dual voices. "Wasn't a whole lie you told us, *de Sombras*. You forgot to mention the details about the real trouble you're in. That's right. We found *you*. Well, the sheriff did. He kept asking around until someone recognized the descriptions, the mannerisms, all of it. We know exactly who you are — *Jack*." His mouth formed each word with precision.

Jack felt his veins pumping in his temples and ringing in his ears. The room temperature plummeted to icy cold, and his feet cemented in place.

Found.

His focus pinpointed to the muzzle pressing into Tessa's flesh.

"I respect you more now. He respects what you did." The gray man added.

"I don't!" Jack threw back before he'd even thought about what he was saying.

"That's too bad. You were willing to do anything it takes — just like me. I bet with your past you have the contacts to accomplish what we discussed earlier. You can bring me into the filthy, modern world. More criminals to dispose of. More uncleanliness. You are my path. With you, I will have the reach to bring real Justice to the world at last, not only to this forsaken dirt pile."

Tessa had hold of the arm that pinned her against her tormentor. Jack knew she wouldn't risk aggravating him enough that he would shoot her, but she was working her grip around, testing his resolve to hold her. Bergman tightened his hold and kept going on about his plans. His voice, the *other* Bergman's voice, overpowered any hint of the man Jack and Tessa met days ago. "I am the Lawgiver. My every thought and word is the Justice of nations."

Jack waited. He refused to believe in power-hungry ghosts and shoved any visual evidence of the last few days into a mental hole. No time for that. Bergman was insane. But there had to be more to what he was thinking up in his psycho mind. Finally, mouth dry, Jack asked, "Yer in charge, so, how do we put our agreement into play?"

"Not '*our agreement*.' That was between you and the sheriff. It was a poor deal, but then, we both know the sheriff is a worthless, ignorant creature no better than those he kills for me. I think that —"

Bergman stopped in the middle of his speech, straining against something painful. The moment was brief, but it lasted long enough that Jack saw the sheriff he knew fighting to regain control. His mouth twisted to the side, opened as if to scream with nothing escaping his lungs. With tremendous effort, tightening his jaw and growling deep in his chest, the *gray* Bergman regained control and refocused his void black eyes on Jack.

Tessa's face paled. She mouthed the words, *Killed for him?*

Jack tried several times to form a question anything to keep the man talking long enough that the real Bergman could get a foothold, force another pause like before and then Jack could strike, free Tessa and get the gun away from him. But nothing worked, and with each question, Jack saw the gun pressed harder against Tessa's head.

He had run out of options.,

"Who am I talkin' to if yer not Bergman?"

"You know who I am, Jack." The monstrous identity inside Bergman forced a wicked grin, turned his head and sniffed Tessa again. "Go on telling yourself, 'There's no such thing as ghosts,' if that makes you feel better. Makes no difference to me. I know who I am."

"Then what do y'all want?"

The monster leered, taking his time, sweeping glances over Jack.

"What the hell do y'all want!"

"You."

CHAPTER FORTY-SIX

JACK'S HEART SKIPPED A BEAT. "No," his voice rasped out.

"I'm looking for an improvement. From piss-poor, power-hungry savage to a brilliant, worldly man, connected to powerful people? Jack, it won't hurt, you know — I will just take over. Since he's no longer needed, *we* will kill this worthless man with ease. Won't that be satisfying?"

Again, for a split-second, the monster inside Bergman wrestled for control. Pain and rage reddened his face as he struggled to hold himself together. This time, barely won, he clutched Tessa more viciously. For her part, she either hadn't noticed the man was at war with himself, or she was too scared to think straight. If that was the case, Jack couldn't blame her.

Jack shook his head. "No. Y'all are crazy. No!"

The monster pushed Tessa forward. "Yes, Jack. Yes. You'll let me because I will release *her* in exchange. You'll let me *re-skin* you in return for her life." He kept pushing Tessa toward Jack. "I've been watching you since before you arrived. You are strong, Jack. Still young. Powerful in ways you haven't learned about yet. I will make *us* into a formidable being — unstoppable — powerful in unimaginable ways."

"I said no."

A shrug was all he got in response.

Jack balled up his fists and stood his ground, forcing the advancing threat to halt or get close enough that Jack could make a grab for the gun. Bergman, either man or monster, stopped a few paces away and glared at Jack as if waiting for something.

My move? Okay then. "What about the rest of the people here?" Jack spat.

"You don't care about them. This place is long since gone. You see, I am the charmer — it is my charisma that tricks the lawless into agreeing to duel. The unclean are easy to manipulate, and the broken are ready to be fed their desires. This town will simply vanish into nothingness, consumed by its own greedy and unjust ways. You and I will have far better game to hunt and slaughter. We will bring Justice and Order."

The monstrous Bergman let go of Tessa and forced her onto the floor between them. "Have her. Take her as a sign of my good will."

At first, he smiled cordially, inviting Jack to collect Tessa from where she'd fallen. Tessa hadn't moved yet, staying low, giving him the room to charge if he planned to.

The sheriff wavered back and forth, tottering on his boots. He strained and grimaced for a moment, clenching and unclenching his jaw before balancing again. His breathing was labored now, and he had to fight to get every word out. "Tell me Jack ... wouldn't you ... wouldn't ... you ... like to have vengeance on those who want to kill you?" His body went stiff and shook with a violent spasm before he settled into himself again. But Jack knew he was still dealing with the monster inside the man. The sheriff's face was a rictus of rage and frustration. He ground his teeth, then said, "... the chance to be respected again?"

Jack looked down to Tessa. She was staring up at him, her lips silently saying, *Don't listen.*

Jack returned his attention to the sheriff.

"That's right, Jack. I know all about your so-called death. The cruel things they said and did. *We* could so easily make things right. *We* will rid ourselves of this worthless sheriff and avenge the wrong that was done to you. To your hard-earned reputation. *We* will be again where your strength and power placed you, but with mine added. Put fear into—"

Suddenly screaming in agony, Bergman clutched his head, and tried to hold himself together physically.

Two forms, one Bergman, the other sheer, spectral, human shaped, began peeling apart. Bergman's struggle to tear the entity away sent him crashing into one of the booths and back toward the agents. A ghastly ripping sound accompanied the parting of Bergman and the Skin Thief.

The gun flew from his grip and slid under a nearby table.

Tessa gaped at the result. "I don't think Bergman likes being called 'worthless.'"

Bergman sneered at her, but turned his rage toward the ghostly monster, flinging one of the bottles of booze at it.

The Skin Thief skittered into the far corner, ill-formed, rocking back and forth, looking every bit an anonymous shadow, until it blended into invisibility.

Jack seized Tessa's arm to slide her over closer to him. "First goddam time Bergman's done anything useful." He was ready to help her stand up, but Bergman grabbed and pulled back on Tessa's arm.

She yanked her arm free and rolled into a crouch next to Jack.

The sheriff glared at them. His skin was pale but natural, his eyes blue and crazed.

Bergman whipped his head side to side, shaking off whatever remained of the Skin Thief's manipulation, then he faced the agents. "Fuck you! Fuck all of you! I made this plan work. Not that thing, me!"

"There is no 'thing,' Bergman," Jack shot back. "But yer right about one bit; this is all on y'all. No invisible playmate to blame. It is yer doing alright." Jack's grin dropped. "What do ya' think, Darlin'? I've learned all I need to learn from this asshole. Split personality. Seriously psycho."

Tessa glared up at him, blinking. "Are you kidding? Jack, you've got to be seeing what I've been seeing!"

"All I see is the bastard who put a gun to yer head. Ya' got this, or shall I? I don't mind handling him, it'll be my pleasure in fact."

"We are going to have a chat about your stubbornness when this is over," she snarled loudly, planting her feet, and knotting her hands into fists.

Bergman's eyes were hard, his hands readied for violence, and the tendons in his neck pulsing. "Bitch, I promised you I'd have what I wanted."

Jack's entire body tensed in rage, until her hand reached out to hold him back.

"Oh no," Tessa growled, "He's all mine."

Relieved he was watching the natural Bergman, confidently reminding himself that the so-called Skin Thief was a result of ... of ... Bergman's split personality, that was it, his own over-stimulated imagination— bad lighting in the diner, Jack held his hands in the air and took one step back. Tessa was about to tear someone a new orifice and she wouldn't take kindly to anyone who kept her from it.

And no, he was not being stubborn, was he?

Before either of them could move, Bergman dropped next to the table and snatched up the gun, bringing it around to aim at Jack.

Tessa twisted and kicked at the weapon.

Bergman fired, but the shot went into the floor.

Jack slid back protectively, never taking his eyes off the fight and making sure to position himself so he could come to Tessa's aid if she needed him.

Tessa popped up behind the sheriff and slammed her knuckles into his back, kidney level. Following the natural flow of her movement, she jammed a right hook under his lowest rib, right over the liver.

Bergman stumbled sideways, then forward, turning at last to fire again.

Jack leaped forward and grabbed the gun in both hands, using it to swing the sheriff around his back.

The man spun and landed on the checkerboard flooring. He managed to control his fall and came back up onto his feet. Empty handed.

Jack held up the gun for the sheriff to see but not reach. "Here now, no cheating. Ya' pissed the little lady off. That was stupid. And stupid's got consequences."

Tessa backed up to open the space between them.

Nothing moved out of the shadows, convincing Jack that he'd been right all along — there was no such thing as ...

Bergman moved in to close the space, then stopped, gripping his head.

He shrieked. Bergman's skin became dappled in gray, and black oozed back and forth across his eyeballs. The damn Skin Thief again. The Skin Thief that didn't exist.

Tessa charged forward with the opportunity and slipped under his reach. One knee drove into his stomach and the other allowed her to roll back into a standing position.

The real sheriff and the shadow tore into two separate entities, again. Bergman howled and cursed at the thing as it tried to regain its hold on him.

It vanished as suddenly as it appeared, and Jack couldn't stop himself from looking into every corner of the room, wherever darkness held sway. *There's no such thing as ghosts!*

Jack heard the stomp of Bergman's boots coming his way. He turned in time to catch the sheriff's shoulders as the man grabbed him in a head-rush and slammed Jack into the wall. The impact knocked the wind and senses out of both men.

Jack dropped the gun, and it slid under the brochure rack near the entrance.

The sheriff fumbled for better footing, dazed. He staggered, finally standing and drawing out a knife to finish with Tessa.

The Skin Thief appeared above Jack, pitch black and so bleak, it was darker than anything he had ever seen. Shadows slithered up the wall behind Jack.

Methodically, the shadowy form wrapped around Jack's neck and chest, lifting the cowboy from prone until he sat helplessly on his knees.

"We will bring Justice to the world," the Skin Thief hissed into Jack's ear. "We are the perfect pairing. My desire for Justice and your physical being. And by our actions, all your crimes and errors are forgiven."

Blackness covered Jack's left eye and something hard probed into it. His pinned arms shook violently, but the spasms didn't release them from the Skin Thief*'s* hold.

Closing his blinded eye and jerking his head did nothing to stop the pain.

"Let me in," echoed in his ears.

The probing ghost-finger scrounged around the eye tissue and socket. Jack's jaw, his teeth — clenched, the scream forcing itself out of his lungs blocked. Another probe entered under his chin and filled his mouth, smothering his tongue. It tasted like decay. He heaved. Something began to wrap around his spine, freezing it. Around his veins. Around his heart.

"We can be greater than you know." With those words, images of the Mesa, different mesa dwellings and settlements appeared in Jack's mind. Bodies everywhere. "Lawless," the Skin Thief cooed. More visions of the dead flooded his brain. Some modern, some pioneer-looking, some so ancient Jack didn't know who or what to call them. "I have been forever. I do not die."

Tessa and Bergman were in a struggle across the room, the knife flashing in and out of sight as Bergman swiped for her and she danced back to avoid the blade.

Jack felt his right leg, exposed to the cold air where the pant was pushed up, to reach the stiletto he kept in his boot.

"Let me in, Jack, and I will guide you to greatness. Let me cover you in a new skin, and I will protect you."

Grasping the handle desperately in his shaking fingers, he tried to use its blade. His head was spinning, the ability to repel whatever it was that whispered in his ear. All the energy to fight was fading.

"No, no, Jack. That won't hurt me," it hissed. "I can't be cut or stabbed. I am smoke. I am air. I am beyond being harmed. I am impenetrable skin."

The Skin Thief gripped Jack's hand and squeezed. The stiletto crashed onto the floor.

Penetrable skin? Like having a hole punched in you? Sid … Sid said …

Jack forced his two good, left fingers into his jeans pocket, and pulled out the deer bone awl. His arms stopped shaking.

He heard someone cry out — a man's voice. Bergman? The Skin Thief? Jack didn't care. His arms were free. The probing appendages pulled back and out, as if hit by lightning.

Striking twice behind his head, twisting, striking another two times at the air where something should have been, Jack began slashing wildly. One eyed. Forcing the bile in his throat to stay down.

The Skin Thief shrieked.

A heavy blanket of darkness covered Jack. It pulled on him. Down. Down. Suffocating. Drowning. Choking.

"I only need your corpse, Jack, not your spirit. I'd prefer you intact, but I'll take what I can."

Jack lashed out with the bone awl.

Again. Again.

Where he struck, he could see slashes opening to let reality burst into the blackness. He felt violently sick again. Closing his other eye, he began ripping and slicing at the darkness, over and over, until he began to fall.

Falling. Falling.

Landing — hard …

… On the Diner floor.

A scream filled the air, along with a grotesque screech of ripping fabric, all echoing away into a roll of thunder.

The kitchen door slammed open and closed viciously. Then the back door.

It was gone? The thing.

Had it fled? Had he killed it?

Opening both eyes, all he saw was Bergman and Tessa exactly as they had been before his wrestling match with the Skin Thief.

Bergman slashed and Tessa leaped out of reach, coming back in with a well-placed side kick to his ribs that sent Bergman back a step. But the man was strong, and it would take more than fancy moves to put him down.

She was half the sheriff's size. He had a knife, but Tessa was faster, meaner, and better trained. She was kicking his ass.

In the relief that washed over him, Jack nearly laughed. What Bergman needed was an army, missile launcher, and a gatling-gun if he planned to beat her. After everything, God, he needed to see that.

Bergman slammed up against the wall near Jack and staggered forward. Jack stayed put, gave a slight lopsided grin, and did his best not to move.

With three powerful steps, Tessa used a chair to launch up to Bergman's shoulder height, lock her legs around his neck, and drop, allowing gravity to pull the big man down. She landed in motion on her knees.

Tessa pushed to close the distance between herself and the sheriff and caught his knife under her arm. She felt the slice in her flesh but didn't stop. The sheriff's momentum kept him moving past.

She locked her arm down on his and dragged him over. He was about to reverse his roll when Jack took the knife out of his hand and staggered out of reach..

"Quit playing with yer food, Darlin'." Damn it, she was going to take things too far.

She'd kept the sheriff's arm locked in hers and kicked out. Her boot heel met his mouth, shoved it to one side and his head promptly followed. Bergman lay on the floor, coughing, spitting the teeth he'd tried to keep.

The murdering asshole had a thick skull. But Bergman was finally down.

Tessa was gulping in air, but otherwise still standing.

Still shaking, Jack put the deer bone awl back in his pocket before Tessa saw it.

He didn't have time to explain what he didn't understand. Hallucination of a fight due to his injuries? Or a real fight with a monster – a ghost? He repeated those questions over and over, as he forced his legs to hold him upright. He didn't want to explain any of it. Not now. Not ever.

Out of desperation for his sanity, he clung to one concept: *there's no such thing as ghosts and Skin Thieves*. Maybe later he could try to understand.

Jack focused on reality — what he could see, hear, and touch. It had been a good call he'd made in taking the knife. Tessa might deserve the chance to pound Bergman into the ground, but the bastard was neither a weakling nor a fair fighter. She was better off taking her revenge and leaving Bergman to other authorities, the kind that would arrest him. No sense in ...

Jack stopped cold.

Tessa was painfully rubbing her ribs. A large blotch of blood stained her left side, where her white shirt peeked out from the slash. Jack looked wide-eyed from Bergman to Tessa and back, before concluding the blood was hers. "Christ, what did ya' do? What happened?"

Tessa looked surprised more than anything. "I got a little cut. I needed him to move closer and —"

"Shit!" Jack had nothing in his pockets to use to staunch the blood. But he had Gin and a horribly incomplete first aid kit in the sack. There was a crushed but yet-unopened package with gauze.

He didn't bother to ask, she wouldn't give him permission anyway, but sternly seated her in a chair, ordering her to keep still. The gauze barely absorbed any of the gin he poured on it.

"There had best be some tonic and lime with that," she demanded.

"Just shut up, will ya'."

She winced when he applied the makeshift astringent. "It's a cut, I tell you. And no, I'm not going to be quiet. I don't like it when men tell me to be quiet or invisible or smile more or—Ow!"

"I need to clean this, and I can't do that when we're arguing."

"Then don't argue with me."

"Yer the most maddening creature —"

"Yes, but do I ever tell *you* to shut up? No. I respect what you have to say. I've never told you, ever, to shut up. And your panic over a little cut isn't doing either of us any good."

"It's not a little cut."

"It's a little cut."

"It's not."

"Oh, for heaven's sake, Jack, let me do this."

"Ya' can't reach it."

"Yes I can ... oh will you stop telling me what I can and cannot do. I can reach that. I can tell it isn't a big deal. I can speak all I want —"

For reasons that eluded him entirely in that moment, he grabbed her in both arms and kissed her. Perhaps a little too hard, but he was caught up in the moment. The moment was so fast and so shocking, even to him, it went by without generating a memory.

The sky lit up, and fewer than three seconds between the light and the thunder.

He let go with a flood of reasons he shouldn't have done that racing through his head. Lots of reasons. Plenty of extremely good reasons. He squeezed his eyes shut and decided that maybe–an apology would be in order. Or, perhaps, he should hold still and let her break his nose. Either seemed appropriate.

Opening one eye, he found Tessa staring at him, eyebrow raised.

She leaned toward him. He was going to get slapped, and damn it, he deserved it.

"I told you, I require tonic and lime with gin." Was she rolling her eyes? "And now that I can see it, I'd say it is a medium-size incised wound, so, we were both wrong."

"Yes, ma'am."

"We can agree on that?"

"Uh, yeah, sure," he trailed off in his Texas twang.

She hesitated, looking over at the sack. "Anything better in there? Honestly, I'm not a great fan of gin, even with the additives." She took the gauze from him and pressed it against her cut ribs, turning it bright pink.

"Mostly swill. I was expecting to use it medicinally."

She sighed. "Just as well." She reached over and tenderly touched his battered, cut lip, and exhausted face.

Tessa's side burned as she pushed her phone back into her pocket. *I deserved that*, she scolded herself. *Showing off. Acting on anger.* She leaned against the dust filled planter boxes, giving her wound some relief.

The rain was letting up, but only briefly. Her senses, her gut, was quite clear that there was more coming. A bigger storm. Literally and figuratively. She would be gone by the time it struck Montejo. For now, the wind was attempting to pick up the soaked dirt with little success. Cool air tickled her skin and prodded her nerves.

Tessa laughed. Her ribs hurt, no, they broiled in livid pain. Yet, she couldn't stop. The preposterous direction her life had taken. *Ghosts, paranormal phenomena, parapsychology?* Her father and his quiet, stoic sensitivities were going to be offended. A chuff burst out before she could stop it and reduced the hysterics to stifled giggling. *Death?* Her father was going to have her committed the minute she told him about *Death*, being *Death's* student, the voice of *Death* in her head. Wouldn't he be right to do so? This was a sort of madness, wasn't it?

She tried her best to control the laughter and clutch her side, and not surprisingly didn't hear Jack come up beside her.

"What's so funny," he asked in a tender whisper.

"You. Me. This whole mission. Mostly me." She grimaced and swallowed back the mirth that begged for the release of tears. "I stirred up quite a mess, but I think it's done now. No more gang fights with collateral damage. You took care of Bergman?"

Jack nodded. "Cuffed and locked in the storeroom. He's so terrified, I didn't even have to force him into the closet. He ran in, to hide. Begged me to lock the door."

She shifted gingerly to face him. *Time to be serious.* "Jack, I called for an ambulance ..."

"I'll take ya' down to Cortez."

"No. I'll go by ambulance — on my own." She paused, noticing just how dry her mouth had become. "My dear Mr. Steed. You need to go."

For a long while, Jack kept quiet. Finally, shaking his head, he replied, "no."

"This is your chance, Jack. Go. Disappear. The ambulance will be here in twenty minutes. Kýrios was already on his way. He'll be here in an hour. He was planning on getting here early anyway, to catch me in the middle of mission failure."

"Y'all succeeded, Darlin'."

"I failed, in the best way." After a long breath, she went on, "I think you already worked this out, but I was under orders to eliminate you. The Agency isn't going to shrug off your survival just because I didn't kill you. You need to go — now. Get as far away as possible."

"I can't do that, Darlin'."

"And I can't let the world go another day without you in it. Even if only a few of us know where you are. Take the jeep, head for your Uncle's or anywhere you want."

"Nope."

"Jack, please, run. Be safe."

"And let ya' face yer boss alone? No. Y'all made a choice, to let me live. And y'all reminded me why I should live. I owe ya'. If y'all are stayin' on this road, I'm not gonna' leave ya' here to deal with the consequences alone."

Tessa sighed. "Someone, possibly wiser than me, said I'm on the wrong path. Perhaps she's right."

"After the last few days … maybe normal isn't workable. Maybe y'all need to follow yer heart, not yer head."

"My gut," she corrected with a smile.

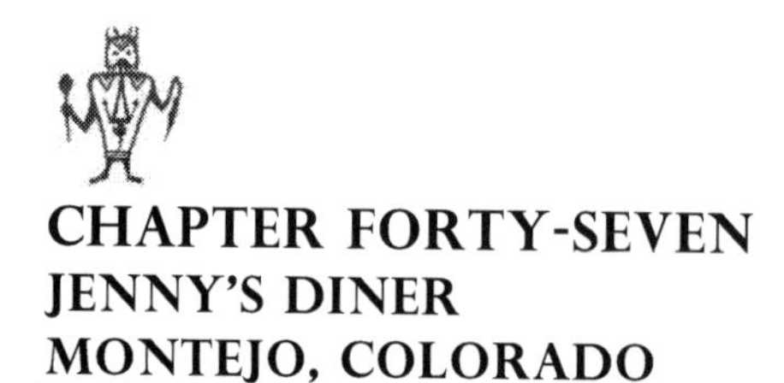

CHAPTER FORTY-SEVEN
JENNY'S DINER
MONTEJO, COLORADO

"WHAT THE HELL IS THIS?" Kýrios demanded. It was the first time he'd stopped to sit down all morning.

The Code Blue Team had arrived purposely too early, to catch Tessa unprepared. Yet they'd found T301 had things under control despite her being away at the hospital. When she returned in triumph – and with everything neatly tidied up – the Code Blue had to be called off. That did not go over well with every agent present, and Kýrios appeared to be one of those agents.

"What is this?" he growled again, pointedly not meeting her eyes but instead staring at the unsealed enveloped on the table in front of him.

"My resignation." Tessa announced and smiled. She settled herself into the Diner booth, slowly. Pain shot through her ribs, but the moment was worth it. Each stitch in her side made itself known, but she pushed through — this was her moment. The pain would pass, the wound would heal. And Kýrios would no longer have claim to her. "It's my way of saying I've completed my mission, Kýrios, and I no longer wish to be employed by the Athenaeum."

"It doesn't work that way, T301."

"Dr. Lancing." Correcting him was petty yet felt delicious. It made up for the pain.

Kýrios patted his brow with a napkin, attempting to appear undeterred. "Agent. When you signed a contract of employment, you agreed …"

"... To many things, yes, yes, I know. But really, we both recognize I'm not suited to this sort of work anymore. I've aged out. Learned the proper use of discretion — what you call 'hesitation'. I have figured out why no one stays with you for very long, and" she leaned in closer to say, "you and your Department 44 solution can go shove it." Tessa actually batted her eyelashes at him. Was he sweating a bit more?

"Ah, that. Since this mission has ended successfully, you won't need to worry about that."

"For now. What about next time, or the time after that? I won't play Damocles for you."

His face cycled through several expressions — surprise, anger, effrontery — finally landing on obsequious. "T301, children get a boogie-man story to keep them in line, we have the threat of Department 44. It is a useful tool. Surly you must agree?"

She held back her ripe comment. Her mouth remained pursed and twisted, her eyes narrowed. After a lag of time that drew more perspiration from Kýrios, Tessa said flatly, "I thought that 'Professionalism' was intended for that purpose. But then, considering who you hire, including myself, that might not occur to you."

"Witty as ever."

"Speaking of professionalism, here is my report. I'm after-mission resigning, not ... ghosting you."

Kýrios cautiously snatched the tablet out of her hand. He scrolled up and down, at first steadily, then wildly. Big eyes glared at her. "I don't see it."

"What?"

"You didn't put it in your report!"

Reaching across the booth table, despite the burning protest in her side, Tessa took back the tablet. She took her sweet time rummaging over the report. "What is it you are looking for? The methodology used to bring criminal leaders here against their own self-interest? Why, it's right here," she gingerly returned the item, sliding it this time.

Kýrios grabbed the tablet again and read. A bead of sweat sat dangerously on his brow.

Behind him, M021 walked up, unburdened by the atmosphere, and read over his shoulder. He studiously ignored her, and she took an interest in the silverware.

As both men's expressions turned from dispassionate to disgusted, she knew what passaged they'd reached.

M021 glared at her.

Guess I'm not invisible after all. "A problem, gentlemen?"

"Are you out of your goddamned mind?" M021 shouted, causing everyone in the diner to turn. State police, other agents, men in suits wishing they were somewhere with air conditioning — all were taken aback by the outburst.

"Agent?" Tessa sounded so ridiculously saccharine that she thought she was going to giggle. But this was not a laughing matter, her ribs and future reminded her.

"M021, hush up!" Kýrios began gesticulating with the tablet. "You want me to accept this?"

"I'd be careful, that's an expensive piece of equipment."

"This is … is … it's bullshit."

"Sir? Language."

"Oh, for God's sake! You want us to believe … that …"

"That you're not getting your magical, mystical, mesmerizing device or secret recipe?" Tessa moved, to settle herself for the verbal fight she was ready for, was hoping for. The pain in her body screeched and she tapped it for all she could get. "No. You're not. There is no device or methodology that the Agency can use or sell." She settled carefully on her arms. "Sheriff Connor Bergman tapped into an ancient power he didn't know how to control. You won't either. As far as I'm concerned, the matter will no longer be a problem. Whatever that being or power was, it has abandoned Bergman and is likely gone. The Athenaeum will not be able to find it or use it."

"An ancient what?"

"It's difficult to explain without bringing up the Paranormal. Which, if you will recall, was the exact reason you chose me for this mission. It is not something any of us will ever be able to discuss without either screaming or laughing. This — let's call it an entity — was the source of control over others as well as the key motivator to the killing. Based on all of the events, there is no reason to believe the entity still exists.

One way or another, it is gone and cannot be recovered for use by the Athenaeum.

"In the meantime, the State Police have taken custody of Bergman on charges of kidnapping, murder, attempted murder … the list is substantial. Our *not* being available for interrogations, depositions, or testimony will neither hinder nor obstruct those efforts. I suspect we will not have to worry about Bergman either." *One, two, three, breathe.* "I believe we can close this mission successfully, as the collateral damage will now cease — at least in those cases directly related to this mission. I'm sure your client will be relieved that his property investment won't be devalued by any further innocent dead bodies."

She had never before left Kýrios speechless. Quite satisfying. *Trust yourself.*

M021 shook his head, slammed his hands down on the table and leaned aggressively towards her. "This is bull! You took whatever it was that controlled those men …"

Kýrios raised his hand and pushed M021 back.

Tessa noted that others in the diner also began moving in, protectively. She didn't need them, but it was nice to know they were there.

"We'll discuss your conclusion when we return to Seattle. What I was looking for, was the situational status of …" He gestured.

Tessa played stupid.

Kýrios gestured again.

A shadow moved across the booth, cast from the side door of the diner.

M021 folded his arms, ignoring all but Tessa.

"Agent T301, where is the proof you promised me," Kýrios demanded.

A strong hand clamped down on M021's shoulder and shifted him out of the way.

"Kýrios, I never agreed to your requirement. I never promised proof."

There was a lull in the noise of the diner. Kýrios let his hands fall off the table and into his lap. "He's not been dealt with?"

Tessa blinked.

"He's right behind me?"

Tessa smiled.

Jack planted his hands where M021's had been on the table. Shifting his hat back and looking as mean and tough, and sexy as she'd ever seen him, Jack put his lips right next to Kýrios's ear. "I'm not dead. And I need ya' to hear me loud 'n clear. Me and this fine lady, we've decided we've had enough of y'all, and by that I mean all y'all in the Business. We're done. We're havin' none of it. So, we're goin' our merry way. No harm nor foul. Live and let live. Y'all do you, and we'll stay out of yer way. And y'all'll leave us be."

"You, sir, are a traitor."

Jack said nothing. His silence was disturbingly effective.

Tessa held herself on her arms, clenching against the pain. "Oh, and I don't suggest you, or your little friend Manny, continue tugging on any loose threads in that fabric, or you might find you're unraveling something big and hideous." She stopped with her solicitous tone. "The kind of big and hideous that will make Department 44 look comfy and charming."

Jack straightened up and stroked M021's tie, then slowly corrected its placement on the agent's neck. "Now, we have all sorts of information that shouldn't go public. Should either or both of us experience anything *unfortunate*, we've made certain that there will be nothing to stop the exposure that each of y'all personally, and the Athenaeum — not to mention several other excellent institutions — will endure. And I guarantee ya' my Uncle, from the CIA, doesn't know anything about how, when or where, so y'all had best not pester him either. CIA gets fussy when y'all start bothering their honored retirees."

M021 knocked Jack's hand away in a pathetic motion. "I have family on the *Committee*."

"I suspected you were behind the sudden Code Blue," Tessa replied. "And my ticking clock. Is that how low the Athenaeum has gone? Can you blame me for wanting to retire? Well, I have family, too."

Tessa was happy to let them think whatever they wanted to. Uncle Mario would have been proud. "And friends and relationships, all over the world. Remember, Manny, I told you it was important to build relationships. Don't count on getting them because of something as banal as birthright."

Outside, someone was shouting. While Jack kept his focus on Kýrios and M021, Tessa glanced out the window. The crowd of officers outside were reacting to the disturbance but not with any great energy. Perhaps it was something they found laughable. Soon, she returned to the brewing storm inside the diner.

"I'm not taking lessons from some old bitch and the traitor she's screwing." The smirk M021 offered Tessa was neither sincere nor natural. She knew that he needed a distinct, public lesson in manners. Ribs and sutured skin screaming at her, she slid out of the booth.

Jack stepped in front of her.

Kýrios held out a flabby, warding arm in front of M021. "Stop it. I won't have my agents brawling in public. This matter is done and closed. There are times when situations have only one option. This is one of those times." He wrestled with the table to get out of the booth, constantly looking to Jack or M021.

The shouting outside had grown more deranged.

Kýrios craned his neck as if interested in what was happening. "Will someone go see what all that racket is! For God's sake, has no one any dignity around here?"

It was Bergman making all the racket, arguing with his captors who had brought him to the State Police car parked at the entrance of the diner. He must have seen Jack and Tessa inside. Although handcuffed, he pointed to them. "He's the One. He's the Justice Keeper now! He stole him!"

Laughter was all that he received for his rant.

Bergman used his enormous size to body-slam the state trooper nearest his right.

"Oh hell," Jack shouted. "That asshole's trying to get loose!"

Tessa and Jack raced through the front door. Officers in the diner split between the two exists, front and side.

Tessa sensed it — a wall of perfume, clattering beads, infinite struggle — she kept moving, clutching her side.

Bergman had the other trooper on the ground.

"Bergman, stop!" Tessa pulled her weapon from its waistband holster. Jack was right beside her. M021 stood behind Jack.

Shoot, girlfriend, shoot now, Death whispered to her.

Now you show up.

Shoot.

No! Not yet.

Classic grip. Aim. Clear view. "Bergman! Stop!"

Bergman pulled the trooper's gun out and spun towards Tessa.

Shoot!

Yes, now.

Two holes, center of mass, Bergman's chest. No hesitation. No joy — only duty.

A round hole burst through the diner's glass window beside him. A second shot entered one side of Bergman's skull and blasted out the other.

Bergman jerked and slumped in the dirt.

Two sharp reports echoed in the distance.

"Sniper!" an officer shouted.

"What the hell," Tessa screamed, diving to the ground.

The crowd outside dove to cover amongst the vehicles. The federal agent seized Tessa and pulled her behind a truck. Her chest and sides burst into flaming pain, effectively immobilizing her.

M021 jerked, fell back from where he'd stood, landing on his side.

Jack dove onto the dirt beside Tessa, demanding to know if she was okay, but all she could see was M021 on his back.

"Agent down!" Tessa shouted, pointing to M021 as he struggled to maintain his basic motor coordination. "Is he hit? Can anyone tell if he's been hit!"

An officer placed his fingers on M021's neck, but stopped, and shook his head. "No, ma'am. I think he got ... punched? Somebody punched him?"

Tessa scowled at Jack, who smiled and shrugged too innocently.

Keeping low and moving wisely along with the officer, Jack crept through the cars with a bevy of other agents and officers.

As long as she didn't move too much, the pain would subside, wouldn't it?

Her gut said they were safe — for now.

Had someone wanted to kill her or Jack, they would be dead. The attack was brutally fast and efficient. Sniper at a distance.

Somebody didn't want Bergman talking. About what?

Who sent him … or her?

Uncle Mario? No. Maybe. She kept breathing through the throbbing.

One mystery compounded by another. That mystery was going to take time to solve.

Tessa wanted to search for a sign of the shooter's location, maybe a flash reflected from their scope, or dust rising from their heels as they fled. Unless the shooter was a true professional, lying prone in plain sight and yet invisible.

So Tessa waited, and she watched, and she hoped Jack would be very, very lucky indeed.

Well done, girlfriend. Well done, my student.

Was it rude to tell *Death* to fuck off?

It probably wasn't smart.

Lady of Death? We are so going to have to define our relationship.

CHAPTER FORTY-EIGHT

THE OFFICER AND JACK stood over Bergman's corpse. One clean shot to the side of the head, another set of shots in the chest care of Dr. Tessa Wells-Lancing. The ugly exit wound on the head was icing on the proverbial cake, though why someone felt it necessary after Tessa neatly handled things troubled him ... briefly. "Sniper used a NATO 7.62mm," Jack said, dispassionately considering the ammunition. He'd recovered the bullet from where it had impacted in the dirt outside the diner, and now handed it to a police officer.

"No sign of the shooter, according to the marshal," the officer added, shaking his head. "Possibly the sniper was up on the hill, though that would be one hell of a shot. No other injuries or fatalities."

"Pretty damn specific shooting," Jack noted.

"Yep. They wanted this old boy and no one else. Smells like a pro hit." The officer quietly put away his patrol weapon.

Looking around at the crowd of law enforcement personnel, Jack could see the mixture of reactions. He figured some were angry, a cop had been shot. Annoyance on the faces of the suits. They were hoping Bergman would testify and make closing this weird case easy. Concern on the face of the state trooper. Hell, he had to tell the politicians what happened, why, and listen to them figure out what to tell the public, if anything. No one, Jack decided, was actually sorry Connor Bergman was dead. His chest ached a bit at the thought. He hoped someone other than Uncle Joe would be sorry Jack was dead when that day arrived. Well, maybe Tessa would ...

"... all these uniforms around and this guy gets hit?" The expression on the officer's face was curious and expectant.

"It prompts the question: who wanted *Bergman* dead? Couldn't have been a cop hater, or this whole crowd would have been a target." Jack played along with the assumption he was one of them. "Y'all'll have to interview the other townies. One of them may have a grudge. One of his deputies would be on my suspect list."

"What other townies?" The man's face screwed up.

"Waitress at the diner?" Jack thumbed back toward the old 50s building. The officer didn't change his expression. "Farmers? Bartender? Garage attendant? We never got his name — we called him 'Gas Guy.'" No change in the officer's glare. "Bergman's deputies?"

The look, which could have meant *you-are-crazy*, only got worse on the officer's face. "Uh, Mr. de Sombras, this town hasn't had any population since the last flash flood."

"Last ... wait ... y'all are ahead of me on this. Flood? No people?"

"Out of towner, huh?" Nodding, the officer carefully explained, "Just before the drought got bad, there was a flash flood in this area. Mud slides, fast moving water, the works. Biblical level stuff. If anyone survived, they moved away. This place hasn't been habitable for ... I don't know ... eight years? A lot of people died."

Ringing filled Jack's ears.

"But Sheriff Bergman?"

"Sheriff? He had oversight on this place. Other than that, his jurisdiction was pretty big. But he wasn't no sheriff. Park overseer, as far as I know. Where he got the uniform and car ... beats me. Always talked big, I hear."

His hands were close to numb. "'Last flood? There was another?"

"Yeah, last night. Didn't you hear?"

"I was with my partner at the hospital in Cortez."

"Everyone was surprised that there wasn't an evac-order last night for all the teams. First rains in eight years. The ground's so damn dry, the water won't soak in, so we got one hell of a flood. Took out the road," he pointed south, toward

Mesa de los Muertos, "nobody's getting back there for a long time. Shredded everything. May have messed up some ancient ruins there too, and I sure do hate to see any archaeological sites get lost. I'm a sucker for that stuff."

Yup, Jack's hands were completely numb now. "I think I get your point now."

"Sure you didn't hit *your head*?"

"I'm not sure of much right now."

Jack returned, looking pale and confused. He relayed to her all the details about the search for the sniper, yet Tessa could tell he was holding something back.

It wasn't the manner of Bergman's death. Jack had seen worse. He'd done worse.

"Very convenient." Jack tried to dust off his arms.

"Too convenient," Tessa said blandly, while he helped her to stand up from the flower bed she'd been sitting on. The dirt was already dry, even after the evening's storm, but a distant thundercloud offered a moment of hope that more might come.

It was painful but comforting to end up briefly in his arms. So what if it was getting hotter out. He was warm, in a way that wasn't measurable.

Oh my, yes, she was emotionally compromised. Whatever he was keeping to himself, she guessed he wouldn't say until they were alone. And she knew he might have some pointed questions for her. Where would this all lead? She didn't know, yet she was happy to explore the possibilities.

Why was she dizzy like a kite cut free and whipping wildly in the gusts? She reached out with her senses. Nope. No *Death* nearby. So very lovely — gut instinct and head were in sync.

"I don't know," he said, as though reading her thoughts, "seems to me this is the first time we've ever been allowed to go our own way."

"It's risky what we're doing."

"Would ya' have it go differently?"

She shook her head. "No. But I do have some big ideas."

He didn't look comfortable.

"What is it?"

Jack helped her into the jeep, telling her what the officer had told him about the dead town, the flash floods, and Bergman's real job.

Tessa stopped him from helping. For one thing, he wasn't helping at all, distracted as he was, he was accidentally manhandling her a bit. For another, he looked like he couldn't digest any of what he'd heard all morning.

But this new information changed *everything*.

"Finally leavin'." Gas Guy stood in front of his garage as though nothing was different from the days prior. His eyes were shadowed, yet he didn't have that threatening aura about him anymore. He nodded politely to them, a gesture of finality as he cleaned whatever it was he always kept in his hands, turned, and walked out on the road toward the Mesa.

Gently pushing Jack aside, she limped around him and into the street, skimming around puddles and hating the grief her ribs gave her with each movement. "Wait!"

Gas Guy stopped but didn't face her.

"Where is everyone? Where have they gone?"

"Back to the Mesa?"

"The road's out."

He shrugged.

"The ... the one who tried to kill us ... tried to possess Jack? Is he gone? For good?"

Gas Guy glanced over his shoulder. His face appeared blurry. "The water's come. Things must be clean now." He calmly walked away, fidgeting with his tool, and nodding his head to a rhythm that was only inside his own mind. "Yeah, must be clean now."

"Darlin'? Who are ya' talkin' to?"

Tessa shot a look at Jack, pointed toward Gas Guy, and turned to see that Gas Guy was no longer there. Not on the road. Not out in the open desert with a huge thunderhead looming across the horizon.

"Figures," she whispered, thinking of all the questions she would have liked to ask. Her wound began to sting, and she held her arm down against it. The jeep wasn't too far away, and she wandered back, mumbling at the opportunity missed.

"Darlin', please tell me you were talking to *someone*?"

She started to reply, then hesitated. "The water's come back, did you know that?"

"Yeah."

"Things must be clean now."

She pushed around to her side of the jeep, clutching her side, hoping the burning would stop.

Jack chose not to comment as he'd focused on helping her with her seatbelt once she finally sat down. He was gentler this time. "*Mrs. Peel*, I don't want to be needed. I want a goddamn vacation."

EPILOGUE
MONTAGUE, RANCH LAND NEAR MT. SHASTA NORTHERN CALIFORNIA

UNCLE JOE SNARLED SOMETHING about a package for Jack. "Something actually addressed to a *John Steed*, whoever the hell that is, Ranch Hand, Montague, CA.

Ranch Hand?

Jack moved his hands away from the item on the kitchen table and stared in momentary horror, from the box to Joe to the box again. Joe waved him off, explained the extreme measures his team had taken to make sure the package was safe, which had included him missing his own breakfast *and* lunch. All the *thank yous* in the world were not going to make Joe happy. Was Joe ever happy? Yes, when he was unhappy or showing off his connections in the dark, power-behind-the-throne world.

For a moment, Jack wondered if that was *his* future. He doubted that it would ever happen. He'd have to live that long for starters. He was certainly putting the mileage on his body though.

Joe kept mumbling and pulling out rod, reel, beers, and tackle box. He mumbled louder, something that included *down to the river*. Joe didn't fish. He napped, listened to the latest ballgame, and drank his beer.

Wishing the grumbling man a good day of *fishing*, Jack again approached the package.

A box. 24" by 24" x 12". No wonder Joe had shown concern. Perfect size for a basic bomb. Ah, but alas, not today. Horses, stall mucking, and more bales of hay to move around so he could move the truck back up to the house were all the items he had on today's agenda. Maybe there'd be a bomb tomorrow. Not today.

If it had once been a neat and tidy box, appropriate for shipping through the post office, it wasn't anymore. All of the tape and paper had been cut. Fingerprint powder still stuck in some places. The cardboard sides had been slashed to make sure no wiring or C4 layers were concealed. The interior package had been sliced open and a faint aroma of the chemicals used in tracing explosives wafted up. The White House didn't get this level of security.

Good old Uncle Joe.

The inner package was marked, *To My Cowboy.*

Jack smiled, first in his lopsided way, then fully, pushing both ends of his moustache upward.

One thin, square box sat on top of the larger box. They had both been opened by Uncle Joe's security detail, and roughly reclosed. He started with the smaller one.

Inside, wrapped in layers of tissue, was something circular, metal, and moderate in weight. Jack kept tearing away the layers. Beneath it all lay a band of silver and leather. Elegant yet tasteful. Masculine. Oval conches of finely tooled sterling were separated by simple silver bars, each attached individually to a leather hat band. It was a work of art without being ostentatious.

Jack opened the second box, not so much surprised by the contents as much as thrilled with how the exquisite, black fur-felt Stetson would look with the hat band. That Stetson was one of the best the maker had to offer, and damn expensive too. The brim was flat. He'd have to start training that, slowly and gently, until it curved into the right shape. Just the way he liked it. That was not something to be rushed.

Yet, he couldn't resist setting the Stetson on his head, to feel the fit. To know the smooth luxury of fur felt under his fingers. The crisply set crown. Tight. Unworn. Solid.

Looking one last time at the gifts before placing them in a secure spot for later, he saw the note, pinned to the top of the bigger box.

Saddle Up.

Jack grabbed his old hat from the stand near the front door and hurried out into the weather. Cold. Crisp. Breezy as usual. The rushing sound of water being faked by pine needles whooshing overhead. His phantom finger pains shot through his hands — he didn't care. His lower back, his still-bruised ribs. He didn't care. He walked as fast as his long legs would carry him until he was near to jogging when he reached the hay barn.

Looking inside, he saw nothing.

He stood, hands on hips, visually rummaging through every inch of the barn. He knew *every inch* of it. Broken slats, the smell of hay and weeds, pickup truck parked from before his adventure. *Every inch.*

No one.

Wait. A new blanket covered something on the truck's flatbed.

The hay fork had been moved over to his latest stack of bales and plunged into one. Dangling off the long wooden hand was a piece of paper tied with a satin ribbon. So *she* was here. Holding back on his amusement, he freed the paper, which read simply, *We're Needed, Mr. Steed.*

"Needed? Right now?" Jack turned to see Tessa leaning against the door frame of the barn, smiling like a cat with feathers from the proverbial canary. "Isn't this supposed to be 'We're needed, *Mrs. Peel*?'"

"Soon. But, before we get started," Tessa started coyly, "I thought you might want to see these." She held out a box and winced.

"Still hurts?"

"More sore than painful," she gingerly patted her side. "You?"

"I'm beginning to feel more like Uncle Joe, and just as old."

Giving the box a brief once-over without opening it, he grinned broadly, both sides of his lips lifting in sneaky satisfaction. "Speaking of Joe, he's been following the aftermath for us."

"He told me when I arrived. Without a steady supply of power vacuums, the street violence have cooled down. Though, sadly, the gangs have found other excuses to keep killing each other."

Jack could only sigh.

"*Quelle surprise*," she mocked.

"Funny how these things tend to get hushed up ..."

"... Especially when the paranormal gets mentioned?" He could tell she was watching for his reaction. "I'd say this is no longer our case, though I may keep my eye on it for a little while longer."

"Not satisfied it's over?" Jack turned his head like a cocker spaniel and put the box on the back of the pickup truck, next to the blanket.

"Possibly." For a long time, she stared out at the white-topped volcano across the valley.

"On to new things?"

"We should review everything thoroughly and make sure we're properly prepared. Rushing into the unknown is rarely wise, though often fun." She strolled past him and lifted the new blanket piled on the back of the pickup. Beneath the red and black Pendleton wool was a nice wicker basket. Swirling the blanket like a matador, Tessa draped it across the lowered tailgate.

The basket, Jack discovered, held a bottle of excellent Prosecco wine, two fluted glasses, an ice bucket, a 2-tier stand of cut sandwiches, and something covered in chocolate. Once she'd assembled everything, she motioned for him to sit.

"By the by, the hat is ..." He couldn't find any word that fit right. "Thank you."

"Perfect for a business gentleman from Texas, relocating to San Francisco." Tessa slid the small box back over to him.

Not sure what to expect, Jack opened it carefully and found business cards inside, freshly packed in tight rows.

"Going legit," he said, a bit too pensively.

"It's only been a few months and already the buzz around your survival has increased. At this point ..."

Jack raised his hand. "I know. I had this discussion with Joe. At this point, there's no hiding anymore." He stared at the box. "These just make it ... well ... real. I know that sounds stupid."

Settling the wine bottle between her knees and staring out toward the distant mountains, Tessa chewed on the inside of her lip for a moment. "This was my doing. I outed you. I will find a way to make it right."

"No, Darlin', I outed myself. I thought I could be fine disappearing from the world, but I ... I hated hiding. I wasn't made to be sittin' around." He leaned back, crossing his legs. "If I truly wanted to vanish, I would have shaved my head or had plastic surgery. Gone off the grid, deep, not headed to my uncle's. I coulda' locked myself away where no man, woman, or satellite could find me. I know how that's done. I've helped others do it. So, maybe, in the end, half of me wanted to be found so I could put an end to the worry and boredom."

Her eyes were wide with hurt. "Joe was worried you might ... might have a suicidal philosophy to all this." She grasped his hand, as if tying him permanently to the Earth. "Too much guilt or fear that you actually are the man they said you were. He doesn't believe it, nor do I."

Jack let that roll around in his head for a moment. "Do ya' trust me?"

"Yes," she replied solidly.

He stood up for a moment, allowing every detail of *that terrible day in his life*, and all the days since, to play like a movie on fast forward. He stretched his back in sympathetic pain with the reminiscences and took a long, deep breath.

Even in the barn, the air tasted good. It smelled and tasted alive. If he didn't trust her now, the time would never arrive. "There are things I can't tell ya', Darlin'. I can't tell Joe. Not one single word of *those things* can be said aloud to either of ya', or y'all're as good as dead. Ya' hear me?"

"I have a bad feeling I know where you're going with this, but yes, I hear you."

The silence was brief, although it hadn't felt like that to him. "After my resurrection became news, I reckoned they would come for me. They haven't." He took in another breath of air, catching a touch of her scent in the mix.

"I thought the same at first. But .."

"They can't risk my getting killed now. Too many folks would start asking too many questions. And, as of now, I don't think they're any too eager to have what we know get out to the public. I also think they want to believe we won't casually throw them under a bus. In fact, I fully expect they will just pretend never to have known us at all. There's going to be a lot of silence and denial. They're waiting for us to act, now, testin' the waters to see if we'll say or do anything to cause 'em trouble."

Tessa closed her eyes and clutched the bottle. "And we won't." Opening them again, she had to look into his and he made certain she kept his gaze. "Unless we're forced to."

"Agreed." Jack sighed. "But I promise ya', on my life, those charges are … not precisely right … it's complicated … but I swear I'm not a traitor." He looked to her, desperate for her acceptance. God, he needed her approval.

"I know that. You are not and you shouldn't... she hesitated.

"Don't go there. And I know ya'," he shook a gloved finger at her. "Ya' want to fix this because that's what ya' always want. To fix things. Darlin', some things cannot be fixed."

She nodded. "And some things shouldn't."

Appreciatively, he bowed his head to her.

Tessa swept a falling piece of red hair out of her face. "You have secrets you have to keep, even from me and Uncle Joe." She found her smile again. "I won't ask. Girl Scout's Honor," Tessa held up three fingers. "Is that acceptable?"

He nodded.

"Besides," she added, "you're much too busy now with our new agency."

He looked at the business card box again. Not nearly as satisfying as the Stetson and silver hat band, still he opened the box as if it were a gift – which technically, it was.

Holding up the dark gray card with black, raised lettering and an elegant, chiseled border, he admired how simple, tasteful, and modern it was. Best of all, it appeared quite serious in purpose, which was going to be important.

They were setting themselves up for some real heartburn. The sides of his moustache rose. They might as well be classy while being sneered at.

Jack N. de Sombras
Owner, Lead Investigator, Consulting Security Analyst

Praetorius Services Group, LLC
San Francisco New York City Denver

Private Solutions & Intelligence. High-level risk assessment, conflict resolution, security consultation, and individual protective services.

"'N?'"

"Nathan or Nathaniel. Your choice."

"Ya' gave me my Mom and Daddy's names?"

"I thought that would be good for your fresher start in life."

He smiled broadly. "Ya' really believe all this is going to work?" Jack turned the card over a couple of times.

"Yes. It's high time." She winked at him. "You said it yourself — I'm a natural born Fixer."

"Y'all can only warn a kid so many times about danger until they stick their finger in the socket and find out for themselves."

She rolled her eyes and turned a sweet hue of pink. "Alright already. Yes. I want to solve problems for people, problems that can't or won't be solved by anyone else."

"I don't know," he teased. "What're the pay and benefits like?"

"Crap and zero: specifically, in that order. However, I anticipate that will change."

He put on his *how so* look for her.

"I'm not going to lie to you. We're going to be taking those cases that no one wants to touch. *Questionable, implausible, and wholly improbable.* In the process, we'll be laughed at, made fun of, and hardly ever put on the invite list to anyone's holiday party. Frankly, Jack, I don't care what our so-called colleagues think."

"Aw hell, if no one else will help ..."

"... We should. I think we'll be up to our asses in very, very strange casework. Very, very soon."

"Let's see if I've got this right. *Questionable*, such as vendettas, old grudges, death threats, a family curse that interfering with the conduct of daily business?"

"Yup."

"*Implausible*, such as in-house corporate espionage by non-in-house persons, or security risk assessment for unique business models that shouldn't actually exist or work?"

"Yup."

Jack hesitated for a moment. "*Wholly Improbable*, as in ghosts, ghouls, and things that go bump in the night, scaring normally reasonable people into giving up industrial or government secrets. And all sorts of stupid human tricks?"

"Bingo!"

"*Paranormal*." After another long pause, Jack sighed so heavily even the persistent wind respected his reticence. "There's no such thing as ..."

"... Ghosts." They finished together.

"We're the goddammed *X-Files* for hire," he playfully snarled.

"Without the government interference they suffered from."

"Or the government budget they worked with." He watched the clouds out near Mt. Shasta drift along. It was all just crazy enough to work. "Bring it on."

Tessa kissed his cheek.

"Fine, *Mrs. Peel* or should I say *Agent Scully?*" He nodded toward her catsuit and boots. "But no aliens! No UFOs, no USOs, no little green men, no motherships, no abductees, nada. If it doesn't happen firmly on planet Earth, we're not touching it. And you can forget about any cults that want to resurrect the dead." Jack settled on the tailgate, arms folded, satisfied he'd made his point crystal clear.

With a soft, controlled pop, the Prosecco was ready to pour into the two fluted glasses. "We have a potential case already. Could be a case of industrial sabotage at NASA or ghosts in the machinery."

"We're not set up to take government jobs yet, how are we taking something from NASA — something *not about aliens*, right?"

"No aliens. Earthly engineers." She handed him the glasses while she poured. "But first, a celebration."

"I'm not dressed for the occasion."

"You are always perfect for the occasion."

Jack's skin warmed while he offered her his lopsided smile and narrowed twinkling eyes.

"Oh, I almost forgot." Tessa reached into the basket one more time and withdrew a perfect pale carnation.

Her delicate hands settled the flower into a buttonhole on his denim jacket, getting close enough that he could smell that light, musky perfume, even over the mud and natural debris. Damn, she was beautiful.

"Now you're all set, *Steed*."

"We're needed, *Mrs. Peel*?" He sat beside her, holding out his glass. "To being needed?"

She lifted her glass to him in a salute. "To being needed."

Jack nodded his agreement and put a hand over his heart to seal the deal. In that instant, he felt the bone awl tucked under his shirt, hanging there protecting him still, from the ghosts he adamantly refused to believe in.

His smile softened, and he added, "And to Sid."

ABOUT THE AUTHOR

T. E. MacArthur, author, artist, historian, amateur cat whisperer, and parapsychologist wannabe lives in the San Francisco Bay Area. She wrote the standout Steampunk series, ***The Volcano Lady,*** and the classic, one-shilling serial, ***The Gaslight Adventures of Tom Turner.***

A Place of Fog and Murder is her Noir-Punk mystery, bringing a fantasy sci-fi 1930s San Francisco to life with her tough-as-nails femme-fatale-detective, Lou Tanner P.I., through exciting car chases and Chandleresque witty repartee. She's even written for several specialized publications, anthologies, and was an *accidental* sports reporter for **Reuters News**.

Her storytelling dramatically shifted direction recently to embrace the paranormal, her lifelong obsession, with the creation of her newest novel, **The Skin Thief**, set in the Four Corners region of Colorado, not too far from where she grew up.

You can find her at ***www.TEMacArthur.com***

Made in the USA
Middletown, DE
18 March 2023

27062651R00187